I0554290

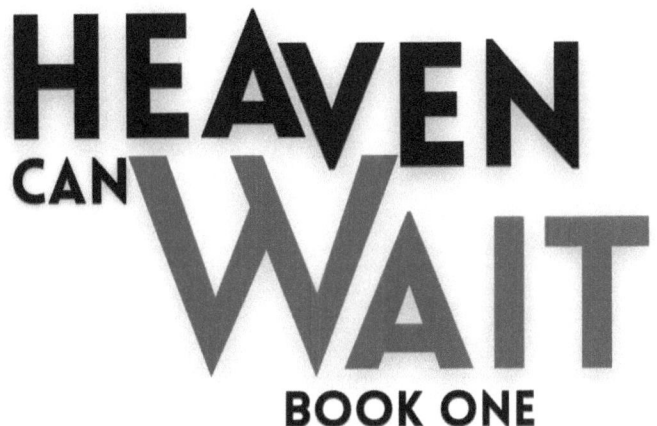

HEAVEN CAN WAIT

BOOK ONE

B.D. HENDRIX

A Novel

Milk and Honey Publishing

Copyright © 2021 by B.D. Hendrix.
All rights reserved.
Printed in the United States of America.

This book is a work of fiction. Names, characters, places, and incidences either are the product of the author's imagination or are used fictitiously, and any resemblance to actual persons, living or dead, business establishments, events, or locales is entirely coincidental.

Set in Times New Roman
Designed by Bria Hendrix

ISBN: 978-1-7367724-0-9
ISBN (e-book): 978-1-7367724-1-6

First Edition: July 2021

.

Acknowledgments

To my loving husband Chaz, daughter Bellarose, sister Shardelle, brother Oolie and the best mother and father I could ask for, Lydia and Orlando Mason. I thank you all for being there for me and blessing me with your wisdom, encouragement, and advice throughout this journey. Thank you all for supporting me and letting me talk you all's ears off as I wrote this book. I love you all.

Playlist

"Crush" – QUIN

"Up" - Cardi B

"Are You in Love" - Kyle Lux

"Nobody's Supposed to Be Here" - Deborah Cox

"Groove with You" - The Isley Brothers

"Fire" - Babyface

"Bloom (Remix)" - K. Roosevelt

"Silly" - Deniece Williams

"Beauty" - Dru Hill

"Lucky Me" - Flwr Chyld, Sebastian Mikael

"Good & Plenty" - Alex Isley

"I Wanna Be Loved" - Eric Benet

"Kissin' You" - Total

"The Agony and The Ecstasy" - Smokey Robinson

"Is It a Crime" - Sade

"Tweety" - Raveena

"Anyway" - Brian McKnight

"Free" - Deniece Williams

"Floating" - Mannywellz

"I Do" - Jon B.

"everybody knows" - Baby Storme

"Still Dreaming" - Raveena

"If Only for One Night" - Luther Vandross

"Heaven Can Wait" - Michael Jackson

Table of Contents

HEAVEN
CAN
WAIT
BOOK ONE

Content Warning
This novel contains discussions and
events that involve sexual violence,
physical violence, and suicide.
Read at your own discretion.

Meet the Characters

As a reader, I love to have visuals of the characters I read about. As a writer, having visuals of the characters help me to write them as people rather than characters. Seeing their faces encourages me to understand who I am writing about and what kind of person they are. So, in hopes of giving my readers an in-depth visual of who they are reading about, without further ado, I introduce you to the fascinating characters of Heaven Can Wait.

THE CHARACTERS

ANDREA ROGERS

Andrea rogers is that chick! Seriously. If you want yourself a woman that's self-made, got stacks for days, and can keep it cute, she's your woman. But she's also a bit of a workaholic, loses touch with reality, and tends to run everything in her life like a business. Including her relationships: A habit that can easily turn out for a lonely and unfulfilled life.

GENESIS STRUTHERS

Genesis Struthers can be a piece of work sometimes and he doesn't even know it. Handsome, smart, well-to-do, and God-fearing, he finds himself in some seriously sticky situations. Though he may act innocent, he knows exactly what he's doing. But sometimes, it's hard doing the right thing. Especially when the right person comes around at the wrong time.

KENDRICK BOWERS

Kendrick Bowers is a gentle giant. Standing at 6'6 and 250 pounds, it isn't recommended to get on his bad side. Have you seen his muscles? Other than his perfect physique, chill personality, and his faithful ways, he remains a mystery to most. Wise, quiet, and trustworthy, Kendrick captures the attention of many women, but seems to only have eyes for one special lady...for now.

WILLIAM ROGERS

William Rogers, a.k.a. Romeo, doesn't let anyone stop him from going for what he wants. He's a go-getter. Romantic. Rich. Up-and-coming celebrity chef. Any woman's dream guy. But one lady has captured his heart. Lola Jones. Consistent and persistent, he's willing to do whatever it takes to build his ideal life with the woman he loves. But dealing with someone as strong-willed and skeptical as Lola, will he get tired of trying to pursue her and instead, pursue his dreams alone?

LOLA JONES

Lola Jones is sassy, fun, loveable, a free spirit, and a fashionista. Everyone is attracted to her, and if someone isn't, then something must be wrong with them. She has a hard exterior, but deep inside, she's as soft as cotton. Not much will sway her from what she wants and how she plans to get it. She's set in her way, and for good reason. But everyone has a weakness. What's hers?

AZRA MCKINNEY

Azra McKinney is lovelorn, shy, and picker than a pecking bird. Trying to find herself, she's tired of acting perfect. Tired of following a guideline of how a Christian 'should' live. She just wants to live. Most of all, she wants love. But like anything, love comes at a costly price. Sacrifice. Compromise. How much will she have to sacrifice for the love of her life?

ONE

LOLA JONES

February 2000

Adrenaline rushed through me. My heart throbbed in my chest. That rise of nausea in my gut encouraged me to run faster and farther than I anticipated. Though the bitterness of the icy snow penetrated my feet as I scurried through the Jackson Ward projects, my mind was more so on my freedom than the frostbite that settled into my bare toes and my bloodstained fingertips. *Oh God! What have I done?*

Present Day

Men aren't worth my time. I have no interest in spending my life under the very species that turned my own mother against me. The same species that stripped me from my innocence and single-handedly destroyed my youth.

But for some reason, they always *tried* it. Tried my time. My womanhood. My patience. My *life*.

And if there is one thing anyone knows about Lola Imala Jones, unless you want to get dropped from my *'I freaks wit'chu'* list, you don't try me. I've been through too much to deal with games, especially those revolving around love.

"Yoo-hoo! Earth to Lola."

Nearly jumping out of my La-Z-Boy recliner, my heart pounds. I redirect my eyes from the flurries compiling on the ledge of the windowpane to the soft, tender voice that enters the door of my Maryland apartment.

"Oh, my goodness, Azra. You scared the crap out of me," I breathlessly giggle and clutch my chest.

My best friend wears an overjoyed grin, one that shows all thirty-two-shining bright. That's odd. She usually seems depressed. Can barely get a smile out of her.

"Why're you so happy?" I ask, puckering my lips into a smirk.

She chuckles. Shaking the snowflakes off her peacoat before draping it on the back of the barstool, she says, "Well, judging by the fact you're not dressed for work yet, your hair is a mess, and you look like a chic raccoon with those dark circles under your eyes…things must've been good." Smiling, she skips over and bounces onto the couch across from me.

She looks cute. Not enough to bring in the money she claims she needs from the club we work at, but…cute. I examine her fit for the night: a black chiffon blouse that teasingly exposes her frilly black bustier top. No cleavage. Her large baby-making hips smuggled into a pair of black jeans, yet no skin. Not even a small rip on the knee.

I battle the urge to drag her into my closet and deck her out in one of my custom-made pieces, but she'd fight tooth and nail. I always tell Azra to not let her religion hinder her from making her coin, but this girl acts like she's afraid to show a little skin. After all, we *are* bottle girls. The more you show, the more money you make. Objectification comes with the territory, and she knew that when she signed up for the job four years ago.

But I digress.

"What are you talking about?" I squint my eyes, refocusing my attention on *her* rather than her overly modest attire.

"Last night? With....William?" she slows her words to give me a chance to recall the date with Romeo, or William for formality's sake. "Was it good?"

"Oh yeah. I mean...It was a date," I shake my head in recollection of why I was in my feelings before she barged into my home.

"So, how'd it go?" she sings in her usual quiet tone that hardly goes over a whisper. She rocks her shoulders side to side in anticipation and glances at my left hand that rests across the back of the recliner.

I pinch the bridge of my nose to release some stress. The idea of breaking the news to Azra gives me a headache.

I sigh, then mutter, "I broke up with him."

Azra's eyes almost pop out of her sockets. "Why? I thought he was gonna pro—"

She quickly curls her lips to stop the words from escaping and tucks her hands between her thighs, looking like a guilty puppy.

"No, finish what you were saying," I take my feet out of the chair and lean forward, "You thought he was going to *what*?"

"Okay," she exhales, "A few nights ago, William came to the club and asked if I'd give him my blessing, since...you know."

"Blessing?"

"Yes."

"Blessing for what? Because last time I checked you weren't God."

She tweaks her lips to the side. "To propose to you."

No wonder why she'd been staring at my left hand. And wait, Romeo wanted *her* blessing? As if this twenty-five-year-old girl was my keeper? My guardian? My mama?

Okay, so...yeah. I don't have any family or other friends for him to ask, and Azra *is* the only person I've gotten close to within the past eight years, but still.

Azra is like a sister to me and knows *almost* every detail about my life, but she'll never understand my mastery of men and how after my thirty-four years of adding, subtracting, multiplying, and dividing them, I always come up with the consistent sum of them...being...the same.

She doesn't understand that my refusal of being chained to anyone is because I've concluded that no matter how good a man looks or carries himself, in my world, he's dangerous. Not to be trusted. Not worth the spit that comes out my mouth.

Well...William might be a *little* different. But not different enough.

I sit back in my chair and scoff. "I can't believe you didn't tell me."

"I didn't tell you because you would've stood him up."

I cross my arms over my chest and glare out the window.

"So, he *did* propose?"

"Mm-hmm," I purse my lips, drag my feet up in the chair and tuck them under me. I watch the snow fall.

Azra's silent.

Neighbors across the street light up their windows with colorful Christmas lights. I shake my head, "I don't get it. Christmas was two weeks ago. Why are people still putting on their lights?"

The sinking air of despair undertakes the atmosphere as Azra's happy-go-lucky attitude fades. She remains silent. You'd think I broke up with *her*. Why does she care so much about my dating life? It ain't that serious. Even if I do feel a smidge of remorse for turning William down, I have to do what's best for *me*, and being someone's lifelong maid is not it.

Snowflakes descend from the grayish skies. Big ones. Like feathers falling from an angel's wings. Ugh...*angels*. Don't care for them. Much like how I don't care for winter. I hate winter. Nothing but hell happens during this season.

Azra sucks her teeth, then exhales. I ignore her.

She does it again, but this time pulls my gaze to her attention.

I ask, "Can I help you?"

"Yes, you can! How could you say no? William is such a sweet guy, and he cares so much about you. From what he planned; it sounds like he pulled out all the stops. The candlelit dinner, the violinist, a photographer, a beautiful diamond ring—"

"That was probably a cubic zirconia he bought from Wal-Mart with his cheap behind. Don't try to play me. Ain't no way a man's gonna put money down on a rock *that* big if he doesn't even want to invest in my fashion line."

"You've been trying to get that so-called fashion line off the ground since before we even met. You can't expect him to do it in a few months."

"It's been over a year. Thirteen months to be exact. And he has a large following. Something could've happened by now if he *cared* to make it happen."

"That's beside the point, Lo. William loves you and he showed that last night. And what do you do? You break up with the man after he poured his heart out to you like a nasty red wine." She pauses and beams pure disgust my way. "Shame on you."

Shame? *Shame*? What have I done wrong? Yeah, Romeo's a nice guy, but they're *all* nice in the beginning. How else will they get you? Hitting you upside the head and telling you it was the wind?

As far as I'm concerned, I'm free to live how I want. I'm on my Beyoncé, and I'm not obligated to marry, be fair, or loyal to anyone but me, myself, and I. Especially after my naïve and early twenties. I'm too grown for the unnecessary shenanigans.

Once my last encounter with 'love' took me for a ride and nearly ended my life, I decided to have fun the same way guys did. No plans on settling down. A few wham-bam-thank-you-sirs here and there. Feelings never got involved, but me being me, I had to make strategic moves. If they couldn't help me further my career as the chocolate Coco Chanel, then I couldn't help them...if you catch my drift.

But somewhere along the line, William Rogers happened. One of the most eligible bachelors in the D.M.V. And boy is he *fine*.

William has been the only man to have the privilege of *almost* changing my mind about the lifestyle I vowed to live. He's single, childless, respectful, and...did I mention the brother is fine? I did? Oh, okay.

Anyway, his heart was set on me from the moment I served him and his crew ten bottles of Grey Goose at the Ace Nightclub, where I work. He was trying to be a big spender. Clearly a front. I've seen my share of celebrities and men of prestige frivolously throw away 10K on bottles and wouldn't blink. But the sorrow on William's face as he watched his wad of cash shrinking before his eyes told me all I needed to know. Crowd pleaser. Frugal Freddie. If he'd spent another dollar, he would have fallen into a deep depression.

Still, he stood out. He remained level-headed and instead of getting tipsy, he sat back and watched little ol' me. Now, I'll admit...it was hella creepy at first. But his brown eyes never skipped a beat as I pranced around the club.

He meticulously examined my every step, bend, and turn as I sashayed around the other ladies who were all at least ten years younger than me. Yet, he didn't mingle with them. He'd slowly wet his full lips with his tongue every time our eyes met, and I'd flirtatiously bat my lashes to let him know I was aware.

When the work night was over, I gathered my belongings, threw my large faux fur coat over my shoulders, and stepped outside into the crisp, snowy night. Glancing around at my surroundings before trotting to my car, the fog of my breath hitting the frigid air revealed a man in the darkness. Like magic. Butterflies fluttered. It was *him*. Mr. High Roller leaning against his 1970 Black Plymouth Barracuda. Had he been anyone else, I probably would've lit him up with pepper spray as he approached me. But since he was cute, I didn't see the harm in entertaining him.

He sauntered near. His black turtleneck, overcoat, and tailored slacks fit perfectly. His scent filled my nostrils: Burning wood with notes of vanilla.

Smoky, yet, satisfying. If I could've breathed in deeper whiffs of him, I would've.

"You know if you wanted to stalk me you could've just asked. I would've added you to my list," I playfully smirked, stopping in my tracks.

"What list is that?" he asked in a deep, softly spoken voice.

"My 'Potential Boyfriend' list. Nothing screams *love* like a man who can't let you out of his sight," I joke, finally face-to-face with him. His pearly white smile exposed the deep dimple in his left cheek. His soft, dark, curls were cut into a fade. His flawless caramel skin and tall, fit stature caused me to gush like a schoolgirl. Suddenly, the frigid bite in the air didn't seem so cold.

"Well, I was actually waiting for my wife to come out the club."

Big yikes.

Blushing, I tried to hide the sloppy egg that dripped down my face. "Your wife?"

"Mm-hmm. Matter of fact, you may have seen her," he bit his lip as he scanned me from head to toe. "She's about your size. Beautiful smile. Long, sexy legs. She got a fur coat just like this."

I grinned and shyly glanced at his black, leather ankle boots. "Don't believe I saw her."

"No? You sure? You look *just* like her."

Lifting my head, I giggled at his coy smirk. "Stop playing."

"I don't play, Mrs. Rogers."

Cocking a brow, I stepped back and eyed him up and down. "I prefer Lola. And I'm not interested in being—"

"Mrs. William Rogers? The wife of the world's rising celebrity chef? You don't want that?"

"Not interested," I grazed past him to continue to my car. He grabbed my hand to turn me back.

"Well, at least let me walk you to your car. It might be some *real* stalkers out here you need protection from."

"I think I can handle myself," I tried pulling my hand from his, only to be tugged back.

His eyes fixed intensely on mine. Licking his lips, he opened his mouth to say, "Trust me. I can handle you a lot better."

Needless to say, we kicked it a few times.

And unfortunately, he's everything I thought he would be. A talented, professional, and surprisingly famous chef, who whips up the best stuffed salmon, roasted potatoes, and onion rings that *slap*. He's captivating. Suave. Funny. But also, eight years my *junior*.

Still had red marks on his butt from the doctor spanking him.

A first-class Romeo. He fantasizes about moving to Switzerland, marrying a slightly older woman his family disapproves of, having five curly head kids running around the house, and living happily ever after. A storybook ending.

But that's all it ever will be. A story. Fake. A fantasy. And we all know those don't exist.

Yet, Azra still doesn't get it.

"Shame on *me*? Chile, please, I told Romeo from the get-go marriage was off the table. We were supposed to be having fun. He was supposed to help me get recognition by posting me and my clothing on his social media. And I was helping him understand love doesn't always go as you'd expect. A life lesson he was gonna learn sooner or later. He just made the mistake of thinking that sticking around would change my mind."

Azra huffs. "Do not use your freedom as an opportunity for the flesh, but through love serve one another—"

"Oh. My. God. Don't go quoting Bible right now."

"*Oh, my God,* nothing. You always talk about how you want to do better and get closer to God. But treating William like he's trash isn't serving him with love. Nor is it getting you closer to God. You led him on. You constantly had your way with him and made him feel special. He kissed the ground you walked on, and you didn't put a stop to it." Azra leans back onto the lavender suede couch as if she just dropped the mic.

Romeo is a good guy. And I do like him. The time we spent together was fun. But I didn't lead him on. I could tell that boy I didn't wash my feet for two weeks and he'd get down and suck them clean. That's how he is. He does what *he* wants to do. And no, I never put a stop to it. I liked it, and in all honesty…it kept me on my toes. No pun intended.

Actually, him *not* listening to me attracts me even more. Maybe it's the chase that intrigues me. The way a gazelle runs from a hungry lion. But no matter how attracted I am to him, I'm loyal to myself first.

"Azra, I have too much living to do, and I can't afford to be tied down. And if you haven't noticed, when I say I want to get closer to God, I'm usually drunk," I chuckle before getting up and going to my room to get dressed for work.

Azra follows.

"A drunk mind speaks a sober heart. And that ain't scripture, but it's true. You need to call him up and get back together. You know you want to clean up your life and find real love. No living, breathing, human being wants to be alone. You probably found it with William, but you're too hurt and blinded by your past to—"

"Listen, Azra," I lift my hand to shut down any philosophical reasoning she has about why I chose the life I had. "First off, William is all the way in Cali right now filming some show. And second, I'm not trying to commit to *anyone*. These dudes out here will have to understand. And if they don't…" I shrug and pivot to make my way to my closet.

"I'm just saying, I don't want you to grow old alone. Your Jordan year is way behind you and you're only getting closer to trading in your Vogue magazine for AARP."

"And you're closer to unconsciousness if you keep calling me old," I untie my ivory-colored satin robe, slip it off and throw it at her.

She chuckles, "Touché."

Silence falls between us. I open the doors to my large walk-in closet full of my designs. I try putting the thoughts of Romeo, the proposal, and Azra's guilt trip behind me so I can focus on what I'm going to wear.

I rummage through tight skirts, sexy dresses, and flowy tops to finally come across a standard, brand new, black, bodycon dress. I put my hand on the inside of the dress and stretch it out to see if I can see through it. I can't stand for a fabric to be so thin and cheap, that my underwear, or lack thereof, is on display for everyone to gawk at. I'm all for being sexy, but I'm not trying to have people say hello to my kitty without me knowing my kitty spoke first. Hence, why I make most of my clothes, except for the clothes I wear to work. I usually buy those from online shops.

Assuring my dress is full coverage, I shimmy into it and yell from the closet, "So, what's going on with you?"

A soft, melancholy sigh permeates the room, "Nothing. Just tired."

She must be perioding.

"I mean, in your life? What's new?"

"Same ol', same ol'," she mutters.

Typical. She never goes deeper into her life than she has to. In the four years I've known her, I haven't learned much *about* her. She's like a turtle. Always sticking her head into my business but retreats when the pressure comes down on her. But that's Azra. I won't pry.

Though she's secretive, she'll never be able to hide when she's PMS'ing. 'Tired' is usually her favorite adjective to use around this time. Plus, we're in sync. Have been since we met.

The rattling of a pill bottle coming from Azra's purse confirms my theory. She pops ibuprofen like candy. I, on the other hand, have a higher tolerance for pain.

I come out of the closet and check myself out in the body-length mirror. "What do you think about our new manager? He's cute, right?" I grab my black and pink makeup bag to throw on some foundation.

"Yeah. He's cute," she smiles.

I slowly turn my head to see her resting her head against the wall and a grin bigger than the one she came in with.

"You like him?" I laugh. Little Miss Church Girl is crushing on a secular club manager and I'm here for it.

"No…I mean," she huffs and puffs with a tantrum stomp, "if you don't swarm in on him first, then yeah. I might."

The shade.

"Chile please, I'm free from Romeo and I ain't getting caught up in another situation again. He's all yours," I chuckle, turning back to the mirror to complete my look with a red lip and lashes.

Stealing a peep at my girl in the mirror, her cheeky grin says it all. The mentioning of that man changed her attitude. And that's the only cue I need.

I need something to get my mind off my reality and that irksome guilt that keeps seeping into my heart no matter how hard I fight it. Hooking Azra up is the perfect task to distract me. Not saying she has a problem pulling guys herself, but with her being so picky and shy, she never has a boyfriend, hence the reason why she's all up in my business. There's even a cute security guard at the club that's head over heels for her. Kendrick. But she friend-zoned him like it was nobody's business.

Shoot, if I was that kind of woman, I might try to make him mine for a weekend, but I'm not that messy.

Anyway, Azra needs a man. Any man. And that manager at Ace might be just that.

"Girl, we better go. We're already running late." Azra pushes from the wall.

I throw my makeup into the bag and toss it into the pink duffle bag I carry to the club in case I need a change of clothes and other emergency items. I grab my perfume from my dresser and douse myself in its chocolatey goodness. I slip my freshly manicured feet into my black pumps and rush to the door.

I'm hot. Don't need any mirror to tell me that.

Looking not a day over twenty-five. Small booty: Poppin'. Waist: Snatched. Face: Beat to the gods! The four-inch scar tracing from my chin to my ear is hardly noticeable. My rich cocoa complexion is hydrated and glistens with each spritz of perfume that melts upon my chest. You can't tell me nothing.

"Lo, let's go!"

"Don't rush me," I lay my fur over my shoulders and snatch up my duffle bag as I jet to the door. Before stepping out, I'm taken aback by Azra standing in the hallway. With her hand on her hip, she taps her foot, looking like a whole grandma going out to party.

With her conservativity, it may be a challenge. But I'm gonna get her the man she wants. And as a perfect distraction from my life at the moment...that challenge is accepted.

TWO

AZRA MCKINNEY

I hate this job. My spirit gets riled up every time I lay eyes on Ace Nightclub. I'd much rather be home writing or trying to get the sleep that's been stolen from insomnia. But nope. Another night of being objectified for a small piece of change is what I'm stuck doing.

The fiery red lights seduce Connecticut Avenue as the upbeat crowds line up to make it inside the hottest club in D.C.

Ace is the spot to be on the weekends, especially nights like this when the hottest celebrities and socialites throw the wildest parties. You'd think since New Year's was last week, people would be partied out. But not at Ace.

I don't see the appeal. If I didn't work here, you wouldn't catch me breathing its air.

Lola and I rush our freezing butts from her car, clock in, and find our way to the common area, where many of the bartenders, cocktail waitresses, and other staff relax before work officially begins. Repulsion grows as the stench of cheap, tart perfumes and burned weave nearly fry the hairs of my nose.

The loud bass from the DJ booth quakes the tacky mirrors that line the dressing room. I catch my reflection as Lola and I beeline it to the little corner of the room where we usually prep for the night.

My five-three, one-forty-pound frame fights to keep my ankles from breaking in these six-inch stilettos. I need to lose weight. Lack of sleep does that to you. Have you gaining fat in places you never thought of before. Overweight or not, these tight clothes are not my style. I'm more of a sweats and sneakers person but working at a club leaves no room for comfort. Not in my clothes, my mind, or my spirit. But I need the money.

"Hey, girl. How you doing?" says hoochie number one.

"I like your hair, Azra," says hoochie number two.

I give a fake smile.

Hoochies here, hoochies there, hoochies everywhere. These girls must spend tens of thousands of dollars for their BBL's and cheap silicone breast, only to be gawked at by dozens of filthy men. All to secure a bag.

I'll never do that.

I already struggle covering my curves with layers of clothes so men don't get the wrong idea; if I wanted to put my goodies on display for a quick buck, I could. But I was raised better than that. My grandmother always told me a modestly assembled woman was closest to God's heart. Never read that in the Bible. But if Mom-mom said it, it was good enough. The less a woman shows, the better off she is. But being a cocktail waitress...that's hard to do.

Sex sells. But I ain't cheap. Only hard work and a wedding ring will open this cookie jar. And I don't plan on giving out free samples.

So, showing no skin left me with no ends.

Fighting eviction from my apartment, taking care of my grandmother, trying to finish my business management degree, and keeping up the Christ-like image as if everything is perfect and God is *so good*, is draining the soul out of me. While the other girls; even Lola—as old as she is—are reeling in the tips and living lavishly, I'm on the verge of saying forget it.

I need a change. Quick.

I take my coat off and sit on the cold, steel folding chair. I spruce up my lightly done makeup, blot my nose and hand brush my jet black, waist-length ponytail.

My phone rings.

Without checking the name, I swipe and exhale, "Yes, ma'am?"

Mom-mom's nasally voice chimes through the phone. *What now?*

"Sugar, I forgot to tell you, but I need you to pick up my medicine."

I sigh. "I dropped your meds off earlier today, Mom-mom."

"I know but the pain medicine is missing. I know you're working hard doing that night shift at that warehouse and all, but I need that medicine, sugar. I'd do it myself, but you know how limited my moving is nowadays."

I puff out a gust of annoyance but try not to let her hear me. "Okay, Mom-mom. I'll pick it up."

"Thank you so much. I love you. And you be safe out there. These devils lurking for some new blood."

"I will, Mom-mom," I dryly chuckle. "Love you, too."

I hang up the phone and take a breather.

Glancing to my left, Lola gives me a side-eye so strong you'd think Picasso painted her.

"What?" I stand from my chair and zip up my purse.

"Girl, you're still lying to Ms. Annette about where you work?"

Mom-mom isn't the kind of person I can be honest with. Matter of fact, she's the single most critical, opinionated, self-righteous person I've ever known. Telling her I work at a club would reserve a special seat in hell before the clock strikes twelve. *And* she'll disown me. But I love her more than anything in this world. She raised me after her daughter left me as a baby. My grandmother didn't have to take care of me after her trifling child decided she didn't want me. She could've put me straight into the system and forgot all about me. But she didn't. Although I'm fed up with having to care for her as if *she's* the child, there's no way I can leave her alone.

She's diabetic, crippled by MS, and after suffering a stroke three years ago, she was diagnosed with advanced heart failure, all at sixty-five years old.

Witnessing her declining health is difficult. We're all we have. No siblings, uncles, or aunts. Just me and her.

So, until the day she's called to glory, *my life* is on hold.

"You wouldn't understand," I mutter.

Lola pouts and eyes me up and down for the umpteenth time tonight.

"What I don't understand is how you manage to be a grown woman, yet *dress* like an old lady, and *act* like a little girl. Who lies about where they work?"

"First of all, I look fine. And second, I don't act like a little girl. You don't know her the way I do."

"She can't be that bad."

"She isn't bad, she's just..." *The most important person in my life and I value her opinion and perception of me.* But even if I tell Lola that, she won't get it. She doesn't care about what anyone thinks about *her*, so she won't understand my plight. I try to dismiss the conversation when a voice through the intercom gathers everyone's attention.

"Ms. McKinney and Ms. Jones, come to the office."

The chatter from the girls goes silent and all their nosey eyes are zoned in on us.

"Why?" my voice quivers and my palms sweat. I glare at Lola who looks just as confused.

"I don't know, but let's fix this, chile." She springs up from her chair and pulls up the bottom of my shirt with her red claws.

"What're you doing? I ain't showing my goodies."

"Well, right now you're looking like an old maid and it's giving me hella anxiety. Plus, you wanna make money tonight or naw?" Lola bugs her eyes as she yanks my shirt over my head and throws it on the back of the chair.

Cold, I fold my arms over my chest and play with the small, gold cross that hangs around my neck.

She scrambles through her makeup bag.

Although I still have more clothes on than *all* the girls here, I feel so nude.

"Here, put this on." Lola holds up a red lipstick to my lips and got the nerve to act like she's gonna put it on me.

"What are you doing?" I push her hand away.

"*Girl…*"

I examine the lipstick and turn my nose up. Who knows where her lips been.

Huffing, she turns around, snatches up a napkin, and wipes a layer of lipstick off before grabbing my cheeks with one hand and spreading the red, buttery substance over my lips.

"Girl, yes! You finna turn all the heads tonight." She smiles and steps back as she pops the top on the lipstick. "Much better."

The fragrant taste of the creamy lipstick grosses me out as I rub my lips together. I frown at myself in the mirror. Not having a shirt to cover my hips and butt makes me look like one of these botched biddies.

My breasts protrude out of my black bustier. The spillage from my side boobs screams thot vibes and it's not okay. But Lord…my heart skips a beat when my gaze lands on my face.

Mom-mom always told me, "A woman who wears red has a toe dippin' in the pits of hell."

Forgive me, Lord is my only prayer when I see that red lipstick staining my plump lips. All I need now is some horns because I'm going to hell.

"Ms. McKinney and Ms. Jones… *Now,*" the voice sternly repeats on the intercom, snapping me from my prayers.

We rush to the office and not a second after the door closes, the noisiness from the club fades.

"You're late," the manager mumbles as he vigorously writes on important papers without looking up at us.

He wears a long-sleeved black sweater. The kind that modestly shows every muscle. A plain baseball cap covers his downward tilted face.

His desk is scattered with spreadsheets and other paperwork. His office is dim, and the aroma of smoked birch wax melts disperses from the luminous wax burners. A comfy, jade-colored couch sits on a dark brown shag rug close to the back of the office. Only the sound of a crooning saxophone plays softly from the Bluetooth speaker on his desk. The laid-back and peaceful ambiance almost makes me forget we're in a club.

"Mister..." Lola pauses to learn his name. It's only been a week since our old manager was fired and none of us formally met this new guy. All we know is he's fine with a capital 'F'. His wavy, clean-cut hair is enough to make any mermaid seasick. His mahogany skin is polished and silky. That coarse black beard that shapes his strong jawline and carves out right around his lips. Oooh...I need to pray.

"Struthers," he answers in a heavy, yet smooth tone.

"Mr. Struthers, we were getting ready when you called for us—"

"No, you were ten minutes late to work."

"No disrespect but the club doesn't open until ten and we clocked in at nine-ten."

"You don't think I know that?"

"Well, clearly you do. But we drove all the way from College Park. You can't get anywhere on time with weekend traffic from Maryland to D.C., especially when you need to look *this* good." Lola winks and puts a flirty twang in her tone as she nudges me forward.

I glare at her and giggle but quickly wipe the smile off my face when Mr. Struthers stops writing and shoots a piercing glance at me.

No expression. His eyes don't bounce around my scantily clad body. Rather, he looks into my eyes and rests there for a moment, taking me in. He traces my features. My round eyes, delicate nose, and full, red lips. He etches them into his brain. He blinks. Glances down to his desk and then back up, directing his attention to Lola.

"I'm guessing you're Ms. Jones?"

"I am, and *this* is Azra," she smirks, putting a hand on my shoulder.

With a stoic expression, he rises from his seat to walk to the front of his desk where he rests on the edge. He crosses his long legs at the ankles, exposing the red bottoms of his eight-hundred-dollar sneakers.

The closer he comes, the more intoxicated I become. His bold, peppery, cinnamon-like cologne causes butterflies.

"I heard a lot about you, Ms. Jones. You seem to be a crowd favorite."

"I do what I can." Lola smiles. He doesn't.

"Let's be clear about something. I'm not here to argue with you. I don't want to have to call either of you in again. I expect you *both* to be on time, or next time…you'll be fired."

"Fired?" Lola snaps, "You can't fire us for being ten minutes late. That's ridiculous."

His gaze leaves Lola and lingers on me. I jitter, tuck my chin in my chest and pray he stops looking at me.

"Do you have anything to add, Ms. McKinney?"

"Uh… I… Um—"

"I'm gonna need you to speak up."

"Uh…I-I don't have anything…to add," I stutter.

"Sorry for wasting your time? It won't happen again? I'll be on time from now on?" he rudely mocks. "You ladies need to have more respect for people's time and money."

"Umm…yes, I-I'm sorry, Mr. Struthers. It won't happen again," I whisper, looking at my shoes before a roar of anger scares the holy water out of me.

"Hold the hell up! Who you think you talkin' to? You *just* started working here not even two seconds ago and you're talking about *respect*? How about having the same respect for *us*? I don't care if you're a manager or not, what you not gonna do is sit here and talk to my girl like she's some snotty nose, second-grader." Lola grimaces.

I glance under my eyebrows at Mr. Struthers whose eyes are still planted on me. I sweat from his burning gaze.

"Thank you, Ms. McKinney. You may leave." He crosses his arms.

Self-conscious, I advert my eyes from his and cover myself. I step backwards out of the room. I don't know who's about to lay into who but all I know is I want no parts.

I walk back to the common area and wait for Lola.

I feel so stupid. Insulted. But I just sat there like my tongue was cut out.

"Girl, what happened?" a fellow cocktail waitress asks. Riley. You can tell she's being nosey because she rarely speaks to me. She and Lola don't get along. Why? I don't know. Typical thot behavior, I suppose.

"Nothing, girl. The manager wanted to talk to me and Lola about something."

"Where's Lola?"

"He's still talking to her."

"Aww shh…shoot," Riley suppresses her urge to curse in front of me, which I appreciate.

"What?" I furrow my brow.

"Well, from what I heard, they firing people left and right. The last manager let a lot of stuff slide and the club was losing money. They ain't taking no prisoners and from the sounds of it, er'body gettin' fired. Looks like you the lucky one out of y'all two."

I shoo her off, "Girl, I don't believe in luck. And Lola's not getting fired. She's been here longer than all of us."

"Exactly why she's probably in there getting her old ahh…butt, handed to her."

"I doubt it."

I turn my back and pick up my shirt from the chair. Pulling it over my head, the elementary *ooohs* from the girls erupt.

"I know, I'm cute. Y'all ain't gotta gas me up." Lola laughs, taking the negative attention, and turning it into a positive, as she always did.

She struts over to me with a smile on her face, but a scowl falls directly on Riley, making her slip away to the other side of the room.

Bypassing me, Lola leans over to close her duffle bag as I explode with anticipation.

"What happened?"

"I have good news and bad news. Which do you want first?" She pivots on her pointy heels to face me.

"Bad?"

"Well, loverboy, a.k.a Genesis *Ace* Struthers, isn't only the manager. He's the *owner* of this joint. And sorry to tell you, I know you're borderline obsessed with him, but he's a disrespectful ass—"

"Language!" I cover my ears.

Lola twists her lips to the side and rolls her eyes, "Anyway, he needs to learn how to speak to women."

"What happened? And why are you packing?" I ask, trying to not become frantic and draw any more attention to us, although everyone is already eavesdropping.

"That's the good news. Effective immediately, my employment at Ace Nightclub is terminated. I guess he couldn't handle a woman coming at him the way his mother should've."

"Told you!" Riley yells from across the room, cackling like a hyena, "I knew they were gonna fire ya' old behind."

"I'm sorry, what was that? I couldn't hear you over all those pills rattling in your purse. Chlamydia, right?" Lola shouts back with a smirk.

Riley's face turns beet red. She flips her blonde synthetic hair over her shoulder. The laughs and taunts from the other girls drive her out the room.

I shove Lola, "How could he fire you? You've been the top waitress here forever."

"I know, I told him. It didn't matter though, and I don't care. He can't think it's okay to talk to *any* woman the way he did. He probably got a wife that walks all over him. Probably paints her face over ours just so he can feel like he's got a backbone."

The wind from Lola pulling her fluffy fur coat over her shoulders fans me. "So, that's it? You're fired?"

Grinning, she touches my arm and gives it a gentle squeeze. "This is great, Az."

"How? You got fired and you don't have another job lined up. *And* you're leaving me here to fend for myself," I lower my voice. "You know I can't stand these banshees."

"Sis, you'll be fine. I promise. And don't worry about me, this is—as you would call it—a blessing in disguise. Now I have time to work on my fashion line." She smiles and an exciting glint sparkles in her eyes. "Everything will be fine."

"Wait, how am I gonna get home?" I ask. I almost forgot we rode together.

"Don't worry, I'll pay for your Lyft."

"Alone? At freaking three o'clock in the morning? You *must* want me to go missing."

"You're hella dramatic, sis." She laughs and rolls her eyes. She opens her duffle bag and carefully digs to the bottom of it. Moving closer to me, she pulls out a shiny black gun. Not just any gun. The woman had the nerve to bedazzle the grip in pink and white rhinestones.

I jump back as if she just coughed in the middle of a pandemic, "Whoa, Lo! What the heck?"

"You know how to use her, right?"

"I don't *want* to know how. I didn't know *you* knew how," I snap.

Lowering her eyes and tilting her head to the side, she chuckles, "Az, it's a *gun*…not herpes. Take it."

"I-I don't—"

"It's either Poppy or prayers and pepper spray. But I can guarantee you, any creeps out past midnight picking up little girls are immune to that stuff." Dangling the weapon on her index finger, she holds it out to me. I grab it by the blinged out handle with the tips of my fingers and drop it in my bag.

"Take care of her for me." Lola presses her cheek against mine, kisses the air, throws her duffle bag over her shoulder, and brushes past me, leaving me alone…with a gun…that I have no idea how to use. God, help me.

THREE

AZRA

In the blood of Jesus. I pray as I lean my shoulder against the club's entrance and wait for my ride to come.

I'm ninety-eight percent sure out of all the good, wholesome ride-share drivers in the DMV, I'm gonna get that *one* aspiring serial killer ready to start making a name for themselves. I can kick myself for riding to work with Lola rather than driving myself. But I wanted to help her work through her feelings about William. No matter how well she plays the *'love is for the meek and uglies'* role, she's in love. She's just being as stubborn as the glue holding down her lace front. No matter how hard you pull it, it won't budge.

Before I get the chance to get mad all over again about how sleazy she treats William, a husky, baritone voice bellows behind me.

"Beauty."

Turning around, Kendrick Bowers, the club's security guard, swaggers behind me. "Heard what happened to your girl."

"Yeah…unfortunate situation," I say through a bitter smile. *Dang*. It's like I can't get away from this man. Three years of shooting his shot and always missing. He just won't leave me alone.

Kendrick is nice, though. And on the surface and beyond, he should be everything I ever would want in a man. But he's not.

Let me explain.

Kendrick is attractive, but *I'm* not attracted to him.

He has some nice dreads that fall down his strong, muscular back, which I love. But my man can't have hair as long as mine.

Muscular, but there is such a thing as *too* many muscles.

A gentle giant, but then it's like…why do you have all those muscles if you're not gonna yoke someone up occasionally?

Tall, but come on, who's trying to strain their neck looking up every time we converse?

Gung-ho about Jesus, which should be a huge plus for me, but something's still off about dude.

He's just not my type. And what kills it for me is that he knows Mom-mom. As a matter of fact, *she* introduced us. Or at least she thought she did.

The fear that rocked me the first time Kendrick spoke to Mom-mom at church, had me thinking the second coming was upon us and I hadn't repented.

A nervous smirk quivered my cheeks as I treaded through the narthex. I marched through the crowds of older ladies who stopped to greet me with wet kisses on the cheek, and men trying to cop a 'godly' feel in the name of Jesus, yet the view of Mom-mom and Kendrick never faltered.

"Sugar, I want you to meet this fine, young man. Kendrick, is it?" Mom-mom said with a frisky grin. She always was keen on young men. Especially when they put on a nice and thick layer of swag-be-gone before approaching her.

Revolted, I crinkled my nose before turning a reluctant eye to Kendrick. My heart hammered in my chest, but I remained calm.

"Azra," I extended my hand to him, playing off the fact that I dodged his advances many times before that day. "Nice to meet you."

"Pleasure's mine." Amusement danced in his eyes as he curled my fingers in his hand and kissed my knuckles.

I shot a glance at Mom-mom to see her reaction. Nothing but a beaming smile stretched her cheeks.

"He told me y'all worked together." Her eyes laid adoringly on Kendrick.

My breath caught in my throat and I blinked uncontrollably. "Oh, yeah...at the *warehouse*...right? You're the guard there?" I stated in the strongest, most confident voice I could find. Giving Kendrick a squinted and meaningful gaze, I prayed he'd catch on.

"Yes, of course. We've only seen each other in passing, but I never knew you were *this* beautiful young lady's granddaughter." Letting go of my hand, he rubbed my grandmother's arm.

"Oh, stop it." She blushed.

Yes please...stop.

I swallowed the lump of fear down. The panic of my innocence being tainted, and the lies I've told, subsided. Luckily, Kendrick knew what time it was. And I'll forever be grateful for that. But still...

It's like he wants to impress *her*. He'd put on his *I Love Jesus* Sunday's best attire because he wants to get *her* approval as if she'll marry me off to him. It's obvious how important Mom-mom is to me, but I hate the idea of someone cozying up to her just to get to me. It's unfair and manipulative as h-e-double hockey sticks.

Moving my position to face Kendrick, I rest my back on the door and check how far my ride is.

8 minutes away

"You need a ride?" Kendrick stuffs his hands in the pockets of his leather bomber jacket.

Avoiding eye contact, I lower my phone, "No, I'm alright. Waiting for my ride to come."

Slightly bending his knees to come to my level and into my view to regain my attention, he smiles. "You sure? You don't have to waste your money. I'd gladly do it for free, especially when that means having a beautiful woman in my car."

His corniness curves a resisting but genuine smile on my lips.

"I'm fine, Kendrick. Appreciate it though."

"*Ahh*," he jokingly stumbles back, holding his hand over his chest, "you know how to break a man's heart, don't you?"

"I don't mean to, it's just…I paid for this ride already. It's nothing personal."

A few lingering partygoers standing outside stumble and shout profanities at one another, drawing Kendrick's attention from me.

"Well, maybe we can do lunch after church on Sunday? You gonna be there, right?"

"Sure. We'll see," I curl my lips inward.

"A'ight, bet. I'm 'bout to get out here and break this up before anything pops off, and head on home. I'll see you Sunday, Beauty."

"Yup. As always," I force a smile.

I watch as he disperses the crowd. He never uses violence and never had to put his hands on anyone. His size alone makes people think twice, which is why he's the perfect guard. Physically, he could be the ideal protector for a little woman like myself. I wouldn't have to worry about anything.

I've tried to picture myself with Kendrick, but I can't see it. Him being all over me? Kissing and touching me? Getting on one knee and propo— no…can't see it.

I grab my phone to text Lola:

Ordered the ride. CashApp me $16. U know I need it.

I slip my phone into my purse and pinch the bridge of my nose. I could smack her. She knows my money is tight. All she had to do was get me after my shift was over but no. Instead, she wants me to die.

I can use the gun that she gave me, but I'm too afraid if I do, I'll hurt myself more than anyone else. Plus, I never even held one until today, so that's a lost cause.

I know I shouldn't be afraid of doing ride-shares alone, but I'm a scaredy cat.

Mom-mom always taught me there was nothing to fear when you walk with the Lord but then countered that with *but only if you live, breathe, think, and eat the word of God.*

In other words, be perfect. Something I've always found excruciatingly hard to achieve. Especially since I started working at the club and lying about it to Mom-mom. Perfection doesn't lie. Yet here I am.

I put on a good face in the presence of other people. Use the right words and act how a Christian should, but every day, I live my life in fear. Not only fear of the Lord but fear of Mom-mom as well.

I love God. But part of me resents being a Christian at such a young age. My life's decisions aren't made from a genuine love for God or because I *want* to, but out of obligation, fear, and guilt. It hurts to admit, but it's true.

It was how I was raised. If you slipped or did anything unpleasing to God, then you were abusing and disrespecting the gift God gave us through Jesus.

I wonder what my life would be if I didn't have the chains of fear on me. I feel like a prisoner sometimes. Not able to do what I want because I always have to remember punishment awaits me on the other side.

I don't feel like waiting for that pie in the sky everyone talks about. I want a morsel of heaven here on earth. That's all I'm asking for. To be free from rules and moral obligation. I just want to live.

I hate to admit it, but that's what I envy about Lola. Not saying I want to be thotty like her, but I love her carefree approach to life. I give her a hard time, but part of me wants to be that way. But the other part doesn't because…love.

I love my girl, and she has her own reasons why she approaches relationships the way she does, but I can't get with throwing love away like it's nothing. For some reason, that muddles with my spirit. Love is so wonderful and precious. When the right person comes along, it's only right to snatch it up and not let go.

Yes, Jesus loves me, and so does Mom-mom. But I need a *man*. Call it having mommy and daddy issues all you want, but I need a love that can take my whole being over and make me forget about the lack of love I craved as a child. One I could touch, feel, see, and hear. Having that would make everything worthwhile. Having that might help me sleep at night.

I mosey to the bench that sits near the entrance and takes a seat. Leaning my head against the wall, I fantasize about my dream guy that always visits me in my not-so-sanctified dreams. The camera in my mind revolves around him as if he's D'Angelo in the *Untitled* video. Ugh, how great would it be to have my Boaz. My handsome Prince Charming. My bae. That's all I want. Am I asking for too much?

"What are you doing here?" a familiar, flat voice echoes through the empty hall, breaking me from my daydream.

Inhaling a shaky breath and slowly opening my eyes with an exhale, my dream man stands right in front of me. Simultaneously, humiliation, anxiety, attraction, excitement, and anger all rush me.

The glow of a car's light shines through the window and puts a halo around his head. He looks like he's sent from Heaven. My knees go weak. Thank God I'm sitting down.

Mr. Struthers stares at me with a faint grin.

My heart drops to my stomach as my eyes meet his. A feverish flush comes over me.

"Hmm?" I purr. Words escape me already.

"What are you still doing here?"

The car's lights remain on him as the muffled sound of a horn blares, yet our eyes stay connected. Since both sides of my brain are preoccupied with trying to process simple language and bodily functioning, I ignore the beeping and straighten up.

"I-I'll be leaving soon, Mr. Struthers."

He quietly huffs and hangs his head low. "Hey listen, Ms. McKinney, I'm sorry about earlier. I shouldn't have spoken to you that way and if I made you feel belittled, I apologize."

I stare. I want to give him the piece of my mind I wish I gave earlier, but the words and courage are M.I.A.

"Do you accept my apology?" he raises his brow.

I massage my dry, red lips together. "Will you give my girl her job back?"

Don't know why I can only think about Lola at this moment, but hey, let's go with it.

He shakes his head. "Listen, Ms. Jones wasn't a good fit here anymore. She was a good worker but sometimes people need to learn their place and—"

"And what? Shut up?" I slither my neck. I stand to my feet and cross my arms over my chest. My words are back and the sass that is backing them up even takes *me* by surprise.

"I didn't say that."

"Lola was the best worker here. She trained most of us and she was here as long as this club has been open. All she was doing was standing up for me. Firing her was completely unnecessary." Mentally patting myself on the back for finally saying something meaningful, I pray these words don't get me fired.

"Are you done?" he asks with a sarcastic smirk.

The cute aggression in me makes me want to punch his beautiful, brown-eyed lights out, but instead, I take a deep breath and nod.

"Now, as I was saying, your friend's mouth got her fired. It's not what she said but it's how she said it. She lacks respect and honestly, if she'd spoken to me the way you did, she might still have her job. But you two can talk about that on your own time. Like I said, I'm sorry for how I spoke to you earlier. You didn't deserve that. You seem like a sweet girl, and I don't want there to be any bad blood between us."

Girl? I hate when guys call me that. Maybe my fun-sized stature gives me a complex. Maybe it's the fact I'm tired of not living my adult life the way an actual adult should be living. Whatever it is, I despise that word coming out of any man's mouth when referring to me. But instead of ruffling feathers any further, I keep my mouth shut and let it pass. *This* time.

"Apology accepted," I mutter, slowly lowering my crossed arms.

"Good. Now, can I ask you why you're the last person sitting out here? Thought everyone would be gone by now."

"I'm waiting for my Lyft," I raise my phone to track the car's distance but don't really pay attention to what's on the screen.

"Lyft? Babygirl, do you know what time it is? That's not safe."

"Hold up. First of all, I'm a grown woman. And second, I'm not your baby," I sharply cut my eyes from him, "Besides, I wouldn't need a Lyft tonight if *you* didn't fire my ride."

He chuckles, "I see you got a little fire in you, too. Just like your friend."

"Lola and I are nothing alike, thank you very much."

The glare from the car's lights disappears from around Genesis and I peer down to my phone.

"Shoot." Scrambling to my feet, I rush to the door. Sixteen dollars I don't have, ride away from me. Close enough that I can see the Ford emblem on the back, but too far to run and flag it down in my heels.

"What's wrong?" Genesis saunters up behind me.

"That was it. Dang! That's sixteen dollars down the drain."

"Where do you have to go?"

"Why do you care?"

"Well, the least I could do after getting rid of your ride…and making you miss this one, is give you one home. You can cancel that—"

"I already paid for it. They don't do refunds."

He sucks his teeth and exhales. "How about I give you that money back and I'll drive you home? At least you know you'll make it safely."

I shift my weight onto one foot and cross my arms. "I don't *know* that."

He chuckles before brushing past me. "Well, I mean…if you don't want to get home, then—"

"Wait," I turn to him as he holds the door open, "you're not a serial killer, are you?

"What?" His eyes crease at the corners.

"You know…Bundy…Ramirez…Franklin Jr. Men that targeted women…preferably smaller than they were to get some sort of sexual thrill out of hurting them?"

He laughs again before running his hand down his face. The dim, dull expression he constantly seemed to wear, lifts. His eyes light up.

"What?" I smile, though I find nothing humorous about possibly getting my head chopped off.

"If you're asking if I'm gonna *kill* you, then no." He chuckles, holding the door open for me.

"Thank God."

"I only do that on Mondays."

"Ha ha…hilarious," I put my hands in the pockets of my coat and walk out ahead of him.

We stroll to the side of the club where a black Escalade starts up and the lights come on at the push of a button.

"So, where do you need to go?"

"College Park," I mutter trying not to steal too many glances at him, but he looks so good. Flurries fall lightly on his brown peacoat. His chestnut, moisturized skin glows as it reflects the sparkle of the twilit night. His eyes, dark. His beautiful bone structure. Prominent cheekbones. Gorgeous.

"Dang, you got me going out of my way, huh?"

"You offered."

We laugh.

He walks with me to the passenger side and opens my door. Butterflies erupt in my stomach so hard it almost hurts.

"Where do you live?" I ask, stopping a grin from spreading across my face.

"Georgetown. Right down the street basically."

He closes the passenger door and walks to the driver's side.

A gentleman. Opens the car door. Handsome. Wealthy. Walking perfection. Second to Jesus, of course.

God, you've outdone yourself with this one.

I hum, taking in the peppery, bergamot scent of the car. Smells just like him.

The fear and apprehension I felt earlier tonight, disappears. As the warmth of the car and the heated seats warm my body from the frigid weather, I lean my head back on the headrest and relax.

Genesis gets into the car. It's comfortable. It feels right. Normal. Like we've done this a million times before.

"So," his eyes meet mine, remaining on me for a moment too long.

My heart flutters. I can't take any more fire-starting stares. I swiftly turn to face the window and bite my lip to hide the smile that tries to break through.

He chuckles to himself as if he knows he's got me. The gear stick clicks, and he finally says in his deep, tender voice, "Let's go."

FOUR

LOLA

February 2000

"Momma, please!" I pleaded. I tugged my mom's leg to stop her from running to the house phone.

How could she do this? How could she not believe her *own* daughter?

"Get off of me!" she yelled, yanking her leg loose and kicking me in my nose. Physical and emotional pain rushed through me. Her hostile, glassy eyes witnessed me crawl into a fetal position, holding my bleeding nose.

All the love I once had for her. *Saw* in her. Was no more if it ever was. Her dark brown eyes shot daggers at me.

Her nose flared in anger. Her fair skin heated with a fierce redness that made her look like Lucifer. Although she was only five-four, the way she towered over me was horrifying. Gut-wrenching.

She was unrecognizable.

This was *not* my mom. It couldn't be.

She ran to the phone.

I gathered myself as much as I could. Wiped my face with my baggy white t-shirt and stumbled onto my feet. The agonizing ache in my chest left me breathless. Tears streamed down my face.

"Please, no!" I screamed, but her frantic wailing drowned me out.

I stood frozen. Time stopped. The world closed in.

The tone of the three numbers my mother dialed finally set everything into reality for me. It was over.

"Hello? Please come quick. My boyfriend's been shot."

Present Day

I gasp, jolting up in what takes me a moment to recognize as my bed. I swallow a dry gulp of air and catch my breath. Sweat beads form on my nose as I try to steady my racing heart. My blood pressure is already questionable for someone my age, so I better calm down before I end up in the ER for having another panic attack.

I can't believe this. My past is *still* haunting me.

After a few deep breaths, I exhale for the last time before a warm hand creeps along my side.

I'm either about to go full-blown Cleo mode and set it off in this piece or have a massive heart attack.

Shoot, I gave Poppy to Azra.

Option two coming into existence in five...four...three...two...

"You okay, bae?" a groggy voice croaks as that hand traces circles around my tatted lower back.

Ugh! I broke my unassailable rule: Never, and I mean *not ever* under any circumstances, let a man stay the night. Why? Because letting a man stay the night was like eating leftover fast food. It's good when it's hot and fresh, but after it sits around for a while, it gets old. The fries get soggy. The drink gets watered down. In other words, once I got my taste, the rest needed to be thrown out expeditiously.

I slowly turn to the side to behold Jeremiah lying beside me. My…*buddy*.

"Yeah, I'm fine…" I huff and swat his hand from tickling my back tattoo. "You need to go."

"What's wrong?"

"Nothing. I'm fine. You just got to go."

"But it's five o'clock in the morning."

"And I need to get some sleep…I have…work," I lie.

After getting fired last night, I came home, took a hot bubble bath, drank a bottle of wine, got desperate, *really* desperate, and called Jeremiah. Yup…had to be pretty desperate to do that. Nothing's necessarily wrong with him. He's cute. Tall. Got the body of a Greek god, makes me feel out of shape when I'm with him. Probably due to the strenuous training it takes to be a fireman. He's fine. But man is he *clingy*. Can't even breathe without him jumping up asking, "What do you need?"

It's been over a year since I last called him over for some TLC. Soon as he got my call this time, he was at my door in 3.4 seconds. Bowing to my every demand.

Though his company is nice for about ten minutes, and I'm being generous, it's time to go. I can't stand a man who doesn't know when to leave. He clings to me like a breastfed baby, which is why I only call him when I'm in crisis mode.

"You gonna do me like that?" He yawns, sitting up on the edge of the bed and hunching over.

"You know the deal, Jeremiah."

With his belt buckle clinking as he pulls his pants over his hips, he dryly chuckles, "Yeah, yeah. I know."

"Thank you," I pick up my phone from the nightstand.

"I'm glad you called. You missed me, huh?"

Oh gosh.

"Mm-hmm," I hesitantly hum as I reply to Azra's text:

Gotchu sis

Before looking up from my phone, Jeremiah's face comes swarming into mine faster than you can say *boy bye*.

"Skrt!" I lean back and press my fingers against his lips, "Bruh, you gotta stop doing that. Now, I said I need my sleep."

He pulls back, looking salty. He knows I don't kiss. The cheek, maybe. But never on the lips. Another one of my rules.

"So, that's how it is huh?"

"That's how it's been."

"I see nothing's changed."

With a sigh of annoyance, I wrap my nude body up in my white satin sheets and gracefully see Jeremiah to the door. For some strange reason, this walk from the bedroom to the door feels like the most disgraceful walk of shame I've taken in my life. I'm getting soft.

About to slam the door shut, he turns around to face me.

"Will I see you tomorrow?"

"No. I got a lot to do," I lie.

"What about tomorrow night? I'm off. Maybe I can stop by—"

"How about *I'll* call *you*?"

"Okay. Just don't leave me hanging for too long this time."

Putting on my fakest smile, I close the door in Jeremiah's grinning face and lean my back against the door.

Big mistake.

Wandering back to my bedroom, my eyes fall on the bouquet of red chrysanthemums that sit in a skinny crystal vase on my kitchen counter. The ones Romeo gave me a few days ago when he proposed.

I stare at them. Before him, I never received a single flower from anyone, let alone a bouquet.

That pesky pang of guilt is slowly creeping back and this time, I can't shake it.

No, I'm *not* about to start feeling bad again. All my guilt was supposed to go out the door along with Jeremiah, but it didn't. Actually, it's getting worse.

You'd think I'd feel bad for doing Jeremiah the way I did but I feel nothing. I forgot about him for over a year and will forget about him for another year…or more, if ever again. But when I do decide to call him up, get what I need, and put him out, does he trip? No. Does he go against the rules and regulations of how I handle situationships? No. Does he try to change or force me to fall in love with him? No.

He keeps his sappy emotions to himself, doesn't challenge me, and obeys my demands without question.

But William? Oh, Willy just can't let it go. He crossed boundaries nobody has *ever* crossed. Kissing me on the lips was strike one. And he keeps doing it.

Staying the night? Well, let's just say he has a spare toothbrush here…for whoopsies. Strike two.

But William doesn't just break the rules. He grounds them into a bag of pretty gold dust he uses to garnish his award-winning dishes. He does too much to prove a point. Like, okay, we know you're handsome and can break barriers only by flashing your dimpled smile. *Whoop-dee-doo*. But proposing was strike three.

So, why am I sitting here feeling guilty for staying true to myself? For real for real, *he* should be apologizing to me for putting *me* through this unnecessary drama.

Sucking my teeth, I roll my eyes from the flowers like it will somehow eliminate William from my mind.

I'm pissed.

I should be happy. I'm free. Free from that degrading job and free from William. But neither feels as good as they should.

Shuffling back to my room with all intentions to go back to sleep, the night light from the second bedroom catches the corner of my eye. Years ago, I turned the second bedroom into a sewing room. A place where I can sew and design in peace. Though I don't have much around to distract me, having a room dedicated to fashion gets me in the mood to create my best designs.

I walk in and glance around at the rolls of fabric and mannequins with pins and needles sticking out of them. Eight years of my life went to that lousy job and I have nothing to show for it other than hundreds of unfinished dresses, skirts, and blouses. I never make pants. If you want to destroy a woman's natural feminine sensuality, make her wear pants for the rest of her life.

This is where I need to be. But finally having the chance to work on my clothing line, I can't help but think about where I'm going to get the money from. My cash cow who ended up being a budget bull, ruined my plans with his stupid proposal. I can't and won't bring myself to commit to another job that will end up taking my time and focus away from growing my fashion line. And I can't start digging into my stash for rainy day rent. So, now what? I'm lost.

Holding back tears from the frustration that fills me, I glance around to see a stack of papers sitting next to my sketch book on my sewing table.

Ugh, here I go thinking about William again. He gave me a business plan template over a year ago when I told him about my dream of becoming a fashion designer.

He should've known then that I just wanted him to promote and sell my designs to his plethora of celebrity friends, but no. Being the *'faith without works is dead'* kind of man, William always found a way to put me to work.

I slouch on a stool and gawk at the first page. I'll never forget the night we brainstormed on what the name of the line should be.

.
**

"If you want to do this, you got to be serious about it," William said, sliding me a glass of red wine, as he sat beside me.

"Romeo, I *am* serious. You're literally the plug. You can ask your friends to wear one of my dresses on the red carpet and boom. Instant success. Don't you know Cardi?"

"That's not how it works," he chuckled, pulling me back by my shoulders to lean against him. He flings his arm around me.

"Why not?"

"Because they have their own people who deal with that stuff. Plus, that ain't my crowd. Yeah, I know a few entertainers, but not on the level where I can slide my woman's services to them."

"*Your* woman? Boy, I'm not anybody's woman but my own."

"You can be your own woman, but you got to share one day."

"With whom?" I quirked my eyebrow.

"Who do you think?" He caressed my upper arm and inched closer to place sweet kisses on my neck.

I giggled at the spine quivering sensation. "Boy stop. You're talking about me being your woman, but you don't even know me like that."

"Well, that's what I'm trying to do. Get to know you."

I cocked my brow and smirked. "You know what I want you to know."

"That's apparent. But I want to know more. I don't even know your whole name."

"Yeah, you do. Lola Jones."

"What's your middle name?"

"Why should I tell you? What have you done to earn the privilege of knowing my gov'ment name?" I joked, turning to face him.

"Well," he leaned forward grabbing the business plan from the coffee table, "I could be the one to put you on track to become a designer to the stars. I think I deserve to at least know who you are."

I tried to stop a grin from cracking my lips but was unsuccessful.

"So, what's your *whole* name?"

I exhaled and bowed my head. "Lola *Imala* Jones," I bashfully turned my face away.

He said nothing. Didn't he like my name?

I bit the inside of my cheek as I waited for him to respond.

"That's it." He placed the stack of papers on my lap and sat back.

"What's *it*?"

"The name for your clothing line. Imala."

"That's stupid."

"How? All the big clothing lines go by one name. Gucci. Prada. Armani. Versace. Imala. Hermes."

"I like how you did that. But my name isn't French or Italian. It doesn't have the same ring as everyone else's."

"Since when have you ever been like everybody else? You're special. That's how you got me."

"Shut up," I playfully slapped his leg.

"Seriously, Bean. You got this thing about you that no matter what you do, or what your name is, you're gonna succeed. I know you will. But *Imala*…that's it. I'm telling you. But you got to put work in. You do that, and you're in there. I promise you."

Smiling, I pick up a pen and write at the top of the first page: *Imala*. This is the only thing I have filled out on this plan. But now, it's official. I need to make money moves. No more working for anyone else. I'm going to be my own boss.

But where in the world am I going to get the money?

I flip through the blank pages of the business plan when my phone rings in my bedroom.

Grabbing the sheet that clings loosely around my body, I shuffle to the room, jump onto the bed, and grab my phone.

My stomach drops.

Romeo

Why is he calling? He's all the way in California, so it must be at least two in the morning there. He usually calls me early because he wants to be the first voice I hear, but that's supposed to be over with now. Isn't turning down someone's proposal considered the end of a relationship? I don't know what to say to him and don't understand what he wants with me after the other night.

Did I forget something? He might want to curse me out for hurting his ego. But then again, he's not that sort of guy. He's a gentleman...yuck. Maybe he's calling to take his flowers back. He can forget that. Those flowers are too nice. Wouldn't put it past him though with how cheap he is.

I'm not answering. But I'm also not one to run from *anyone* and I can't start now.

I exhale, close my eyes, and swipe the green button.

"Hello?"

Silence.

I pull the phone from my face to see if he hung up, but then his deep, penetrating voice draws me back.

"You know, for a second I thought you were gonna ignore me."

Chills run down my spine.

"Thought about it."

"Did I wake you?"

"Nope. What's up, William?"

"Whoa," he chuckles, "since when do you call me that?"

"Since you pulled that little stunt the other night."

"Stunt? You mean proposing to you?"

"If that's what you call it," I put my phone on speaker and lay it on the pillow.

William's cool and sexy chuckle vibrates through the phone. All I want to do is get off and go back to trying to not think about him, but that's gonna take a load of willpower.

"What?"

"You never cease to amaze me, Bean." He laughs.

I still don't appreciate that nickname. All because I'm tall and skinny, he thinks it's funny to call me 'beanstalk'. But I hate it. And I can't get him to stop. We're talking about William here. The same man who thought it was cool trying to trap me in a marriage. Nothing but a sly dirty trick. And he's got the nerve to still give me butterflies? How dare he?

"What's funny?"

"I never met anyone like you."

"And you won't ever again."

"Which is why I need the original."

"Dang, you're telling me rejecting your proposal with that Cracker Jack ring wasn't enough to get you off my case?"

"You thought that was enough to push me away?"

"Hoped so."

"You cold," he chuckles.

"Isn't it like two over there?"

"Yeah, I was about to go to sleep."

"Then why are you calling me dumb early after I turned you down?"

Silence. The suspense kills me until he says, "I don't give up that easily, woman."

"Well you should, *man*."

"Maybe…but you know you don't want me to do that."

"Says who?"

"That smile that's been on your face since answering the phone even though you're trying to hide it in your voice."

I pucker my lips to restrict the smile that *definitely* is on my face.

"You don't know me," I say trying to take any happy inflection out of my voice.

"I know enough. And once I peel back those tough layers, you'll be happy I didn't let a rejected proposal stop me from making you mine."

I huff, "Whatever, William."

"So, you agree?"

"On what?"

"You're gonna be mine one day."

I huff. "The number you have reached has been disconnected or is no longer in service. Please *don't* try again."

Turning on my stomach, I pick up the phone and hover my thumb over the end button.

"Okay, you got jokes huh? That's cool, Mrs. Rogers."

"Bye, William," I raise my voice.

"Hold on. I wanted to ask you something."

"You got two minutes," I sigh, tossing the phone back on the pillow.

"What'chu doing on the twenty-third?"

"Probably be in the middle of my 'swearing off men who do stupid crap' ritual. Why? What's up?"

"Well, after all that swearing off, you might be hungry. I'm coming by to make you dinner."

Scrunching my face, I squint at the phone, "Uh, excuse me, what makes you think you're invited? *You're* the one I'm swearing off."

"You know you want to see me, woman."

"We're. Not. Together. You messed that up."

"Did I?" There's a delight in his voice as he pesters me.

"Yes, you did."

"Okay, so what time do you want me to come over?"

"Are you deaf or dumb?" I snap. Sitting up, I take the speaker off and bring the phone to my ear.

"I'm a fool for you," he laughs.

"Never, William. You can't come by. We are done, done."

"Seven?"

"What the—"

"Alright then, seven it is."

"I'll call the cops on your pubescent behind."

He sniggers, "You gonna call the cops on me, woman?"

"If I have to."

"I'll take that risk."

"Suit yourself. They'll be waiting for you."

"As long as I can lay my eyes on you before they turn me away."

I grit my teeth to suppress a smile. "You're crazy."

"Well, tell me you don't like it and I'll stop."

"No, you won't."

"Yes, I will. Say it and I won't bother you anymore."

I bite my lip. He's serious. I can tell him to leave me alone, but for some reason, those words fail me.

"Bye William."

"Ah," he chuckles one last time before saying those horrific words he takes pleasure in saying without my prompting, "I love you, too."

My thumb hits the end button and I fling the phone beside me. Ugh, I hate when he does that. Isn't he tired of getting his heart broken?

I lie in bed to get some shut-eye, but every time I close them, all I see is my Romeo.

Oh God, shoot me now.

FIVE

AZRA

At a stop light, I glance at my reflection in the sun visor's mirror. My red-tinged, sunken in eyes tell it all.

I barely slept. Which isn't unusual. Sleeping pills are usually my friend during times like these but I didn't want to sleep.

He's been on my mind.

His gleaming white teeth that contrast against his beautifully dark skin. Those deep-set eyes. Strong arms. That cologne.

Lord forgive me. I can't believe the thoughts I'm thinking about a man I'm not married to.

Is it a sin to find someone attractive? It isn't like I'm lusting after him, I'm just *admiring* his physical appearance. The Bible doesn't say you can't do that.

I just can't stop thinking about the fuzzy feeling I felt being so close to Genesis.

Last night, I could've died from the flipping my stomach was doing as he drove me home.

I scrolled down my Bible app. The ride was pretty quiet aside from The Isley Brother's *Groove with You* setting the mood for us as we merged onto I-495. The streetlights lit the inside of the car just enough to catch him glimpsing at me in my peripheral. My body trembled with chills every time our eyes mistakenly met.

I was smitten like a kitten. I kept trying to focus on the scriptures and prayed to keep it together.

Genesis is everything. He's a bonafide *man*. It's in the way he carries himself. He stands tall in his tailor-made attire. He pronounces his words clear and precisely. He's so well-groomed. Not a strand of beard hair out of place. And the way he gazes at me through those pretty brown eyes. I'm in love.

While we were riding, he was texting someone. It was four o'clock in the morning. Who in the world was he texting?

I had the mind to peek, but I refrained because it isn't my business...*yet*.

"Here." He held out his phone to me.

He reads minds too? The man probably thought I was delusional, desperate, and deviant with the conversation I was having about him in my head. Thankfully, when I looked at the screen, I saw Google Maps pulled up. *Whew.*

"What do you want me to do with that?" I asked.

"Put in your address so I know where to take you."

"Nah, that's okay. I'll tell you where to go," I politely nudged his phone away.

He laughed, "You really think I'm gonna come back and gut you or something?"

"Anything's possible. Take Exit 25A and follow US-1 North."

He chuckled to himself before putting his phone on the phone cradle.

"So, you're a Christian?" he asked.

"I am. How'd you know?"

"I peeped you reading the Bible on your phone. Plus, you got that cross around your neck."

"Oh, yeah. My grandmother gave me this when I was a little girl."

"That's what's up. So, do you have a favorite scripture?"

Without hesitation I cracked a smile and recited one of the thousands of scriptures that were drilled into me as a child, "Count it all joy when you fall into various trials, but let patience have its perfect work, that you may be perfect and complete, lacking nothing."

He shot me an impressed glare. "What'chu know about that? That's a seasoned saints scripture right there."

"Well, I was raised by an elder of the church. My grandmother served at The First Baptist Church of Mount Moriah longer than I've been alive."

"That's what's up. So, you grew up in church?"

"Yeah." *Unfortunately*, I wanted to add, but that wouldn't be right.

"So how do you relate to that scripture? You can't be no more than, what? Twenty-one? Twenty-two? What trials have you been through that makes that your favorite?"

"That's a deep question to ask, Mr. Struthers," I huffed and crossed my arms, "and my age is none of your business."

"Genesis," he corrected me. "And my bad. You just look so young. Thought you couldn't have been through too much."

I hated when people discredited my struggle because of my age. I may not have had traumatic experiences, but he didn't know that. He equated youth to naivety. Flat out foolish.

"All because I'm young, doesn't mean I haven't had my share of trials to overcome."

The corners of his lips curled downward, and he nodded, "Sayless."

Feeling bad for coming off a little abrasive, I uncrossed my arms and adjusted toward him. "What's *your* favorite scripture? And since you want to be all in *my* business, how old are you?" I smiled to let him know I wasn't trying to be rude.

"Well, I'm thirty-seven. I don't have a problem saying it because age ain't nothing but a number," he peered at me with a smirk.

My heart quickens. *Well, call me Aaliyah.*

"And that's easy," he continued, "Make allowance for each other's faults, and forgive anyone who offends you. Remember the Lord forgave you, so you must forgive others."

"Mmm…interesting," I tilted my head. How was it possible for this man to be gorgeous *and* accurately quote Bible like it's a second language? I thought it was impossible for him to get more attractive but apparently, I was wrong.

"How?" he asked.

"It's about forgiveness. That's specific."

"Well, I had to forgive a lot of people in my life." The smirk on his face weakened.

"Like whom?"

"Look who's being nosey now! Nah, I ain't telling you nothing," he laughed.

"Fair enough."

"Nah, if you want to know. I grew up in the church too. Let's say, God brought me through a lot. I had to forgive a lot of people so I could get where I am today."

"Got'chu. Oh, make a left at this light," I reluctantly pointed to the stop light ahead when I realized we were close to my home. I wanted to keep riding. I didn't want the night to end. Yet, I directed him until we pulled up in front of Lola's apartment building. Shoot, he might be fine, but I need to feel a person out before I give them my address.

"This is me," I said looking at my gray, 2004 Honda Civic parked to the right.

Gathering my bags and unbuckling my seatbelt, I remained in the car. Genesis frowned. "What's wrong?"

"I'm getting out of the car."

"Oh…kay…"

"The door—"

"Oh, wait. You're waiting for me to open the door for you?"

"Well, you opened it for me to get in. It's basic car etiquette at this point."

He chuckled before getting out of the car and walked over to open my door.

I hiked my bags over my shoulder and hopped out. "Thanks, Mr. Struthers," I smiled.

"Absolutely." He quickly cast an eye over me from head to toe, still holding the car door open, "So, you forgive me now?"

"For what?"

"For firing your ride?"

"She's my *friend*, and I don't know. I'll let you know tomorrow," I tipped my head to the side and gazed at him. Our eyes met and my breath caught. I shivered. Not from the frosty snow hitting the back of my neck, but from the look he gave me.

He licked his lips and redirected his eyes to my car. "Well, I won't hold my breath. Long as you don't quit on me, that's all the forgiveness I need."

"I'm not quitting," I said.

"Good," he smiled at me and grazed his hand on my shoulder. "Have a good night, Azra."

My knees weakened. The way my name rolled off his tongue made me wish he'd whisper it in my ear. On loop. My new favorite song. I shuddered at its sweet melody.

"You too, Mr. Struthers."

"Genesis," he corrected me again.

"Noted."

His eyes bored into mine for only a second more before his phone rang in the car.

Glancing over at the infotainment system 'Her' showed on the screen.

Oh Lord, someone's trying to steal my man.

My spirits crashed into the snowy pavement.

"I'll see you tomorrow." He moved aside to lead me on my way before sauntering over to the other side of the car.

I stepped to the driver's side of my car and hopped in.

Looking outside the window, he smiled at me as he spoke to whoever *Her* was before pulling off.

I sat in my car and let it warm up, thinking about how sucky I felt.

Now, I feel the same I felt five hours ago. He's supposed to be *my* man. But unfortunately, he's got a woman.

Ugh! Am I going to be single for the rest of my life?

I jump as the sounds of multiple horns blast behind me. I wave 'sorry' as I hit the sun visor up and pull off.

Making it to Mom-mom's quaint home, the smell of bacon and eggs fills the house. Makes me sick.

"Hey Mom-mom," I sing, entering the small kitchen to find her flipping that nasty, lardy bacon. It seems like every day I see her; her skin gets darker, and she becomes thinner. Like a shell of herself.

All the body I got, I got it from my mom-mom. She was always thick and shapely. But over the years, her sicknesses have eaten her up. It's painful to watch.

She fried her eggs in the bubbling, black bacon fat.

I turn my nose up and try to hold my breath. I want to take the pan and throw it out the window. Exchange it for a nice leafy green salad. I've been trying to convert her to become a vegetarian, especially after her stroke. But God forbid I tell her about how unhealthy she eats. Lord knows she'll pop me back into Leviticus for touching her dirty swine. If she did it before, she'll do it again. She's done it before.

I hand her the small white bag that holds her pain medication.

She takes it and places it on the counter. "Hey, sugar. Thank you so much for getting my meds. I was afraid I might be in pain all day."

"You alright?" I give her a half hug and frown at the pan of fried eggs. Though she slaves over the stove, she smells of lemon and vanilla. Her signature scent from Bath & Body Works. I love it. Nostalgic.

"Oh, I'm fine," she shoos me away, "just need to get these meds in me and I'll be fine."

I take a seat at the small, round kitchen table and watch her cook.

"Missed you on the prayer call today." She raises her eyebrows.

"I know, Mom-mom. I'm sorry, I got in late last night."

"They're working you too hard, baby. This the second time you missed Saturday's prayer."

"I know, but I need the money. I have to pay rent for this month *and* last month. On top of that, I've got debt to pay back to the school from last semester, *and* I need to save so I can pay for this coming semester. It's a lot. But I'll be leaving that job soon."

"You sure you don't need any money, sugar?"

"I'm sure, Mom-mom. It's fine. I just have to do what I have to do. I'll be fine."

I'll never take her money. Not because she's my grandmother, but because she'll have a field day talking to her church buddies about how she's taking care of me and keeping me off the streets. It's weird. She wants people to see her in this perfect light, yet she'll stretch the truth until it becomes saran wrap thin.

"Mm-hmm," she hums, "You just make sure you don't stray too far from the Lord. It's the end days. You need to stay in prayer."

I prayed on my own time.

All because she doesn't see me praying, then to her, that means I'm not doing it. It's like nothing I do is good enough for her. This is why I don't like being around her for too long. She tells me I need to pray. Judges whether my spirit is right based on my church attendance. And makes me run errands. I love her more than anyone on this earth, but I'm getting tired of trying to please her. But I don't know how to stop.

I can't have an opinion, so I don't even try to defend myself. As usual, I bite my tongue and grit my teeth.

"Yes, ma'am," I say, chewing on the side of my cheek.

She continues to ramble. Talks about how young folks are going to hell. How most of my generation is demonic and doesn't have a chance of entering the Kingdom of God. Which is only half true. Apparently, only people sixty-five and up are saved. The rest of us? We're on our own. She then goes on to allude to how perfect we must be, but then rebuttals by saying it's impossible because fleshly beings will never be as perfect as Jesus. Contradictions and confusion. The typical conversation with her.

I've been hearing this nonsensical speech my whole life. I just zone out now. I glance at the bible in front of me.

Second Timothy. My eyes fall on verse seven.

'For God gave us a spirit not of fear but of power and love and self-control.'

Amen to that! Love and self-control. At this point, I don't have much of either.

The last twenty-five years of my life have been nothing but a facade to uphold this image of perfection and Buddha-like discipline. But the desire to put on for people is waning every day. The more I meditate on that scripture, the more it clicks.

It's time to take control of my life. Take control of my actions. Stop letting the fear Mom-mom instilled in me control what I do. Last thing I want is to be scared into being just like her. Couped up in a house eating greasy food and blaming the doctors and everyone else for the diseases *I've* caused.

They say if you want something you never had, you've got to do something you've never done. That's what I'm going to do. I'm going to live my life, and I'm not going to let anyone damn me to hell for it.

"Sugar? You hear me?" Mom-mom sits across the table with her head tilted. A piece of burned bacon crumbles in her mouth.

"Yes, ma'am. I'm just—"

"Tired. I know those doctors put you on that medicine so you can get some sleep, but I'm telling you, all you need is a bacon sandwich and some ginger ale, and you'll be knocked out in no time. Why don't you go to my room and lay down for a couple hours? I'll wake you up before Bible study."

"It's okay, Mom-mom. And I told you before, I don't eat meat. And even if I did, I'd die before I eat that nasty bacon. I can't even stand the smell of it. The grease. The saltiness—"

"That's 'cus you don't know good cooking. You used to eat this stuff every day when you was a little girl. You ain't complain then."

"But I'm not a little girl anymore."

"Mm-hmm. All you want to do is eat that tutu stuff."

"It's *tofu*, Mom-mom," I giggle, "And it's better than that smelly bacon. At least you won't die from eating it every day."

"I wouldn't be too sure about that. You know I read on one of those news articles on the internet that *tufu*, or whatever you call it, can cause cancer. It turns men into women, too. Something about lowering their testosterone. No wonder why boys your age out here wearing dresses and stuff."

I chuckle, "That's what they say but that's a myth. But I'm sure it won't clog your arteries the way that swine does."

"If you say so, sugar."

Yawning, I stand and push the chair in under the table. "I'm gonna get going, Mom-mom. Go home and try to get some rest. You need anything?"

"Just a ride to Bible study later."

My eyes water but I blink the blurriness away. "Alright, I'll come and pick you up."

"Okay sugar, you be safe. Don't fall asleep on the road. Lord knows I can't take that kind of news right now."

"I'll be fine, Mom-mom," I chuckle to myself as she walks me to the door.

After giving hugs and kisses, I mosey to the car, throw my purse on the car seat, and pull out my phone to text Lola:

U home?

Shoot. I forgot. Sending you the money now.

No. It's fine. But can I come over?

U ever ask b4?

Nope. Be there in a jif.
& u betta have some clothes on

Don't forget to knock!

I toss my phone to the passenger seat and pull out of Mom-mom's driveway.

SIX

LOLA

February 2000

"Come here." The stench of whiskey and rotting teeth stung my eyes as his face neared mine and his hands tightened around me.

"Let me go, Randy," I wriggled to loosen his grip on my arms.

"Stop!" he violently rattled me, "If you don't keep it down, I'ma tell yo' momma what you do to me right next to her in bed. You wan'er to know?"

I bit my lip to keep myself from bawling.

I shook my head.

"That's what I thought. Now, be a good girl and lay down," he grumbled.

Lying face down on the bed, I quietly sobbed.

This would be the last time he'd tell me to be a good girl.

I slipped my hand under my pillow. The cold piece of steel I found in Randy's drawer felt so big in my little hands.

Randy's weight pinned me beneath him. His sweaty body imprinted on my back, making it hard to breathe.

I squeezed my eyes shut as he lifted my shirt above my waist. He leaned his face into the nape of my neck and whispered, "Don't worry. I'll make it quick this time."

The tears streamed down my cheeks as he yanked my underwear down.

Wrapping my finger around the trigger, I pulled it from under the pillow. "No!" I screamed, turning around and kicking him away from me.

He hissed, "Keep ya damn voice—"

I pointed the gun at him. His eyes steadied on the opening of the barrel.

"What'chu gon' do wit' dat? Huh?" He tried snatching it away.

I tumbled back and hopped to my feet. Standing on the bed, I aimed the gun at his cratered face.

He slowly footed backwards, "Lil' girl, gimme the damn gun 'fore I take it and off ya' mo—"

Bang!

His eyes bulged. He stumbled back as he held his bare stomach. Blood gushed through his fingers as he pressed against the bullet hole.

He reached and staggered forward to take the gun.

Bang!

He dropped to the floor.

My ears rang. My hands tremored, rattling the gun from my grasp. A single tear trickled from my eye.

The door flung open. My mom plodded into the room. She slammed herself into the doorframe. Her eyes, red and droopy. She sniffed and wiped her nose.

"What the hell is—" She zones in on Randy sprawled out on the floor. A puddle of blood streamed from underneath him.

"Oh, my God!" she shrieked, dropping to her knees. Crawling over to Randy's dead body, she held his head in her hands. "Lola, what did you do?"

***

Present Day

"Hey, Lo."

My phone jumps out of my hands and falls on my chest as Azra busts into my bedroom. What is wrong with this girl? She knows my nerves are shot.

"I told you to knock!" I sit up on my bed.

Azra trails over and sits silently on the edge. Worry lines crease her brow.

"What's wrong?"

"Nothing. Tired," she says with a tight-lipped smile. "How you doing? Now that you're unemployed and all."

"Best decision I've ever made."

"You didn't quit, Lola." She chuckles.

"I didn't? Shoot, with how good things been going, I forgot it wasn't my idea."

"It's literally only been twelve hours but go off, sis."

"Twelve hours and already making moves, boo," I grab my business plan from my nightstand. I filled out the sections I thought I understood.

"What'chu been doing?" Azra asks, lying over the foot of my bed.

"Well, I've been filling this out," I toss the papers over to her.

She flips through but doesn't read anything. "What's this?"

"A business plan. I've been thinking too small. I want a fashion line, but I also want a place people can come and actually try and buy my clothes. So, after thinking about it, I've decided to open my own boutique."

Azra places the papers on the bed and looks at me through lowered lids. "Really?"

"Yes, really. Girl, it's time to be my own boss. I don't have time to be working for other people."

"That's great, Lo. But where you gonna get the money?"

"You know who you're talking to?" I snatch the papers away, "I am Lola 'Mother Make Do' Jones. This is what I do, sis. I might not have it now, but I'm gonna find a way."

"Okay." Azra laughs, but I'm serious.

I made my way in life with little to no help. This new journey I'm embarking on is going to be no different. Forget a rich man. I'll figure it out. Always have.

As I place the business plan back on my nightstand, Azra's phone chimes. Her face brightens.

"What're we doing tomorrow night? It's my first Sunday off and I'm finna get turnt," I say with a shoulder dance.

Azra sighs, looking at her phone. "I have to work."

"But it's your day off."

"Genesis just texted me and told me I have to work. I guess because you aren't there."

"*Genesis*? You on first-name basis now?" I knit my eyebrows as Azra goes googly-eyed. "What the heck is *that* face?" I shrill, nudging her with my foot.

"Nothing," she smiles.

"Even after last night you still like dude?"

"He's not that bad."

"How do you know?"

"We may have talked a little when he...gave me a ride home."

I grin. "*That's* why you didn't accept the Lyft money."

Bouncing off my butt, I lay next to her. Resting my chin on my hand, I ask, "Girl, tell me everything?"

"Nothing, he just gave me a ride. That's all."

"Mm-hmm. That smile on your face is saying more than that. Looks like you wanted to go full equestrian on him."

"Shut up," she giggles, nudging her shoulder against mine.

"I'm just saying, I never saw that face before."

"It's not a face. I…I just don't think he's a bad guy. You can't judge people based on one encounter."

"It's *definitely* a face. And you can *certainly* judge them by first impressions," I raise my brow. "Is he gay?"

"Wha—No!" She slams her hands on the bed.

"How do you know? He fired *me*. I never met a straight man that turned me away."

"Not everyone is into you, Lola." *Could've fooled me.* "He's just a nice guy. He's not like the dudes you're used to dealing with."

She's so innocent. All guys are the same in one way or another. But instead of popping her bubble, I'll let her live out her truth.

"Listen. You know I'm all for you exploring your options and having a good time. But don't get caught up with a man that talks down to you. Trust me. It never goes well."

She nods.

I want the deets. But trying to get information out of Azra is like pulling gold teeth out of an old pimp's mouth.

"How old is he?" I ask.

"Thirty-seven…I think."

"Oh, he's too old for you."

"Too old?"

"Yes, that's like…" I count on my fingers, "a twelve-year age gap, Az."

She sits up on the bed with one leg bent, "Last time I checked, you were dating someone ten years *younger* than you."

I scoff, "Seven and a *half*, thank you very much. And Romeo is different. He's…mature for his age."

"And I'm not?" she frowns, crooking her head to the side, "William is only two years older than me. And at least nobody is *engaged* in this situation." She rolls her eyes.

"First of all, Romeo and his fiancé were estranged. And second, it isn't my fault my good looks and charm was stronger than the hold she had on him. He was fully capable of making his own decisions," I sit up and grab my phone, checking to see if he texted me. I catch myself and throw my phone down like it's hot coal. I will not become that girl. Checking her phone every time she thinks about a dude. *Nope.*

Azra hums, brushing off what I said.

"And you better hope Genesis ain't married…with his ugly self," I roll my eyes.

"He's not. I haven't seen a ring. And you were just talking to me about how cute he was last night."

"Well, not his attitude. And a ring never stopped a man from cheating. Plus, he's got tendencies about him that's not cool. Kendrick seems like a better fit for you. He's only thirty, way younger than Genesis. And at least you know he's not married."

"Genesis isn't married, Lo. And Kendrick…stop with that. We'll never be more than friends." She slowly massages her temple and stands from the bed. I've never seen Azra so defensive. I chuckle at her disturbed demeanor.

"He bet not be, 'cus I'm not trying to save you from being dragged by someone's wife."

She bunches her brow and crosses her arms, "Do I have home-wrecker written across my forehead or something? Even if he was married, why would I willingly go along with it?"

"Chile, even Mary sinned. What makes you any different, Becky? Or should I say Beckham? 'Cus he might play for the other team?" I laugh, cracking myself up.

Azra remains stone-faced.

In all seriousness, I don't trust Genesis. I don't appreciate the way he spoke to Azra or his pretty boy fashion sense. It's unsettling. But if Azra wants to have fun and not get in too deep with dude, she'll be fine.

"Let me leave before that Jezebel spirit you got hops onto me." Azra backs out the room. We share a laugh as I walk her to the door.

Walking back to my room, I stop in my tracks as a knock sounds at the door.

Checking the peephole, two police officers stand outside.

I swing the door open. "Yes, officers?" My heart hammers in my chest.

"Are you Lola Jones?" the tall, male officer asks.

I nod and hold my nervously aching stomach.

"I'm sorry to inform you, but your mother was found dead."

SEVEN

AZRA

"Ms. McKinney, please come to the office," Genesis's voice sternly summons me to his lair.

I clocked in late again. That's only because my beater of a car was giving me a hard time starting. But come on; I'm not even a full two minutes late and he's already calling me in?

I sigh as my stomach drops to the floor. No matter how annoyed I am, I'm more afraid I might be next to get the ax. I'm in no position to let that happen. But judging the way Genesis did a one-eighty after giving me a ride, I'm sure I'm about to be panhandling for money.

After our ride together, he changed. He barely speaks to me when we cross paths. He darts across the room to avoid me. Even when we had our weekly meeting, he didn't catch the flirtatious shots I was throwing. And that is *not* like me. I like for the guy to chase me. But he acts as if I'm invisible.

Maybe Lola was right. His wrists might be broke. Or he might be married and is avoiding me to stop himself from doing something he'll later regret. Either way, I'm in a mood behind it.

I trot to the office and lift a fist to do a courtesy knock before it flies open. The waft of his irresistible cologne hits me like a sedative. All angst sweeps away. His eyes beam into mine. I melt like the Wicked Witch of the West.

"Ms. McKinney," he smiles, welcoming me in his office before closing the door behind him.

His formally addressing me makes me nervous. Maybe that's his way of being professional. "You know why I called you in here, right?"

I shake my head. I would mention my tardiness but that pleasant smile on his face confuses me. I decide against incriminating myself.

"I wasn't eavesdropping, but I couldn't help but overhear you talking to a couple of the ladies here the other day."

My heart sinks. The only thing I ever talk about with the girls is how much I hate working here, so whatever he heard, can't be good.

"You don't like it here?"

"No! I didn't mean it like that, Mr. Struthers. I love my job," I lie. "I'll work hard, even on weekdays at the bar. I just don't—I *can't* lose this job."

"Ms. McKinney. Breathe," he chuckles, placing his large, comforting hand on my shoulder. "You're not losing your job. Relax."

He gently squeezes me, and I relax but my heart is in overdrive.

He continues, "I called you in because I feel you may want a different opportunity here."

"Like what?"

He walks behind his desk, sits, and leans back in his seat.

"Well, when you started here, you had on your resume that you were a business major."

"I still am. I'm trying to finish but I need to pay my debts before I complete my last semester."

I feel like a broken record every time I explain why I haven't finished school yet. Not having money sucks, but it really sucks when you have to choose between keeping a roof over your head and getting an education, so you don't have to work a degrading job. And moving back in with Mom-mom isn't an option.

His eyes narrow before he looks down and folds his hands together.

"What if I can help you with that?"

"What do you mean?"

"Pay your debt so you can finish. That's the only debt you have, right? One semester's worth?"

"Yeah, I was on a payment plan throughout college, but since my rent when up last year, it's been hard keeping up with the payments."

"Well, Ms. McKinney, your work ethic impresses me. As you know, we had to get rid of a lot of people because they got too comfortable. I know you don't like this job, but you still grind and do what you gotta do. I like that. So, I want to offer you a manager's position here. But you need to have your degree before I can do that."

"M-me? A manager? Over th-this club?" I stutter like Elmer Fudd.

What does he want from me? There was no way a man will pay for a woman to finish school, give her a position making twice the money, and not expect *anything*. What do I have to do for it? Because if he thinks he can simply sit here and look like a whole meal, all while using his power and good looks to get me to succumb to his deviant desires...well...he's right.

"I could definitely use your kind of help. You're smart. Driven. Beautiful. I don't see why you wouldn't qualify."

I giggle and shield my face, "I don't think beauty has much to do with qualifications, Mr. Struthers."

"You'd be surprised," his eyes linger on me. He parts from whatever thoughts are floating through his head. "But until you get your degree, you'll be my assistant manager. That means you'll get a raise, *and* you don't have to worry about putting yourself on display anymore. Sounds good?"

I clasp my hands together, "Of course! I'd love to work under you." Oh gosh, did I just say that? I wince at the thought of possibly making things awkward, but he seems not to notice. Or at least not mind.

"Perfect. Well, you start tonight." He sits back in his chair and folds his arms.

"But I don't know what to do."

"Don't worry, I got you. But before we do anything," he stands and drifts over to me with a stony expression.

My knees shake.

His glare weakens me. *What is this man doing to me?*

He continues, "Do I have to walk you through being on time again?"

"I'm so sorry, Mr.—"

Shaking his head, he chuckles, "I'm messing with you."

My heart settles. This man is aiming to give me a heart attack.

He holds his hand out to me, "Welcome to your new position."

Shaking his hand, I smile.

Lola was wrong. Genesis *is* a gentleman. And by the rate things are going, my time at Ace Nightclub is about to get a little more interesting.

EIGHT

LOLA

Lady of Sorrows. That's what my mother named me. She kept me only because she couldn't afford an abortion. But I loved her the same.

I brought her days of misery. And she did her best to remind me.

She was always that woman I saw the day Randy died. But as a child, I didn't see that. I saw my loving mother. Rose-colored shades will make you see diamonds when in retrospect, it was nothing but a pebble.

Regardless of everything that's transpired, it's a new day.

For the first time in years, I woke up void of a cold sweat. I slept through the night. Peacefully. A clearer mind than before her death.

A weight lifted when the cops came knocking at my door. But oddly, there's still a piece of me that feels like it died along with her.

An overdose.

Supposedly, she was clean for a few years. Then, one day, she was back on that stuff again.

I want to cry. Laugh. Scream. Dance. But I can't bring myself to do anything but carry on.

Life happens. People die. But the living must live on. But I still need time alone. At least one good thing came out of her demise: my nightmares ended. A win for me, I guess.

Although I have the mind to tell Azra about my mother, it's useless. She knows I despised the woman, but she doesn't know why. Never asked either. No one knows about my childhood or what I did. I prefer it that way. Besides, there's no need to tell anyone now. My childhood is dead and gone.

I told the funeral directors to throw my mother's ashes away. I buried her in my past. I'm moving on.

I let Azra know that I was taking a couple weeks to do some major self-care, but instead, I utilized this time to binge on junk food and Netflix. But being a brownie away from wallowing in my woes, I make myself go into my sewing room.

Designing is my safe haven. The one thing that lets me know all is well in the world. The one thing I've done my entire life. The one thing I can thank my mother for introducing me to. She was a fashionista. Got me into sewing at a young age, although she never liked anything I made.

I made her a dress once. Brown with yellow polka dots. Ugliest dress I ever laid eyes on, but as a child, I made it out of love. She faked a smile; said she'd wear it one day. The next day it was in the kitchen garbage with leftover spaghetti dumped over it. I always hoped it was Randy who did that.

Pushing my thoughts away, I turn up my Bluetooth speaker to vibe to some Raveena. Grabbing my black charmeuse silk, I close my eyes, rub the lustrous fabric in my hands, and envision a beautiful dress: A floor-length, marigold macrame skirt with a strapless charmeuse silk bodice that cinches the waist, creating a gorgeous hourglass figure.

"Yes, bih."

I open my eyes, snatch the scissors from the sewing table and go to town. As I cut, my worries vanish. Then a knock at the door shakes me and my hands. I rip the fabric.

Shoot! I throw the scissors on the table, trample out the room and peep out the peephole.

"What the…" I mutter.

William's happy behind stands on the other side of the door, smiling. He holds two large brown paper bags of groceries in his arms.

Dang, I totally forgot he was coming by today.

This man is gonna make me deal with him whether I like it or not. But I'm not ready. I look so homely. Changing is an option but that'll take too long. Not answering is a choice, but I can't leave him hanging.

Sucking it up is my final resort.

I smooth my hands over my crop top and brush off the Dorito crumbs that are sprinkled over my tights.

Opening the door, William's smile disappears. He examines me without the beautiful fixings he usually sees me in.

"Wow..." He smirks with an enchanted glint in his eyes. I watch as they inspect every inch of my face, even the scar that traces the left side of my mouth to my ear.

Feeling self-conscious, I turn away.

"Why do you wear all that makeup again?" he asks.

"Why not?" I cross my arms.

"You're gorgeous without it."

My heart sinks a little, but I keep my cool. I chew the inside of my cheek to curb a stupid smile from appearing on my face.

"Well, this look was supposed to work as F-boy repellent but apparently, it ain't strong enough."

He sweeps an eye down my body and chuckles. Brushing against me, he backs me inside and makes his way to the kitchen.

"So, what you been up to, woman?"

I hold up my destroyed silk and knit my brows. "Trying to piece back together what you ruined."

"How'd I do that?" His cheeks dimple as he set the groceries on the kitchen counter and unpacks.

"By banging on my door like you wanted a cap in your behind. You know I got a mean trigger finger; you can't be popping up on me like that."

"I told you I was coming over."

"I never said you could."

"You didn't say I couldn't either."

I roll my eyes and take a seat on a barstool. There's no winning with him. He thinks everything is a game.

"Anyway, you owe me forty dollars now."

He smiles, "I'll give you forty-one."

"You know, for you to be so-called 'rich', you sure are cheap."

"It ain't *so-called* woman. I spend on what I need, and I don't brag and boast about what I have."

"Well maybe if you were bragging and boasting about *me* then we'd still be together."

William carries on. He grabs *my* pans from *my* cabinets and used *my* water to fill up a pot. How dare he? The fact he knows where everything is in my kitchen has me high key bothered. But that's what I get for making him feel comfortable.

"You work on the business plan I gave you?" he inquires, putting the large pot on the stove with his back facing me.

"I did."

"When?"

"Over the weekend. I'm done."

He turns around. Confusion twists his face, "You finished it?"

"Yup."

"Nobody finishes a business plan in a couple of days, Bean. It takes months to do."

"Well, I did."

"Okay," he chortles. He comes closer and holds his hand out. "Let me see it."

Skipping to my room, I grab the papers, come back, and smack them in his hand.

He flips through like Azra did. But at least he looks like he's reading it.

"I see where you're going with this. A boutique is a great idea. But you need to develop this...a lot."

I seize the papers and throw them on the counter. "Why can't you just give me the money to do this, William? You act like it's gonna hurt your pockets."

"Who's to say people even gonna like your clothing? And even if they do, who says they're gonna buy it?"

Oh no he didn't. I step back and squint my eyes, "You're saying my designs are ugly?"

"I didn't say that—"

"That's what it sounds like."

"Listen, Bean. You need to know the business behind owning your own boutique. You need to know your customers, prices, expenses, location. This?" he picks up the papers and flutters them, "This doesn't tell me anything, other than you want people to love and buy your clothes—"

"Designs," I snatch the papers back.

He laughs.

"What's so funny?"

"Nothing." He turns to continue cooking.

"No, humor me. You know I've been passionate about fashion ever since we met. I took courses to learn what I already know about it. You know how much this means to me. You have the money. Why don't you want to help me?" I yell.

"Calm down."

"Don't tell me to calm down! This isn't a game, William. This is my dream! I've been wanting this my whole life."

"Lola—"

"No. You already know what I want from you. You know all I ever wanted was your help. But you act like I got to be your wife before you give me that. I'm telling you now, I'm not marrying you. I'm *not* giving you what you want because I don't know if you will *ever* give me what I want. So why are you here? You still trying to trick me? You just want me to be your little stay-at-home wife. Somebody you can carry around on your arm like that freaking faux-lex watch you got. Brag to your whack friends about how you pulled yourself a cougar? Is that it?"

He lifts his head to the ceiling and lets out an exasperated laugh.

"Stop laughing!" I scream, banging my fists on the bar.

"I can see you got everything you wanted as a child, didn't you?"

My eyes narrow. "You don't know me," I mumble.

"You were that little brat that didn't have to work for nothing to get what she wanted, huh?"

My eyes water.

Not everyone grew up with a silver spoon in their mouths, but William doesn't understand that. He doesn't know that sometimes, the only way to survive was to find or steal what was needed. Some of us had drug addicts for parents and not doctors. *He* grew up wealthy. Not me. How dare he assume?

I flutter back tears. "William, stop."

"Nah. You think because your daddy gave you your way as a child, then that's what *I'm* supposed to do? Let you use me to get your way while you give *me* the bare minimum."

"Shut up," I shout. "Yes, I'm gonna use you and as many men as I can to get what the hell I want. And I'm gonna get it, you know why? Because I deserve it! You don't know what I've been through and you're not gonna sit here and act like you got me figured out, because you don't."

"That's what I mean, Lola. You expect me to open my wallet to you, but you can't even open up about your past. I told you about why I became a chef. How my Aunt Andrea helped me learn to bake and cook so I could eat while my parents were constantly working. How I felt when I got accepted into Le Cordon Bleu and lived in Paris. I told you where I came from and how I got where I am today. But you haven't. I don't know where you came from because *you* kept it that way. You won't even let me know little things, like why you decided to get angel wings tatted on your back. But Lola, I want to help you. I want you to achieve all your dreams. I want you to go places you never thought you'd be. But I need you to be serious. I want you to open up but if you can't do that, then at least show me you're willing to put in the work. Not just into the clothes but into the *business*. Once I see you're serious about that, I'm already ten steps ahead of you. Just show me something."

The pent-up emotions I've been holding in for two weeks, trickle out as tears of angst. I cross my arms and focus away from William's unwavering stare.

His brows pull together, and his body relaxes. He ambles near, pulling me into a bear hug.

I should shove him away. Even throw him out. But I can't. His warmth is so calming. I feel secure.

I lean my head on his shoulder and sob. He embraces me. Eager to squeeze out every ounce of agony that's possessed me since childhood.

After a few moments, I squirm from his arms and dryly chuckle. "You think you're my father now?" I pat my eyes dry with the bottom of my shirt.

He softens his tone, "I'm just trying to give you direction, woman. I know I'm younger than you, but I need you to trust me on this."

Trust? Trust means more than love. Trust is giving someone your heart. Being vulnerable and knowing the other person won't hurt you in the long run. Blindly following someone into a fire and not questioning their intention. Love, for me, is a no-no. But *trust* is a foreign impossibility.

I twist my lips and walk to the barstool to sit my overemotional behind down. Blinking back the last of my tears, I flip my emotional switch. "What'chu cooking?"

William glares at me like he's trying to figure me out.

"You good?"

I chuckle, "I'm fine. Just…got me worked up. That's all."

He backs away with a worried smile. Taking a deep breath, he returns to the kitchen to finish cooking.

"Uh, I'm making your favorite," he says, "Shrimp stuffed Tuscan salmon, roasted garlic potatoes, and…since you can't live without them…onion rings," he shivers and playfully gags.

The first time he made that meal for me, he made it with some bougie asparagus on the side. That was before he learned my favorite veggie was onions…dipped in batter…and fried. Twice. He always teases me because I had no idea what a five-star meal looked or tasted like until he made it. Until him, I was happy with a sandwich and a soda. After all, I got by with less as a child.

I'm classy, not bougie. I make do with what I have. But I'll never complain when it comes to William's food.

"Mmm," I hum, gradually beginning to enjoy his company. The distraction from thinking about my mother doesn't hurt either. Maybe taking his advice isn't so bad. He is a businessman in his own right. It can't hurt to follow his lead…I guess.

NINE

LOLA

I struggle to make out Azra's text as I blink and rub away the sleep from my eyes.

Lo, I miss you!
Meet me at CocoDrop. 8 a.m.
I got news!

It's been two weeks since the last time I've seen my girl. With the lack of staff at Ace, she's been working overtime. Barely even had time to text me. So, I'm excited to see her today.

Before the sun fully rises, I slip out of my nightie, get myself cleaned and dressed, talk to William for a few moments, and ride to CocoDrop, the best bakery and café in D.C.

Early risers bustle along the busy streets, getting their morning coffee and pastries. The woody, crisp air gusts through my hair as I trample from my car to the cafe through the fresh coating of snow.

The morning French jazz playing through the café puts my heart at ease as I wait for Azra to arrive.

I don't know if it's typical CP time, or the fact her stride isn't long enough, but Azra is *always* late. *I'm* surprised I'm the one who got fired and not *her*.

A soothing voice captures me, distracting me from my thoughts.

There he is. Sitting at a bar by the window. William looks as if he was waiting for me.

Without hesitation, I ruffle my hair and strut over, until a flowery scented woman nearly bumps into me to get to him.

Oh, *hell* to the naw.

Pulling back the right hook that's spiraled up and ready to spring, I sit back in my chair and slouch so he can't see me. I keep an eye on them.

The way they smile at each other heats my skin. She flings her arms around his shoulders. He grabs her, picking her up off the ground.

I can't believe my eyes.

She resembles a young Vonetta McGee. Clearly, older than me. There's no comparison. I'm obviously better. But I can't help but marvel over her brown faux fur shearling coat. And the boots! I mean I wouldn't wear my suede knee-length Manolo Blahniks in a foot of fresh snow, but that's her choice.

I attempt to eavesdrop but hear nothing. The doorbell jingles and Azra comes in. She swarms me with a hug.

"Girl, it feels like it's been forever. I've been waiting to tell you all week but....what's wrong?" she asks, looking in my eyes as we pull away.

I force a smile and sit up, "Nothing."

"Well, you look like someone boo booed in your Balenciagas."

"I'm fine," I swat her away. "You're in a good mood. What's the big news?"

"Okay, so," Azra takes her coat off and sits across from me, leaving William and his old lady in perfect view, "I got a new job making double the money."

Ecstatic, I reach across and hold her hand, "Seriously? Where at?"

"Ace! I'm assistant manager now."

"What? Girl, congratulations. I didn't know you applied."

"I didn't." Her eyes grow innocently big. A cheeky grin spreads over her face.

I pull my hand away. "Oh, Lord."

"What?"

"I know you're not telling me Mr. Struthers just *gave* you that position without you even asking?" I drift my eyes to William and his woman.

"Yeah, he knew I was getting my master's in business and said he likes my work ethic. He hired me on the spot. He even said he'll pay my debt for school so I can go back and finish my degree. Isn't that crazy?"

I hear Azra but can't peel my eyes from William. He's smiling way too hard. The nerve. I got a good mind to go over there and pop him upside his head.

"Lo," Azra calls my attention, "You hear me?"

I snap my gaze back to her, "Yeah, it is crazy. Kind of too good to be true. You sure this job doesn't have any strings attached? And how're you gonna run a club when you can't even defend yourself against Genesis?"

She sighs. The light in her eyes dim. "I can assert myself when I need to, Lola. And Genesis isn't like that. He's not trying to get anything out of me."

"Mm-hmm. I hear you. Be careful, Az. I know you like him but I'm telling you now, that man ain't your Boaz."

"Oh, my goodness, Lola. I literally was telling you this because I thought you'd be happy for me."

"I *am* happy for you. But you're getting financially wrapped up with a man who doesn't know you but is paying off your debt. It sounds fishy to me. I'm just saying. Don't get too close to him."

"Why not? He's just being nice, Lola."

"Have I taught you nothing?" I roll my eyes back to William. He grins at his new—I mean old woman. I'm sick.

"I know, *they're all nice*, but he's genuinely nice to me, Lola. Why can't I just enjoy that? Why do I always have to have my guard up?"

I snap, "Because men will run all over you if you let them. That's why. And a grown man like Genesis will do hurdles over your behind. Shoot, he's about to have a complete relay race on you," I snatch my eyes back from the cougar fest that has my blood boiling.

This is why I don't trust men. William was just cooking dinner and comforting me the other night. Now, look at him. In a café, early in the morning *kiki-ing* with some biddy old enough to be his mom.

Azra huffs, "You must really think I'm stupid or something. I'm not some helpless child, Lola. I know how to handle myself. And if I did want to get close to him, then that's *my* prerogative."

"I guess."

She sucks her teeth. "Why can't you just be happy for me?" she snaps, standing from the chair and snatching her coat and purse.

Everyone in the café stares, going silent.

"Lola?" William zeroes in on me.

Shoot.

"Azra, don't leave," I tug her hand. My heart thumps as William and his lady saunter over.

"Nah, sis. This is why I don't tell you anything. The first thing you do is treat me like I'm some sort of child. Never again." Azra pulls away and storms out.

Left facing William and his smiling geriatric side piece, I cringe.

"Lola, what's up?" he asks.

Lola? What happened to Bean? Woman? Now I'm just *Lola*?

I rise from my seat, "You seriously gonna sit here and flaunt your old flavor of the week to me? We *just* talked on the phone this morning. You got some nerve," I bark. To think I was about to trust his adolescent behind.

He smiles. Then she smiles. Then they lose it.

"What the hell is so funny?" I blow up.

"Woman," he grabs my hand and pulls me close, "this is Andrea, my aunt. She just got back in town from France. This is actually her bakery. She's a business owner and I was meeting with her to talk about getting you some help with your business plan."

There's that egg again.

My face warms. I cover my mouth with my hand, "Oh, God, I didn't know—"

"No worries, I understand it probably looked a little strange." Andrea smiles, holding her hand out to me. Shaking my hand, she continues, "Almost a strange as it was when I found out my nephew was seeing someone *so much* older than him."

Well, *that* shade is well received.

I giggle and squeeze her hand, "Well, not as strange as it was when I thought he was dating his grandmother."

She snickers, taking a tap at my upper arm with a little more force than I expect. She cuts her eyes from me and glares at William.

What's her problem? I want to lay her out. But I'm already too embarrassed as it is. I lost my couth for a moment, but it's back now.

I suck it up and keep pushing. After all, as awkward as it is, this might be what I need to get my boutique started.

TEN

AZRA

"I didn't see you at church yesterday. Everything cool?" Kendrick's mellow voice echoes through the phone.

Sprawled out on my bed and battling writer's block for a poem I've been trying to finish; I stare up at the ceiling. I huff, "Yeah, I'm fine. Tired. Got a lot of work to do at the club. It's a little stressful."

And stressful it is. I missed church for the first time ever. Now, I have to work on Sundays. Mom-mom's not happy about that. Thinks the devil is on my heels. But being an assistant manager is no joke. Managing grown folks and trying to put my foot down, all while not wanting anyone to hate me, is a struggle. But thank God, Genesis is right there helping me through it all. Instead of rushing to get a new manager for me to work under, he said he'd stay until I feel comfortable in my position. Under those conditions, that would be *never*.

I enjoyed the eye candy. The money isn't bad either. I'm able to go back to school and keep my apartment, so I can't complain.

"Wanna talk about it?" Kendrick asks.

"Not really. It's not that interesting, just work stuff."

"Anything dealing with you is interesting."

I giggle. Kendrick's shots always go nowhere, but he keeps shooting. I open my mouth to respond but my phone beeps with an incoming call.

Genesis

It's Monday afternoon. The club is closed. What does he want?

With the quickness, I sit up. "Kendrick, can I call you back? My...*Mom-mom* is calling," I don't know why I lie. It's just easier to do sometimes.

"Sure, I'll talk to you later, Beauty."

Barely muttering goodbye, I switch over to Genesis's call.

"Hello?"

"Hey, Azra. I was going through the schedule and noticed you double booked us for Friday after Cinco de Mayo. Drake had that spot first, but it doesn't say who the other party is."

"I know. It was a mistake, but I straightened it out. It probably didn't process but trust me, it's handled. The other party is DJ EXO. They said they wanted to remain anonymous and didn't want promotion or anything. But I let his people know we were available the previous weekend."

"And he was okay with that?"

"Yeah. They said it worked better. Amazingly, we were able to fit them in *that* early, since we're booked every weekend until October."

"That's Ace for you," he chuckles.

Silence falls.

I remain quiet, enjoying the time on the phone with him.

My mind wanders. I wonder what our babies would look like. I bet they'd have his thick, dark hair. Probably his perfect, deep brown complexion, too. As long as they carried on my doe eyes and his chiseled cheekbones, I'm gucci.

He finally speaks, "You mind meeting me at the club?"

My ears perk. "Sure," I beam. No hesitation. If Genesis needs me, I'm there.

I find a pair of jeans and scour my drawers to find a shirt that isn't Mom-mom approved. It won't hurt to show a little collarbone. I have to look good for him. It's a must.

*
**

Walking into Ace, the stillness is uncanny. No music. No lights. No cheap perfume permeating the place. It's kind of nice.

Reaching the office and opening the door, the aroma of Thai food fills the room. My stomach growls.

Beauty by Dru Hill softly plays. Always reminds me of Kendrick. He dedicated this song to me when we first met.

"What's all of this?" I smile, closing the door behind me.

"Lunch." Genesis grins.

"For what?"

"You've been doing a great job here. You've been taking a lot of stress off me having to run this club and manage it alone. And honestly, you're doing better than I expected."

"You didn't think I could do it?"

"I never doubted you. But I'm pleased. You're doing a really good job."

"Thank you, Mr. Struthers—"

"Genesis," he interrupts with a motion of his hand. "Only when we're off the clock though." He chuckles.

"Well, thank you, *Genesis*. Flattery and food will get you everywhere," I cock a flirty brow.

I don't know what consumes me when I'm around him, but I can't regulate my thoughts. Tingles roam through my chest and other places that will remain nameless. My mouth waters at the mere sight of him. It's uncontrollable. I can't stop it.

We sit across from each other at the desk and eat. Carefully forking some lo mien into my mouth, he peeps at me. I slowly chew and swallow my food. Feeling self-conscious of how I look eating, I poke around the plate to find smaller pieces to eat without looking like a pig.

"What are you doing here on a Monday?" I ask, breaking the ice.

"Just making sure everything is in order. Can't always do that during business hours. Too many distractions."

I nod my head and nibble on a noodle.

"Are you enjoying your new position?" he asks.

"Yeah. It's good. Can't complain. Better than being objectified all night long," I mutter with my hand covering my mouth.

"I can imagine," he chuckles.

I smile. Swallowing the small amount of food in my mouth, I ask, "How long have you owned this club?"

He wipes his mouth with a napkin, "I opened it twelve years ago."

"All by yourself? No partners?"

"Actually, uh…no," he glares at his food and chews on his bottom lip, "I started it with my wife."

"Your *ex*-wife?" I question, glancing at his naked ring finger.

"Umm. Nah. My *current*…wife." He avoids eye contact, stuffing a forkful of rice in his mouth.

Sugar honey iced tea. You telling me *Her* is wifey?

Lola *was* right. *Dang!*

I sigh. "Oh. That's…nice. How long?"

"Ten years, this August."

Pressing my lips together, I eye the food I suddenly have no appetite for. "Congratulations," I mutter.

"Thanks, but…never mind."

"What?" I ask, perking up. I sip on some water to hide the smirk from spreading across my face. I sense trouble in paradise.

"Nah, they say don't talk to anybody about your marriage so, I'll pass," he laughs.

"Well, I'm hardly just *anybody*. I know why your favorite scripture. That's deep stuff to tell someone on the first car ride home so I'm practically your therapist at this point. You can tell me anything," I sit back and cross my legs, giving Genesis the floor to tell me *all* his business.

He dryly chuckles, mimicking my position. "Well," he sighs, "people change."

"Care to elaborate?"

"I didn't believe in God for a long time." He takes a deep breath, "I mean, I knew he existed, but I didn't believe in Him, if that makes any sense. Growing up, my dad was a preacher and away from home most days of the week. Not having him around, made me grow up a little faster than I should've. I basically became the man of the house, looking over my mom and my little brother."

"How old were you?"

"Six."

"That *is* young," I lean forward and rest my chin in the palm of my hand, "So, what happened? You said your father *was* a preacher," I ask but quickly retract as his expression grows dark, "Oh my—I'm sorry, I didn't mean to—"

"No, he's not dead." He chuckles. "He messed around on my mom with a woman at church. You know those so-*called mothers of the church* women can be a trip. So can the preachers."

"You sure he doesn't know my grandmother?" I joke.

We laugh.

I take a drink of my water and admire him as he continues his story.

"But he got that woman pregnant, and my mom took me and my little brother and left."

Speechless, tension builds in my brow.

"Mm-hmm. So, when I was ten, I started getting paid under the table to work at this diner to help my mom. Long story short, I was playing husband and father before I was a teenager. After what my dad did to my mom, something happened to my faith. I couldn't understand why a man of God would do what he did. It made me question everything. I started straying away from God and focused on making money. So, around thirteen, I got some turntables and me and my brother started DJing at weddings and events like that. We made a good living from it for a while."

"That's cool. Where's your brother now?"

He smirks, "DJ EXO is actually *Exodus* Struthers."

"DJ EXO is your *brother?* Why didn't you tell me earlier?" I squeal.

Genesis laughs as I fangirl over his brother, "Because I knew you'd give me this reaction. I think you spoiled his surprise."

"How?"

"Because he wanted to remain anonymous so I wouldn't know he was coming. This year—the weekend before Cinco de Mayo—is my birthday. May eighth. I guess he wanted to surprise me since we haven't seen each other in a few years."

"Aww, that's so sweet. Well, I'm sorry I ruined the surprise. I didn't mean to."

"It's cool. I'm not the surprising type anyway."

I bow my head, "I can't believe y'all are brothers."

"Well with how different we are, I find it hard to believe, too. We promised each other no matter what we did, we would be the best at it so our mom wouldn't have to work again. He's better at DJing, and I'm good at selling, promoting, managing, booking places to play, stuff like that. So, as we got older, we got deep into the careers that offered that. He likes the attention and I like to be behind the scenes, so it works for us."

I'm mesmerized. I'm actually having a conversation with this man. He's so fine. And the fact he's being so open with me makes me want to throw my moral compass away. Take it.

"Anyway, about fifteen years ago, I met my wife. She just graduated from college after getting her business degree. We linked up, and a couple years after that, Ace opened. My brother DJ'd here for a while and we were good. But I was still lost in my faith. I didn't have a relationship with God, and I was making moves on my own."

"So, what brought you back home?"

He laughs, "Back home? You sound like an old woman."

"Shut up," I blush.

"But life made me come back," he continues. "It took some time, but something was missing. So, a few years ago, I went to church and that was it. I asked for forgiveness. Repented. Prayed. And now I'm here."

I gaze at him. He's perfect. He's everything. Unfortunately for me, he isn't *single*. But is he *available*? Oh, Lord. What am I thinking?

My longing desires are chipping away at my conscience. Bad is beating Good's behind but I can't let Bad win. Now, *that* would be sinful. He's married. He's not mine.

Pressing my lips together and pushing my yearnings away, I look down and mutter, "You had a hole in your heart only God could fill."

"Exactly. God…and a godly woman."

Glaring at him from under my brow, I meet his eyes. His expression filled with aspiration. *Is he coming onto me?*

"Well, you seem to be set then. You know, with having a godly *wife* and all," I remind him.

He chuckles and scratches his head.

"What?"

"I said, *I* went to church and prayed. My wife didn't do that with me."

"Why not? Isn't she a Christian?"

"She believes in God, but she's not religious. Or spiritual for that matter."

"Okay, now I see. When you said *people* change, you meant *you* changed."

"I mean—"

"*I mean*," I mock. We share a laugh, but I continue, "It's alright to change, as long as it's for the right reasons. You changed for the better."

"Yeah," he trails off.

"Penny for your thoughts?"

"Just thinking."

"About?"

He glances at me. "Nothing."

"Genesis…" I reach across the desk and place my hand on his arm.

He looks at my hand over his, then back at me.

Hesitantly, I pull away. "I-I'm sorry."

"Don't be. I don't bite." He smirks. His teeth draw back on the smooth flesh of his bottom lip as he bites down.

My core tightens. A strange desire comes over me. I can't pull my gaze from his mouth. His lips. That sexy nibble.

Leaning both elbows on the desk, he sits for a moment. Draws both hands into a fist and places them over his mouth, blocking my view.

I bounce my eyes from his lips to his intrigued stare. He blinks away and smirks.

"If I tell you. You got to keep it between us. Don't go around telling the girls about it or anything."

I breathe, pushing the lewd thoughts from my head and *really* praying he doesn't read minds. "Whatever you say," I giggle.

Sitting back in my chair, I take a sip of water to douse the fire burning inside of me.

"I should've known things weren't gonna be right when we got engaged," he says.

Swallowing, I ask, "Why?"

"She proposed to *me*."

My eyes bulge out and I hide a smile with my hand. "Really? She got down on one knee?"

"The whole nine."

I snicker, "Oh. Sounds like quite the gentleman."

He chuckles. "I knew something was wrong then. That ain't the way it's supposed to be."

"But you said yes. So, there had to be some love there."

He groans. "In a lot of ways, marriage is about alliance. Prosperity. Stability. Financial support. Not love."

"But you *do* love your wife…right?" I ask, partly hoping he says no.

"Well, that's hard to say right now."

"Why?"

He stares at me. "I really shouldn't be telling you this."

"I'm just here to listen. I won't tell anyone. Promise," I smile.

He sits back in his seat and rests his arms on the armrests. He sighs, "I'm not sure if I love her. But like I said, that's hard to say because we're in a rough patch."

"Well, every marriage goes through those. What makes this one so bad?"

"Because I want to sell the club and she doesn't."

"You want to sell Ace? Why?"

"Have you seen this place? God ain't pleased with all of this. And being the mastermind behind it…I can't live like that. Not if I want to get all the way right with God, you know?"

I don't know what to say. I nod and shrug. All I know is if Genesis sold the club, I don't think I'll work here any longer. He's practically the only thing keeping me in here at this point.

Sighing and clasping his hands together, he sits back. "But, enough about me. Since you're doing all this 'love talk', are *you* in love? You probably got a few men trying to holla at you around here."

I suck my teeth, "I wouldn't say all that."

"I see these dudes checking you out. Especially Kendrick."

"Trust, *all* they're doing is looking. Nobody tried talking to me except Kendrick, and he's not my type."

"No?"

I pout and shake my head.

"So…" he smirks, "what *is* your type?" He licks his lips, waiting for me to respond.

I leer at him. Getting lost in my thoughts. He knows what he's doing. But he's *married*. It's unfair God only made one of him.

"That's uh…" I swallow the excess saliva building up in my mouth. "That's hard to explain," I coyly smile.

"Oh, I see. You're one of *those* women, huh? Got a list longer than the constitution. Print finer than the woman sitting right in front of me."

Oh my gosh! He's *definitely* coming onto me. My heart races and I melt. Not even the power of Pine-Sol can mop me up right now.

"No," I giggle, tugging at my earlobe. I gaze down, trying to stop my heart from hammering out of my chest.

Feeling him observe my every move, I keep my eyes set away.

He chuckles, "Mm-hmm…okay."

ELEVEN

LOLA

My brain is hurting.

Starting a business is hard, and I'm not even to the fun part yet.

I pinch the bridge of my nose as Andrea takes a break from lecturing me on owner's equity, liabilities, and a bunch of other gibberish that has my head spinning.

After our little run-in at CocoDrop, she begrudgingly invited me to meet her here during off-peak hours to work on my business plan.

The tension is *thick*. Wishful thinking is telling me it's because her first impression of me wasn't stellar, but I know better than that. She and William are close. After she heard I turned down his proposal, she was pissed. And according to the eye roll and limp handshake she gave me when I came to meet her today, she *still* is. She doesn't want to help me. But it's clear she can't say no to William either. As much as I didn't want to accept her help, I sucked up my pride and took it.

Now here I am. Glancing around at the gray, pink, and white décor, and marveling over the framed photographs of different celebrities who visited this bakery. Tyra Banks, Usher, Nicki Minaj, even Michelle Obama. I've been here at least fifty times and never realized how nice it is. Vanilla and cinnamon fill the air. I understand why this place stays packed. CocoDrop Bakery is a hot spot in the DMV. It's even been featured on those food shows as one of the most delicious bakeries in the country. A café by day. Lounge by night. Serving up wine and cocktails alongside of different cheeses, hors d'oeuvres, and their famous cupcakes and pastries.

Although Andrea's the owner and doesn't lift a finger in the kitchen, according to William, she's breaking grounds in multiple areas of business. So, she can definitely help me get on the right track.

"So, let's start with the basics. Who's your target audience?" she asks.

A staff member places two fresh complimentary cups of coffee and a taster platter of mini cupcakes on the table.

"Thank you," I smile and snatch one up. "Well, of course, people like Beyonce, Rihanna. J. Lo—"

"Whoa, whoa, whoa. Slow your roll…Those are your *prospects*. Not your audience." She giggles. "Take Vera Wang, for instance. Her audience is middle to upper-class women, ranging between twenties and forties. Most may be looking to get married since that seems to be her niche. Then you have Chanel, which targets predominately women, between the ages of twenty and eighty. Usually of the middle to upper-class woman as well. Elegant. Luxury. So, I ask again, who is *your* audience?"

Stuffing my face with my second creme-filled lemon and mint cupcake, I furrow my brow and shrug. I haven't thought that far. I just enjoy making clothes.

Rolling her eyes, she sits back and puts her hand out, "Let me see your portfolio."

I hand her my large, white binder that contains countless designs and swatches I've built up over the years.

Her eyes light up as she flips through the plastic pages. Slamming the binder on the table, she takes my business plan and writes in big letters.

"What's that?" I ask, twisting my head to make out what the writing says.

BOHO CHIC

"That's your style." She holds the paper up to me, "So, who's your audience? Who do you want to see wearing your clothes?

"Everyone," I say, "But if I had to be specific, then women like me. Twenties to fifties? Sixties, maybe? Middle to upper class…I guess."

She looks underneath the table at my jade and black, floral, pleated skirt and black slip-on booties. She raises her eyebrows and twitches her lips to keep from laughing. "Well, I wouldn't wear it but…we all have our own sense of style, right?"

Oh, no she didn't.

"Next time we'll get a list of different suppliers to look into and figure out what other lines you'd like to carry—"

"Uh, I'm sorry but I don't want any other lines in my store. I understand it's a boutique and all, but I want this to be high-end. Selling Imala designs only."

"Other lines will help you expand your audience and revenue."

"I don't care to do that. My audience is my audience. I may not know them just yet, but I don't want any other name in my store."

She rolls her eyes, "Listen, if you think you got the manpower to make different designs that will appeal to people without them all looking the same, then that's your choice. It's a lot of work. But if that's what you want, we'll get there. One thing I don't do is fail, so…" She huffs and sloppily stuffs my business plan back in its folder.

My leg bounces with annoyance. I'll show her. Imala will succeed without the help of other designers. You don't go to Gucci and find Versace. Hell, you don't even go to Target and find the same clothing brands that Walmart sells. Her disbelief in my vision is sickening, but I compose myself.

"Thanks. You know, at first, I thought you were a stuck up, bougie heifer, but…you're only *half* bad."

"You mean, *not* half bad."

"No," I grimace.

"Well, the feeling is mutual."

We share an exaggerated laugh, and she rolls her eyes.

"So…" she begins, "Shall we talk about the real issue here?"

I sigh and sit back. There's no way I can avoid this conversation about William and me. But boy I wish I could.

"What about it?" I ask.

"I heard he proposed to you and *you* turned him down."

"I did."

"So..." She crosses her arms.

"Listen, no disrespect, but what's going on between me and William is none of your business."

"Well, *he* made it my business when he asked me to help the woman who turned his proposal down."

"What does one have to do with the other? He asked you, not me."

"But you accepted the help."

"So? This is business, nothing else. I wouldn't be surprised if William is paying you to help me."

She narrows her eyes and leans on the table with her elbows. "Do you know who I am? I don't need Will's money, nor will I ever take it. I'm here because my nephew asked me to help you. I will do anything for that boy, but I will not let an old woman take advantage of him—"

"Old woman?"

"Did I stutter?"

"You gonna wish you did," I say, standing from my seat.

She smirks, "Lola, sit down, darling."

"Don't you *darling* me."

"Lola…" she gives a meaningful gaze and smiles. "No one is here to fight. Honestly. Take a seat."

Folding my arms, I slam myself down into the chair.

"Listen," her expression softens, "I don't have a personal issue with you, Lola. But you've got to understand, Will is like a son to me. He told me about you and how he thought he found *the one*, but we didn't even know you. His parents and our family invited you to dinner how many times? And you always turned us down. We never even got a chance to know you. So how do you expect us to *like* you?"

I sink in my seat as she reminds me of the countless times William asked me to meet his family.

"I didn't mean to get this deep with him."

"Yeah, well, you did. And you broke his heart."

I sit up. "Broke his—William's heart is not broken. If it was, I doubt he'd still be talking to me. Besides, I told him from the beginning that what we had was just for fun. He decided he wanted to fall in love and propose. I never intended on marrying him nor did I give him that idea. So, if it's anyone you need to talk to about this, it's him. I just stayed true to myself."

She raises her eyebrows and shakes her head. "Look," she sighs, "I'm not coming at you, Lola. But I just want what's best for Will. I know he can be downright stubborn when it comes to getting what he wants. But he doesn't fall easily."

"No?"

"Nope. That's why we can't understand how he fell for you so quickly. Especially being so much older than him."

"I'm not that much older than him."

She twists her lips and lowers her eyelids.

"What?" I ask.

"You're in two different stages of life, Lola."

"No, we're not."

"Clearly you are. He's ready for marriage. He wants to settle down. Have a family. *You* on the other hand, are still stuck in your early twenties, trying to have a hot girl summer."

I put my hands up in surrender. "As I said before, I'm staying true to myself."

"As you should. But the least you can do is let him off the hook."

"I have."

"*Have* you though? Have you told him to leave you alone and find someone he'd be better with?"

Sitting back, I clear my throat and peer down. "It's not that simple."

She scoffs. "Of course it's not. I know Will. He makes it really hard to say no to him. Which is why I'm sitting here with you right now." She chuckles. "But all I ask is that you don't break his heart. You don't have to be with him. Leave him. Let him go. But please don't break that boy's heart. He's already had it broken before. But I'm sure you already knew that."

I pout and shake my head.

"He didn't tell you?"

"I mean, I knew he was engaged but I never asked what happened between them."

"Well, *you* happened between them. You practically stole him from his fiancée."

"I did not steal—"

"Pipe down, darling. It's not that serious. None of us liked her anyway," she says, swatting her hand back and forth. "Anyway, they dated for like nine years. High school sweethearts."

"Why didn't y'all like her?"

"She was a stuck-up little whore—uh…excuse my French, darling. But she was. She treated William like crap. He was on the verge of breaking up with her anyway."

"So, how'd y'all find out about me?" I hesitantly ask.

"He told us after he broke the engagement off with his fiancée. I was the first to know about you. He told me your name and how good you looked. But when he told me your *age*, he got the side-eye. And honestly, I thought you just wanted him for his money and fame."

Which is true. But I won't tell her that.

"But I will say this," she continues, "I've never seen Will go this hard for anyone. Ever. No matter how much I tell that boy to leave your tail alone, nobody can stop him. He's gonna go for what he wants and that's it."

"Well, don't get mad at me. I've tried to get him to leave my *tail* alone, too. But he doesn't want to. I can't make him stop."

"That's because you like it," she says, sliding my portfolio across the table to me. "Listen, whatever you decide to do with him, don't wait too long. Il faut qu'une porte soit ouverte ou fermée. You can't have it both ways. He's still young but he wants what he wants. And if you can't give that to him, let him know. But if you don't, let him go. Ghost him if you have to. It'll save him the heartache in the long run. Now, I know he's helping you get your boutique ideas together, and business is business. But a heart is a fragile thing. Please don't play with his."

Feeling defeated, I sigh, "I won't."

Andrea is only protecting her nephew. Something any good person would do. And *I'm* sitting here trying to use him for material gain. Ignoring the fact he has a family behind him that wants him to win.

I'm trash.

I flash a weak smile and stand to leave the bakery. Andrea and I say our goodbyes and plan to meet again. Walking out and thinking about all she said, that common tinge of guilt brews in my spirit.

I'm getting soft.

TWELVE

AZRA

Not sure if it's because I've been stressing at work, running errands for Mom-mom, or juggling school and personal time, but I've lost weight. I like it.

Ten pounds lighter and I already got that definition I've always wanted. It used to not matter what my body looked like. It was gonna be covered up by piles of clothes anyway. But now, things are different. I really like my body. And I'm not going to be twenty-five forever. I need to enjoy it while I can.

I've got a new attitude and a metaphorical fresh start on life.

I haven't attended church like I used to, but to be honest, I'm happy about it. Mom-mom's not though. She thinks the devil's out to get me. But I'm legit just working. Any change in life is a red flag to her and it's frustrating. Being away from her and church is a weight lifted off my shoulders. Though

I know she's judging me from a distance. I still feel free. It's better than being around that negative energy all day. I'm getting a much-needed break from everyone's opinions about how I ought to be living my life. I still pray. Mostly in writing and usually in a poetic form, but it's still prayer. I do it every day. And knowing Mom-mom, she has me covered in the blood, so I'm good.

Everything seems to be on track. I'm enlightened. Happy. Able to breathe. Only thing I need now is a new wardrobe.

I jump in my car and prepare myself for an awkward encounter with Lola. Since that day at CocoDrop, we've been distant. It's been over a month. We text and call here and there but something's off, and I'm not talking about that wig she's abandoned since being axed from Ace.

She's getting older. Changing. Usually, her only judgment of me was about my outfit or the color I painted my nails. But that day she called me out instead.

It seemed like she was jealous or something. She's so accustomed to men falling at her feet, she doesn't understand how a man could dislike *her* but actually be nice to *me*.

Either way, it doesn't matter. Genesis is married and I'm as single as the last piece of chicken at a buffet. But I have noticed at work, his eyes wander in my direction more than not. And even though he doesn't like talking about his wife, that doesn't stop him from making frequent disapproving comments about how she controls everything in their lives. He's fed up with her. So, we'll see how long their relationship lasts.

I knock on Lola's apartment door. I hope she isn't mad at me for being away for so long.

The door swings open.

I smile.

Shifting her weight to one side and crossing her arms, she looks me up and down. "Can I help you?"

"It's an emergency," I open my peacoat to reveal my loose-fitted jeans and white t-shirt. Fashion is Lola's niche. It excites her. So, what better way to reconcile than with a terrible outfit?

Her mouth drops open and she quickly drags me into the apartment by the lapels of my coat. "Oh girl, get on in here before someone sees you."

I giggle and stumble in. "Do you have something I can wear?"

"I don't have many potato sacks laying around, but anything is better than this."

"Shut up!" I laugh, hitting her on the shoulder, "I missed you, Lo."

Her lips slowly turn as she drops her mad act. Pulling me into a tight hug, she croons, "I missed you, too. It's been a month and some change. Where've you been?"

That was easier than I thought.

We pull away. "Just working. It's busy at the club. A big party every weekend. It's crazy."

"I bet. Still lying about where you work to Ms. Annette?"

"She knows I'm an assistant manager. Not at a club, but at least she knows what my job is now."

Lola laughs, "I can't believe you. Little girl in a woman's body."

I tilt my head and suck my teeth, "I'm not a little girl, Lo. I wish you'd stop—"

"Yeah, okay. So, what's going on with this?" she asks pulling my coat off.

I shake off the vexation and breathe. "I need a new wardrobe. Maybe something a little more...form-fitting?"

"Where's that Bible at?" she jokes, frantically looking through her kitchen drawers, "Do I need to call a priest so we can do an exorcism or something?"

I sneer, "Ha, ha. I'm not possessed. I just want to try something new. Besides, DJ EXO is coming to Ace in a couple of months and it's gonna be this huge party. I have to look good. You should come, too" I flop on her couch. I leave out the *Genesis and EXO being brothers* part. She'll ask how I know, and I'd have to tell her about the lunch with him. She'll go on a rant and I don't feel like all of that.

"Would love to but I'm not stepping another toe in that place again. And are you trying to catch something?" slowly walking over, she grins, "Because I know you're not changing your style just for a party. You finally gonna give Kendrick a chance?"

"Not exactly," I snatch my gaze from her and stare into my lap.

"Then what is it? You met someone?"

I tighten my lips and shake my head. My body is saying one thing, but my eyes scream guilt.

She stops and stares at me. Her eyes widen and then narrows. I feel like I have an electric red sign above my head that flashes the name GENESIS.

Disgust grows in Lola's face. She moans, "Oh goodness, Azra…"

"What?"

"Him? Really? You still like that man?"

"I'm not even thinking about him, Lo," I lie, "Besides, he's married anyway," I resentfully elaborate.

"See! I told you something was up with him. Well, good. Now, you can move on," she says.

I roll my eyes. She thinks she knows everything.

"Why don't you want to give Kendrick a chance? Ms. Annette likes him and everything."

"But *I* don't like Kendrick like that."

"But you like Genesis like that?" she simpers for a moment, then her face grows still, "Wait, hold up, don't tell me you're changing your style for *him*?"

My temperature rises. I take a deep breath and bare my teeth. "I'm not changing for anybody, Lola."

"Then who are you getting sexy for then? 'Cus last time I checked you were two steps away from rocking nun couture—"

"Me, Lola! Myself. Damn, I can't even dress the way I want without you thinking I'm changing? What are you? My Mom-mom?" I snap. I can't hold it in anymore.

She steps back and clutches her imaginary faux pearls, "*Damn?* I know you're on your period and everything, but you need to chill out, sis. Since when do you curse?"

"Since you stopped being my friend and started mothering my every move."

"What? Nobody is mothering you, Az. I'm just curious what's going on."

"Seriously? Something's got to be going on because I want to dress differently?"

"No. It's because *you* are different. Your face, your body, your demeanor, this attitude. It came out of nowhere," she sits beside me and rests her hand on my knee, "Azra, what's going on? Ever since that day at CocoDrop, I barely see you. It's been a month. You never went a day without barging in here."

I feel a knot rise in my throat. I don't know why I want to cry, but I do.

She continues, "Girl, you know I'm all for you bustin' loose and having fun, but you just told me he's married. If this is for him, girl, it ain't worth it."

"*See*" I snatch her hand off my knee, "That's exactly why I haven't been around. You're always assuming. You act like I have no sense. No morals. This is why I don't tell you anything in the first place. You always belittle me like I don't know anything. Not everyone is out here thinking about men twenty-four-seven like you. And all because you got hurt before don't mean you gotta stop *me* from living."

"I'm not trying to stop you. You can say you're not changing for a man, but I wasn't born yesterday. And glowing up for any man, especially a married one, ain't the look. If a man wants you, he'll want you for *you*, not what you think he wants you to become. Trust me, I've been through hell behind men—"

"And you don't think *I* have? I grew up without a father too. You're not the only one whose parents are trash. I've lived my life knowing my father *and* my mother didn't want me. Didn't even care. At least you knew your mom. I had *neither*. But the only difference between me and you is that *I* didn't turn into a hoe behind the crap I went through. So, I think I know how to handle myself," I hop up and stomp to get my coat.

Silence.

Okay, so, the *hoe* part slipped out. But there are only so many men you can sleep with before you start making a name for yourself. Lola surpassed that. So, I'm not lying, but it *was* harsh.

Resentful, I turn back. Lola's eyes are glossy. Her face is pinched into a scowl and she grumbles underneath her breath, "Get. Out."

I slowly step toward the door. Lola remains on the couch.

I want to bite my tongue, but I can't tame it.

"All I'm saying, the life you chose for yourself a.k.a. growing old and dying alone never experiencing love, that's your life. Not mine."

"Get out."

My tongue continues, "Keep acting the way you do and trust me, you're gonna grow old without any friends, too."

"Get the hell out of my house!"

I open the door and slam it shut. Taking a deep breath, I cover my mouth and nose with my hands. Tears well up in my eyes.

Oh, god. Why did I say that?

THIRTEEN

AZRA

Whoever said April showers bring May flowers must've prophesied my bloom season.

Because baby; Azra McKinney is coming out of her shell. And with the weather heating up, probably a few other things.

I ransack my bedroom looking for the perfect outfit to wear to work. This isn't just a normal day at work. DJ EXO is coming. So, I have to look good. But since I'm assistant manager, I have to maintain a somewhat professional look for the sake of my position.

It's a struggle. Fashion isn't second nature for me. These are the moments where it'll be beneficial to have a girlfriend who doesn't make me feel like the world's most disgraceful human being for wanting to primp up my style.

I miss Lola, and I know I should apologize for calling her a hoe, but I'm not ready to talk to her. Because though it pains me to admit it…she's right.

I know. It sounds bad. But I'm not trying to take Genesis from his wife. I'm not that kind of woman. But who wouldn't want to draw his attention? What's the harm in flirting? It's not like we're sleeping together. We just talk. There's nothing wrong with that. Most of our conversations involve God and that's because he can't talk about faith to his wife. As a matter of fact, from the way he speaks of his wife, she's a borderline atheist. I don't think God approves of that union. That's why it's falling apart. They're unequally yoked.

Genesis didn't know any better when that woman forced him down the aisle ten years ago. But now that he's met me, he sees they aren't meant to be. He now knows he needs a woman who values his faith. Someone in his corner to support him in what he wants to do with his life. All his wife needs to do is stay in her place and have his back. What's so hard about that? Apparently, she's gotten comfortable. She's blind to the treasure she has in him and puts more time and energy into her businesses rather than her marriage.

He told me everything. People say you shouldn't discuss your marital problems with anyone else, but sometimes Genesis just needs to vent. So, I give him that space. He calls me. He talks. And I listen. Something his wife never does.

Since I've been promoted, we've gotten close. Like *being a step away from leaping off the Jesus train and hopping on that midnight train like Gladys Knight*, type of close. I swear I'll do it if he asks me. Even if he just blinks it in Morse code, I'll do it.

But until then, he has to deal with his control freak of a wife, keeping him from expanding his family, and holding him under lock and key until he decides to call it quits. Maybe she feels like she'll lose him to someone younger and more attractive. But her low self-esteem and demanding ways do nothing but drive him farther away and closer to me. All you have to do is see the way he looks at me when he thinks I'm not watching. That man emotionally checked out of his marriage the first day he laid eyes on me.

Genesis has so much more living to do, as do I. So, why not do it together? He knows he wants to. And I'm ready for him to show me what I've been missing all these years. It's about time.

After a desperate search for something to wear, I come across a red matching spaghetti strap set, with a tight, mini skirt that I bought from one of those fast fashion sites. For professional sake, I throw on a cute blazer. I grab my makeup bag to choose what to finish my look with. I usually wear lip gloss, but lately, I've been obsessed with red lipstick.

I know. Mom-mom would have a heart attack if she knew I was wearing red. But what she doesn't know, won't hurt her.

I throw the lip gloss back in the makeup bag and slick the lipstick all over my lips. I turn around in the mirror and check out all the hard work I've been putting in on my backside. It's funny. As assistant manager, I'm dressed more like a cocktail waitress. Ironic. But one thing I do know is that if I was still prancing around the club serving up drinks, the other girls wouldn't stand a chance.

To be honest, I like the newfound attention I've been getting. I'm twenty pounds down, body on snatched with a new confidence that *clearly* was hiding somewhere in the shadows of that heavy cross I was carrying. Before, I was just *cute*. I didn't embrace my full potential. Now, I'm curving dudes left, right, front, and back. But I'm only focused on one guy. The only thing that keeps me coming to work every day. The one that gives me that adrenaline rush just by the way he looks at me.

Without a touch, he makes me feel alive. I've been doing the right thing for so long. If this is wrong, then God should at least give me a pass on this one. I just want to feel good for once. That's all I want. I deserve it.

I grab my purse, my notebook, and Genesis's birthday gift, and head out.

Ace is lit. I'm not a party girl but with DJ EXO guest emceeing and DJing, I can't help but feel the electric waves pump through the crowd.

Though today is another workday, the vibe is much more relaxed. The staff is dancing, drinking, laughing, and having a good time. I stay on the outskirts of the crowds. A few frisky hands sneak down my lower back and up my thighs a few times but for some reason, I don't mind tonight. Patrons aren't supposed to touch the staff, but we all know a slick hand in a crowd full of drunks and freaks is inevitable.

I scan the club. Genesis is sitting up in VIP, looking down on everyone having a good time. Skimpily dressed girls prance up to his blocked-off section with flashing lights and sparklers in bottles.

He glances at them, smiles, and cuts his eyes back to the crowd below him. In a crowd full of dancing people, Genesis scopes me out.

Our eyes meet.

I admire him. God, I can look at him all day. Those cat-like eyes that always dodge away from staying on me too long. He's quick. But I always catch him.

His wife comes up behind him, pulling his eyes away from me.

She smiles. He doesn't. She kisses him on the cheek. He pulls away. She rubs his back. He acts like he's stretching to stop her crumby hands from touching him. She offers him a sip of her drink. He walks away from her and jogs down the steps, ignoring the bottle girls and other floosies that saturate the club. He does *not* like that woman.

She watches him disappear into the crowd. She doesn't see me. Just skims right over me.

Looks young. Pretty. Short hair. Probably will look better if she got a weave but that's just my opinion. I haven't seen her up-close-and-personal yet, but from here, she a'ight.

I back my way down the hall and into the office. The noise fades. I flick on the light switch and sit behind Genesis's desk. I pull out my notebook from my large purse and flip it open. I grab a pen to begin to write. Something that's been tricky to do since work has taken up all my free time.

Just as I write the first letter, the door opens.

Genesis comes in. He's casual. A black fit polo shirt and dark blue jeans. As casual as he is, he's so clean. So debonair.

My cheeks heat up as he closes the door behind him, locking it. Something he never does.

I smile, "Hey."

"What's up," he mutters, avoiding my gaze.

"Having a good time?"

He saunters in with his head down. Pinching his chin and rubbing his facial hair, he sits on the other side of the desk. "Yeah, you know…it's a party. I'm not into the club scene like that anymore. Ten years ago, it was a different story, but I'm getting too old for this kind of stuff."

I reach under the desk and pull out his birthday gift. A gift bag that has his favorite cologne by Dior, a study Bible, and a few pairs of socks.

I hand him the bag. "Well, I hope this can make it better. Happy birthday."

His eyes brighten. "McKinney. What'chu do this for?"

"I wanted to give you a little something for your birthday. And a little thank you for how sweet you've been to me. I really appreciate you paying my debt in school and putting me through another term. I just…wanted to give you something special."

He holds the bag in one hand and puts the other up to his chest. "Thank you, Azra. You didn't have to—"

"I wanted to," I reach across the desk and grab his forearm.

He narrows his eyes, and we connect. *Sparks*.

Pulling away, I clear my throat, "Um…Looks like your wife's having a good time," I smile, waiting for him to respond. But he just stares and breathes. His blinks become limited. Soaking in each ounce of my desire through his greedy gaze. My heart races.

His lips look so soft. His tongue breaks the surface to wet them. Heat rushes through my body. I shift in my seat, breaking eye contact. Straightening my blazer out, I sit back in the chair, grab the mouse, and click away at the computer.

I glance over.

His eyes remain on me. He's lost. I don't even think he realizes what he's doing.

A smirk curls my lips as I tilt my head down. "Mr. Struthers?" I whisper, "You're staring."

He stirs in his seat. "Uh…Sorry. I wasn't…I'm sorry," he laughs.

"Did you hear me?" I giggle.

"What did you say?"

"Your wife—"

"Oh right. Yeah. Uh, she's having a good time. She loves when Exodus comes around. Loves parties even more. I'm surprised she didn't plan this one."

"She's a party planner too?"

"Nah, but she gets off on being in control, planning things. You know."

I slowly nod and skip a side-eye his way. "Sounds lovely," I pester.

"You have no idea," he laughs. "So, you sure you want to be in here all night? Everything is handled. We can stand for you to have a little fun on the job."

"No, I—"

The doorknob rattles the office door.

Without a flinch, Genesis gets up and unlocks the door.

"G! Wassup my mans." Exodus comes in, dapping Genesis up.

"Yo, E. Nothing much, man. Just coming back here, making sure everything's running smoothly."

"Man, it's ya' birthday. You still working?"

"Always." Genesis chuckles, closing the door as Exodus walks in.

My heart flutters as Exodus comes closer. Now that I know they're brothers, they look exactly alike. Genesis is a little taller, bronzer, and has more muscle mass, but Exodus is a cutie. Gold chain, black T, and a matching leopard-print suit. I'm no fashionista, but you can tell he's the loud one.

"I see what you workin' wit'," he glares at me with a smirk on his face but directs his words to his brother.

I stand and smile.

Genesis chuckles, "Nah, bruh, you gotta chill. It's not even like that. This is Azra McKinney," he comes in between us, "she's the new assistant manager."

Exodus scans me. He undresses me with his eyes, but I kind of like it. My palms feel sweaty. My heart stalls at the sight of him. I'm a bit starstruck but I handle it well. He extends his hand and I take it without delay.

"It's a pleasure to meet you, Ms. McKinney," he rubs the back of my hand and kisses it.

I giggle and glance at Genesis. He rolls his eyes away and shifts his position. His jaw jerks with irritation. Jealous much?

I pull my hand away, "Nice to meet you, too."

Exodus walks back and pulls Genesis with him. He whispers, "She assisting and managing something, but it ain't the club. Damn, she sexy."

"Man," Genesis snaps, looking back to make sure I didn't hear. I play it off like I didn't. "She's a respectable woman."

"Well, you know I got a lot of respect to give."

"E," Genesis places a hand on his little brother's shoulder and squeezes, "Where's Crystal?"

Exodus's face grows somber. "Man, I been meaning to tell you."

"What's going on?" Genesis asks.

Exodus lowers his voice to a mumble, "She told me she's pregnant."

Acting like I don't hear a thing, I click the mouse and ruffle through papers on the desk. Keeping busy.

Genesis doesn't respond, rather, he takes Exodus by the shoulder and leads him out into the clamorous club.

Genesis glances back, "Uh, Azra, you good?"

"I'm fine. You have a good time. Say hello to the Mrs. for me," I tease.

He shakes his head, "You're a trip," he chuckles, "And aye, thank you for this. I appreciate it," he says lifting the gift bag.

"Don't mention it," I smile and bite my lip.

He zeros on my mouth and breathes. "Yeah, uh," he snaps out of his head and looks behind him like he's about to get caught checking me out.

He looks back at me. "Alright then, I'll see you later. Have a good night, Azra."

"You too, Mr. Struthers" I grin.

I sit back and throw my head back. Did Exodus just call me sexy? DJ EXO?

He sees women all over the world and for him to say I'm sexy is a big effin' deal. Genesis said they are completely different, but I got a feeling they can agree on one thing, whether Genesis admits it or not. He's into me.

His stare tells the depths of his heart. I can feel it and he sucks at hiding it. But I'll get him to say that he wants me. That he needs me. Just so I know I'm not the only one having these thoughts. These feelings. I just want to hear him say it. That's all. It's just words. No harm in that.

FOURTEEN

LOLA

"And that's it!" Andrea says, dropping the finished business plan on my coffee table.

"Oh, my goodness, Andrea. I don't know how to thank you," I utter, hopping up and reaching across the table to hug her.

Over the months, we've worked hard on finishing my business plan. But during that time, we've gotten to know each other. After we talked everything out about William and me, she understood where I was coming from and she actually slipped up and called me an *ami*. That's *friend* in French. Even got a little nickname she calls me: Belle. Means *beautiful*. Better than what Lola means, but that's a story for another day.

I'm not the type to collect friends, but Andrea and I have so much in common. She has style; I'm a designer. Neither of us have a relationship with our mothers. She's an ambitious boss, and I'm on my way to opening my boutique.

I'm so glad William got us together, because in such a short period of time, I found a friend in her. Especially since Azra wanted to go rogue on me. I'm not sure if missing a few Sundays in church had her thinking she was going to hell, so she might as well make the best of it, but I'm not feeling her. She can go sleep with a married man and get her wig snatched by his wife for all I care. She's grown.

"Belle just keep doing what you're doing. We're gonna make this boutique happen. All we have to do is settle on a supplier, get a staff, a manager, all that jazz," Andrea says, taking a seat on the couch.

"Oh, my goodness. This is really happening," I join her.

"It's happening, darling. And for good reason. You're talented. Your clothes have a…je ne sais quoi. It's something people will catch onto. I have to say…you've got potential to be the next Coco Chanel. Even better."

"Get outta here!" I push her shoulder and laugh.

"Seriously. As a matter of fact, that's why I wanted to come over, so we can talk about your first investor."

My eyes widen and I almost jump out of my skin. I *just* finished my business plan, and someone already wants to invest in me?

"Who?"

Andrea stands and does a cutesy twirl. Holding her arms out, she sings, "Moi, ma chérie."

"Are you serious?" I dart up, grabbing and squeezing her hands.

"I don't lie. I'm all about making money and I can already see this boutique doing wonderful things the minute it opens. I know I gave you a hard time in the beginning, but I'll admit, I see what Will sees in you now. You got what it takes, but you had to learn it for yourself. So, to make things a *little* easier for you, I've reached out to a couple of friends in high places and…are you ready for this? Evvie King is going to be your first celebrity client."

My knees buckle and sends my butt straight into the chair. "You're joking," I whisper.

"I'm as serious as that heart attack you're about to have," she giggles.

I'm floored. My heart is beating out of my chest. This is a dream. All those years of wanting and wishing to be a designer, and it's finally happening.

"Andrea, you...I...," I stammer before covering my blushing face with my hands.

"You don't have to say anything, Belle. I know how hard it is getting things off the ground. Trust me. Before opening Ace, it was hard getting *two* people to come to the bar. It was a struggle to take on such a large load, especially with it being my first business venture. Now, look at it. It's one of the biggest clubs in the country."

Ace? I furrow my brow and steady my eyes on hers. My overjoyed tears are quickly wiped away.

"Wait, *you* own Ace Nightclub?"

"Yeah. William didn't tell you?"

"He said you own a few businesses, but not *Ace*. I worked there for eight years."

"That boy has so much on his plate with traveling and filming shows; he's not thinking about what I got going on." She laughs before continuing, "But I don't focus much on Ace like I used to. Right now, I'm focused on expanding CocoDrop and helping you with Imala, so, I'm not familiar with the people that work there. That's all on my husband."

My eyes widen. "Your husband?"

"Yeah." She smiles and bunches her brows.

"What's his name?" I ask.

"Genesis. Well, Genesis Struthers. I didn't take his last name."

What in the small world is going on? My smile fades and my heart feels like it's crawling on the ground.

"What's wrong?" she dryly chuckles.

I force an exaggerated smile, "Nothing. Just surprised. I had no idea you were married to him. You know he's the reason why I don't work there anymore."

"How's that?"

"He fired me for being late."

"Ugh, are you serious?" she rolls her eyes and laughs. "I'm so sorry. Genie's always been a stick up a monkey's behind."

"It's fine. If it weren't for being fired, I wouldn't be here opening my own boutique. Everything worked out."

"Yeah..." she says as her smile wilts away.

"Now, what's wrong with you?" I ask.

She sits and casts her glare to the floor. "Belle it's...nothing."

I chuckle and tap her leg. "What? Tell me."

She stares at me for a second. "You've got to promise you won't tell anyone. Not even William."

"Promise," I hold my hand up like I'm taking an oath, "So, what's going on?"

She takes a deep breath, "Genie and I've been going through a rough patch these last few years."

"How so?"

The atmosphere shifts and I feel like I stepped onto a landmine.

"Well...Many years back. A lot of mess happened between us. I'd rather not go into it all right now, but it took us some time to even get where we are now."

"I'm sorry to hear that."

She shakes her head, "It's fine. But since then, I just can't get over this feeling I've been having."

"What is it?"

She blows a breath. "I...I think he's seeing someone."

My stomach drops but I'm not surprised. I think I know more than she does. But I still play along.

"Why would you think that?" I ask in the most concerning tone I can find.

"He's been different. Just a few months ago when he fired the manager, he didn't even want to step foot in that club. He was hellbent on finding another manager, so he didn't have to manage it himself but after a few weeks, his tone changed. Now it seems like he *wants* to be there. Every day he's dressing nice and smelling good. I just...I don't know. He seems happier now. And it all happened out of nowhere."

"Well, what's so wrong with that? Happy husband, good loving, or whatever they say."

"I guess. I don't know. Something just doesn't feel right. And on top of it all, for years he's been talking about selling it, but suddenly, that talk stopped. Which I guess is a good thing because I don't want to get rid of Ace."

"Why does he want to sell it?" I ask, hoping to segue into a different subject rather than him cheating on her with my best friend...or ex-best friend.

"I guess his religion or whatever. He got saved a couple years back and claims the club is the work of the devil." She chuckles and shakes her head in disbelief. "His relationship with God is his business. I love God too, but all I'm saying is the club is one of our most successful businesses. That's where the Struthers' empire started. If we get rid of that, we won't be able to pass it down to our children."

"You have kids?" My eyes bug out.

"No. God, no. Not yet anyway."

Whew. I exhale a slow and steady breath, hoping she doesn't notice my nerves. Why am I nervous? I'm not the one messing with her husband.

"He wants kids, but I don't think we need them. But that may be the wrench that's driving us apart. He always talked about having a big family, but I never wanted that. Besides, I'm getting up in age."

"Girl, it's so much technology nowadays, you could probably be post-menopausal and still pop 'em out," I joke but find myself to be the only one laughing.

"Yeah…kids don't seem like my style, though. If I did have a child, it'll only be to pass on what we've built. He wants a bunch, and I don't think I have the patience, time, or eggs for that now."

"I feel you. Kids are a lot of work."

"And money. That's what Genesis doesn't get. I love kids and all, but I don't want to go through all that pain again, just to have what I already have with Will. He's my baby, you know? Plus, I don't want to mess up my figure. I've worked too hard to get here and I ain't gonna let no baby mess that up."

"Well, surrogacy is always an option."

She bucks her neck and turns up her nose. "Please. I'll be bewitched if I let any woman that close to my man. With *his* baby? No. We ain't about to have no crazy chick up in my house trying to take me out."

The mood lightens a smidge as we share a good laugh, trading ways we'd handle a chick if she tried to kill us to take our men.

After babbling on and on about randomness for a couple hours, she stands to leave.

"Thanks for listening to me, darling." She hugs me.

Her sorrowful vibe overtakes me as we embrace. I hug her tighter, partly to make her feel better, but also to make me feel less guilty for knowing who her husband's mistress is. I want to tell her it'll be okay, but I can't promise that.

"Listen," I pull away, "if Genesis is being an f-boy, girl, you got the looks, the money, and the personality to get yourself someone ten times better than him. And whenever you need to talk, just give me a call," I say, rubbing her shoulder.

She smiles and whips her Gucci bag around her arm, "Thanks, belle. Qui vivra verra."

She reads the confused look in my squinted eyes and laughs.

"We'll see how everything plays out," she clarifies, "but I'll be in touch for us to talk money this week."

"Ayeee! I'm getting a boutique; I'm getting a boutique," I merrily sing and dance Andrea to the door.

As she steps out the door, my phone vibrates on the kitchen countertop with a call.

"Let me guess…William?" she grins with her head tilted to the side.

I glance at the phone. Don't recognize the number, but the 804-area code tells me it's from home, and instantly I feel sick.

Other than my mother, there's only one other dealing I have in Richmond. I swallow and answer the phone.

"Hello?"

"Lola," a familiar gruff voice says, triggering memories of a time I wish to forget, "He's getting out early."

My eyes concerningly meet Andrea's as she stands by the door.

"How early?" I ask.

"In three weeks. Just thought you should know."

My ears ring. The wind has been knocked out of my lungs. Before I can process what I've been told, the phone hangs up.

I freeze. Trembling, I place my phone on the counter and collapse onto the barstool. Goosebumps prickle on my skin.

Andrea places her bag down and rushes over to me, "You okay?"

I inhale deeply and exhale through my mouth. "I-I'm fine. Just feeling a little sick."

"Oh Lord," she steps back, "you ain't pregnant, are you?"

"No," I scoff. How I wish it were only that simple. I had a target on my back. And no matter how bad I want to run, it's useless. Angel is coming. And if he's anything how I remember, he's going to find me.

FIFTEEN

AZRA

Walking into Ace hours before the Sunday staff files in, I catch my reflection in the black marble wall before stepping into the office. This white cut-out bodycon dress clings to my curves like an extra layer of skin. Lola would be proud. Or be hating. Either way, I didn't come to play. Genesis is going to gag.

I open the door and let it swing open. For dramatic effects, I poke my hip to the side and place my hand on it. My naturally curly tresses drape over my right eye and my luscious red lips have me serving Jessica Rabbit realness for centuries.

"Hey—" Genesis pauses as he looks over from the computer screen. He gawks at my moisturized thunder thighs and scans up to my heightened chest. "What are you wearing?" he asks with a puzzled expression. He leans back in his chair, eyes fixated on me.

I strut to the jade couch and teasingly tug at the bottom of my dress before sitting. "Clothes," I say in a *duh* kind of tone.

Breaking his gaze, he straightens up and continues typing, "You look like your friend dressed you."

I crook my neck. I may look different than normal, but I don't look like a walking thirst trap.

He lifts his hands in surrender, "I didn't mean it like that, McKinney. I'm just saying. It doesn't look like you."

I cringe at his semi-formal acknowledgment of me. He never calls me by my last name but insists on keeping it *professional* at work. Although, professionalism went out the window four months ago when he began calling me *just to talk*. I call bull.

"Mm-hmm," I press my lips together. Taking a seat on the couch I open the laptop sitting on the cushion next to me and log in. I toss my hair, ruffle my hands through it, and peep Genesis's eyes darting back and forth between me and his computer. He's beguiled. It's obvious. But I can't fault him. The new Azra's pretty amazing.

He heaves a sigh and sits back in his chair. "Alright, McKinney. What's up?"

I quirk an eyebrow, "What do you mean?"

"This? The way you've been dressing. It's a lot different than how you were a few months ago."

I smile and peep at him out the corner of my eye, "I...like it? Why? Is there a problem? Am I breaking any dress code or something?"

"No. I just thought you were a sweats and sneakers kind of girl."

"See, that's the problem. I'm a grown woman and I'd like to be *seen* as one. Besides, a woman can change up her style whenever she wants."

"McKinney," he twirls himself from behind his desk, demanding my attention. "The clothes you wear...or lack of...don't make you a woman. *You* do. You don't need all of this. You're smart. You're getting your degree. You're in a higher position now. So why are you dressing like these girls here?" He stands and walks to the couch, "You got brains. You don't need to show all of *that* to get anybody's attention. Don't change for these dudes out here. They ain't worth it. And if they don't understand you're more than just body, then they ain't the one."

He speaks to me like a father would. It kind of creeps me out because though I appreciate the sentiments behind it, he still not getting it. I don't want a daddy. I want *him*.

I turn my body in his direction as he sits on the edge of the arm of the couch. Crossing my legs, I watch as he squirms. He tries to stop his eyes from traveling up my thighs but that's an epic fail.

A lopsided grin shines upon my face, "What if these dudes aren't the ones I'm trying to attract?"

He narrows on my mouth and I seductively bite my lower lip. He mindlessly mimics me before breaking from his trance.

"All I'm saying is I wouldn't want Andrea walking around the way these girls do, and I don't think *you* should either."

Oh gosh! If he brings this woman up one more time I'm going to scream. *Andrea*, he calls her. Not *An-dree-uh*. But *Uhn-dree-uh*. Like she's royalty. Knowing doggone well her mother named her a basic behind An-dray-uh. No matter what her name is, I'm tired of him bringing her up.

I sigh and roll my eyes. "Why is that?" I sit back, jutting my chest out ever so slightly.

His eyes are focused on mine, but this time with more determination to not divert his gaze elsewhere.

"Because some of these dude's imaginations ain't cool. Some women are too good to be reduced into a fantasy."

"But I'm not your woman. So why does it matter whether guys fantasize about me?" I bat my lashes.

He adjusts his seating on the armrest and tugs at his pants. "I'm just telling you how men think. My brother was attracted to you and you didn't do all this. You capture attention just by being you."

"Well, why didn't you let him shoot his shot?" I smirk.

He rubs the back of his neck, becoming agitated. "Unless you want to become a baby mom, I don't think you want him to shoot his shot. I love my brother, but he don't care about these women. He wants them for one thing and that's it. So, I couldn't let him get that close to you. You deserve better than that. But dressing like this ain't gonna attract the kind of man you want."

I chuckle. He speaks a good game but his eyes have slipped below my collarbone more than he'll admit in the last thirty seconds.

"So," I stand from the couch and spin, stopping to look at him over my shoulder. I stick my booty out to give it that extra pop, "you're telling me *this* wouldn't attract you?"

Catching his gaze rise from my buttocks, he shoots his eyes back to mine, "It'll attract a lot of dudes."

"I asked about *you*," I pivot on my heel and shimmy my blazer off my shoulders. I throw it on the couch.

"Did I catch yours, Mr. Struthers?" My eyes draw to his.

The muscle in his jaw jerks before he heavily breathes, "What's gotten into you?"

My question exactly. I have no idea what's crept up in me. Time and energy spent around this man make all my senses react. I need to know he feels the same. I've obsessed over Genesis. He's taken possession of my mind. I can't stop thinking about him. All I want is him. My body, my mind, my soul craves him.

It's wrong. I know God will probably strike me down where I stand if I lay one little hand on him. But I can't stop. I saunter closer, floating like a character in a Spike Lee Joint. Genesis's magnetic pull draws me towards him.

I whisper, "It's a simple question. Just answer it."

He chuckles like he's about to risk it all. He slides his hand down his face, "Simple questions can get a man like me in trouble."

Standing a foot away from each other, heat radiates between us. I lick my lips and let my eyes do the talking. Scanning over his mouth, down his neck, back to his eyes. Intensity builds.

He's so still. Like he's afraid to touch me. Afraid to think. To breathe. If it weren't for that thirst in his eyes as he leers into mine, I'd think he was a statue. His arms flinch a bit to refrain from grabbing me closer, but his willpower is gradually withering away.

"You know I'm married," he whispers. His words are faithful, but his guards are frail and fickle. He wants to give in. He yearns for the possibility of what could be. For what would be if he weren't taken.

My fingers dance up his arms. His body languidly slumps into my grasp. He surrenders. I snake my hands around the sides of his neck.

"And we're just friends, Genesis," I murmur, "Answer the question."

His nose flares, "You already know the answer to that, Ms. McKinney."

I smirk and step back, "See, that's all I wanted to know. And I like it better when you call me Azra," I giggle before tearing my eyes away from his stoic expression.

Reaching for my blazer, a strong hand yanks me back by my waist. Spinning me into him, we meet again. Eye to eye. Chest to chest. I place my hands on the solid physique that lies under his jean button-up shirt. His heart is pounding as his chest rhythmically inflates and deflates. His clutch around me tightens.

I'm about to spaz. My breaths become thin. My fingertips tingle at the touch of him. It's electric. This is what I've been wanting. This is what I've waited for.

I smirk, but he only meets me with a passion in his eyes and a tenseness in his jaw that shakes me to my core. Closing my eyes to relish in his hold, I drift further from my morals and deeper into his tantalizing presence.

His breath tickles my lips. I wreath my arms around him, closing the bittersweet distance between us. Chests to chest. Hearts throbbing. Creating a beat only we march to. Butterflies erupt as his mouth parts mine. My knees buckle but thankfully it goes unnoticed as he tightly holds me.

He draws his head back.

Reluctancy and confusion riddles his expression. If there is any more blood left in his brain, he'll probably push me off him and fire me on the spot. But he doesn't do that. He stares at me. An unfulfilled thirst in his eyes, in his touch, grows. Waiting to be quenched.

I grab the back of his head and lean his forehead against mine.

You know I'm all for you bustin' loose, but all for a married man? It isn't worth it, sis.

I rake my fingers through his beard as our eyes burn into one another.

These devils lurking for some new blood. You gotta stay prayed up, sugar.

I wrap my arms around his neck and rise up on my tiptoes.

For God gave us a spirit not of fear but of power and love and self-control.

Ignoring the constant badgering of my spirit, I press my lips against his and lose all sense of self-control. The ravishing attack on each other is movie-esque. It's life-giving. If this is what it feels like to be free and not living by any rules, then what was I doing before? Kissing Genesis. Being in his presence. I relax and react at the same time. My legs shake, so I squeeze them together. The beating through my chest is making me think I might have an arrhythmia. The oxygen to my brain is cut off. I want more. More. *More.*

I'm his and he's mine. Alone. Secure. Comfortable. Oblivious of the time and place. I love it. The temperature rises and the need to cool down leads me to unbutton his shirt. He moans and I lose it. He lifts the bottom of my dress.

Boom, boom, boom.

Jumping apart and mindlessly adjusting our clothes, my heart pounds as knocks rattle the door.

Genesis and I swallow our guilt and clasp back the aches of our needs and desires. We turn toward the door to see Kendrick bobbing his big head in.

Steadying my breath, I sit on the edge of the armrest and tightly cross my trembling legs. Genesis struggles as he widely trudges back to sit behind his desk. On the corner of my eye, I see him casually buttoning up the rest of his shirt.

"Yo boss, I—" Kendrick knits his brow as he watches Genesis lick and pinches his cherry-stained lips with his finger and thumb.

Shoot! I knew I should've worn lip gloss.

Kendrick's eyes shoot over to me. I'm flustered. Lipstick smudged over my face. The hem of my dress risen a few centimeters higher than what it should be. Breathing still trying to steady to a reasonable pace. I can only imagine what he's thinking. He's probably putting me in Harlotsville right now.

Oh God, what did I just do?

I bow my head to avoid the disappointment that riddles his face.

"What's up, Ken?" Genesis asks, drawing Kendrick's attention back to him.

"Yeah, boss. Um...Riley. She's out here throwing a fit talking about she's Godzilla and drinking from the bottles at the bar. I don't know if you want me to kick her out, or..."

"I'll handle it. Thank you." After a few moments, Genesis gets himself together and stands to head out of the office, not looking in my direction. He slaps hands with Kendrick and quickly embraces him before he walks out the office.

I peep up at Kendrick who remains in the doorway, shaking his head.

A begging glint in my eyes pleads for him to not say anything, but he slowly backs out of the office.

"Kendrick, wait," I call out. Crossing my arms and keeping my head down, I saunter over to him. "Please don't tell anybody."

"About what?" He leans against the doorframe and stares at me, knowing darn well he knows what I'm talking about.

I shrug and chew on the side of my cheek.

"Nah, Beauty. That's *y'all* business," he says backing out, "I'll see you around."

As the door closes, I drift to Genesis's desk and flop into the chair. Leaning my elbows on the desk and holding my head in my hands, I shut my eyes and take a deep breath.

Am I that far gone? I'm going completely against what I know is right. *He's married, Azra. What are you doing?*

I know I'm wrong for this. All this messiness is about to make me quit my job and go to nun school, and I ain't even catholic. I don't need this in my life. I'm not built for this.

Alright, Azra. Breathe. Inhale—oh my goodness.

I pop my eyes open, and my inner thoughts go blank. I lift my wrists and smell them. I grab a loc of hair and smell it. I pinch the tight fabric of my top and bring it to my nose. Oh, my goodness. I smell like him.

Genesis's scent awakens my senses and I forget why I felt guilty.

Why should I feel guilty for this kind of pleasure? Why does this feel so good if it's not right? Now, that's torturous. God, why?

I close my eyes and try to get understanding from the One who knows me best. But the prayer I have stored in my heart becomes faint and distant with each whiff of Genesis's essence. It numbs my brain. It numbs my heart. And all I want right now…is more.

I can't keep denying myself. I'll go crazy. I'm so tired of doing that. I need to live. I need to be happy. I need to be free. I need *him*.

I'm done resisting.

Genesis is it. He's the one for me.

He gives me what I've been missing. I'm in paradise. And I didn't have to die to get it.

SIXTEEN

LOLA

"Azra, I don't know why you're avoiding me. If anyone should be mad, it should be *me*," I yell through the phone at Azra's voicemail. "Listen, I need to talk to you. It's important. Please…call me back, sis."

I sit on the edge of my bed and gather my thoughts. Just when I'm on a high in my life, here comes my past creeping back. When am I gonna catch a break? Even the hardest diamonds crack under pressure and with the news of Angel being released from prison, the pressure's wearing down on me.

I haven't left my apartment in six days. I know he isn't out yet, but I don't want him sending one of his goons to find me.

Tears well in my eyes. I tilt my head back to keep them at bay, but they find their escape. Ugh, I hate being so doggone emotional. I feel like I've been crying over everything lately. I should be happy. I should be in my sewing room finishing the unfinished pieces in my closet. But not even sewing can make me feel better. I need guidance. Someone to tell me what to do.

Azra's the only one who knows about my tumultuous relationship with Angel. And she's acting like a simpleton for not answering my calls.

There's no way I can outrun an angel. And Angel Burgos is just that. Easy on the eyes. Smooth. Irresistible. Crazy. Possessive. Utterly *terrifying*.

See how quickly that turned? That's Angel for you. Predictably unpredictable. You know he'll snap, but you'll never know when.

He's an angel, but *not* God's angel. He's the embodiment of unadulterated evil. Everything I loathe. The one person I'm petrified of. I should've known what I was getting myself into when I laid eyes on him at the diner I served at. His long, blown-out ponytail cascaded down his neck as he captured me with his green eyes. The white tank top should have been a dead giveaway, but I was only sixteen. Being too busy trying to flip through hoops to stay out of the system, I missed all the warning signs. I thought it was impossible to run into someone like Randy, but Angel proved me wrong. He's worse.

He's gunning for me once he's released. If it weren't for me, he'd still be free…and I'd probably be pushing up daisies. Looks like I just prolonged the process.

What am I gonna do? Of course, I don't have Poppy when I need her the most. The least Azra can do is send her to me in the mail.

I grab my phone to text Azra for the ninth time, but William's name minimizes the text screen.

Blinking away tears and exhaling a shaky breath, I answer, "Hello?"

"I want to show you something," William cheerfully says.

Desperately wanting to meet his level of glee, I can't. I groan and lie back on my bed, "What?"

"I can't tell you *now*. It's a surprise."

"Romeo, I'm not in the mood to play around, so can you just tell me?"

"Oooh," he chuckles.

"What?"

"You called me *Romeo*."

I press back a smile only he's able to put on my face in the midst of distress. "What do you want?"

"I want you to come out with me on Friday."

I don't feel like putting up a fight. Besides, I can use something to take my mind off my current situation.

I sigh. "What time?"

"What time are you getting up?"

"Whenever you call me at the butt crack of dawn."

William laughs. He knows I'm not a morning person, yet he insists on calling me at the vile hours of daybreak.

"Well, that's when I want you to get ready. I'll get you shortly after."

"Where're you taking me?"

"Didn't I tell you it's a surprise, woman?"

"You know I hate surprises. Plus, the last time you mentioned a surprise you proposed, so this better not be another trap."

He laughs, "Nah. Not this time. Just know you're gonna love it, okay?"

"Okay," I grumble.

"A'ight, I'll see you then, Bean."

"Wait," I beg, trying to stop him from hanging up, "What'cha doing?"

"*What*? You want to know what *I'm* doing?"

"Oh God, why'd I even ask," I grin.

What am I turning into? The stone-cold walls I try to maintain are slowly melting as the days go by. I feel like I'm turning into a big pile of mush when I talk to him. It's disgusting. Like, I'm repulsed. Offended. Appalled. What is he doing to me? Better yet why am I *allowing* myself to fall?

"Nah," he laughs, "I'm at the airport right now, about to take a quick trip to L.A. for this show. But I should be back Thursday night. Why? You wanted to see me, didn't you?"

"Please. What show are you taping now?" I bite back a smile.

"Some competition show. I'm a guest judge. Since I'm the only young, Black, successful, and handsome dude in the game, you know they had to call me."

"Don't forget *modest*."

"You already know, woman."

Although William boasts about how great he is, he's genuinely humble. He can be flashy sometimes, but what twenty-six-year-old that makes as much money, has as much fame, and looks as good as William, isn't?

"Well...good luck," I mutter, mad that I can't have him with me right now.

Instead of staying on the phone, getting in my feelings, and accidentally spewing out things my heart's been daring me to say, I cut the conversation short.

As I lie in the dark, scrolling through the same videos on YouTube that I've seen at least ten times today, a message pops up.

Jeremiah

Since you don't want to call nobody, I'ma be off at 12. Lemme slide through.

Eggplant emoji.

Bruh. Is he serious? First, let's not compare what he's working with to an eggplant because that's fraud in the first degree. Second, he must've gotten the wrong message when I mistakenly let him stay the night. But he needs to go.

I drop my phone to the side and massage my temples. I get up, take a cold shower, and slip on one of William's t-shirts he left here months ago. Still smells like him. Woody and sweet.

I lie on my bed and hold the neck of the shirt to my nose to sniff it like some weirdo. It calms me.

Jeremiah's the furthest thing from my mind and the last set of arms I want around me. The only arms that can take away my anxieties are headed to L.A. And if I can't have those, I'll settle for my own.

It's finally Friday, and I didn't sleep a wink.

Thankfully, my sleep deprivation is from excitement rather than the fear that's fortunately dissipated as the week crept by. William's back from L.A., and I'm ready to see what he wants to show me.

After getting his morning call, I feel like a kid going on a field trip.

I want to look my best, so I laid out my outfit last night: A jade Bardot floor-length dress with a long split up the left thigh. It might be a little extra, but come on, Lola Jones is known for drippin'. I'm dodging Angel and his goons, but being on point when I step out is a non-negotiable.

As I exit my building, I chuckle.

If people think *I'm* extra, they must not know William. He sits in a brand new, all-white G-Wagon. The bass of the music reverberates through the apartment complex. With the windows rolled down, he sits in the driver's seat with his sunglasses on, looking like he stepped out of a GQ magazine.

Slowly click-clacking my way to the car, I check it out. I never understood why men go crazy over cars, but this Mercedes may have changed my mind. It's clean.

Like clockwork, the May breeze flows through my hair as William finally notices me. He slides off his shades and ogles at me for a minute before jumping out and rushing to open the car door.

"You tryin' to hurt me today, huh?" he scans me from head to toe.

"That's all you. Riding around like a star," I brush past him to get in the car.

"Only when I got you with on my arm," he closes the door.

Taking in the crisp and citrusy, oceanic aroma of his new cologne, I glance around at the peanut butter and wood interior. It's nice. Real nice.

I just find it funny that he splurges on cars and toys whenever he wants to show off, but never thought to invest in my business. Although I'm grateful he introduced me to Andrea, I still don't understand why he hasn't help me out himself. Andrea became an active investor only after a few months of knowing me. She understands my vision and knows I'm serious. William and I have been together for over a year and he still hasn't mentioned anything about investing.

But what's done is done. If there's anything I learned in life, it's to depend on myself. I know if I want to make anything out of my life, I have to take matters into my own hands. And that's just the way it is.

"So, how'd everything go?" I ask, taking a peep at William as he drives. He's swagged out, wearing his fitted tan, short-sleeved, mock neck shirt, and his dark brown plaid pants. A single gold chain hangs from his neck as usual, and I swoon.

"It went well. The producers said they're gonna give me a call to do another show in a couple months."

I widen my eyes and smile, "Oh? What will you be doing?"

"Well, they want me to be *in* the competition this time around. So, you know, I already got that in the bag."

"Well duh."

"You know they need me."

Opening my mouth to intentionally knock him off his high horse, I glance out the window for a second as we stop at a stoplight. I freeze. My heart flashes with an aching pain as my eyes glue to the back of a man. His puffy, long, black ponytail and white tank top debilitates me. My insides tremor but my body is stuck in place.

"You okay, Bean?" William's mutter barely stirs me from what I pray is a hallucination.

I can't speak.

All I see is *him.*

The fright.

The pain.

The blood.

How could they let him out early? I follow every gesture. Every strand of hair that blows in the wind. Every minuscule muscle movement he uses to slowly turn around. The relatively older man's dark brown eyes connect with mine as he stands on the corner, waiting for the bus. The warm smile that shows on his face instantly puts me at ease.

Heaving for air, I clutch my chest and steady my pounding heart.

"You alright, Lola?" William leans in, grabbing my shoulder and giving it a firm rub.

"I-I'm fine," I say patting his hand.

"You sure? You've been kind of aloof lately. You feeling okay?" He lowers his hand to rub my stomach, "My baby a'ight?" he smiles.

I slap him away with the quickness.

"Boy, please," I giggle, "I'm fine. I'm just not in the most talkative mood. That's all."

"Well, aren't you happy about having Andrea as an investor? That's something to talk about."

"Yeah. We've been speaking over the week and I'm excited," I unenthusiastically mutter. I want to be excited right now, but fear of the past is stalking my present.

"You know you can talk to me, right? I'm here for you, Bean. Whatever it is, I got'chu."

"Thanks, Romeo," I say, glaring over at him and smiling. He's always there for me, but I fear he'll eventually get tired of me putting him on the backburner. Keeping my truths to myself and not letting him in. It's only a matter of time for him to find someone who isn't so stubborn. I won't blame him if he left. But the thought of it makes me want to cry.

We ride in silence for some time, taking in the scenery. I huff back the thoughts of my past and focus on the beauty of D.C. The enormous buildings resemble the architecture of classical Greece and Rome. The winding and confusing roads make me feel like we might get in an accident if we aren't careful. The most amazing part about D.C. to me, is how much it's changed.

Chocolate City is no more. Taken over by gentrification, it's sad how one side of the street can have rundown apartments, while the other side has booming businesses and hotels that the people across the street can't even afford to stay in. A sad shame.

After getting well into D.C. and passing so many different monuments and buildings that all begin to look the same, I ask, "Where are you taking me?"

"We'll be there in a couple minutes." William chuckles.

Driving up Eighth Street, he parks the car and points to a beautiful storefront with large windows. "What do you think about this place?"

Taking a glance at the empty store, I envision my boutique. A large sign with my name on it. Fall line on display. Lines as long as those outside of the Apple store when a new iPhone drops.

"I think this is exactly the kind of place I need for my boutique. It's in the middle of the city. People would be busting the doors down," I smile, making a mental note to tell Andrea about this spot once I got home.

"It's a good spot," he mutters, staring at me with raised eyebrows and a smirk.

Furrowing my brow and tearing away from his gaze, I ask, "Did you bring me here just to ask me what I thought about *this*? You could've just pulled it up on Google maps."

He laughs and leans in to put his arm around my shoulder, "Woman, look closer," he points into the store, his lips centimeters away from my ear. "You see that?"

Fighting the glare from the sun hitting the windows, I squint my eyes to see the back wall of the inside of the store. It all becomes clear.

There it is. Big, black, sleek letters, I-M-A-L-A are beveled out of the wall, visible for the street to see.

My eyes grow large, and my lungs deflate all the oxygen in my body. "Oh my God! Romeo, are you serious? Stop playing!" I screech, hurting my own ears.

"This would be an expensive joke," he laughs, leaning back over in his seat.

Nearly jumping into his lap, I fling my arms around him and squeeze. Loosening my grip and giving him just enough space to breathe, I scream at the top of my lungs and judder his shoulders.

"Whoa, woman. We haven't even gotten out the car yet." He laughs, pulling my hands off of him. "Wanna go inside?"

"Yes!" I shriek. I jump off William's lap and out of the car in one clean motion.

I run to the door and nearly press my face against the spotless glass, like a kid at a candy store.

Not a millisecond after the door swings open, I fly inside. Spinning around and taking in the smell of fresh paint, I find myself in the middle of the store. Carrara marble floors, strategically placed spotlights, and the tall ceiling that holds a beautiful, spiral, raindrop chandelier, gives the store the high-end look I've only dreamed of. It looks more like a small department store than a boutique.

Chuckling, William walks behind me and wraps his arms around my waist.

In awe, I lean my head back on his shoulder and stare at my middle name on the wall. Exhaling, I turn around to face him.

"How? Me and Andrea just finished the business plan last week. How'd you get this place so fast?"

"I told you I stay ten steps ahead, didn't I?" he smiles, "I had this place secured back in February when I knew you and Andrea were getting your business plan together. Andrea ain't no joke. She owns this building and a few others around here. When she told me this place was for sale, I snatched it up and got it remodeled. Knowing you, I knew you wouldn't want to wait too long to open. So now it's time to get things rolling. But I'm telling you, it only gets tougher from here. This is yours now. You got me and Andrea here to help you, but this is all you."

"I don't care," I grin, "this is what I've always wanted. I'll work day and night if I have to."

"Well, make sure you make some time for me," he smiles, wrapping his arms around me.

I swallow the growing knot in my throat and glance at my feet before meeting his eyes again. "Thank you so much, Romeo," I blink back tears.

He smiles, shaking his head and pushing a few strands of hair from my face. "Oh, I almost forgot," he says, backing up. He takes my hand in his and places the keys to the store *and* car in my palm.

Hesitating to grip them, I peer into his eyes.

"It's all yours," he whispers.

His eyes fix on mine as he searches for a response, yet all I can do is point to the $180,000 car sitting out front to make sure I heard him correctly.

He chuckles, "Yes, woman."

Taking my hand in his and curling my fingers over the keys, he plants a tender kiss on my forehead.

"William," I whine, only making him laugh harder. His dimples deepen as his lips rest into a smile.

I'm speechless. After all I did to this man and he is unmoving.

I wrap my arms around his neck and gaze at him as he holds me close.

"Why are you so sweet to me? After how I've acted. All the things I've said and done. Why are you still here?" I ask, tightening my embrace.

I don't understand William. I can't figure him out. But that's what intrigues me. Anyone else would have dropped me the moment I told them to. But he didn't. He supports me, even when he knows he'll get nothing from it. It's foreign to be treated well with no conditions. With such chivalry and respect. I don't know how to handle it.

He takes a deep breath. "Because whether you like it or not, I see those cracks in your armor. Funny thing is *you* aren't even aware of them. You think you're bad, and strong, and got everything on lock, but I know you. That's why I do what I do for you. I know the person behind that wall. I might not know the details, but I'm gonna keep on breaking through until it all falls apart. Because I want to get to know you more. But most of all, I want *you* to see what I see in you, Lola."

My lip quivers. I bite down to keep from crying, but with the gentle swipe of William's thumb wiping away a single tear, it's too late.

"You care about me that much?" I croak.

He holds me snug in his arms. His expression remains soft and heartfelt. "I *love* you that much, Lola."

Cue the waterworks.

I lower my head and bite back the words. Unable to control the emotions that spill out.

He tilts my chin up to face him, his lips inch closer. We kiss. The world disappears around us. Gravity lifts from beneath our feet. I'm on cloud nine. No one can make me feel the way William does. He's in my heart. Nothing can change that.

SEVENTEEN

AZRA

"Shoot!" I hit the steering wheel of my car. After turning the key so many times, the whirling sound of the engine makes me lose hope.

This is what I get for ignoring Lola. She's the only person I can rely on in my time of need but I'm not talking to her.

I can hear her now. *"Oh, so now you wanna call, huh? Where's Prince Charming? Home cheating on you with his wife?"*

I don't feel like hearing all that, nor do I want to *think* about Genesis.

Who cares about that cornball anyway? Not I. Not after he went and hired a new manager and didn't tell me about it. Didn't even have the decency to give me a heads up. After he went to *'handle'* Riley, he never came back. The next day, I came into work with my list of apologies, only to be greeted by a pretty brunette, in a blue suit, sitting at Genesis's desk.

Trish.

She was the one to tell me about Genesis leaving. She told me he had other business to tend to and couldn't manage the club. She also told me she was hired on the spot, which instantly made me feel less special as I thought I once was to him.

He just left me. I was so sure he would call or text or something, but no. He vanished. Vamoose.

Me and Lola are on the outs. Kendrick is dodging me for breaking his heart. And Genesis is ghosting me like Space Ghost. Now my *car* dies on me? Just my luck.

I roll down my windows to get some air. Picking up my phone to google AAA's number, a large vehicle slowly drives up next to me. I already know who it is: Mr. Casper the *Cowardly* Ghost.

"Hey." Genesis turns down his music and flashes that gorgeous smile I haven't seen in ten days. "You good?"

"I'm fine," I say sitting back in my seat. I sneak my hand to the window controls and pull up the button to roll the passenger window up. I don't even want to look at him. I refuse to get caught in his beauty and forgetting about how he ditched me.

"Hold on, Azra," he utters, only to be cut off by the shutting window. As hot as it is at three o'clock in the morning, I have no problem with burning up in my car to avoid sitting through another one of his disappearing acts.

I hesitate to call AAA until Genesis pulls off, only to park in the parking spot in front of me.

He gets out of his car and swaggers over to mine. Although I'm not a fan of his antics, I surely do miss the sight of him. *Lord ha'mercy!*

"What's going on, Azra?" he asks, bending down and gazing at me with those dark eyes.

Cutting my eyes away and lifting my phone to my face, I scoff, "I should be asking you that."

He sighs and straightens up, placing an arm on the roof of my car. "Your car broke down, huh?"

"No. Just take pleasure in making myself living clickbait for serial killers," I cock my head to the side and mindlessly scroll through Instagram. How'd I get on here? I'm supposed to be calling AAA.

He chuckles, "Lemme see something." Moving to the front of my car, he pops the hood to see what the problem is.

Trying not to enjoy the view of Genesis working under my hood, I continue to swipe through Instagram. I double back up the screen to see one of the few photos Lola's ever posted. A picture of her in front of a storefront that has her middle name in the background. The caption makes my stomach cramp.

And y'all thought I couldn't do it. #Issabusinessowner
#itsthesuccessforme.

Wait, is that William taking the picture? I study his loving smile through the reflection of the glass window.

I swallow the rising anger fighting to burst out into a boiling rage.

How?

I dare not address God in this kind of anger I feel cycling through me, but why is she blessed like this after all the crap she did in her life? She ain't no saint.

And what do I get? Twenty-five years of living my life so dedicated and faithful to God. Getting on my knees, day and night. Praying. Keeping my honor because if I didn't, I'd be punished for the rest of my days. All of this...all for nothing but a degree from the University of Hard Knocks. She's done nothing to deserve that store. The man. The looks she puts absolutely no effort into. Yet, she gets it all. What is going on?

"That's the problem," Genesis says slamming the hood shut, jarring me from my hateful thoughts. I throw my phone in my lap.

"You got a crack in your distributor cap."

"Never heard of that but okay," I say in a flat tone, crossing my arms, still not looking at him.

He leans his forearm on the roof of the car, lowering his head to see inside. "It basically sends the voltages to start the car's engine."

"So…"

"You got to get it towed. You got AAA?"

I nod and pick my phone up.

"Well, call them tomorrow. They'll pick it up for you. Until then, let me give you a ride. It's late. You don't want to sit out here all night." He reaches into my car and unlocks the door to open it.

"Excuse you?" I roll my neck, keeping my gaze from falling on him. "What makes you think I want to ride with you? How do I know you're not gonna go missing in action in the middle of 295?"

"Azra," he sternly utters, stepping back and motioning for me to get out.

He must have strings attached to his fingers because like a puppet, I grab my purse, get out the car, and walk to his car without a single word.

Riding in silence, his usual sexy old-school R&B plays. All I want is a quiet lift home but because I'm petty, I use this opportunity to ignore him, giving him the same punishment he gave me. But apparently giving him the silent treatment isn't enough for him to take the hint.

"So, how've you been?" he asks, turning an eye to me.

"Fine," I peer out the window.

"I know it's been a while, Azra."

A while? We spoke and saw each other every day for the past four months. For all communication to stop for almost two weeks without explanation is wrong. It felt like an eternity.

Exaggeratedly scoffing, I keep my thoughts to myself.

"Azra, you got to understand. It's hard being around somebody like you. The other night…I can't say I didn't want it to happen, but it wasn't okay. You know that, right?"

Of course, I know it was wrong. But that's what makes this thing so genuine. Exciting. The raw passion that we felt that night can't be faked. That's chemistry. He knew he liked it and if Kendrick's big head didn't barge in, he would've *loved* it. But instead of responding, I keep my eyes from wandering over to him and remain quiet.

"Listen, I want to apologize for putting us in this position. I'm the one who's married, and I should've had more self-control," he pauses for a moment.

His voice is sincere. Makes me feel a little bad for bringing out a side of him he doesn't want uncovered. But I'm two seconds away from falling in love with this man and his virtuous ways make him even harder to resist.

I huff a deep breath but allow him to continue.

"I also want to apologize for ignoring you and not letting you know I was leaving. I just needed to get away for a while."

Gradually turning to face him, I swing my right leg over my left and lean my elbow on the center console. I can't stay mad at him for long. He's trying. Besides, the connection that's felt when our eyes meet, disarms me.

"We all make mistakes," I smirk, "And don't worry, my lips are sealed. It'll be our little secret," I zip my lips and throw away the invisible key. I reach over to pat him on his muscular arm and his body stiffens. He clenches the wheel, and his glare grows intense.

Feeling his tension, I pull back and adjust myself in the seat.

He flashes a quick smile then directs his undivided attention to the empty road. "So, you didn't see me tonight, huh?"

"You were at the club?"

"I was. Laying low. Checking things out. Making sure everything was running smoothly on the outside. That's what you got to do sometimes. Pop up and see how things are running when nobody expects you. Get a good idea of how the customers view everything."

"So, you're a pro at being a ghost, huh?"

He chuckles, "You're not gonna let that go?"

"Nope," I pop my lips and cross my arms. With every smile he sends my way, my guard comes down. "I know it hasn't been a whole two weeks, but with the way you left, I thought you might actually be going through with selling the club."

He stares ahead with knitted brows, "I'm still thinking about it."

I lower my head. The past few days without Genesis at the club were terribly boring. I can't see myself staying if he left. But I want to encourage him and not be like his demanding wife. "Well, you got to do what makes you happy. Live the life you want to live and not feel like your gonna resent it later," I say, partially speaking to myself.

"Thanks, Azra. At least somebody's got my back on this." The corner of his lips curl. "Speaking about resentment. Do you still resent working at the club? I know you didn't want to be a bottle girl, but are you happy as an assistant manager?"

"I mean…it's alright. After I complete my degree, I'll probably move onto something else."

"Of course, I should've known being a manager wasn't your dream job." He smiles. "So what do you wanna do?"

"Probably go into the entertainment field. It's been something I've wanted to do my whole life. Something business related since that's what my degree will be in. But I wouldn't mind dipping my toes in songwriting."

I never told anyone about my hidden talent as a writer. It's a hobby. A guilty pleasure if you will. Mom-mom always told me that writing false things was nothing but the devil because they insinuate lies. She said I should only write about the Lord. About how good God is and nothing more. But I love writing. Not just about God but about life. Things I haven't experienced but want to. Feelings that I've never felt but I yearn to. Uncharted territory.

Songs. Poems. Short stories. You name it, I write it. But lately, songs have been capturing my creative senses. It's euphoric. Sitting on my bed and writing whatever comes to my heart. Making up tunes on my keyboard to sing to. Everything in the world gets quiet while melodies and harmonies play around in my head. It's just me, my notebook, and my keyboard. It's part of the reason why I'm an insomniac. My creative juices flow at night and they can't be stopped.

I never felt it was possible for me to go into entertainment and serve the Lord at the same time. But now that I'm seeing the world differently, nothing is off-limits. No matter how farfetched my dreams may seem. I'm ready to get mine. Enjoy life. Encounter everything this world has to offer. And I mean *everything*. Well, maybe not everything, but you get the point.

Turning an eye to Genesis, his face brightens with an impressed look.

"You write?" he asks.

"All kinds of things. I sing, too. I always wanted to be an R&B singer. Singing in front of thousands of people. I would sneak my mom-mom's radio in my room late at night and lip-sync the lyrics. Then sneak it back before she woke up," I giggle as I reminisce.

"What kind of music?"

"Stevie, The Gap Band, Teena Marie, Luther Vandross. Michael Jackson. All of that."

His brow furrows and he laughs, "This the *elder* of the church we're talking about?"

"Mm-hmm," I roll my eyes and shake my head, "she made it seem like it was a sin to listen to secular music, yet the whole time she was doing it herself," I laugh, "but when I was six, I asked to be in the children's choir. I loved it. I could be as loud as I wanted to be and not have to worry about getting popped for it, so that was nice. And when I couldn't sing, I'd write. When my mom-mom thought I was studying the Bible; I was actually writing songs and poems and stories. She never found out."

"So why aren't you a singer or writer now?"

"That don't pay the bills. And according to Elder McKinney, not singing or writing for the Lord would land me in hell for eternity, so…" I sarcastically shrug and twitch my cheek with a smirk as I recall my grandmother shamelessly condemning me as a child.

Genesis laughs, clearly not understanding the mental torment I went through. Mom-mom told me so many falsehoods in my life. So much so, that over the past few months, I've stayed away from her. As I'm coming into myself, I need to learn who I am. No interference. No judgment. Just getting to know what I want without the restrictions of religion and her disapproval for not being perfect.

I love God. And I pray. But I've been so good for so long, if I eff up along this journey of finding myself, so be it. I'm tired of not going for what I want. Not being able to enjoy the fruits of life. After all these years of devotion, and seeing people like Lola prosper, it's time to try something new. A dip in the wave pool of liberty.

As we approach the intersection that divides my apartment complex from Lola's, I quickly direct Genesis to turn right into mine.

"I thought you lived over there," he points to Lola's complex entrance.

"I…I might have lied?" I grin, baring my bottom row of teeth.

He chuckles, "You really thought I was gonna track you down, huh?"

I giggle.

We've gotten so close since that first ride. I was so shy around him, so guarded. But that night hooked me. Since then, all I can do is think about Genesis. And as quiet as it's kept, he's hooked too.

Driving up to the entrance, he extends his hand for my key fob to get past the locked gate.

I smile. He does the same back.

"What?" he asks.

"I don't have a key fob," I lie, unbuckling my seatbelt.

"So, what are you gonna do?"

"You have to put a code in to unlock it," I say, pointing to the dial box.

"Cool, what is it?" Genesis puts his arm out of the car to begin punching in the code.

"I'm not telling you," I titter.

"Why not?"

I smirk and roll my eyes, "I don't know you like that."

He laughs, "Oh, you don't, huh? Still think I'm gonna come and get you or something?"

"Mmm. You never know," I grin. "I got it," I touch his arm and adjust myself.

Leaning my trim body across the center console, I reach over him, using his thigh as leverage to hold my body up. His leg muscles tense and he pushes his body back into the seat. I chuckle to myself and punch in the code.

Hovering across his legs, I linger a bit as the gate opens. His gluttonous eyes briskly skim my body as my tank top rises up my waist.

Rolling myself back into my seat, I excuse myself and haul my top down.

He scoffs, fighting back a grin. "What were we talking about again?"

"Writing and singing," I giggle.

He's all types of distracted.

"Right. Well, maybe you can sing me one of your songs someday."

"Sure, but I can't sing without my keyboard," I say, leading him in the direction of my apartment building.

"Wait, you play piano, too?" he asks with a grin, "What *don't* you do?"

Leaning my head on the headrest, I make sure to capture his eyes. "Disappoint," I playfully wink.

He glances my way with wide eyes.

"I'm kidding." I giggle.

Turning his head, he chuckles, grips the stirring wheel, and focuses on the narrow roads of the complex. A nervous smile rests on his face.

"This is me," I point to my building to the right of us.

Genesis puts the car in park, probably pondering on my last comment.

"I mean, I could sing for you right now? It won't take too long," I say, nodding my head towards my apartment.

"Nah. It's late and I got to get home before Andrea—"

"Listen," I roll my eyes, "it isn't like we work together anymore. And with you planning to sell the club, we may not see each other after tonight. Besides, you offered the ride. Now, it'll be *very* impolite if you decline my ever so kind offer to give you the experience of a lifetime. My voice will leave you changed, Mr. Struthers," I coquettishly grin and flutter my big eyes.

Groaning and running his hand down his face, he chuckles, "You're persistent, aren't you?"

Biting the corner of my lip, I smirk, awaiting his answer.

His eyes focus on mine. Like he can read my mind. Picture all the things I long for at this moment. His eyes glaze over my body.

I try calming my thumping heart, but as his eyes trail up to mine, all sense disappears.

Killing the engine with the push of a button, he grabs his keys from the cupholder and leaves his phone in the phone cradle. Looking me over once more, he licks his lips and shakes his head before murmuring, "Let's go."

EIGHTEEN

LOLA

Red or green? I boggle over what sauce to get for a dinner I'm making William. We've been spending so much time together I thought *I* was the chef. Chile, you can't tell me nothing. Fourth of July was four days ago, and William taught me how to marinate steaks and flip burgers. When I'm not being the grill master of the year, I've been whipping up the slappiest fried turkey and cheese sandwiches on this side of the coast. So, after all Romeo did for me, I want to cut him some slack in the kitchen and give him *my* version of a gourmet meal: Tacos, and my take on William's onion rings. I know they don't go together but that's my choice, dammit.

I throw both sauces into the shopping cart and roll down the aisle.

Whitney Houston sings throughout the grocery store about how she wants to dance with somebody, and I croon and bop my head along with her. I love me some Whitney.

An older woman smiles at me as she passes by. Probably thinks I'm a little on the coo-coo side, but I don't care. I'm so excited. I'm a boutique owner. I have a celebrity client already. My staff is hired. Years of designs are on display. And the grand opening for Imala is only one week away. It's a dream come true.

Andrea is the plug. She not only has the stage set for me to come out into the fashion world with a bang, but she's planning the opening herself. All within six weeks. I'm not sure what kind of super blood runs through the Rogers family's veins, but they're a different breed.

"Lola?"

Turning around to see who's calling me, Kendrick's fine self walks up. He has a few items in his hands. Nothing exciting, just wheat bread and unsweetened peanut butter. Gross.

But *sheesh*. When did he get so fine? He's always been a good-looking brother, but he's different now. He cut off his dreads and now has a low-cut fade, and he's letting his facial hair grow in; something I told him to do years ago.

"Hey Ken, what's up?" I say nearly breaking my neck to greet him. If this man isn't a giant, I don't know what is. And I'm five-ten.

"Long time no see," he smiles, wrapping one strong arm around me, "Congratulations. I heard you're opening a boutique."

"Word travels fast, huh?"

"Everybody's talking about it at the club. Saying you're the one that got away."

"Well, in the words of the illustrious Mike Jones: Back then they didn't want me…you know the rest."

Chuckling, he glances down my frame. "They always wanted you…trust me. You're looking good. Ace lost a good one when they got rid of you," he smiles.

I feel nude beneath his gaze. I kind of like it.

But…William.

Quickly diverting my attention to the shelves of tortilla shells, I keep quiet.

"I'm proud of you, Lola. I knew you had it in you."

"Aww, thank you, Kendrick," I grin, switching topics in the most unawkward way possible. "Have you seen Azra lately?" I ask.

"At work. But we don't vibe like that no more," he says, with a sour expression.

Mmm, no wonder why he's flirting with me. Must've gotten his heart broken. And though I'm not positive, I've always been able to smell a homewrecker-high from a mile away. My senses are telling me Azra is smoking bongs of that drug called lust. She must be tripping, which is why Kendrick ain't messing with her anymore.

"Why?" I ask as if I didn't figure it out in three seconds.

Laughing, Kendrick shakes his head, "Ain't that your best friend?"

"I haven't spoken to Azra in months. I've tried calling her but she's ignoring me. I just want to know if she's okay."

"She seems fine. Busy," he raises his brow.

Kendrick knows something. But with how in love he is with Azra, he won't tell me what's really going on.

I swat the air between us to take the pressure from him. "Well do me a favor? Next time you see her, tell her to give me a call. We need to talk."

Agreeing, Kendrick hugs me goodbye before walking away.

As he trots his tall, muscular statue down the aisle, the perfect idea pops into mind.

"Wait, Ken," I hoot, stopping him in his tracks, "you only work nights, right?"

"Yeah, Thursday through Sunday. Why?"

I sweetly grin, "Would you like to work for me at my boutique?"

"As security?"

"Yeah, I can definitely use the protection, and the looks won't hurt either," I teasingly wink and feel like trash afterward.

He chuckles as I shake off the embarrassing gesture.

"We're opened from nine to seven and we're closed on Mondays and Tuesdays, so it won't interfere with your schedule at Ace. You'll just be working all day for a few days," I giggle.

"I ain't worried about that. You know I don't turn down a job offer. Especially from a woman as beautiful as you," he toys back.

"Oh, stop."

Walking back to me, he digs into his pocket. "Let me know when you want me to start," he says, handing me a business card. His name, number, and security services he offers are on the front. His picture of him in all his buff glory is on the back.

I blush. "Sure will." Smiling I break my gaze at the card and tuck it in my purse.

He walks away and I can't pull my eyes from him. His broad shoulders sway back and forth with his swaggered walk. I wonder how much he can bench. That is a fine piece of male tail Azra's skipping out on. But if she won't take advantage, I will. With his height and strength, he's all the security I need. Angel could never.

The zestful Latin guitar plays softly from the Bluetooth speaker as I place the wine flutes on each side of the table.

Lighting the candles around the apartment one by one, I fight butterflies. Although the saddle is worn and the cowboy dominated *this* bronco, I still feel like it's my first rodeo with William. I don't know what he does to tame my heart, but I can't stop gushing. My glow is different. My walk is different. I'm smiling more. I feel secure. And although it's hard to switch off what is now becoming the *old Lola*, I like this change. I guess what I'm trying to say is, love doesn't stink. But the thought of uttering those dreaded three words to William scares me. How do I know I won't be hurt again? How do I know he's truly different?

His melodically tuned knocks make me pounce from my thoughts.

I run to the bathroom to dab the sweat off my nose. I tap my underarms with some tissue and perk up my boobs. I take a deep breath.

Why am I nervous? It's just William.

I rub down my sapphire, V-neck, ruffled mini dress, before I reach for my perfume on the countertop. Spritzing its jasmine and citrus mist over my chest, I steady my racing heart.

"Get it together," I whisper to myself before stepping out of the bathroom.

Click clacking in my *completely-unnecessary-for-eating-at-home* heels, I come face to face with the door.

Turning the knob, I bashfully avoid his gaze.

"My Lord!" William grins, stepping back to get a fuller picture of me. He acts as if every time is the first time he sees me.

"Shut up," I grin, shielding my face.

He grabs my hands from my face and pulls me close, "You look gorgeous," he says, planting a sweet peck on my lips before twirling me around and wrapping his arms around mine.

"I got a meal that will knock your chef's hat off," I giggle. We waddle to the table like a high school couple. Inseparable.

"You're telling me I'm not looking at it?" he whispers, nibbling on the lobe of my ear. A spine-chilling shiver scurries down my back. William always knows what to do to turn me on, but tonight, things must be different. I want to see what I'm getting myself into when it comes to four-letter-wording him. And the only way I can do that is by not letting carnality control me.

Nudging him with my shoulder, I playfully push him into the chair and switch over to the kitchen to grab the plates I prepared.

"Your, viande dans une tortilla?" I say in the best French tongue I can muster. I place the plates on the table.

"They just call it a taco," he laughs, "But that French accent is sexy on you."

"Bon appétit, monsieur," I tease with a curtsy.

He pulls me in by my hips.

Resting between his legs, he flowers my collarbone with kisses, "I'm ready for dessert," he growls.

My body is weak. And boy, does his lips feel good. I shake with pleasure but quickly snap back to reality. I did not slave in this kitchen and nearly burn it down for us not to eat.

"Stop it," I giggle, begrudgingly backing away. "Listen, every time we're together, we do *this*. I want to try something new for a change."

"What's that?"

Taking my seat on the other side of the bar table, I shyly glance down and smile. I know I'm going to regret this. There's not a second of any given day that I don't need my Romeo fix. But things must change.

Unbeknownst to me, my heart already fell for William back when we had our *first* one-night stand. Now, it's my *mind* that's playing catch up to see what's going on because evidently, my heart does what it wants without my permission.

"I thought we'd just talk. Eat. Maybe watch a movie—*not* Netflix and chill. But kick back, eat some popcorn and candy. You know, change it up a little."

As I glance up to meet his gaze, a smile slowly spreads across his face. "I'm cool with that."

My heart warms.

Over a year of being with William and *this* is the first time we're spending time together *not* getting it in.

Looking at how kissable he is, I kind of wish I could take the suggestion back, but it's only right I get to know him platonically...I guess.

"Cool," I glare down and begin wrapping up my soft-shell taco. Preteen jitters bubble in my stomach.

"Onion...*rings*?" He chuckles, looking at the crinkled and lightly Cajunéd onion bits next to his perfectly decorated taco.

Yeah...kind of effed those up. But minus the charred taste, they're pretty good.

I shrug and shake my head, "Not everyone can be a top chef *and* look this good. It's impossible."

Laughing it off, William picks up his taco and takes a bite. At least he looks pleased with how that turned out.

"I see you been spending a lot of time with Andrea. Picking up on that French."

"Why does she speak French again?" I giggle before taking a bite of my taco.

"She visited a lot when I was in Paris and picked up the language," he says, wiping his mouth with a napkin.

"So, in other words, she's just extra."

"Pretty much," he laughs, taking a sip of wine. "But are you excited? The store opens next week. You ready?"

"Beyond ready. The staff is ready. The manager's ready. The schedule is set and ready. I'm ready. It just needs to get here *already*." Glancing up, I met William's stare. "What?"

He shakes his head, "Nothing. Success looks good on you, Bean." He smiles before taking another bite of his food.

Blushing, I twist my lips to stop my big Kool-Aid smile. "Well, I couldn't have done it without you," I say, unable to look at him.

"This is all you. It's no need to thank me. I just stayed true to my word."

"Well, I owe you."

"You don't owe me anything. How many times do I have to tell you? I do this because I want to. Stop trying to pay me back."

"But I want to do *something*. I mean, I know I made you dinner. But I don't feel like it's enough," I say, taking a drink of wine.

I can't lie. I feel so guilty.

It's terrible how I've treated William. I know it might sound like I'm only coming around because he's literally making my dreams come true, but it isn't my fault extravagant gifts are my love language. But I honestly feel bad. For indirectly kicking him to the curb. For pushing him away from me. For denying my feelings for him. I thought I didn't want a man in my life. But now I don't want to lose him. Although there's plenty of fish in the sea, William is a blue whale who willingly swam right into my net and will not leave. And I don't want him to. I want to give him my best. I ain't suggesting marriage. Hell to the naw. It's gonna take more than material things to commit *me* to lifelong maidhood. But I want to be better. And though I'm trying my best, It's not good enough.

"You want to do me a favor?" William asks.

"Yes. Please."

"A'ight. Simple. Tell me how you got that scar." His eyes travel down my face to stare directly at my deepest insecurity.

My heart drops as I'm reminded of a time I've tried to forget for eight years.

"You said you owed me. All I want is to know more about you."

Through pleading eyes, I beg for him to choose something else to talk about. To dare me to strip down naked and streak around the complex. I'll do anything. But his eyes plead back.

He's been waiting a long time to get to know me. And though I don't want to tell him, it'll probably be good to let some things off my chest.

Pushing my plate away and sitting back in my chair, I down my glass of wine like a shot. I'm as ready as I'm going to be to travel down nightmare lane.

"When I was sixteen, I was homeless for about four years." As the words fall out my mouth, William's eyes bug out. His gold spoon upbringing probably taught him 'homeless' was a made-up word. Now he knows it's real.

"I had a job as a waitress at this diner in Virginia," I continue. "A lot of guys would try to get at me, but I never paid them any mind. Until one day, when my shift was over, an older man followed me to a group home I was staying at, if you want to call it that. It was a place where homeless teens would stay. An underground thing. But anyway, this man grabbed me and took me in an alleyway and tried to…you know. Little did I know, another guy from the diner followed him and beat him up. Real good.

Afterward, he made sure I got home safely, and that was it. I fell in *'love'*," I say with air quotes and a nervous titter.

William's face never changes. In fact, it makes me feel hella awkward that he's so attentive to every word I say. But that's him.

"Anyway, after that, he drove me home every day. One day, I told him I wanted to go to his place. He was five years older than me, but I mean, all I saw was a man who I cared about. So...he was my *first*," I falter, careful to not expose too many secrets at once. "Not even a week later, I moved in with him and his roommate at the time, who just happened to be a corrections officer. He was the first guy that was ever attentive to me. He acted like he cared. He bought me everything I wanted. We even got tatted together. He got my name on his arm and I got angel wings on my lower back."

Tears brim my eyes, but I blink them away as I meet William's softened expression.

"He was everything I *thought* I wanted in a man," I scoff, "what did I know? I was only a teenager. Anyway, as the years went by, I realized he wasn't the dream guy I thought he was. He was jealous. Possessive. A cheater. And he was super anal about everything. If there was a sprinkle of lent on the table after I cleaned the entire apartment...h-he'd hit me," I stutter, looking everywhere around the room except for William. Though I don't see his face, his agitation is exuding across the table.

"One night, he couldn't get me from work. So, one of the guys I worked with drove me home. When I got home, he already got word that I was in another guy's car, and...he snapped. He accused me of sleeping with the guy. Shoved me against the wall. And usually, he'd just slap me. But this time...he punched me. I could usually take a slap...but...this time...I couldn't take it anymore."

*
**

November 15th, 2013

"Who the hell is he?" His nose flared with anger as he pinned me against the refrigerator.

"Angel, baby, you're reaching. He just gave me a ride home, that's it," I begged.

I just wanted the old Angel back. The sweetheart. The man I was in love with. He knew I'd never cheat on him. No matter how many hoes he paraded around me. I didn't show any emotion when he'd stay over another chick's house, but anytime a man popped up in my life, he felt his dominion over me was being threatened. That's when the brass knuckles came out.

"Don't lie to me, Lola." Pulling out a pocketknife from his baggy pants, he lifted it to my throat. "I saw the way you looked at him," he whispered in a tone so deep, it sounded like Satan himself.

I slowly raised my hands to his arms. He was overreacting as he usually did. He pulled out a knife on me before, but he never used it. All I had to do was use a little charm and I'd be fine. I softly spoke, "Angel—"

"*Are. You. Sleeping. With. Him,*" he yelled. His green, cold, vacant eyes pierced me just as sharp as the knife directed at my jugular. But he wouldn't hurt me. He couldn't. He loved me.

"No, baby," I said calmly, trying to lower his arm to relieve myself from danger.

"You liar," he bellowed, slamming his fist against the refrigerator, and scaring me into a panic attack. "I'm sick and tired of you lying to me, Lola."

My heart pounded. My palms moistened. I could hardly breathe. He wasn't letting up. My puppy dog eyes and soft voice wasn't calming him. This time was different. Was he that threatened? All over a car ride? Angel should've known he was my one and only, but there was no convincing him at that moment. But I still tried to argue my case through my labored breathing, "I'm not…sleeping…with anyone…but you—"

"Lie to me again," he snapped, spinning me around and squeezing me in his arms. With the knife still pointed at my neck, he whispered in my ear, "Oh, you scared now, huh? This what I gotta do for you to tell me the truth?" Trailing the knife from my neck to my jaw and up my face, he flicked my lip with the flat end of the blade.

"I'm…not—"

I screamed. A sharp splitting pain rushed through me. Before I could finish explaining, Angel slithered the steel into my cheek. Reflexes used my fist to hammer him in the genitals, making him fall to the ground.

Wriggling free, I found my escape and shifted into survival mode.

Running for the door, a yank on my ponytail pulled me to the floor.

Struggling to stand he yelled, "¿Estás loca?"

He tried pinning me beneath him. Tussling and dodging his jabs with the knife, I managed to snatch it from him. Whipping the knife back and forth to keep him away from me, I accidentally sliced the 'Lola' tattoo on his upper arm in half. The last thing I wanted to do was hurt him. But he pushed me to my limit.

My eyes grew big as I watched the blood gush from his arm. I had the mind to help him. To make him feel better. But the shriek of agony and look of death he fired my way made me trample to my feet and out the door to run for my life.

I sprinted like Flo Jo, making it blocks down the road before my legs buckled. Swiveling and disoriented, my footing slowed, and my vision blurred. Finally looking back, all there was, was an abandoned, snowy street. No Angel in sight. Just my barefoot tracks and a trail of blood.

I stumbled over to a bus stop bench. I grazed my hand over my cheek to feel it nearly split in half. The back of my shirt was soaking wet. My hands shook. The panic was worsening.

"Ma'am, what happened? You okay? You're bleeding." A woman wearing scrubs came beside me. As I glared up, the red emergency sign hazily glowed behind her. I trembled as she hiked my arm around her shoulder to walk me into the hospital. I uttered desperate nothings as my words flowed together. While she called for assistance and a wheelchair, the world spun around me. My head pounded through my skull, and before I knew it, everything went black.

*
**

Present Day

"When I woke up the next day, I had stitches from the corner of my mouth to my ear and could barely move. Apparently, while we were tussling, he stabbed me. Two centimeters away from puncturing my lungs," I say, blankly staring at the table.

I haven't spoken about that night since I told Azra, but the wounds still feel fresh. The fear resonates with me as if a day hasn't gone by, though it's been eight years.

"Did they arrest that motha—" William's face hardens as he bites his bottom lip to compose his anger, "Did they arrest him?"

I nod. "After the police got my statement, they went to the apartment and found him being patched up by one of his hoes. He confessed to what he did and that was that. Open and closed case. But it didn't stop. He wrote me love letters for two years. He knew how I felt about him, and he took advantage of that by keeping me bound to him while he was in jail. He said he forgave me for telling the cops and he told me that he wanted to be with me when he got out. But I couldn't let myself be abused anymore. I never responded to any of the letters and after I moved to Maryland, I got a gun and vowed if any man ever tried it, they wouldn't live to see another day."

I breathe deeply, wiping away a sole tear breaking from the lid of my eye.

William shakes with rage, but he keeps his cool. He brushes his clothes off and sits back. "How long did he get?"

"Twelve years but it doesn't matter," I shrug. "You know that corrections officer I mentioned? Angel's roommate?

"Yeah."

"Well, he never really liked Angel. He moved out of the apartment soon after he noticed bruises popping up on me. He tried to convince me to leave, but…I couldn't. Anyway, he works at the prison Angel was at, and promised to keep me updated on him. A little over a month ago, he called and told me he was getting out early."

Bracing his jaw, William's eyes narrow on mine as he asks in a deep whisper, "How early?"

Sinking into myself and glaring at the cold tacos, I utter, "He's been out for about a month now."

Pausing a moment before nodding his head, he mumbles, "Okay." He pulls his phone from his pocket. Tapping on the screen, his chest rises and falls with a perturbed breath.

"Okay?" I ask.

This situation is everything but *okay*, and by the way William's temples are bulging with the clenching of his jaw, he's pissed.

"You ain't gotta worry about nothin'."

Sitting up and reaching across the table, I try to reason with him. "Honestly, Romeo. I'm not worried. He doesn't even know where I live. If he hasn't come for me yet, then he ain't coming." I wish, but no level of hope can keep Angel away.

I know him. I know his obsession with me. And I know his thirst for vengeance. His thrill for mental and physical affliction. He gets off on it. But I have to talk William off the ledge. I can't let him come into my mess and play Superman. Angel is more dangerous than kryptonite. And the last thing I want is for William to do something that will take him away from me.

"Let me handle it, Lola," he says, typing on his phone.

"I didn't ask you to, William. I'm a grown woman. I can handle my—"

"Let me handle it," his voice deepens. He cut his eyes from his phone and draws into mine.

"William—"

"Dammit, Lola, what I just say?" he bellows.

Jumping, I sit back. Hugging myself, I gaze away. I know he's angry. So am I. But he's never raised his voice at me like that.

William's attitude switches as he sees me shaken up. He places his phone on the table and steps over to me. "Listen, Lola," he runs a hand down my hair before tilting my chin up to greet him.

Unable to meet his eyes, I try to keep myself from pouting.

"Look at me, woman."

I tighten my lips to finally look into his tempered eyes.

"I'm never gonna let anybody hurt you," he continues, "I need you to trust me. You don't have to handle everything. You didn't have me then, but you got me now. Let me protect you. You got me…" he trails his thumb across the scar on my face, "and *I* got this. You understand me?"

The painful lump in my throat grows and my breath catches as I nod.

I'm not sure if I'm just a sucker for love or if William is Angel 2.0, but I'm so confused. I contemplate on kicking him out of my life but the unbearable thought of losing him keeps edging in. My naivety in men is on a new level. I took pride in knowing the makings of a man before he opened his mouth. Now I don't know what to think. I can't tell if he's being true, or if he's just playing the 'hero' card to continue with his grand scheme to win an underwear washing machine for the rest of his life.

Stroking my cheek and gazing into my eyes, he slowly leans down. His cushioned lips caress mine.

I hesitantly kiss back. Doubt runs through my mind. My heart sinks with the desperate desire to fight the unknown. To not give in to what I have such a hard time trying to comprehend. While my mind is whispering *don't give in*, my heart and lady parts scream for me to let go.

Ignoring my mind and choosing to listen to my heart like I've done too many times before, I fling my arms around his neck. He picks me up and wraps my legs around his waist, backing me onto the kitchen countertop.

Here. Kissing him. Holding him. He releases me from every constraint. Physical and emotional. Every barrier that keeps me grounded and logical. And that's what scares me. The same blissful feelings I used to feel with Angel, constantly come back when I'm in William's arms. That love that kept me from leaving such a toxic, deadly situation. It feels so good, it hurts.

Addictive and petrifying at the same time. I'm defenseless. Overwhelmed. I want to stop my distorted idea of love, but I'm confused if this is true love, or if it's what my mother, Randy, and Angel taught me love would be.

I hope William is who I think he is. My Romeo. My Superman. The man who has come to change the game without using unnecessary roughness. The only option I have is to wait and see. Time will tell. Until then, his hands continue to explore my body in ways I didn't know were anatomically possible.

I'm drowning. Slowly. But I don't want to come up for air. I moan and let myself go. Let myself enjoy this time and hope it doesn't blow up in my face.

Breathing heavily, I say through a muffled kiss, "So much for changing up our routine."

NINETEEN
AZRA

Back at it again, blood pumping through my veins,
You make me feel things I never felt.
This is sin, but it's hard to detain,
The single thought of you makes me melt.

For you, my heart beats relentlessly,
But how far can we go when you're vowed to another?
This feeling I have is heavenly,
It's purposely fulfilling me.

Please don't call me a monster,
Cus at the end of the night you'll go back to your lover,
The one you promised to love and cherish above all others.
So forgive me if I'm selfish and think of myself it's,
Just too painful to walk away.
My heart beats for you, so for my life, I'll stay,
After all, maybe heaven can wait.

My pen bleeds. Leaking my emotions over my notebook for the man I never knew would really be mine. My Genesis. My first. My beginning. The period to my sentence.

If only that paper that seals him to another could be burned. That's all his marriage is at this point. Paper. The connection we have is stronger than matrimony.

It's been about a month since I finessed Genesis into my apartment. He came for the song but stayed for the performance if you know what I mean.

It was an experience of a lifetime. With each word that streamed from my heart, I captured his. My fingers stroked the keys of my keyboard. Every melodic note that flowed brought him closer to me.

Once my serenade ended, our eyes met for what seemed like an eternity. A sudden bloom of warmth swept me as his fingers traced my hairline down to my jaw. Shivers of titillation shook my insides as his gape steadied on my lips. His tongue painted his. Intertwining our fingers, I petted a kiss over his lips. He pulled back and tried to leave. I guess his conscience was getting the best of him. But it felt too good. Who could walk away from that? I needed him. He needed me. It was too late to stop. I tore him from the doorknob.

Aching, saturated with an appetite he can only satiate. His body pulsed. Hardened as he tried to resist. Standing on tiptoes, I grabbed his face and kissed him. His guards fell. He weakened yet became stronger than ever. His brawny arms lifted me and carried me to my bedroom. He laid me down. Kissed me. And took everything from me. My sense. My morals. My mind. My spirit. My clothes. My body. My edges. And I loved every moment of it.

My life was changed.

Everything building up to that moment might've been paradise, but that night, and many nights since, have felt like I've been raptured over and over and over again. I saw heaven. Though a little different than what I imagined, it was still the best thing since water turned to wine. I'm still drunk.

"Azra," I jolt from my intense writing and dart my eyes to Trish, who's sitting across the desk. "You listening?"

"Yeah, Trish. Everything you said is…" I connect my finger and thumb to give the a-okay sign. I don't give a squirrel's tail about scheduling and health inspectors popping up, but I just nod and smile in agreeance to make the day go by faster.

I've been an oblivious mess for weeks. I can't stop thinking about Genesis. And when I'm not daydreaming about him, I'm writing about him. I feel the urge to tell everyone that I did it. I want to shout it to the world that Genesis is *mine*. But that wouldn't be smart. Good thing I'm on summer vacation from school because I'd fail miserably.

I didn't know falling in love would be so easy. I didn't know I'd fall so hard. But it feels good to know I'm not the only one. He feels the same way. Ever since that night, he's been insatiable. Not just physically but he wants to spend all his time with me. Although he doesn't show up to the club anymore, I see him nearly every day. And the days I don't see him, he calls me. We'll talk for hours wishing we were together.

But let's acknowledge something here: I'm gifted. Like Cardi B and Megan Thee Stallion gifted. Everything I'm doing now is new for me. But I got a man like Genesis addicted. What other explanation is there? I mean, sure. I *did* spend twenty-five years with pent-up aggression begging to bust loose. And he wasn't getting none at home. So? Still doesn't take away from my natural talents. Any man would be lucky to have me. I'm just glad it's Genesis. It's just this so-called wife that's in the way.

I know it's wrong. We both do. But at this point, I don't care. I found the real deal. It was all in the look in his eyes the morning after our first time. That's how I knew it was real. Waking up next to him in my little full-sized bed. I didn't think I'd ever have anyone in it before I got married, so I never upgraded to a queen. Anyway, hearing him say the cliché, "Good morning, Beautiful," made my heart burst.

"You sure?" Trish asks, "because it looks like you're just writing. What do you write in that thing anyway?"

"It's nothing. Just…stuff," I say, putting my pen in the notebook as a bookmark and sliding it into my purse.

"Well, I don't mind you writing, but we need to make sure everything is running smoothly here. I don't want either of us to be on Genesis' bad side. He's counting on me to not mess up like the last manager," Trish says, pushing her glasses up on her nose.

She's cool, but she takes this job way too seriously. I guess everyone doesn't have dreams like I do. Without Genesis here, I'm contemplating leaving and pursuing bigger and better things, like songwriting. What's the point in staying here anyway? I already got my man. Once I finish my degree in the Fall, I'm out of here. But the Christian in me still wants to see Trish succeed, even if I'm not around to see it. So, I'll do what I can to help her.

"I understand Trish. Don't worry I got everything you were saying. We got this girl."

"Thank you."

I smile.

The door opens and grabs both of our attention.

"Azra," Kendrick says as he comes into the office, carrying a long black box.

I won't lie, Kendrick's been looking like a whole snack lately. I won't go as far as saying I'm second-guessing choosing Genesis over him, but not being hankered by him anymore kind of makes me miss him.

"This was dropped off for you," he says, walking past me and Trish. He's barely looked at me since he caught me and Genesis in our compromising position. But he nods at Trish and that just tells me he's ignoring me.

He places the box on the couch at the back of the office and turns to leave.

I stand from the desk and touch his shoulder to stop him from walking out. "Hey. Thanks. Did they say where it was from?" I ask as he turns around and acknowledges my presence. Man, he's looking good without his dreads.

"Nah. Must be from one of your boyfriends."

"Ha, ha," I roll my eyes, "listen, Kendrick, how've you been? I feel like I haven't seen you around much. You haven't texted me in a while either,"

I say, touching his hard biceps. A vein pokes out without him even flexing. Someone's been in the gym.

"I got stuff going on. But I'm sure you understand that," Is that a read? "I've been good, though. Oh yeah, I saw Lola the other day. She wanted me to tell you to give her a call."

That floozy.

"I'll see what I can do. How is she?"

"She looks like she's doing *real* good," he says rubbing his hands together, "Time away from this place did her justice."

Excuse me? Is he seriously crushing on Lola in my face? What is it about that woman that makes men flat-out stupid? I can't understand it. She *ain't* all that.

"Good for her."

"Oh, and you might wanna call Ms. Annette."

Shoot. I almost forgot about that lady. It's hard to believe there was a time my life revolved around her. Yet, that was until my life turned up somewhere between Genesis's legs. I'm focused on myself. For once. But I'll be lying to say I don't feel bad for throwing Mom-mom on the back burner like some old chicken grease.

"She said you've been busy with work and I've tried explaining to her how things could get at the *warehouse*, but she just wants to hear from you. She understands you work on Sundays and are busy, but she's been asking me to run errands because she doesn't want to burden you."

"Oh no," I cover my face.

She's lonely. I mean she *did* judge everyone away from her. Nobody wants any parts of that. But other than me, Kendrick is the only one that seems to like her and is willing to do things for her.

"Kendrick, I'm sorry. I'll talk to her."

"Nah it's fine. I honestly don't mind it. But I do think you need to drop by. Let her know you're good. She said she hasn't seen you in months."

"Yeah. I will," I huff and rub my forehead. "Thank you, Kendrick."

He leaves, without another look back. Not even a *bye*.

"Oooooh, secret admirer, huh?" Trish asks as Kendrick closes the door behind him. She saunters over to the couch with me to see what's in the box.

I shrug and smile. Picking the little card from the top of the box and opening it, I intuitively know who it's from.

Wear this Friday night. Bring that singing voice I love so much. (Especially those high notes) I'll pick you up at 7.
-G.

High notes? *He nasty.*

But Friday? Genesis knows I work on the weekends. There's no way I'll be able to make it. Unless…

"Who's it from?" Trish asks, trying to read the card from over my shoulder. I nudge her away and hide the card against my chest.

"Personal space," I giggle, "Am I on the schedule this weekend?"

"No. Remember? You texted me a couple days ago and requested this weekend off."

That sneaky man. He must've texted Trish from my phone the other night while I was sleep. I hit the jackpot. He's like the men out of those old chick flicks.

"Duh. You know, the days have been running into each other. I totally forgot I took off," I play it off. "I have this…*thing*. It's really important, actually," I open the box and unwrap a silky, red, lacy dress. This must've cost a fortune.

"Well, if you're wearing *this*, it must be," Trish says, taking the dress from my hands and putting it up to herself.

I chuckle and snatch it away. "Give that back."

I press the dress to myself and turn around. This is going to fit me like a glove.

"It's beautiful. He must like you, girl," Trish says.

Correction: He must *love* me. This man is something else.

*
**

Sitting in the car as we prepare to go on Genesis's mystery date, I goggle at him.

His black tuxedo fits him like a cloak of glory that was laid upon him by the Lord himself. *Amen.* He's so hot, steam fogs up the space between us. No, wait…that's a hot mug of tea sitting in the cupholder. Why does he have hot tea in the middle of the summer? Random. Instead of asking him about it, I lean over and place a hand on the side of his face. Turning his head to me, I tenderly kiss him. *Sparks.* My legs tremble as he reaches over and runs his hand down my side. I push off, leaving him desperate for more.

Buckling my seatbelt, I smirk. This man is wrapped around my dainty little finger. I stroke my hands over the dress that hugs my curves.

"I'm glad it fits…in all the right places, too." A flirty smirk plays on his lips.

Chills run down my spine and I squirm in my seat. "Where are we going?"

He puts the car in drive, and we roll off. "Well, it was supposed to be a surprise, but I'm giving you an opportunity to be a singer. Andrea needed a singer for this event she's got going on."

The words fall out of his mouth as if he told me I'm singing at a karaoke bar with a bunch of drunkards. And wait…*Andrea's* event?

"Wait, what? Genesis I can't do that!" I shriek.

"Why not?"

"Baby, it's your wife's event. Why would you think that's okay?"

"Babygirl, you're the party singer. It's not that much of a big deal. She's not gonna be worried about you. Probably won't even realize you aren't the original party singer."

"Well, what happened to the original one?"

"She got sick. Andrea just needed someone to take her spot and it was on short notice. I told her I knew a singer, and that was that. She's not gonna be suspecting anything. All she's gonna see is a fine, young woman on stage doing what she's getting paid to do."

"Does she know who I am? Is she one of those women who can see right through lies? Because if she is Genesis, we can't do this."

"Babygirl, calm down. Stop worrying. She doesn't know who you are. All she knows is that you're from Ace. That's it."

"Ugh, god," I drop my face in my hands and my stomach turns. "Genesis, what if I was one of those mouthy side chicks that wanted to let all our business out to your wife?"

"Stop calling yourself a side chick."

"Well, that's what I am, isn't it?"

"No, you're not."

"Then what am I?"

"You're my woman, okay? And you're not gonna tell her anything because that's not even like you. Why would you do that?"

"*I* won't. But side chicks are crazy."

"Well, you're not a side chick, so…"

I sigh and throw my head back on the headrest. Covering my face, I muffle out, "I don't even know the songs I'm supposed to sing. I'm gonna get up there and make a whole fool out of myself."

He puts a hand on my bouncing thigh and squeezes.

"You don't think I got you, babygirl? It's all songs you know. Classics. You got it." He takes his hand off my thigh and reaches for the cup of tea to hand it to me.

I drop my hands and eye the cup. "Genesis this isn't something you can just spring on me," I say, taking the tea and sipping its hot liquid. The intense taste of honey infuses my mouth as I clear my throat.

"It was all short notice."

"Short notice my foot."

He laughs.

I cut an eye to him and roll them back. "How big is the event?" I ask, wiping my red lipstick off the rim before sipping.

"I think about two-hundred—"

Choking and nearly spitting out the tea all over the dashboard, I wheeze, "You're joking, right? Genesis. I'm not ready for this. Do you realize I'm about to eff this whole thing up?"

"You're not gonna eff anything up, Azra. Just relax. This is your shot. I'm not putting you out to embarrass yourself, I'll never do that. I'm just trying to help make your dream come true. You said you wanted to sing in front of thousands. This is only a couple hundred. You got this. Just have the same confidence you have when it's just us."

"Well, a heads up would've been great."

"I told you to have your singing voice."

"With how ambiguous the letter was, I didn't think you meant my *actual* singing voice. You know my Minnie Riperton is reserved for the *bedroom*, not the stage," I take another sip and shake my head.

He laughs.

"Listen, baby," he says, laying a calming hand on my thigh, "the first time you sang for me was insane. You're amazing Azra. You've got talent. You're beautiful. You're perfect."

My heart flutters at his confessions.

He continues, "If you don't get someone who wants to sign you tonight, you can at least get your foot in the door. It might not happen right away, but it's about who you know. People who know people. Somebody might want to get ahold of you later on, but this chance is just to get exposure. You can get put on with songwriting and everything. That's what you want, right?"

"Yes, but—"

"But nothing. You don't have anything to worry about. Okay?" he says, taking the mug from my hands and placing it back in the cupholder. He grabs my hand and brings it to his lips as his eyes remain on the road.

"I'll make it up to you tomorrow night, okay?" The heat of his breath warms the skin on the back of my hand.

I shudder, biting my lip and intermingling my fingers between his. As much as I want to punch him in the face for putting me in this position, I can't say no.

"Fine," I mutter through my teeth.

He kisses my hand before giving it a gentle squeeze, not letting go.

My heart fills with anxiety as we near the venue. To calm myself, I turn to look out the window and take in the excitement that fills the streets. Right as my heart begins to beat at a normal rate, the bustling crowds thicken as we slowly approach what looks to be a red-carpet event. Limos and chauffeurs escort their passengers along the sidewalk and into the place where I'm sure to be making a fool of myself in a moment. My stomach curls.

Lord, I know I haven't spoken to you in a while. But please don't let me faint on stage. Give me the strength to do my best and to not make a complete idiot of myself, I silently pray.

After neglecting prayer and dodging the conscience that tries to stop me from living my best life, I don't expect God to answer my prayer, but it's worth a shot.

Genesis parks the car in the parking garage across the street from the venue. He gets out of the car and opens my door. Grabbing both sides of my face, he kisses my forehead.

"Everything will be okay," he says.

I want to kiss him so badly. That'll take my mind off these nerves. But that would cause an indecent exposure dilemma the world ain't ready for.

As we exit the garage, Genesis navigates the way with his arm wrapped around my waist.

"Listen, when we get up here, we have to go in separately."

"Why?"

"Photographers will be taking pictures of everyone who's attending. Andrea knows I'm bringing you, but we can't be seen in any photos together. It's bad for business."

I resent every time he mentions her.

"Fine," I mumble, pulling away from him.

"Don't be like that, babygirl."

I roll my eyes and cross my arms, looking ahead as we near the flashing lights and security guarding the doors. Without another word, I walk ahead of him and get a better view of the inside of the venue. My heart pounds and my feet stop in their tracks.

"This is the place," Genesis says, pointing where everyone is waiting. His hand is on my back to push me forward, but I'm as still as stone.

"What's wrong?" he asks.

A pit grows in my stomach. I slowly lift my finger and point, "This is Lola's boutique," I say. The large letters IMALA stare me straight in the face.

"Who?"

"Lo—The one you fired the day we met," I finish, shaking my head and moving aside to the building next to Imala.

"Your friend?"

"Yes, Genesis. Why didn't you tell me this was at her boutique?"

My stomach tightens and my fingers tingle. I can't show my face in there. Not only have I been ignoring Lola but showing up with the guy she told me *not* to mess with, ain't it. Especially when his *wife* is here. I know Lola is locked and loaded with some words of worldly wisdom she can't wait to spew onto me. I'll admit, I'm not ready to be convicted. I need to live just a little more before that happens and I pray to God, Jesus doesn't come back before then.

"Azra I had no idea whose event this was. This is Andrea's venture. Usually when she has an opening for one of her businesses, I just show up. I don't have anything to do with *this*. I didn't even know she was working with your friend. She just told me she needed a singer for an event she was hosting. You know she doesn't tell me everything."

I take a deep breath and inhale sharply to try and clear my mind. But that doesn't work because the tension is building in the middle of my forehead. I gently tap between my brows and exhale.

"I thought that was your girl?"

"Yeah, well I haven't seen or spoken to her in months,"

"Why not?" Genesis leans against the wall next to me. He's a respectful distance away, but close enough where I can smell his delightful scent. It awakens my hormones.

I look at him and eye him up and down. "Because of *you*."

"Me? What I do?"

I sigh, "I think she knows I'm seeing you. The last time we spoke, I kind of snapped and called her out her name because she read me like a newspaper. She knew I liked you but really came down on me when I told her that you were married. I guess she hit a nerve and…that was that."

Genesis leans his head back on the brick wall and breathes in deeply. Exhaling, he says, "Damn. So, she knows about us?"

I turn my head to him, "She *thinks* she knows. She doesn't know anything for sure. I haven't even spoken to her since then. It's nothing to really worry about though. She's not the type to go around, telling everybody's business. But still, this isn't the look. Coming to her spot. Being around you. It just…It looks bad. She's gonna judge."

He lifts his head from the wall and glares at me. "How do you know she won't say anything?"

"Because…Lola's not like that."

Quiet, Genesis ponders. My heart flutters as the unnerving silence stands between us.

"Listen," he finally speaks, "if you don't want to do this, you don't have to—"

"Good, let's go," I push off the wall and grab his hand to walk back to the car in hopes of getting that *woosah* I'm in desperate need of right now.

"Whoa, hold on," he says, pulling back, "I have to stay."

"Why?"

"She expects me to be here with her. I can tell her you couldn't make it or something. In that case, we can just rely on the band. But I can't leave. Not tonight."

I cross my arms, "I hate everything you just said."

He chuckles.

"So, you *want* to be here with her?" I whisper as if someone will hear us out in these crowded streets.

"Trust me," he whispers back, slowly closing the space between us, "I'd love to leave with you. Take you out on a real date. Spoil you. Take you home, and..." he smiles and glares down my body.

My breathing is shallow. Just thinking about what we could do if we didn't have to hide makes my temperature rise.

He lifts his head and runs his hand down his face. He huffs, "But it's more about business than it is pleasure at this point. It's a lot of people we know here. I can't leave her alone."

Even though I want to go home and wallow in my side chick sorrows, I don't want to leave him. I'd rather make a fool of myself than spend the rest of the night without him. It won't be so bad.

I inhale and exhale before meeting his eyes. "What songs do I have to sing?"

He grins and his eyes widen, "You're gonna do it?"

His smile brings joy to my heart. Unmatched by anything in the world. I tentatively nod.

He stops himself from pulling me into a kiss...or a hug...or whatever he wants to do and just bites down on his lip. His eyes darken as if not being able to touch me is about to drive him crazy.

"You're amazing, Azra," he says.

I giggle. Walking to his side, I glare into his eyes, "You just focus on how you're gonna make it up to me," I whisper, looking him up and down and walking off to go onto the red carpet.

"I'm already ahead of you."

TWENTY

LOLA

My phone vibrates on my desk, but I don't have time to check it. It's probably just DMs from people who don't really care about my success but want to have some sort of connection with me when I blow up.

Being famous has never been a dream of mine. But after tonight, it might be a reality. I don't think I'm ready for it. All I want is to make money off my clothes. I prefer to keep my circle tight and my business between me and those I choose to share it with, hence, why I don't share anything personal on social media. I even had to argue with Andrea and William about posting about the opening because I didn't want anyone getting a whiff of my whereabouts and relaying that information back to Angel. Though it's been weeks since his release and he hasn't popped up yet, I'm still shaken about him being back on the streets.

I reapply my brown lipstick and comb through my lashes with my long, red nails. My phone vibrates with another message. I look over my shoulder and try to peek to see who was blowing me up, but the screen dims. Oh well.

I turn back and continue to primp in the gold embroidered vanity Andrea insisted I have in my office.

"'L'habit ne fait pas le moine'. Looks can be deceiving. But I say you can't expect people to model your clothes if you look like a pimped-out possum." Whatever that means.

I giggle as Andrea's raspy voice plays in my head. Without asking, she had my office/workspace decorated to fit the sleek, yet royal décor of the store. Her intentions are good, but she has it twisted to think Lola Jones will ever be caught slipping. I stay right. Even now. I stand and look over myself in the mirror. That dress I made after hearing the news about my mother's passing, is beautiful. The floor-length, marigold macrame skirt, fits snug around my hips and legs, spilling out around my feet. The strapless charmeuse silk bodice has me snatched, giving me that gorgeous coke bottle shape that looks like I had to break a couple ribs to achieve. I even built in some cups so my boobies could get a much-needed nudge up. I've outdone myself before, but this time I'm fit for the Met Gala and the theme is Show Off or Show Out.

But this rumbling in my stomach is not cute. Bubble guts ain't no joke. It must be a mixture of nerves and hunger. I should've eaten before the makeup artist beat my face like Ali. But after my edges were laid and my lace front was secure, I couldn't blink without feeling like I'd ruin everything. Until the hors d'oeuvres are served, I'll just have to laugh and talk louder than my growling stomach and hope nobody hears.

"Knock, knock," Andrea's flowery voice whispers through the crack of the door of my office. I look through the mirror to see her shimmying her way into the room and shutting out the noise of people setting up downstairs.

"There she goes!" she hoots, looking like a disco ball. She's wearing a long, silver, sequin, trapeze dress, which in my opinion should never be worn by *anyone*, but especially someone who has curves like Andrea. My face tends to speak before I do, so I consciously force a smile, so I don't hurt her feelings, because today ain't the day. I mean she doesn't look *terrible*. But she's giving me very much seventies aesthetic vibes that would look much better on someone a decade younger, but that's a choice.

I stand to greet her with a hug.

"Wow. I knew you had talent with a sewing machine but *Lola*. This is *you*?" she asks, putting her hands on my shoulders and turning me around to get the full effect of my dress.

I spin around like a black Barbie on display. Flipping my hair over my left shoulder and peering over my right, I strike a pose. "Did I bring the smoke? Or the fire?"

"Chile you brought the smoke, the fire, the lighter fluid, and the match! You sure the sprinklers working in here?"

I laugh and shake my head before she pulls me into a tight hug.

"Are you ready? This is it," she says as we pull away, holding each other's hands.

"I'm a little nervous."

"Don't be. Everyone is so excited to see you."

I squeeze Andrea's hands and give her a pouty grin. I look up to the ceiling and bat tears back as the door swings open.

It's William.

My heart thumps as he nears me. Since that night we had dinner, I kept my distance. I sort of lied and told him the reason why I was M.I.A. was because I was busy, which I was, but I also didn't know how to deal with him. I've dealt with getting yelled at too many times in my past and I won't stand for it anymore. But I'm a sucker. And I'm still holding out hope that he's different. Besides, I never met someone who makes me lose my breath at the mere sight of them...except for myself of course.

"You look amazing, Bean."

"Not too shabby yourself," I smile as he leans in to kiss me. Pulling back, I examine his white button-up and navy-blue slacks. "Not what I'd call black-tie but...you look good."

"You two...I just...I can't." Andrea lifts her hands in surrender and chuckles as she moves to the door and cracks it open. She stands on her tiptoes and peeps down into the crowd of people rallying up in the boutique. "Oh, there he goes."

"Who?" I ask.

"Genie. I didn't tell you because I didn't want you to worry, but the party singer got sick, and I was killing myself trying to find another on such short notice. Genie said he knew someone who sang but her car wasn't working so he had to pick her up. Thank God they're here."

"That's what happens when you wear too many hats, Ms. Investor."

William laughs, "I keep telling Andrea she needs to sit back and let people work for her sometimes."

"Listen you two, I know the way things need to be. Nobody does it like *me*. I just might open my own event planning business one day, but I'll be bewitched if I let someone do what I do best."

"I feel you. I still can't believe how you got this kind of turnout in just six weeks. You must know people," I tease.

"Impossible n'est pas français. Nothing's impossible. I'll be back though. I'm gonna see what's going on with this singer and get her set up with the band."

I shake my head and wave as she leaves.

William turns to me and swoops me into his arms. I wrap my arms around his neck. He kisses me with such passion.

Our lips unlock and he leans his forehead against mine.

"You've been distant lately. You okay?"

"I've just been busy trying to prepare for this opening. It's been stressful. Sorry I haven't been available like that."

My phone vibrates again, urging both of us to glance at it on the desk. The screen dims. He kisses my forehead and backs away.

"Don't apologize. I understand. Well, while you were gone, I got a security system installed. Extra cameras, alarms, a Glock in your top left drawer, motion detectors, hold up button—"

"Whoa, whoa, William," I laugh, "all of that is unnecessary."

"The hell it is. Lola, I don't think you realize that after tonight, you're gonna have people from across the pond trying to see what Imala's all about. You have to have protection. Not only for yourself but this place—"

"Alright, William, I get it."

"Listen, I'm just trying to look out for you. Security is a necessity. We need to make sure you, your clients, and customers are safe."

"How're you gonna do that? With cameras and an armless alarm system? That won't protect me from everything. It's impossible, Romeo."

"You're right. Which is why that guard you hired from Ace. Kendrick? He's not going to be enough."

"What do you mean?"

"I hired someone to keep an eye on you."

"Are you serious?" I squint my eyes. Not a hint of a smirk cracks his lips.

"You need a bodyguard."

"Okay, William, time out. You're taking this too far. The security system and Kendrick are enough. I'll be fine. Don't nobody got time to look after me all day. I'm not that important," I laugh, finding my seat behind my large desk and flopping into the big, black, and gold swivel chair that looks more like a thrown.

"Too far? Lola, didn't you just tell me you got a crazy ex that just got out of prison?"

"I didn't say he was *crazy*."

"Okay, *abusive* then? Better?"

I roll my eyes and shake my head.

"Listen woman, this is *your* night. We're not gonna get into it because it is what it is already. I got'chu. Kendrick already agreed he'd be security, and I got a professional bodyguard to watch over you while you're in and out of the store. His name is Clyde and he's gonna take good care of you when I'm not around to protect you."

I suck my teeth, "Romeo, not to crush your ego but you're a chef. When we're together I could probably take an entire army and come out without a scratch. What're you gonna do? Slap somebody with your spatula?" I giggle.

He chuckles.

"I'll turn into Samurai Jack and slice somebody like deli meat if they try messing with you, woman. You just be glad you never had to see me in that way."

"Mhmm, whatever," I laugh. "Where'd you find this bodyguard of yours anyway?"

"Through this company called *Bulletproof Guards*. They reached out to me about a year ago when I started getting more traction. They saw I didn't have any protection and felt I might need some, but at the time I didn't think it was necessary. Not for me, anyway. I told them I'd get at them when I felt I'd need it."

"So, this is that time, huh?" I cock my brow.

"It is Bean. You need it and they're available. Ain't trying to break the bank with their services either."

I roll my eyes and cross my arms.

"Just take it," he says, unfolding my arms. "He'll only make sure you get home and to work safely. You'll still have your freedom and probably won't even know he's there."

I cross my arms and roll my eyes. Going back and forth with William is useless, so I just huff, "Fine."

Getting a bodyguard sounds ludicrous, but I have to admit...I feel like Beyoncé right now and I low-key like it. Am I that important? Probably not, but still.

William chuckles to himself and comes behind me in my chair, "I know you probably think this is all nonsense, but I just don't want anything to happen to you. It might seem extreme but it's all for the best." His warm hands graze over my bare shoulders and he leans in close to my ear. "I love you, Lola."

I wince and shiver, shrugging his hands from me.

"You okay?"

"Yeah, your hands are just...cold," I deflect, swirling around in my chair to face him. "So, enough with the safety talk. You gonna help me celebrate tonight? You know *after* the party?" I pull my bottom lip with my teeth.

The brightness in his eyes dim and he drops his head.

"What's wrong?" I ask.

"You remember that competition show I told you the producers were gonna call me for?"

I nod.

"Well, filming takes two weeks. And they want me to be there by tomorrow morning."

"Oh, so you gotta leave right after? That's fine. I'll probably be too tired to do anything later anyway—"

"No, Bean, I—I should've told you before, but I have to go...now."

"What?" I stand up, meeting him eye-to-eye, which is rare for us, but the four-inch heels that are squeezing my big toe and probably forming bunions on my feet as we speak, put us at the same height. "So, you gonna miss all this? It's the *opening*, William."

"You don't think I know that?"

I watch his every move as he backs away and walks in front of my desk. He leans on the table with both hands, his head down.

"Why didn't you tell me earlier?"

"I didn't tell you because I didn't want you moping around because you knew I wouldn't be here."

"So, telling me right before I walk out in front of all those people and not being able to have you by my side is better?"

"I didn't think of it like that."

"Of course, you didn't," I scoff.

The phone vibrates again and lights up beneath William's face. He stares at it for a second, then he grabs it. He straightens up and his brows bunch.

"What are you doing? Who is it?" I ask, leaning across the desk and unsuccessfully snatching for my phone.

He pulls away. The swiping sound of my phone being unlocked makes my heart ache. He's never looked at my phone, so I never put a lock on it. But now, I wish I did. I have messages I never erased and if he gets into any of them...Oh god, that crease between his eyebrows is deep. His jaw is so tight.

"Romeo, give me my phone."

He scoffs an unhumorous chuckle and throws my phone on the desk. The screen is on a particular message board.

"Looks like you don't need me anyway."

I can't breathe. My face warms and my hands shake. I can't even bring myself to look at him.

He backs up and heads towards the door.

I grab my phone and skim over four new messages:

Hey beautiful.

And...

I miss you.

And...

I see people talking about you and your new store. Congratulations.

And...

I just texted you because I had to let you know I can't get you off my mind. I know you probably been busy, but I wanted to know if I can slide by tonight when you're done with your opening and everything.

All text messages from Jere-freaking-miah

"William, wait!" I yell, throwing my phone and stumbling over the train of my dress. I beat him to the door, blocking him from leaving. "William, I don't even talk to him. You gotta believe me."

His apathetic stare stabs my heart. He's disgusted but a slight smirk turns his lips.

"Romeo? You got to believe me," I plead, placing my hands on his shoulders.

He breaks eye contact and turns his head away.

I run my hands down his arms and grab his hands. They loosely sit in mine. Giving up on hand-holding, I place both hands on his cheeks and turn him to face me. Our eyes connect, but he's checked out.

"I haven't seen that guy in...I don't know how long. I can't get him to leave me alone and he just keeps texting me. You clearly saw that I don't respond to him. I don't deal with him anymore."

I beg him to believe me. Tell him how sorry I am for not deleting Jeremiah's number. But he acts like he's deaf.

Tears form in my eyes. William looks away. Uncaring.

I'm seconds from falling onto bended knees. My body weight feels too heavy for my legs to hold.

He peels my hands from his face and backs away. Brushing against me, he reaches for the knob.

Not knowing what else to do, I move aside.

As he opens the door, Andrea jumps back from nearly bumping into William.

"Hey! You're leaving already?" She asks, moving aside to let William out of the office.

I turn away, wiping and blinking back the tears from my eyes.

"Yeah, my flight is at nine," he says.

"Oh wow, okay then. Well, you be safe and let me know when you get there. And tell those people raisins don't belong in potato salad and it's more seasonings out there than just salt and pepper."

William dryly chuckles, "I will."

I take a deep breath and clasp my hands together, so Andrea won't notice my nerves getting the best of me.

"Belle," she calls, closing the door, "you alright?"

"Yeah."

"No, you're not," she says as she faces me, "What's wrong?"

"He just told me he wasn't staying," I dare not tell her what's *really* wrong. Not with how protective she is over William.

"I'm sorry. I thought he told you already. He doesn't like letting people down. I'm sure he didn't do this to try and mess up your night. But it comes with the territory. Will is a busy man and you're about to be busy too. It's gonna be moments where you guys can't always be together and celebrate with each other. But one day, it'll get better. Trust me."

I smile and nod. Andrea's always optimistic. But when I think about her failing marriage and how unhappy she is with Genesis, I don't know if I want to take her by her word.

"How's everything going?" I ask, trying to toughen up. I feel like a chunk of my heart has been ripped out.

"Great..." Andrea's face tightens.

"Oh, god Andrea, please don't tell me something else is wrong—"

She lays her hand on my shoulder and uses her other to signal for me to calm down. "Nothing is wrong, Belle. The caterers are here. The DJ is set up. Photographers are on standby for your entrance. The party singer is here," her face drops, "Genie's...helping her get acquainted with the band," she tightly smiles, "Everything is fine. Matter of fact, would you like to meet him? He's just downstairs."

Before I can answer, she shoots out of the room to gather the pieces of her husband that she's managing to hold onto.

I stand here. Frozen in place. Everything is happening so fast I don't even have time to thi—

"Lola, this is Genesis," she covers the side of her mouth with the back of her hand and whispers loud enough for him to hear, "you know, the husband I got on the side," she chuckles to herself. "Mon amour, this is Lola. The woman I'm putting a lot of my money and faith into."

"I'm afraid we've met before. But...charmed," I present him my hand with a bent wrist.

He laughs and grasps my fingertips in his hand. "It's wonderful to see you're doing well, Ms. Jones." He bows his head.

I wiggle my fingers away and roll my eyes.

"Duh! I forgot you used to work at Ace," Andrea chuckles.

A gentle knock nudges the door open, capturing all our attention.

Before I see who it is, Andrea's voice screeches with fake excitement. "Oh, and this is Azra. She's our party singer. Isn't she a doll? Looks like she just finished playing with them yesterday." Andrea teases, taking a shot at her age.

Genesis gives Andrea a stern glare as Azra walks in between them. Yes, Azra. The same chick who's been ignoring my calls, texts, and cries for help.

"Hey Lo." She nervously giggles in a high-pitched tone.

What is this wench doing here?

I grind my teeth and flare my nose. Taking a slow, steady breath, I try to calm myself, but all I see is red. Literally, Azra is wearing a red, slim fit, lace number, that makes her look like...wait...she actually looks...good! Almost better than me. Oh, hell naw. What the...is that a thigh I see? This can't be the Azra *I* know.

"Y'all know each other too?" Andrea asks. She looks so confused. If only she knew to what extent I knew her husband's mistress, she'd probably stroke out.

"Uh-uh. I don't know her," I say, cutting my eyes from the little skeezer.

My gaze falls on the *true* homewrecker and I just roll my eyes at his sorry behind. He can't even keep himself from mentally undressing Azra, and I'm not okay with it. He's wrong for bringing his new flame around his old candle. Just messy.

"Lola—"

"Isn't it time for me to go out?" I ask Andrea, cutting Azra off.

"Yes, it is. Um...Genie?" she grabs Genesis by the arm and pulls him towards the door. His eyes linger on Azra a little too long for my liking. "Azra, let's get you set up," Andrea says.

"I'll be right there. I'd like to have a word with Lola, please?"

Andrea looks at me and I shrug to give it the okay.

"Alright, you know where the band is. Just remember you go on at eight-thirty sharp."

As the door closes behind Andrea, I pivot on my heel and step my way to my desk to sit on my throne.

"Lola, listen…" Azra begins, "I know you're pissed—"

"Pissed ain't the word, *sis*. What the hell are you doing here? Because I know you're not planning on singing at *my* event? Not when you've been ignoring me for months? Are you kidding me? And you know how to *sing* now? Since when? Did Genesis's magical dipstick give your little behind some supernatural talent or something?"

She scoffs and crosses her arms, "There ain't no talking to you."

I sit back in my seat. "No, there isn't. Because I've been *desperately* reaching out to you, Azra. Begging to talk to your sorry behind. And you just pop up here and think you can lead the conversation in *my* place, and I'm supposed to be okay with that? Hell no! You must be out of your ever-loving, praise dancing, holy ghost catching mind to think *that* was gonna fly. You don't have a clue what I've been through these past few months. You haven't even tried to find out after the countless texts I sent you. Do you know how bad that hurt me? I thought we were sisters, Azra."

"We are, Lo!"

"Nah. Not from what I heard. You said I was nothing but a hoe."

"I didn't mean that."

"Like hell, you didn't."

"I didn't. Lo, I was just upset. It's been hard. I've just been trying to find myself. I can't do that with too many strong forces pulling me in different directions. Can't I do that?"

"You can do whatever you want. But dumping your family because you stole a piece of discounted and partially eaten meat, isn't worth it. And I hope you know Andrea is William's *aunt*," I inform Azra.

She gasps.

"Mm-hmm," I say, nodding my head, "but you would've known that if you didn't ignore me. But too late now. So, thank you for putting me in the middle of your bull crap."

She tucks her head down.

"I can't believe you have the balls to sit around here and flaunt your stuff around that man's *wife*? That's a new low, Azra, and you know that. How foul can you be?"

"It's just…it just happened, Lo. I didn't mean for all of this to—" she inhales and closes her eyes. She exhales, "He asked me to sing…and I couldn't say no. He…I…I don't know."

I narrow my eyes and cross my arms. "Are you sleeping with him?"

She stares at me. Her eyes, cold. Not a peep comes from her mouth. She just stares.

I nod and glare down, avoiding the uncomfortable stare down. "Well, if I wasn't sure before, I am now," I scoff. Bringing myself to glare back into her eyes, I articulate every syllable. "When that man breaks your heart, or when his wife drags you through the mud, sand, and Rocky Mountains, don't say I didn't warn you."

I unfold my arms and stand from my seat.

The room is silent. Not even her guilt speaks. She's quiet but harsh. Ruthless. Unbothered. She stands there as if I didn't even ask her a question. Like she's waiting for me to say something else.

I shake my head.

"Ladies and gentlemen," Andrea's amplified voice echoes throughout the place and just barely cuts the tension between Azra and me. "I want to thank you all for coming tonight to the grand opening of Imala, the new high-end fashion boutique that is set to take over runways and red carpets across the world."

Loud roars and applause from the crowd strangely puts my nerves, and now irritated heart, at ease.

I quickly rush to the vanity and dab my under-eye with my beauty blender, reapply my lipstick, and spritz myself with perfume. I forget Azra's in the room until I see her somberly staring at me through the mirror.

Wow. Some emotion.

I almost feel bad for her, but I don't know why.

Andrea continues, "I don't want to keep you all waiting so I won't. I'd like to introduce you to the vibrant, gorgeous, vivacious designer and owner of this exceptionally beautiful boutique; Lola Imala Jones!"

The exhilarating ovation rumbles the boutique. I rise from my seat and glide to the door.

Unable to deny her foggy air, I glance over my shoulder at Azra to give her an assuring look that says: *I still love you and we'll talk later.*

I open the door and it's like the movies. The spotlight follows me down the wide-set spiral staircase. Flashes and shutters of cameras almost cause a severe migraine. The cheers from what seems like thousands of people rooting for me. The smiles of nameless faces warm my heart. The nerves are gone. I can get used to this.

Approaching the temporarily built-in stage, Andrea stands in the middle with a beautiful bouquet of pink chrysanthemums in her hands. An ecstatic and comforting grin graces her face. She passes me the flowers and hugs me as a mother would hug her daughter. She whispers, "Will wanted me to give these to you."

My heart sinks and my eyes sting with tears at the mentioning of William's name, but I have no time to get caught up in my feelings. Andrea pulls away and rubs my shoulder before stepping back and giving me the floor.

I adjust the flowers in my arm and try to keep the tears from falling. I bat my long eyelashes and look up at the bright spotlight.

"Speech!" someone screams from the crowd, making everyone else laugh. I chuckle as I sniff back tears.

"Everyone," I say as the mic gives a little feedback, "I would like to thank you all for coming out tonight to celebrate the opening of Imala. Ever since I was a child, it's been my dream to become a fashion designer. I would've settled with designing clothes for fish if I could've just figured out how to get the sleeves to stop slipping off their fins," the crowd generously laughs at my terrible joke.

"But thankfully, I found someone who saw in me what I couldn't see in myself. They had great faith in me. And although they challenged my patience to no end, they not only helped me become a better designer but a better person. Although that person isn't here right now, I'd like to thank William Rogers for helping make all this happen. Without him, I wouldn't have met this beautiful woman behind me, Andrea Rogers, who I'm sure all of you know," I step aside and look back at Andrea. She smiles and shoos me away. "She's a great woman, and I'm forever grateful for her and her overwhelming contribution to Imala, and the friendship she's given me over the short time we've known each other. Thank you so much."

She blows a kiss and mouths 'thank you' back to me.

"And although I didn't think I'd want to, it's only fair I thank her *very* generous husband, Genesis Struthers. If it weren't for him firing me from Ace Nightclub, I wouldn't have had the motivation to pursue my dream. So, although we started off on the wrong foot, thanks, I guess," I say halfheartedly while trying to find him in the crowd. Unsuccessful, I chuckle along with everyone.

"I'm sure many of you can relate, but I've been through hell, y'all. Faced unimaginable demons that I thought would take me out for good. And though I'm not an overly religious person, I still recognize that it's only through God's grace that I'm still here. Without those trials and tribulations, I wouldn't be here now. And I'm grateful for that." My heart palpitates and tears make their escape. "Let me stop before I ugly cry," I chuckle. "I hope y'all have a great time tonight. Check out my designs on display and if you feel ever so compelled to buy, feel free to find me or one of my associates with your inquiries. Thank you all."

After stepping off stage, swarms of beautiful people rush me. Some look like models. Others look like wealthy, Italian designers trying to see how they can steal my styles. I love it.

Through the excitement, I spot Azra flirting so hard with Genesis. They're trying to stay low-key, but sheesh. Right in front of Andrea?

She stands on a step of the staircase, overseeing her husband's interaction with Azra. She slowly sips on a drink but never looks away. I can only imagine what she's thinking.

I dismiss myself from a few people to make sure Andrea is okay. While I make my way over, a tap on my shoulder turns me around.

Two large security guards stand on each side of a small young lady in a gray, floral kimono, and big rose-colored glasses. Her beautiful curly tresses overs her right eye, and that small mole that sits above the left side of her lip gives her identity away.

"Lola Jones?" she speaks.

My jaw drops. "Oh. My. God. Evvie King?"

She giggles and shakes her head, "No, no, no. I'm just a client of the up-and-coming Lola Imala Jones. Call me Evelyn. Please."

"Evelyn, I'm so glad you were able to make it. I didn't know you were coming."

"There's no way I'd miss this. Andrea couldn't stop telling me about you. I love your designs. Definitely my style. Is there somewhere we can talk that's quiet? I'd like to see what's up with this dress I was promised to wear to the VMAs."

"Y-you mean *the* VMAs?" I stammer.

"Yeah. I'm sure Andrea told you that's what it's for, right? Or has she been busting her behind as always and forgot to mention that small detail?" she smiles.

"You know Andrea," I chuckle, trying to wrap my head around what is happening. "Just follow me this way and we'll talk in my office," I say leading her to the stairs.

Stepping closer to Andrea, who's still speculating from the staircase, she turns to us and gasps. "Evelyn. Ma chérie, comment vas-tu?"

Evvie responds to Andrea in French and they speak for a moment before we proceed to my office. I invite Andrea to join us, but she decides to get another drink and says she'll be up soon.

Evvie and I go into the office while the security guards shield the doors.

"So," I sit on my throne, feeling on top of the world as I watch Evvie sit across from me. I smile and close my eyes. An unusual feeling comes over me, and *'thank you, God,'* crosses my mind while I simultaneously say, "Let's get started."

TWENTY-ONE

AZRA

I snatched wigs tonight. Killed it. Even surprised myself. I know I can sing but with the nerves I felt, I didn't think I'd do as well as I did.

Once I finished dealing with Lola, I went over the songs with the band and was set. Genesis was right. All old-school classics. Exactly what I'm used to.

I ripped the stage apart once I opened the set with *Free* by Deniece Williams. Everyone was in awe. Especially Lola. And to think she tried to play me by asking if Genesis gave me some sort of singing power. She's such a hater. But she learned today. Mouth dropped. Eyes wide. And for a split second, I swear I took her breath away. Though, in proper Lola fashion, she was too stubborn to give me props and ignored me the rest of the night.

Genesis was mesmerized. He couldn't keep his eyes off me, though he'd blink away from time to time to make sure Andrea didn't catch him watching me. She didn't. Ms. *I'm-so-busy* was too preoccupied ordering different cocktails from the bar. By the way, up-close, she isn't all that. She's cute but not exactly who I'd see Genesis with. She was feeling the booze though. Maybe that's what gave her stank-eye syndrome because she couldn't stop staring at me.

Every time I caught her looking, she'd force a smile and tried to be cordial. But overall, the vibe was strange. She asked where I learned to sing but quickly got distracted by the lemon in her drink having too many seeds in it. I think it was a Long Island Iced Tea, but I couldn't be too sure. I don't partake in fermented libations.

Anyhoo, now she sits in *my* seat in the front of the car, and I sit in the backseat like a kid. This is not okay. She should've taken the same transportation she took to get to Lola's boutique, but nope. She just *had* to ride with *Genie* to drop me off. Ugh, such a stupid nickname.

She grabs his hand while making phony googly eyes at him. Though she'd drank to her heart's content and is *acting* like she's drunk, she's too coherent. Too stable. I can't tell if she's really drunk or just putting on so she can say what she wants and then blame it on the alcohol later.

Genesis pulls his hand away and the faux attempt at romance ends. He adjusts the volume knob to turn the music up and leans an elbow on the center console.

"So, you don't want to hold my hand?"

Genesis takes a deep breath. His eyes meet mine in the rearview mirror and he gives a *do-you-see-what-I-go-through* look.

I raise my brows and hide a grin.

"Fine. Don't. I'm tired of putting on these charades with you anyway." She flings her hand toward him before rotating around to me, only to slur out the same question she asked earlier.

"So, Ezra, where'd you learn to sing like that? When I was younger, I had pipes that would blow away a plumber, but my music teacher wouldn't let me be great. You know she had the gull to tell me I had the tendency to sing through my nose instead my dia...diagram...dia...frame? You know what I'm talking about. Boy, did she have the ugliest set of teeth on her. And her breath smelled like Colgate said the hell with it. She wasn't one of *us*, though, so she wasn't used to the soul I possessed in these vocal cords. She just wasn't ready for all this honey. She wasn't ready for all that ho— did I just say that? Ooh, that reminds me, why wasn't there tea at the party? Every party needs coffee."

Is that a British accent?

Genesis shakes his head in embarrassment.

"Well, my name is *Azra*. And I always knew how to sing. And the word you're looking for is dia*phragm*."

"Mmm, that's it," she sloppily wags her finger and glares at me with droopy eyes, "you're a genius. I see you. Beauty and brains. *And* you can sing? The whole package. Reminds me of myself, though...I'm rich of course," she chuckles, "I'm surprised my husband never mention you before."

Is she being nice or sarcastic?

"Dre?" Genesis says, trying to tell her to stop, but she doesn't.

"What? You don't agree? You're usually the first to notice a pretty girl when you see one. What makes her any different? The fact she's young enough to be your little sister? Ain't stopped you before."

Sarcastic.

She rolls her eyes from him and tilts her head back to me. "How do you two know each other anyway?"

"I told you she works at Ace—"

"The child can answer herself."

"She's a *woman*, Dre. And this is the reason I tell you to stay away from the bar, you act like you don't know your limits. Why don't you just lay back and rest until we get home?"

"Are you implying I'm drunk?"

"You're acting like it."

"No! *You're* drunk! Let me be and stop acting like you care so much," she dramatically shoos Genesis away. "So, Asha—"

"It's *Azra*," Genesis says.

"That's what I said," she hiccups, "where're you from?"

"Maryland," I mutter.

"Is that so? What city?"

"That's not your business, Dre. Leave her alone," Genesis intervenes.

"What? It isn't like I'm asking her what her blood type is."

"It's fine," I chuckle, enjoying this spat a little too much.

By this time, I can see that Andrea's planning to blame the alcohol once this ride is over, but I'll see how this plays out. Besides, the more she talks, the more she looks like a fool, the more Genesis loses his attraction to her; if there's any left.

"I'm from Hyattsville but I live in College Park."

"Hyattsville? Is that so?" she raises her eyebrows.

I nod.

"Where are *you* from?" I ask as if I care.

"Oh, honey I'm from Potomac. I'm sure you don't know anything about that. That's where the Richie-rich folk are from," she dismissively states. "You know I always wondered what it was like to be poor. No offense or anything. I just wonder...like...this party must've been a bit of a culture shock for you."

"A'ight Andrea, you need to chill."

"What? I'm just asking her a question."

I meet Genesis's eyes in the mirror and roll my eyes, not at him but the fact this tramp got the nerve to ask me such a question. I turn my gaze back to her and mutter, "I'm not poor, thank you very much. My grandmother and I lived in a peaceful and well-to-do neighborhood when I was growing up. And College Park is nice...so...I don't know what you're trying to say. Potomac isn't even a forty-minute drive away from where I'm at now."

"Your *grandmother*? You didn't have a mother or father growing up? No wonder why you had to live in poverty—"

"Dre—"

"No, Mr. Struthers. It's fine," I glare at Andrea as if looks could chop a head off and serve it on a platter, "I didn't have parents, but my grandmother did more than what she had to, to make sure we were good. She's twice the mother *and* father any biological parent could ever be, so—"

"Have you been?"

I scrunch my face, "Been? What're you talking about?"

"Potomac? Have you ever been?"

No, this ho didn't just act like I wasn't talking.

"No, I—"

"Well, you wouldn't know what you're missing. Potomac…it's rich. But don't worry, one day you may get to ride through or something. If you stick with that singing thing you do. You just might meet an executive that'll discover you and you can hit it big. Especially if you keep singing at my events."

I tightly nod and sit on my hands to stop myself from knocking her big, fake British accent having, head off her shoulders. "Thanks, but no thanks. I'm not interested in being a party singer for the rest of my life."

"Then what *are* you interested in doing the rest of your life?"

Don't look at Genesis. Don't look at Genesis. Don't look at Genesis.

"Song writing," I blurt out. Man, with the way this woman is looking at me, as if she *wants* me to break her heart, I should've just told her the truth.

"Song writing? What's the reward in that? You'll be doing all the work for someone else to take the credit."

"Well, what you're thinking of is more like ghost writing, which I wouldn't mind doing either, for the right price."

"So, you don't mind someone taking credit for *your* work?"

"Oh, I do, but with ghost writing, you know what you're signing up for. You can't get mad when someone comes along and takes credit for making something you created, better. It's like a relationship. If you don't mind me asking, how long have you and Gen—I mean, Mr. Struthers been married?"

She pulls her brows together and lifts her head off the headrest while Genesis glances between her and me in the mirror.

"Um…nine, almost ten years next month. Why?"

"If someone offered you a million dollars to take him and make him rich and famous. Put him in the position to make a real difference in the world and bring joy to people's lives, would you take it?"

"No, a million dollars is pennies to me, I'm not doing that, after all the work I put into him."

"So, you'll hold him back from becoming a better man?"

"No, I'll make him a better man *myself*. It's apparent I already have."

"That's the difference between a song writer and other people. A songwriter who writes for the love of it, learns when to let go. They work hard, love it, nurture it, sacrifice for it. Then when you can't do anything else to better it, they know they'll need to either sell it, or give it to an artist to sing it for it to become greater. Sometimes, you might get paid to release the rights of the song to the artist which enables them to take full credit for writing it, but because it was written for the love of writing, it's okay. A song writer doesn't limit the song's potential by holding onto it in hopes of being acknowledged for the work they've put into it, because they understand all the good the song can do. They realize it's bigger than them and their own ego. We all have a bit of that songwriting trait in us, we just have to identify what we love more than our own glorification."

Her eyebrow cock and her face twists as if she doesn't understand my analogy.

I glimpse to the back of Genesis who is trying to hide a smile by drawing in his bottom lip with his teeth.

For a second I wonder if I said too much. By the look on Andrea's face and the burning side-eye she gives Genesis, I may have. But I'm talking about *songwriting*…not her tight hold around Genesis's neck.

"I don't mean to offend anyone. I'm just saying—"

"I know what you're saying," she declares as she turns around to sit straight in her seat. She leans her head on the headrest, *"If you love something, you let it go.* But darling, marriage is *not* songwriting. *Life* is not song writing. You've ever heard the saying, *Il ne faut rien laisser au hasard?"*

So, she's French now?

"Well, I'm just a poor girl from Hyattsville so—"

"Leave nothing to chance, darling. Life. Marriage. You're career. It all deserves well planning. You must know what you want before you go into it. You must understand every decision you make affects the way your life turns out," she pauses before glancing over at Genesis, "that's why I married *him*. I've made Genie a better man. Do you know where he came from before I got ahold of him? Chester, Delaware. Do you know where that is?"

"No, I—"

"Exactly. But I'm sure it's the same as Hyattsville," she cuts me off which I'm sure is solely done to irritate the crap out of me at this point. "But all of that doesn't matter. I saw his potential and I knew one day he would be great. That's one thing you may learn in life. You don't always get the pleasure of doing things out of pure love. You must analyze things. Invest in your future. Think about 'what's in it for me' before you take your next steps. That's what got me where I am today."

"Of course, which is why your *businesses* are thriving. It must feel great to get all the accolades for your hard work," I try to be as sarcastic as she's been, but her condescending pretentiousness overshadows every attempt.

"It does. And maybe one day when you grow up and learn songwriting will not get you *anywhere*, you'll find a real career and work it until you feel the same satisfaction I feel. Something you can say you'll want to do for the rest of your life."

Catching Genesis's eyes in the rearview once again, I smirk, "I think I know what that is."

Chomping on some carrot sticks, I flick through the guide to see what's on TV.

I should be sleep right now, but I don't want the night to end. It was magical. Besides, I can't go to sleep without my sleeping pills and if I take them, I'll feel like crap in the morning and tonight will be a vague memory. I don't want that. So, I'll dose off naturally if I can.

After searching 500+ channels and finding nothing to watch, I go to my bedroom and sprawl out on the bed in the dress I've failed to take off. I grab my notebook from a stack of books I have on the floor next to my bed and start writing.

Just thoughts. Reflections. The day. Journaling my life in lyrical harmony.

I check my phone for the time as a knock at the door startles me. I drop my phone, notebook, and pen on the bed and jump up. It's two a.m.

Who the heck is that?

I tiptoe to the door, careful to not make any noise. I stand on my toes and peep out the peephole.

It's my baby.

I swing the door open and grin.

"Hmm, well it's a surprise to see you here. I thought it was just gonna be you and Lady Tremaine the rest of the night."

He remains stone-faced. "Why'd you have to say all of that in the car?"

"What do you mean?"

"Andrea had a fit after we dropped you off," he says, coming in and walking to the love seat we anointed a few weeks. Maybe I shouldn't use that terminology, but goodness, it was glorious.

"Why?" I walk over. We sit together, practically on top of each other.

"I guess what you said hit a nerve."

"Really? So, wait, before I ask anything else, was she really drunk? And why does she speak in a British accent?"

He shakes his head, "She's crazy. And if she was drunk, she sobered up right after you got out the car."

I knew it.

"So...what did she say?"

"She asked if I thought her leash on me was too tight. Told her it was, but she wasn't trying to hear it. I don't know why she was so surprised about it though; it isn't like this is the first time I said that. I always told her she can't be my mother *and* my wife. That ain't how this works. But I guess what you said struck a chord."

"All I did was tell the truth. Holding someone back or treating them as if they're property isn't love, and she's doing exactly that. She said how she feels about you. That woman doesn't love you like you think she does, Genesis."

He shakes his head in denial, "Nah...Nah, she was just a little tipsy."

"Tip—Genesis are you serious right now? A tipsy tongue trots the truth and her *truth* said you ain't nothing but a project to her. Just another one of her businesses. You think that's okay?"

He sags into the couch and slowly shakes his head. I almost feel like a therapist at this point.

Mom-mom always told me: *the softest and biggest part of a man is his pride. It's my job to boost it.* Though she probably meant for me to do that for my husband but that's beside the point.

I fling my legs across his lap and hike myself up on his thigh.

I place my arm around the back of his shoulders and lean my cheek on his head.

"Baby, you're so big and strong. You're a man of God. Yeah, you're not perfect but nobody is. You still deserve a woman who will respect you for who and what you're trying to become. Andrea's not that. But the only reason why she's able to treat you this way is because you allow her to. You're the man, baby. You need to take control and stop letting her run you."

Oops! Not the best way to stroke someone's ego, but hey, I haven't had much experience, okay?

"Listen, don't nobody *run* me. I just don't need more drama in my life. All this fighting and fussing. I'm getting too old for this."

"So, what're you gonna do?"

"That's part of the reason I came over," he picks my legs up off him and stands up, "I'm going to take some time to myself. You know, just to clear my head."

"Oh…where to?" I stand with him.

My heart sinks. I don't know what it is, but I shouldn't feel this attached to this man. Though I don't like her, I can feel Andrea for not wanting to let go of him. Him talking about taking time to himself makes me upset. I can only imagine losing him forever.

"Just up to my condo in Baltimore."

"Oh?"

"Yeah. It's got a beautiful view of the water. Heated floors. Shower is about the size of your kitchen. California king bed." He draws closer and slides his hands around the sides of my waist, making my body tingle.

"Sounds…nice. But why are you telling me all of this?" I say with my eyes cast down.

"I was wondering if you would be interested in joining me."

I double-take to see a slight smirk on his face.

"Joining you? To clear your head?" I grin back, "Genesis, I have to work. I'm not rolling like you are. I still need to get myself a car."

"Last time I checked; you got the whole weekend off. And there's nothing going on at the club that requires you to be there. Whatever happens, Trish can handle it. I'll pay you for your time off. And we'll talk about that car real soon, babygirl. I just need you to come and help me clear my mind. Will you do that for me?" He draws me closer and stares into my eyes while wetting his lips.

I do the same, attempting to keep my body from trembling. "I don't even know what to pack or for how long."

"It'll only be for the weekend. You don't need anything. I got everything you need there. Just do me a favor and be spontaneous with me, baby. Please. I need this."

Lost in his eyes, I smile and giggle out, "Okay."

TWENTY-TWO

LOLA

"You have reached the voicemail box of—"

Click.

I carelessly fling my phone on the fuzzy white carpet in the middle of my office. Sitting on the floor, I pick up the draft pieces of Evvie's dress and glance over them before I get sewing, but I keep getting distracted by a nagging feeling. It's like my heart is being ripped out.

He's ignoring me. William is the first to pick up the phone and call me, yet he hasn't given me my morning call since the day of the opening. That was a week ago. After finding those messages in my phone, he texted me *once*, and that was just to let me know he made it to Cali safely. Since then, I've been the one trying to get ahold of him. Trying to explain myself and those stupid messages. I left a voicemail telling him the truth about Jeremiah. And I told Jeremiah to leave me alone. He, of course, acted like it wasn't a big deal, but then texted me last night to see if he could *slide through* again. Needless to say, he's blocked and a hundred feet away from being served with a restraining order with his clingy behind.

Why are guys the way they are?

With the crazy success Imala has seen the past week, and the incredible opportunity to work with one of the hottest celebrities in the industry, all my lovesick behind can do is think about a man.

This is why I say they ain't no good. All they do is mess with your head. Get you all loopy and dumb, and the next thing you know, they're gone.

I can't blame anyone but me. I should've kept my heart buried with not a vessel exposed.

The chiming of the store's doorbell rings. It's Monday. No one should be here.

I push myself up from the floor and run out of my office to see who it is.

"Yo, Lola?"

"Kendrick? What're you doing here? You know we're closed Mondays and Tuesdays."

"I know, but I was getting some food and saw that flashy car sitting outside, but no black SUV around. Ain't your bodyguard supposed to be around at all times?"

"Ugh my god!" I wail and turn to go back into my office. "I don't need that freaking bodyguard. I can handle myself. I'm fine. Besides, I gotta get this dress done for Evvie before mid-August, so I don't need any distractions."

"I was just asking a question. My bad," he chuckles as he comes up the stairs.

I laugh a little to myself. I need to take a chill pill. I've been super snappy and on edge since I haven't spoken to William. I need to stop allowing these men to have so much control over my emotions or I will single-handedly become my own downfall.

As I sit on the floor, Kendrick appears in the doorway and leans against the frame. He stares at me while I put my hair up into a messy bun on top of my head. If I put a little lip gloss or mascara on today, I wouldn't mind him enjoying the view. But not in a tied-up Guns N' Roses shirt and some leggings. I'm basic at best and feeling hella uncomfortable.

"What?" I furrow my brow.

He shakes his head, "You look extremely beautiful today, that's all."

I bow my head. If I were White, I'd be blushing.

No. Not fair. He can't do this right now. Not with me feeling vulnerable and confused about William and me. Because if we are *really* over, Kendrick could get it Monday through Saturday and thrice on Sunday. But who am I fooling? I'm in too deep with William. I can't even picture myself with anyone else.

"You're too kind, Ken. Now, leave," I smile, "I got work to do and I don't need any more distractions."

"So, I'm a distraction?" he flashes his pearly whites.

I slowly grin back but stop myself. "*Bye*, Mr. Bowers."

"Alright, then," he laughs, pushing off the doorframe, "well, I'll be down the street getting some food. You want anything?"

"Just a little peace and quiet."

He chuckles and backs away, "If you need me just hit me up."

"Don't worry, I won't."

Laughing, he jogs down the stairs and exits the store.

I get off the floor and go to my sewing desk in the corner of the office beside the vanity. I pull out some red tulle from the large wooden dresser that sits next to the mini-fridge and carry it to my workspace when I hear the doorbell ring again.

"Kendrick, what did I tell you?" I yell from my office.

No response.

I *did* just hear the bell, didn't I? I haven't slept in a week, but I know what I heard. I pause every bit of movement and listen. Footsteps slowly tap downstairs, but I stay put.

"Ken?" I call again.

No response.

I smirk to myself. That ain't nothing but William trying to sneak up on me. Maybe he didn't have to be in Cali the whole two weeks. Or maybe he heard the message I left him and decided to come back early. Either way, I knew he couldn't stay mad at me for too long.

I jump out of my seat and rush out of the office. "Romeo is that—"

Bouncing back into my office after hitting what feels like a brick wall, my heart stops. A pit the size of a basketball grows in my stomach. Chills shoot through my spine. My skin goes cold. I'm frozen. It's as if my soul left my body. But I'm not dead. Yet.

"Nah, ain't no Romeo. Just me."

His voice has gotten deeper. Gravelly. Not even a second passes and I already see how much he's changed. His hair has grown. Two large, neat braids flow down his pumped-up chest. Veins pop out from his hands and forearms. His hulk-ish arms have that *just released from prison* swell to them. He towers over me and all I can do is cower in his daunting wrath.

"Well, damn! I heard you had it going on, but I didn't know it was like this!"

Backing me into the office, Angel circles me. A hellish heat radiates from him.

My heart thrashes so hard I feel it in my ears.

He stops in front of me and sneers, "¿Qué pasa? Here I go traveling this whole way to see you and I can't even get a *hi*?"

I forget how to breathe but still find some air in my lungs to croak a tremulous, "Hi..."

"Hi," he mocks as he grabs me and wraps his huge, crushing arms around me. "Why you acting so scared? Ain't you glad to see me?"

His arms tighten around me. As much as I want to fight to free myself from his hold, I don't budge. A gleam of deviltry rests in his eyes, though it is awakened when I mistakenly meet them.

"I-I I'm just sur-surprised."

"I ain't ask you that."

"Yeah. Yeah, I'm happy," I lie.

He glances at the scar he created and smirks. "You healed up good," he says staring back into my eyes. "So, who's Kendrick and Romeo? They ain't nobody tryna steal my girl, are they?"

He releases me and I lose my balance, catching myself on the corner edge of my desk.

"No, no Kendrick is just the security guard. And Romeo is…he's…uh…"

A subtle smile curls his lips. It's like this man knows when I'm lying. "Cat's got ya' tongue?"

I shake my head, "He's an investor. He helped me get this place."

"That's your final answer? 'Cus I know you got a habit of lying to me."

"I haven't lied to you Ang—"

"Shhh," he places his dirty finger on my lips, "You don't want to get yourself in any more trouble than you're in, do you?" He runs his finger down my lip, leaving a salty taste on the inside of my mouth. "I see life's treatin' you good. Saw people talking about how Imala's blowing up. Little did I know, my girl *is* Imala. Social media can be a bitch when you try to stay low-key, huh?" he laughs. *I hate social media.* "So, what's up?"

"Nothing," I lighten my voice, "I've been—"

"Hold up. You must got me confused. You think I'm asking what's up with *you*? Nah mami, I can see that online."

I gulp. "What do you want, Angel?"

"Don't act like you don't know what I came for."

I know exactly what he's here for. Other than my head, $10,000 is in question. Something I took to get away from all the hurt and pain *he* caused me for years. That's the least he owed me for the crap he put me through. My little money from the diner wasn't cutting it. I needed money to leave Virginia and leave it for good. Yeah, I took it. But why would I tell him that? I'm damned if I do *and* if I don't.

"Angel, I didn't take any money."

"Mami, no me molestes. Don't lie to me, Lola, you know I can't stand that shit."

"Angel, listen. If you want money, I can just give it to you—"

"Mistaken again. I mean I know you're a successful business owner, but I don't think you got ten G's on you right now. Even if you did, you think that'll be enough? You don't think you owe me a little more than that?" he says slowly screening down my body. He licks his lips and a raging desire squints his eyes.

He comes closer and my stomach clenches. I slide around to the backside of my desk to get away from him, but he corners me. Backed against the wall, I scan the room. There's no way out. I'm as good as dead. I look at the drawer and it all comes back to me: *Extra cameras, alarms, a Glock in your top left drawer.*

William got me another gun. But is it loaded? If it is, is the safety on? Is it in eye's view or is it buried under a bunch of romantic love letters? Because that's what William does.

As Angel inches closer, my shoulders tighten. I close my eyes and calculate how long it'll take to pull the drawer open, locate the gun, load, cock, and shoot. I open my eyes and Angel's nose is nearly touching mine. His breath reeks.

"Angel, you can't do this," my voice shakes.

"Do what? If nobody around to see then nothing happened right? Ain't that what your stepdad used to say?"

I gasp. I can't believe I told him that.

"You are so *evil*," I whisper.

"I'm not evil, mami," he laughs, "I just know something nobody else do. *I* got the upper hand now."

The hair on the back of my neck stands, and my hands shake. "First of all, Angel, he was *not* my stepdad and you know that. And second, there's *nothing* you can do to me. There're cameras all throughout this place, so whatever it is you're thinking about—"

"Cameras?" he laughs, "You think Angel is afraid of a couple cameras? Ha! What the hell they gonna do to me? Man, I'll wipe them bitches clean after I…" he scans me up and down then back into my eyes. "Nah, I ain't even here for that, baby."

"Then what are you here for then, Angel?" I say with as much stability in my throat as possible. My way out is right in that drawer, but he stands so close I can't figure out how to get around him.

"Well, unlike you, I keep my word. I don't say shit to nobody 'bout nothin'. But I don't forget nothing either. If you read my letters, you would know I ain't tryna hurt you. Not physically at least. So, you can relax. For now. But I do want mi chavos." He pushes off the wall, "So, you know there ain't no statute of limitation on murder. Don't matter if it happened yesterday or twenty-sum years ago. Be a damn shame for that to come out."

His eyes break from mine and he turns to sit on the edge of the desk.

"What the hell do you want, Angel?"

He snaps his head to me. Bulging eyes and a clenched fist. That devil's just waiting to emerge despite his white collard way of threatening my livelihood.

"Who the hell you talking to, bitch? Don't make me take flight on yo' ass." He blinks. Shakes his head like he didn't mean for that to come out. And he's back to normal...well...*his* normal. He sits on the desk. "So, as I was saying. You give me five hunnit grand by Friday, and I won't say shit. You stay out the cage. You get to keep ya' little shop or whateva. I get my money back *with* interest, including what was supposed to be put on my books. And we good."

"Five hun—how am I supposed to do that, Angel? Nobody has that kind of money on them. You can't even take that out of the bank at once."

"William? Or Andrea? We can go all the way to Genesis if you want to baby, but I know y'all ain't really like that. But somebody got to have some money stowed away somewhere. Especially if they helped you get this place."

Oh god, no. Nausea turns my stomach. My heart races with each pump of blood. My legs weaken. But instead of buckling, I jump forward to the desk, fling it open, and reach for the Glock.

Angel grabs me by the arms and slams me against the wall. Twinkles blur my vision and my head throbs. The gun falls from my hand and underneath the table.

Eerily calm, he chuckles as he pins me to the wall.

"Damn! You still a fighter, I see," he breathes in my ear, "I like that."

"Get off me!" I try to break loose, but his grip on me is too strong.

"Calm down." He grips me tighter and tighter, squeezing my arms against my sides until my ribs feel like they'll cave in.

I stop squirming but my chest pounds. I can't breathe. Light-headed, I steadily inhale through my nose and out of my mouth.

"You calm?" His hot breath makes my ear sweat as he whispers.

I rattle my head and try to keep myself from going into a full panic attack.

He lets me go and I slide down the wall and onto the floor. My chest aches and my body feels like pins and needles. My hastened heart only relaxes when I see the gun sitting right beneath my desk.

Watching me, Angel cackles at my distress. "You ain't shit. Look at you. You can't touch me, Lola." He backs away from me and heads towards the door. "You just worry 'bout how you getting my money. If I ain't got it by Friday, then...you know what it is." He lifts the base of his shirt, revealing a gun on his hip. He turns his head and smirks, "Might even pay little Romeo a visit."

Oh, *hell* no.

As quickly as I catch my breath, I move with such swiftness to retrieve the gun. Sliding underneath the desk as if I'm an extra out of "Mission Impossible," I seize the gun, cock it, take my best Hail Mary shot, and hope with all my heart, it's loaded.

Bang!

My hand jerks back. Blood splatters on the pure white wall.

Shaking, I drop the gun on the floor as his body plummets to the ground. One shot. Just one.

My life flashes before my eyes. I press my hands against my ears to stop the ringing from the loud blast of the gun.

I can't go to jail. I can't lose everything because of him.

I trip over my own two feet but unable to get my footing right. So, I crawl.

Numbness takes over me. "Angel?" I whisper.

His leg flinches a few times before it abruptly stops.

I inch closer on my hands and knees and whisper again, "Angel?"

No response. Not even a twitch.

Jumping up on my feet, I run over and fall by his side.

What just happened? What did I do?

My arms feel like stretched-out rubber bands as I try to turn him over, but I stop as soon as the store's bells chime.

"Lola, I got you some food just in case you were hungry!" Kendrick yells from the front door.

My breath quakes. The ringing in my ears continues. The room spins but all I see is his body. Still. Leaking. Lifeless.

"Lola?" Kendricks quickened footsteps travel up to the office.

I blankly stare at Angel's corpse. Somehow, my face becomes drenched in tears dripping into my lap. Why am I crying? What am I upset about? This man beat me for years on end. He harassed me from prison. He threatened my livelihood. My freedom. William's life. And I'm crying for *this* piece of trash? What is wrong with me?

Slipping on blood and whatever brain matter that spilled from Angel's head, Kendrick catches himself in the doorway. His eyes grow wide, "Oh, my God."

"I-I…I don't…what do I…" I hysterically bawl. My heart wrenches as I throw myself over top of Angel's body. I can't believe this. He's gone. Oh, God. "What did I do?" I scream.

"Shh. Hey Lola, come here." Kendrick softens his voice. His eyes widen in terror. He rushes to peel me off the body and carries me downstairs. My legs are as good as gone. I feel nothing. Nothing but a pain so bad it's numbing.

"Are you okay? Are you hurt?" he asks as he sits me down behind the checkout counter.

I try to keep the shrills of agony in, but I can't. I'm so stupid.

He hugs me tight and rubs my head pressed against his chest.

I'm going to jail. That's it. My life is over.

Kendrick's soothing voice repeats, "It's gonna be okay," and, "Just tell me what happened."

I'm still trying to figure that out.

TWENTY-THREE

LOLA

Dammit! Why do I have to be such a good shot? If I would've just been a few centimeters off I may have just grazed him. Not killed him.

I try to sum up to Kendrick what led me to shoot Angel. From the first time he hit me, to now. I give Kendrick the rundown as fast as I can. But he's not buying it.

"Lola, you got to tell me what *really* happened. He's got a gunshot wound to the back of the head. You can't tell me that was self-defense."

Drained, I can't even find the words to plead my case. I sigh as the tears fiercely trickle down my cheeks.

He lays his hand on my back and rubs it back and forth.

"Listen. I know why you did it. Trust me. I fought my hardest to stop my father from putting his hands on my mother. I wasn't as big then so I couldn't do as much damage as I can now. Until she decided to leave and take me and my siblings away, I regretted every day I wasn't able to put a bullet in his head myself. So, I understand *why* you did this. But the cops are on their way and they're not gonna go for self-defense when there's a bullet in the *back* of this man's head. William got this place littered with cameras so unless you want to go to jail you need to let me know what happened so we can figure this out."

I take a deep breath and sop up my tear-soaked face with my hands. I tell him everything. The truth. The truth that ended in the loss of *two* men's lives.

Sirens blare in the distance and as if a light bulb came on in his head, Kendrick runs upstairs without another word. I sit behind the counter, numb. Yet, tears are still falling and it's pissing me off. A queasiness emerges in my belly, but I focus on my breathing. In and out. In and out.

Kendrick runs down the stairs before the cops pull up.

"What are we gonna tell them? What about the cameras? They'll know it wasn't self-defense and they'll probably give me the death penalty. I'm not ready to die—"

"Hey," he puts his hands on my shoulders and bends his knees. He looks me deep in my eyes, "Don't you worry about any of that. Just tell them *exactly* what happened. But tell them I came. I found him attacking you. I pulled him off you. We tussled. He pulled away and reached for his gun, but I got him first. Okay? It's a foolproof explanation. They'll believe you, okay? Don't worry."

He's taking the blame for this? I stare deep into his eyes. He's sincere.

I nod and swallow the lump rising in my throat. I'm sure I look like the damsel in distress, but the tears might be too much. Will they think I'm guilty because I'm crying so hard? Will they see past the lies I'm ready to tell to keep my butt out the electric chair? Am I overthinking this? I mean a man just died right before my eyes. Anyone would be a crying mess, right?

The doorbell chimes and three police officers come in.

"We got a call about a trespasser and a shooting."

"Yes officer," Kendrick begins to lead a couple of officers up the stairs. He looks at me and mouths, "You okay?"

I nod but I'm not.

"Hey beloved," an older, Black, female officer approaches me. She reminds me of an auntie or the mother figure I always wanted in my life. All I want is to cry on someone's shoulder right now, but I can't. And I can't help but to think this wouldn't even be happening if my mother was a *mother*. I wouldn't had been alone. I wouldn't had needed protection. I wouldn't had met Angel. I wouldn't have had to kill him. Everything would've been normal.

"You alright, sweetheart?"

I know she sees this kind of crap every day. But I actually feel like she cares. My throat locks up and that lump rises again. My stomach convulses and I can't even open my mouth to answer. The only thing that comes out is a wailing , "Oh God!" I drop down and bury my face in my hands. Tears drench my face.

"Beloved, it's gonna be okay," she rubs my shoulder, "I just need you to come outside with me for a moment. I have a few questions to ask you about what took place here."

Helping me from my squatted position, she reminds me that it's gonna be okay. I wipe my face with my shirt and stagger outside.

My nerves are shot. I stare out the window. The hazy morning glare settles on the window screen. It's still early. Eleven o'clock or so, I don't know. Time stopped hours ago for me. After being questioned and asked to go to the police department to give a formal statement, Kendrick brought me home.

I sit on the edge of my La-Z-Boy, bringing my tea mug up to my lips. The liquid sloshes around the edge of the cup as I attempt to steady my shaking hands to take a small sip of this bland chamomile tea Kendrick made. Rocking back and forth, I take deep breaths. Breathing through my nose. Exhaling out my mouth. Something I taught myself every time Randy snuck into my room.

I keep my eyes from closing because every time I do, it happens all over again. Randy. Angel. Hemorrhaging from their wounds. That last breath. Dying. Dead. At my hands.

This is crazy.

Years of waiting for this man to die so I wouldn't have to look over my shoulder anymore. Sitting and bedazzling my gun while listening to love songs that once were our favorites. I waited for this day. Prayed for it. Thought I'd be overjoyed. Should've blown away the gun smoke like they do in the cowboy movies. I just knew I'd be relieved. Alleviated from the hauntings of the past.

Yet, it's quite the contrary. And I hate it.

Kendrick turns on my large 75-inch TV that's mounted up on the wall and the news comes on.

"Tragedy strikes in D.C., once again. A man shot and killed in D.C.'s up-and-coming fashion boutique," a nasally voice draws me to the screen, "Imala, the brand-new boutique that has captured worldwide attention in such a small period of time, was broken into this morning, while the owner, Lola Jones, was there. Authorities told us a domestic dispute broke out between Jones and recently released from prison, and armed, Angel Burgos. Not many details are being shared about what happened inside of the boutique; but luckily, a security guard that works at Imala, came just in time. Burgos was shot by the heroic guard, saving himself and Jones. We've reached out for further information from the guard and Ms. Jones. Both have yet to respond. Back to you."

The hell? Why are they putting this on TV?

"Can you believe this? They can't even wait until the six o'clock news," Kendrick fusses, shaking his head.

"What about my store? People are gonna be afraid to come now."

A loud knock at the door steals our attention. My heart pounds.

Kendrick glares at me and puts a finger up to his mouth to keep me quiet. Pulling out his gun, he moves with his back against the wall and yells out in a heavy voice, "Who is it?"

"Man, open the door!"

"Romeo!" I screech, sprinting off the couch.

Pushing past Kendrick, I unlock and swing the door open. William stands there. Brow creasing. Waiting to receive me. Without pause, I jump in his arms and wrap my legs around his waist. He grabs me tight. One arm holds my body while the other grabs my head. He massages the back of my head and all the nerves and fears slowly whittle away. Feeling his rapid heartbeat thumping against my chest, I lie my head on his shoulder and stick to him like Velcro.

"I'm so glad you're alright," he whispers in my ear. "Yo, dude, why y'all ain't answer the phone?"

"My bad, man. I left mine in the car when I was helping Lola up here. And her's is in her bag." Kendrick responds.

My tears stop. Pure joy along with the gentle heat from him breathing into my hair, warms me. For a moment I forget what's happened.

His legs bend underneath me as he sits on the couch. Now straddling him, I open my eyes. Kendrick stands by the door with a slight smile on his face but doesn't notice me peeping at him. He slides his gun back in the strap and walks over to the kitchen to gather his things.

Azra's a fool to not want that man.

"I'm gonna go ahead and leave y'all alone," Kendrick says.

"Hold up, man," William double taps my butt before helping me off him so he can get up. "Yo, I appreciate you, bruh. Thanks for what you did. You came through. I don't even want to know what would've happened if you weren't there."

"You ain't gotta thank me, man. Something told me to get her some food and bring it back," he stops and looks at me from across the room, "just got there in time."

"*Perfect* time. Oh, yeah, if you haven't already, we gotta give the footage over to the cops, so they don't have any questions."

Looking over the back of the couch, my mouth parts and my eyes widen. *What did Kendrick do with the footage?*

"They already checked it, man. They said nothing's been recording on that thing since it was put in."

"For real?" William's head flinches back. So does mine, "I checked them after they were put in though. They were working just fine."

"Something must've happened, I don't know," Kendrick mumbles, rubbing his eyebrow. "That's just what the cops told me when they checked it." He glimpses over at me and I skip my gaze down to avoid his.

If I would've known church people were as devious as Kendrick and Azra I might've joined their church a long time ago. He's a *convincing* liar, too. Just slides right off the tongue. All in the name of saving me. And my toxic behind sitting here thinking that's attractive. Oh, God...I need help. Like now.

"Damn," William says. He reaches into his pocket and pulls out his wallet. "Either way man, I appreciate what you did. I wish I could do more, but..." he opens his wallet to pull out some money before Kendrick stops him.

"Nah, bruh. You ain't gotta do all that, for real. Anybody would've done it."

"But *you* did it," William says, pulling out what looks like a few hundred dollars. He places them in Kendrick's hand before pulling him into a dap type of hug.

After Kendrick leaves, William swaggers over. His eyes sweep the floor as he comes to the couch.

"Bean. Can I ask you something?"

I nod, "Mm-hmm."

He glares at me. "Why didn't you call Clyde? Lola, I got that bodyguard so people like that can't even make it that close to you."

Breaking eye contact, I shrug.

I'm dumb and feel like I can take matters into my own hands without anyone's help, I think. But instead, I say, "I don't know—"

"Lola, things could've turned out completely different today, you know that, right? I nearly got into *two* car accidents after reading you were attacked. You didn't answer your phone. Andrea was calling me crying because she didn't know if you were hurt. All you had to do was call Clyde—"

"Okay, William!" I yell, curving my back and slouching over with my elbows on my knees. "Please, I really don't need your lecturing right now. I'm sorry. I wish I called him, but I didn't. It's over with now. A man is dead in my boutique. I might lose it now because people are gonna be afraid to come. Everything we've worked so hard for is about to be stripped away because all of this sh—"

"Alright. Alright, I'm sorry. I don't mean to come down on you, Bean. It's just…I was worried. Everyone is. We don't care about the store. We care about *you*. Your boutique ain't going nowhere. People not gonna stop coming. We'll work this out. I promise you, Bean. Okay? I just don't know what I would do without you." He rubs my back before pulling me into him.

He holds me. I rest my head on his chest and listen to his heartbeat. Sniffles capture my attention and I raise my head to look at him.

He pinches the bridge of his nose and squeezes his eyes shut. Is he crying? I move his hand and make him look into my eyes. Tears brim his lids.

I pout, climbing over him and kissing him to stop both of our tears from flowing. Losing ourselves in one another I feel the safest I've ever felt. Covered. Shielded by love. Invincible.

I pull away and kiss his nose.

"I've never seen you cry before," I dryly giggle, swiping a single tear away from his cheek.

"Yeah. And you won't again." He laughs.

Hunching my back, I rest my arms on his shoulders. "I'm exhausted, Romeo," I drag my fingers over my dampened eyes. "I can't stop crying. I've got a headache. I'm sure I'm gonna need therapy within the next hour so I don't lose my mind."

"Oh, trust me, we're gonna get you some. For real. This ain't nothing to play with. Just tell me when you're ready and we'll go."

I sit back and force a smile. The last thing I want to bring up is what happened the last time we saw each other, but honestly, anything is better than what transpired today.

"I'm so sorry, William." My lip quivers.

"About what?" he asks, caressing my chin.

"Everything. I know I messed up by not deleting Jeremiah's messages, but you have to believe me, Romeo. Not hearing from you this week has made my life hell. Everything—other than today—was going so well but I couldn't get you off my mind. I just wanted to talk to you and—" I squint my eyes, "Matter of fact what *are* you doing here? I thought the competition wasn't over until Saturday?"

"Well, apparently I couldn't get you off my mind either." He chuckles. His brows knit together, "I got your messages, and to be honest, I was embarrassed by how I handled everything. I felt bad for how I treated you. After I thought about it, I don't have a reason to not trust you. It was just that…the woman I was with before you, cheated. We were both chefs. Went to school together and everything. When we got back from Paris, we worked at different restaurants and I worked almost every night. Was pulling around seventy hours most weeks. But once I started auditioning for shows and being recognized, she couldn't handle it. So, she chose to test the waters—or should I say, the *wine*, with the sommelier she worked around. Long story short, I found out. She wanted to work things out. I considered it for a while. We actually continued planning the wedding. But that night I saw you at the club, I realized I was missing much more being *with* her than without her."

My heart leaps out of my chest. I bow my head and a rush of heat warms my cheeks. How is this even possible? Tears that were just falling for a man I thought I once loved, are now replaced by tears of joy.

"You never gave me a reason not to trust you," he continues, "you've always been open and honest. I knew you were telling me the truth that day. I was just afraid of being hurt again. So, I shut down. It's just..." he closes his eyes, resisting tears. "I don't know what I'd do if I lost you. And when I landed and saw the news I...I thought the worst."

Though his eyes are dry, mine cry for the both of us.

"But I'm here, William. I'm here and I'm not going anywhere. I lo..." I hesitate, catching my feelings from slipping out my mouth. "I'd *love* for us to work this out. I honestly don't know what I'd do without you either and I don't want to find out."

His cheeks dimple as a smile rises on his face. "That's why I ain't willing to throw all this away. Not over some stupid text messages. I don't care who he is. As long as you ain't seeing him no more, we good." He wipes my dampened eyes with his thumb.

I bite my lip and smile. "So, you're not mad at me anymore?"

He chuckles. "A little bit."

"Why?"

"Because! You made me lose, woman."

"Lose? The competition?" I laugh, but I try not to. "Is that why you're back so early?"

He nods. "I was whoopin' 'em too, until we had to make a Southern gourmet meal."

"Well, that's right up your alley. Why'd they eliminate you?"

"I put onion rings on top of stuffed salmon and potatoes. Guess they didn't like that." A smirk grows as he stares lovingly at me. "You were on my mind heavy, woman. Funny thing, I've made it that way for you so often, I forget what went with it before."

"Some nasty behind asparagus," I chuckle, love tapping him on his chest.

"Ah, that's right," he laughs, "had I made that I probably would've won."

"Well, maybe you should make the onion ring version a *thing* at your own restaurant one day."

"Maybe I will. But until then, I want you to stay with me. Just until this stuff dies down about Imala. Okay? If you don't want Clyde around, I'll get rid of him for now. But until my next gig, I'll look over you myself. I'd feel better with you staying with me than being alone."

I lean in and kiss his cheek before laying my head on his shoulder.

There's no place I'd rather be.

TWENTY-FOUR
AZRA

Trying to catch my breath, I swirl my index finger on my man's firm chest. I admire him from a different angle every day but lying on his chest is my favorite. With his eyes closed and his pulse throbbing in his neck, I melt. I can get used to this. Afraid I already have.

My head follows the rising and falling motion of his chest. The heavy pounding of his heart rate normalizes. Our hearts beat in sync. I close my eyes and relish in the snugness of his body. The comfort of his sensual grasp. I want this forever.

I ask, "Do you love me, Genesis?"

He rests one arm behind the pillow he lies on and rubs my shoulder with the other. "Of course, I do."

"Well, why haven't you said it? I always tell you how much I love you, but you never say it back."

He lifts his head and looks down at me with a half-smirk. Kissing me on the forehead. He says, "I love you, Azra."

"How much?"

"Enough to spend almost every night with you." He chuckles.

I suck my teeth.

"What do you want me to do? Make you breakfast in bed or something?"

I sit up and snort, snatching up the covers to hide my goodies.

"What's wrong?"

"Don't ask me that *stupid* question."

He sits up and looks down. A few seconds pass before he asks, "You feel bad about this too?"

"About what? Us?"

He nods.

"I didn't say all that. Why? Do *you*?"

"Well, yeah…"

A hardness settles in my gut. I clutch the sheets up to my chest.

"We know this is wrong, babygirl. We both know God wouldn't approve of this if we were to die right now."

"So, what do you want to do *Reverend* Struthers? Why are you here if it's so damning to your soul? You wanna leave? Then go! Nobody's stopping you."

"Did I say I wanted to leave?"

"That's how it sounds," I swallow the lump in my throat and turn my head toward the sunlight shining through the window. The yellow light bounces off the sparkling bed of water. Sailboats float by. So peaceful. If only I could enjoy this without the drama.

"Babygirl, listen," Genesis leans forward and moves my chin to face him, "I'm not saying that I want to leave. But we can't ignore that this is wrong."

I frown, "So, what do you want to do then?"

His eyes drop from mine for a second. His mouth moves as if he's going to say something, but instead, he shakes his head. "I don't know."

Our eyes reconnect as his finger traces my chin with his index finger. "But…even though it's wrong, there's nowhere else I want to be. I don't know what you do to me. Can't put my finger on it. But I want more of you. I can't get enough of you."

I bite back a smile. A surge of warmth takes over my body. "Well, I've been thinking. How long do you plan on putting up with this?"

"With what?"

"This. Us. Sneaking around. You don't love Andrea anymore, right? Y'all haven't been happy in years. She doesn't even see that you're unhappy because she's too busy with everything else. Why are you still with her? Y'all don't even sleep together anymore."

"Azra—"

"Please? Baby can you just tell me? Forget all the morals that we came in with because they're gone. Pandora's box is opened. I don't want to hear all the guilty rhetoric. We're past that. Now, it's time to figure out what we're doing. Where are we going? I'm not trying to be the side chick for the rest of my life."

"Stop calling yourself that."

"What am I then, Genesis? Okay, so I'm your *woman*. But that's not enough. I want more. I want to be your wife baby—"

"And you will be."

"I *will be*?"

"You know I want you to be my wife Azra. I love you, baby. I want to spend the rest of our lives together. I want you to be the mother of my children. There's nothing I want more than that."

I blush. "You want me to have your kids?"

He stares into my eyes and nods his head. "But we just got a few things to sort out first. I need to figure out everything with Andrea and…it's a lot, babygirl."

"Just leave her," I spit out. "Divorce her. Have her served. Do something. Why is it so hard?"

He motions his hand to tell me to calm down, "Hold on now. It's a lot that has to be done. Me and Andrea got businesses together. Assets. It's not that simple to just divorce in our situation. Things can get messy. Especially if she finds out I'm leaving her to be with someone else."

"So don't tell her. I understand what you're saying," I nod, "but divorce is the only option here. You can't stay in a marriage you aren't happy with just because of money."

"It's…it's deeper than that babygirl. I don't think you understand. But listen," he grabs my hand and searches my eyes. "You're right. I haven't been happy. So, I'm gonna talk to Andrea. Okay? And I'll speak with a divorce attorney to see the different avenues I can take without being wiped clean. I can't promise you when, but I'll take care of all of this. I just need you to be patient with me, alright? I want to make this right. I want to spend the rest of my life with you, Azra. I just need you to trust me."

God hates divorce. But for some reason, none of what I've read or know seems to matter at this point. It doesn't make sense. This feels too right to be wrong. I need him.

I smile and grab his face in my hands. "I want to be with you, too, babe. I trust you," I place a kiss on his lips before trailing kisses all over his face.

He laughs.

Pulling back and looking into his eyes, I ask, "You don't think we're moving too fast, do you?"

He shakes his head as he takes my hands off his face and holds them firmly in his. "Nope. If only I was single months ago. I would've made you mine the minute I saw you."

I bite my lip as my eyes bounce from his lips to his eyes. We kiss. Climbing over top of me, he grazes kisses down my neck. I arch my back and giggle at the tickling sensation. Aches and yearnings of pleasure flush through my body. He draws his lips back to mine. Stares deep into my eyes and hovers over me. I prepare myself. Wrap my arms around his neck. He lowers, and everything comes to a screeching halt.

My phone rings.

We moan and groan. The use of a colorful variety of expletives expresses our irritation. We laugh. He leans over to the nightstand and grabs my phone for me. Rolling off, he lies back down and rests his eyes. I stare at the unrecognizable phone number, frowning before swiping to answer.

"Hello?"

"Hey, Azra. This is William. How are you?"

"Hey, I'm fine," I sit up and furrow my brow. "What's up? Everything okay?"

Genesis glares at me and mouths, "Who's that?"

I hold my index finger up.

"Well…I know this is gonna sound weird, but do you think you can come over my place? Lola's here and…she needs you."

"Me? Why?"

He hesitates, "Can you just come? It'll be better if she tells you. I don't know why y'all haven't been talking, but she needs you right now."

"Sure," I say, swinging my legs off the bed. I bend to grab the white terrycloth robe from the floor. "Just text me the address and I'll be over."

I throw the robe over my nude body and place my phone on the nightstand.

Genesis sits up, "Who was that?"

"William. Lola's boyfriend."

"Andrea's nephew?"

"Yeah, I guess," I roll my eyes, tying the robe shut. Does he have to keep bringing that biddy up? "Something's wrong with Lola. He asked me to meet them at his place, so I need you to take me. You know where he lives right? Since that's your *nephew* and all."

"I do, but that wouldn't be a good idea. That boy ain't ever like me, and if he sees me dropping you off, he won't hesitate to tell Andrea."

I suck my teeth, "So, how am I supposed to get there then, Genesis? I don't have a car—"

"Calm down, babygirl. Listen, I can get you a rental and drop you to get it. I would take you but for all I know Andrea's already over there, and we can't risk getting caught. That won't look good, especially with me talking to her about a divorce." He shakes his head.

"Ugh," I growl.

I storm to the bathroom to get ready. Throwing my hair back in a ponytail and forcibly rolling up my sleeves, Genesis comes behind me. Wrapping his arms around my waist and glaring at me in the mirror, he kisses my cheek.

"Don't be like that, baby."

"Like what? You said you'll take care of it, so…" I press my lips together and try nudging him off. He grabs my arms and crosses them over my stomach as he hugs me from behind.

"You trust me, don't you?" he asks, looking at me in the mirror.

"Sure," I shrug. I try to ignore his body pressed against mine.

He nibbles on my earlobes. Then my neck. My eyes flutter. The stimulation weakens me. If I don't get this man off, I'll never make it to see Lola. I reluctantly wriggle from his grasp and shake him away.

"I trust you, baby. But I need to go," I raise my brow.

"I got you. Just be patient with me."

"That's hard dealing with a man like you. But I'll try. Don't wait too long, though. Because if *you* don't handle it…I will."

He arches his brow, "What does that mean? That's not even like you to do something crazy."

I shake my head and smile. *He must not know me.*

"You should go. Wouldn't want Mrs. Struth—sorry, *Rogers* to get too upset after being gone all weekend," I bitterly tighten my eyes at Genesis through the mirror as I turn the golden knobs on the white marble sink to wash my face.

"Don't do that, babygirl."

"Do what? She doesn't have your last name. That's not my doing nor my fault."

"Well, neither is it mine, Azra. Are you gonna act like this until the divorce is finalized or something? What do you want me to do? Call her up and say, '*we're done, I got somebody new?*'"

"That'll work."

He cuts his eyes with a heavy sigh.

"I have to go, *Genie*. So, if you don't mind, please get ready so I can see what's going on with my friend. Thank you."

Unfortunately, I knew everything I needed to know before I popped up on William's doorstep.

While we were getting ready to leave Genesis's condo, I overheard him talking to Andrea about Lola's situation today.

"Calm down baby, it'll be okay," he said as he ignored me putting on one of *her* jumpsuits he gave me permission to wear. He said she bought it years ago and never wore it. Still had the tag on it and everything. Saint Laurent. Fancy.

But *baby*? Only baby he needs to be referring to is me. It didn't help that he got off the phone with a loving, "I love you. Be home soon."

Humph. Doesn't sound like a couple on the verge of divorce to me.

All that talk he was doing this morning about how he's going to leave her and how much he loves me and wants to marry me, just to turn around and give me the ultimate slap in the face. He's testing the force of my hand and he doesn't want that. I'm not a violent person but listen…something's got to give. This woman is in the way.

After Genesis got off the phone, he let me know everything that happened with Lola and told me that Kendrick was her knight in shining armor.

I didn't know how to respond. I didn't have anything to say to him after that joke of a phone call he had with his Massa, so I brushed him off and endured a long and silent ride back home.

In the car, I anxiously texted Kendrick to make sure he was alright. He let me know everything was fine in a very not-like-him kind of way, and I left it at that. He's still upset with me.

I watched the news about the shooting and the second we got to the car rental place, I hopped in the car and shot over to William's.

"Thank you so much for coming, Azra." William opens the door and moves to the side for me to come in. The instant fresh wood smell hits me as I walk in.

"Of course. Is she okay? I just saw the news on the way over."

"Yeah, she told me you were the only one that knew about him."

"Yeah, but I didn't know he was out. I guess that's why she's so upset with me. Does she even want me here? I don't want to make her more upset than she already is."

"She knows you're here. I know it's only been a few hours, but she needs to talk to you. Y'all are like sisters, and it's only so much I can do for her right now. She'll deny it, but she needs you. She fought me tooth and nail and cussed me out for calling you over here but it's all good. She'll thank me later."

He laughs. I nervously chuckle too.

I follow William deeper into the living room where not a seat cushion is wrinkled or out of place. This condo is giving me Architectural Digest vibes and I love it. Who would've known William had such fine taste in interior design? He must've hired a decorator. Then again...Andrea probably did it. It does look similar to how Genesis's condo is decorated. I don't like the floozy, but she *does* have immaculate taste.

Looking out at the wall of windows that oversee the beautiful skyline of the National Harbor and the large Ferris wheel that slowly spins around, makes me think. Shoot. I need to get on my grind. Genesis and I can have all of this and more if he stops playing. He doesn't need her money. We can build together. I don't want a trace of that floozy around if I can help it. The more stripped away Genesis is from her, the better.

"But, uh," William says, breaking me from my trance, "I'm gonna step out. Let y'all talk. She's right in the bedroom, just make a left down the hall and another left. It'll be the first door on the right."

"Thanks. Big place any time you have to give directions to the bedroom."

"Yeah. I got this place thinking I was gonna spend more time at home but turns out I'm at Lola's place or on the road more than I'm here."

"Not surprising. Lola's always been stubborn when it came to lounging around other people's homes. You know she don't like following nobody's rules but her own."

"Tell me about it. Took me a half hour to make her take her shoes off at the door."

We laugh because Lola is a fighter. She calls it strong-willed but it's cold-cut stubbornness. If things weren't her way, she didn't want it. But that's her nature. That same fighting instinct probably saved her life today.

"But I'll see y'all later," William says, "And if y'all start scrapping, don't break nothing. That's an expense I ain't paying for."

We laugh once again as he makes his way out of the condo and I walk to the bedroom.

I slowly push the door open to see Lola lying in bed, scrolling on her phone. She clearly knows I'm here, but she keeps from acknowledging me.

"Hey, Lo."

"Hey," she mutters.

"I heard what happened. How you doing?"

"Fine."

"That's it?"

She sits up and throws her phone to the side and crosses her arms. Staring at me with red, puffy eyes, she asks, "Where's Poppy?"

"Seriously? I don't know, Lola. Under my bed somewhere. Is that all you can say right now?"

"Mm-hmm. I'm gonna need that back ASAP."

"Lola! Come on," I flare my arms and flop on the king-size bed, "Please? I'm trying here, Lo. I'm sorry, okay? I don't know what else to say. I'm sorry for ignoring you and not returning your calls or texts. I'm sorry for calling you a hoe. You know I didn't mean that. I'm sorry for not being there for you through all this mess. I'm sorry, I'm sorry, *I'm sorry*. But Lo, we can't stay like this. I know it's my fault but the last thing you need right now is to be mad at me for something I wish I could take back. I'm here now. I'm trying to fix this. I *want* to fix this. I'm sorry. Can we just talk? Please?"

Through half-lidded eyes, her gaze wanders around the softly lit room, "You sure are sorry..." she cuts a glance at me, "but where did this drip come from?" She pushes a smile back as she pulls at the spaghetti strap of the floral jumpsuit that I was slaying in. Andrea could never.

"This old thing?" I chuckle, getting some sort of laugh out of her. I hold her hand, "I miss you, Lo."

She bites her bottom lip, "I miss you, too, Az."

Her eyes well up with tears and within seconds, she bursts out crying. I hop over on my butt to hug her. She squeezes me tight and cries into my shoulder as I rub her back.

For years, I knew Lola feared her ex-boyfriend. She rarely spoke about him, but when she did, the darkest cloud came over her. Still, through all *the I hate him's, I wish he were dead's,* and my favorite*: somebody needs to cut off his you-know-what and feed it to him,* I knew she still loved him, no matter how insane it seemed.

How could you love somebody who beats you like a drum and plays you like a violin? It's beyond me. But she did. So, I understand that although she's relieved he's dead, seeing her first love get shot down, had to be traumatizing.

"Oh, god, Azra. Oh, my God!" she cries.

I grab her tight, holding her head on my bosom. "I know. I know it hurts, Lo. But it's gonna be okay. You're strong. You'll get through this," I say, holding back tears.

Her pain penetrates me. I hold her. Rock side to side to soothe her. Her wails slowly fade, and she pulls away.

Reaching over to the near-empty box of tissues on the bed, she wipes her eyes then blows her nose. "I just don't know what to do," she says.

"I know. But although it hurts now, you just got to remember that things could've been worse. If you think about it, this is the best thing that could've happened. I know you loved Angel, but he can't hurt you anymore. He never loved you and you know that. But the man you have now…" I shake my head and grin, "all I can say is that I wish someone would love me the way William loves you," I drop my gaze and my smile goes with it.

If only I wasn't Genesis's little secret, we could have what Lola and William have. I wouldn't have to hide. We could love each other freely. That's all I want. Lola has that opportunity amongst so many others, and she's not taking advantage of the blessing that's sitting right in front of her. She's blind to it. But this isn't the time to get annoyed with her.

"You okay?" she asks, drawing me back to the issue at hand.

"Yeah. I'm fine. Just saying, William will do anything for you. He's a wonderful guy and…just be grateful for what you have. Angel didn't love you. He wanted you dead. But thank God Kendrick got to him first, right?"

She drops her chin to her chest, "Yeah. Don't know what I would've done without him."

Aside from Lola's sniffles, we sit in silence for a few moments.

"Well, um…I'm glad I'm able to see you," I smile and rub my thighs. I guess this is it.

She flashes a smile, "Me too."

I stand to leave. "Once again, Lo. I know I've been a first-class butthole these last few months. I-I didn't mean to be, it just…it's been a lot going on. I'm sorry for not—"

She waves her hand, "I don't want to talk about it. What's done is done. Life is too short to be so focused on the past. It isn't worth it. Besides, friends argue. They fight. They stop talking. But they wouldn't be friends unless they came back together again. So, we're cool."

"Really?" I smile, sitting down to grab her hand.

"Yeah, I guess." She laughs.

"Thank you, Lo. Listen, I don't want to fight again. I missed you and I just feel so bad that I wasn't—"

"What did I just say?" she chuckles, "It's over. As a matter of fact, these are the last tears I'm crying over this situation. So, if I can stop the tears from falling, then we can move on. Okay? Life goes on."

"Okay," I smile.

I lean in to hug her before she holds her hand out to stop me. "Uh, not so fast."

"What?"

"You know what, missy."

Uh-oh. Here comes that diamond studded elephant trampling through the room.

I sit back and cross my arms.

"Don't get an attitude with me," she giggles, but that's short lived. "You still messing with him?"

"You gonna let me talk?"

"I don't know. It depends on the level of thot-lish you're talking. I might need to brush up on my lingo so I can follow."

"Oh, shut up! You're not gonna let me live that down? I didn't mean to call you a hoe!" I laugh but then again…is she calling *me* a thot?

"It's dead, sis. You can talk. I'll keep my comments 'til the end."

I drop my head and nod, "Yeah…I am. But it's not *messing around*. Genesis loves me—"

"Oh God—"

"No, I'm serious, Lo. And I love him, too."

I wait for her to say something, but her silence allows me to continue.

"I know you and his wife are friends, but this isn't something we planned. It just happened. And now, we don't know how to stop. And to be honest, we don't *want* to stop. I found someone that loves me. No if, ands, or buts about it. He showers me with so much attention and although he wants to give me more, all I want is *him*. Lo, he's even helping me rent a car since my old one broke down. It's got a sunroof and everything. He really cares about me," I glance up to see her with her lips pursed to the side and her eyebrow cocked. "Stop looking at me like that!"

"Like what? I'm just listening, sugar baby."

"I'm not a sugar baby. Seriously, we're in love. And maybe once you're in a better headspace I'll be able to tell you more. But trust me, I wouldn't be in this situation if I were the only one feeling this way."

"You wouldn't be in this situation if you would've stayed your little butt in church with Kendrick and Ms. Annette."

"Oh, so you're Mother Teresa now? You know what, I'm gonna let that slide because I love you and you're going through it right now, but it's not even like that."

She sucks her teeth and rolls her eyes. "I'm just saying."

I'm not getting into it with her today, so I brush off the conversation. We sit around for a while to catch up on little things like reality TV show fights and the drama at Ace between the girls and the scandalous hookups in the bathrooms. We laugh and *kiki* until William comes back.

I take my cue to leave, hugging Lola and William goodbye.

When I get in the car, I check my phone. Genesis texted me. Spending time with Lola has me feeling so great, for a split second, I forget I'm supposed to be mad at him.

I swipe my phone to read the message:

Babygirl, I'm sorry if I hurt your feelings. Things are just easier said than done. But I promise you, I'm gonna talk to her. Tonight. Sounds crazy but I can't stand you being mad at me. I want to be with you. Hope you're still not mad. If you are, I'll make sure it won't last too long. I love you. Don't forget, you're my future.

I collapse back into the driver's seat and hold the phone to my chest. A smile emerges on my face. His *future*. I'm gonna give him the best years of his life as soon as he makes me Mrs. Struthers. Mm-hmm. Something Andrea will never have the privilege of being.

TWENTY-FIVE

LOLA

I stitch together the skirt to Evvie's dress. It's almost done. I've been working day and night making sure everything is perfect. Creating new designs and working on dresses for my other clients has made my office a second home. I'm surprised I'm able to work in this place and not feel creeped out or sad about all that's happened here.

Since Angel has fallen off the face of the earth, I've been at peace. No more looking over my shoulder and walking around afraid he'll find me one day. He's gone. I can breathe.

Not to mention, the publicity has been wonderful. The fact that people are drawn to my boutique *because* of a shooting is on a different level of *I-just-don't-get-it*. But hey, who am I to complain? Sales have gone through the roof and requests from more celebrities are flooding in. I can barely keep up. My manager, Sarah, is phenomenal at communicating with my clients and keeping my meetings in order, but soon, I'm going to need an assistant. I'm a busy lady.

The door to my office opens, "Knock, knock."

Andrea sounds happy, but I don't turn around. It's been about two weeks since I saw her. She's been in a funky mood lately. Hasn't spoken to me or William like she usually does. She says she's working on a new project, but something is off. Maybe it has to do with that sorry husband of hers.

"Hey, Andrea. I was just thinking about—" I turn to see that it's not Andrea at all.

Azra scoffs. "Oh, gosh, don't tell me I sound like that wench."

She walks in and closes the door behind her.

"Az, what are you doing here? How'd you get past Sarah?" I ask, turning around in my swivel chair. "Aren't you supposed to be at work?"

"Well, first things first: Kendrick is looking mighty fine these days, isn't he? Standing at the door looking like a melanated Clark Kent. My goodness. And Sarah? Girl, I just said I was your sister and I needed to tell you something private. Far as Ace goes, you know there ain't nothing going on, on a Wednesday morning. I said I'll be in tomorrow. Trish is cool about it, so." She sits on the white, padded guest chair at my desk and crosses her legs.

She wears a cute pink sundress with heels that make my ankles hurt just by looking at them.

Where did all this swag come from? Who taught her that this is cute? Because it is. But wait…this is *Azra.*

"Trish?" I ask.

"Oh, yeah. Trish. She's the manager there now, but girl that's another story."

"Wow. A lot has changed, huh?" I lift the rest of the long fluffy skirt of the dress off my legs and place it on the sewing desk. I swivel my chair around to give Azra my attention.

"You're not missing anything, trust me. Shoot, I've had more fun sitting in on a prayer call on a Friday night. The tea that's served up on those calls be having my tongue burnt. Can't taste for weeks."

I laugh. *She's charismatic too?*

She chuckles, "What?"

"That was pretty funny. You should've told jokes at my opening, rather than sang."

"Girl, whatever. You know I did my thing."

"You did. I was surprised. Didn't know you could sing like that. But goes to show, you don't know people the way you think you do."

She smiles and tucks her head as she gets up from the seat. She walks over to the drafting wall that holds different sketches of Evvie's dress: A red, asymmetrical, fluffy red skirt, with a gorgeous tassel draped brassiere. A showstopper.

"So, what's been going on? This dress is fire, by the way. I'll take one in a size two. You know I lost weight?"

"Hard to not notice. You almost look like a different person. I realized how small you got the night of the opening. I can't lie, you look good, girl."

"Thank you." She grins, floating over to the body-length mirror near the door.

She turns around to check out her backside. No matter how many squats I do and calories I eat, I'll never achieve the booty she has. It's like the weight loss made her butt even bigger. How is that possible?

Azra's gorgeous. Always been a pretty girl, but there's a glow about her now. Seems happy, but there's an undeniable darkness surrounding her at the same time.

"What're you making now?" she asks.

I snap from admiring Azra's beauty and direct my attention to the dress mannequin she stands in front of.

"It's actually a dress for one of the biggest soul singers in the industry," I grin.

"Who?" Azra asks.

"The one and only, Evvie King, of course. She was at the opening but was under the radar. It's for the VMA's. Can you believe that?"

Azra's jaw falls to the floor and her eyes glow. "Oh. My. God. Are you serious? I love me some Miss King. Oh my God, her song, *Remember When.* Ugh! That song is on repeat as we speak."

I laugh. "She *is* good. And she's such a sweet person, too. Her vibe is everything. I can't lie. I was a little star-struck when I met her."

"No. Lola? Star-struck? Years of celebrities trying to holler at you at the club, and you were star-struck over Evvie King?"

I nod and giggle. All the glitz and glam from the men who tried to get with me never fazed me. I may be an opportunist, but never have I been a groupie. I never understood that logic.

"You're doing it, Lo," Azra smiles. "And see! You were worried about people not coming anymore but seems like the Angel situation worked out for the better. People love a victim."

"Excuse me? Uh-uh, sweetie. I am not a *victim.* I hold my own."

"Oh, gosh, Lo. You know what I mean. Either way, it didn't take business away. From the looks of it, it boosted it." She waltzes over to the guest chair and plops down. "So...How's William?"

My heart flutters and I stupidly grin. "Good. Got me going to therapy and what not."

"That's good," Azra raises her brow. "You should be happy you got a man that cares enough to make sure your mental health is intact. He a real one."

"Yeah. He told me there's no need to sit around and wait. So, we started going last week. We have another session tomorrow actually. It isn't bad but going into my past is just...I'd rather not."

"He's going with you? Girl, you got a keeper. And I'm sure it'll get easier the more y'all go."

"Hopefully," I smile. "But anyway, you want to chill? Like, have a girl's night or something? I know with our schedules being so different now, it's kind of hard, but we should plan something soon. It's been a while since we hung out. There's a lot to catch up on."

She wrinkles her nose. With forced elation, she screeches, "Yeah, sure. We can figure something out."

The hell was that?

"Listen, Az, don't feel pressured, okay? Sheesh, I thought you might want to have some girl time after all these months."

"No, Lo, it's not even like that. It's just…" she glances down and plays with her long, oval-shaped, acrylic nails.

"What?"

"Don't judge me, okay?" she begs. I bug my eyes out and she finally says, "Genesis is staying with me."

"What do you mean he's staying with you?"

"Exactly what I said," she rolls her eyes.

This little girl is about to make me pop her.

I lean my elbows on my knees and interlace my fingers, "Am I missing something? Last time I checked, y'all was just messing around, now he's *staying* with you? Does Andrea know about this?"

"Why would she? She doesn't care about Genesis. Hasn't even called him to make sure he's okay. She's no kind of wife to him. And why do you care if she knows? You gonna tell her or something?"

"Azra, I'm serious. How do you feel getting in between a family?"

"They aren't a family. Trust me, she's making sure of that. She knows Genesis wants kids, but she refuses to give him any. That ain't right. That's part of the reason he doesn't love her anymore. She's stupid for trying to hold onto a man that doesn't want her."

"That's her *husband*, Azra."

She mumbles something under her breath and pulls her phone from her purse.

I can't believe her. Little Miss Church Girl has gone to the dark side. I never thought I'd see the day. I'm shocked.

Squinting my eyes, I glare at her. "How do you sleep at night?"

"Oh, my god, Lo," she puffs, "I thought you weren't gonna judge."

"I'm not judging. I'm asking a legit question. You don't feel bad about what you're doing?"

She lowers her phone and glowers at me. "Honestly, the only reason I'm telling you this is because I don't want us to fight anymore. Besides, I need someone to talk about it with." She takes a deep breath, "It's not easy. It's been killing me, especially since he's been staying with me. I can barely sleep, even with him right next to me. I've been taking sleeping pills just so I can get some sleep. I can't stop thinking about it. What's worse is that something my mom-mom always used to tell me keeps on haunting me."

At least she's showing some remorse. I sit back and breathe. "What did she tell you?"

"She always told me when it came to men: *You lose them the way you get them.* I just can't help but worry, like…what if Genesis does the same thing to me? What if he cheats on me in the future?"

"The future? Are you high?"

"On love." A hefty belly laugh shakes her.

"Chile you must be on something if you think he's gonna leave Andrea for you. That never happens."

"He *is* going to leave her. He doesn't want her anymore. He loves *me*, Lola."

"Of course, he does. And I'm sure he's telling you that a lot more now because he needs a place to stay."

"No, he's telling me he loves me because he loves me. Why do you think everyone has a motive, Lo?"

"I don't. I'm just saying…ugh, never mind. I really don't feel like arguing with you right now."

"Me either," Azra whines and tilts her head to the side. She rolls her eyes.

Silence rests between us. I conceal what I want to say: that Genesis is a fad. That this is not love, but infatuation. That the deeper she gets, the harder it'll be to break away. That the minute he breaks her heart she will hate him for the rest of her life. I keep it all to myself. Won't matter what I think anyway. She's in too deep.

I sigh. "What happened? Why is he staying with you?"

She straightens her head and blows air out her mouth. "He's divorcing her."

I suck my teeth, "Yeah right."

"He is. That's why he's staying with me. They got into it a couple weeks ago. He told her he wanted a divorce. She got mad. Threw a tantrum. Told him to get his things and get out."

I shake my head. "Are you serious? Didn't they just celebrate their wedding anniversary?"

"If they did, it wasn't much celebrating going on because he's been with me. All they do is argue. It's been like that for the past few years. She doesn't care about him. She puts her business ahead of her marriage and treats Genesis like crap. I don't even think she understands why he doesn't want to be with her anymore."

Her nonchalant attitude makes me want to give her an old-school, big momma smack down. How could she do this? This is Azra. But it isn't.

"What happened?" I ask.

"I just told you."

"No. What happened to *you*?"

She rolls her eyes. "Oh goodness. Not the melodrama."

"I'm not being dramatic, Azra. I'll probably kick myself for saying this, but I used to look up to you. You used to walk around with that moral compass so close to your heart, I kind of wished you would loosen your grip just so I could at least have a glass of wine with you."

"I still don't drink. I'm actually really proud of myself—"

"Azra," I stare at her with the *shut up and listen* look. "Are you crazy? Seriously, this just doesn't seem right. Men like Genesis, they'll have you doing backflips off the Eiffel Tower. It's dangerous, Az. I mean, look at me. I just had a nervous breakdown over a man who beat me for years and finally got what he deserved. I'm literally in therapy behind him. That first love will have you liable to lose your mind. Throwing away everything. But trust me, all that glitters ain't gold. Don't let that man drive you insane. That's all I'm saying." I sit back in my chair and swivel around to my sewing desk.

Azra's checked out. Looks down at her phone and acts like she doesn't hear me. A rebellious smirk quirks her lips.

"So, I'm talking to myself now?"

She chuckles. "No, I hear you, Lola. I won't let him drive me *crazy*."

That ship has sailed.

TWENTY-SIX

AZRA

I stand in line at the gas station to check out some snacks and beverages for me and Genesis's movie night. It's been a month since he's been staying with me and I love it. We've made Mondays our movie night since I don't have to work. We choose a movie, usually scary. Pig out on junk food. And before the movie's over, we indulge in each other.

I'm addicted. The more I have, the more I want. I love the way he makes me feel. Light. Like I'm flying. Resting on a cloud.

The line moves. I hold onto my goodies piled in my arms. Doritos, candy of all sorts, a mango Arizona for me, and a Red Bull for him because…well, you know.

"Azra?" a familiar voice calls me from behind.

Turning around with my arms full, I see Andrea.

"I thought that was you. How've you been?"

Better before I saw you. "Good. You?"

"You know," she shrugs and forces a grin.

She looks bad. No makeup makes her look *different* to put it nicely. Her eyes are so sunken in. Red. If I didn't know any better, I'd think she was high.

"I'm glad I ran into you. Must've been meant to be because I was coming from my condo in Baltimore and had to get some gas. But I've been thinking about you. Especially how terrible I treated you the night of that party. I was a little tipsy and…I'm just sorry for how I treated you. I wasn't in my right mind. The next day, I woke up and all I could think about was how bad I felt talking to you the way I did. I was rude and I'm sorry."

"No harm, no foul," I huff, placing the junk food on the checkout counter. Pulling out my wallet from my purse, I feel Andrea looking at me. Why is she acting so weird? I avoid eye contact and pay for my items.

"Well, um. It was nice seeing you again," she mutters, with her plastered-on smile.

"Yeah," I flash a fake grin and rush out the store.

What a creep. If she's anything like that with Genesis, I completely understand why he's ready to jump ship.

I sit in my car and watch Andrea fill her tank. As she pulls off, I follow her. At first, I do it to make sure she isn't trying to follow me, but once I follow her onto the highway, I realize she probably *is* just going back to Georgetown. Still, something comes over me, and I keep following.

Like the twilight zone, nobody else is on the road but us.

Why is she driving with her hazards on? The tears of lost love must be blinding her to the point she can't see. Shame.

Hmm. I wonder if she'll be able to identify this car? Does she even know Genesis is paying for my rental? Probably not. The man could probably commit a murder right in her face and she wouldn't notice. She doesn't care about him. She only cares about herself. Just selfish. Holding on to a man because of her own personal glorification. Makes me sick. She needs to let him go. Better yet, *he* needs to let *her* go. For good.

I turn my lights off and gradually creep up behind her, just like those big cat shows Genesis watches all day long. I've learned a thing or two from them, though. First, is to blend into your environment. That's what tigers do. They go undetected by their prey. Blending into the dark environment of the empty road, I then lurk behind my prey. That's step two. I check out all avenues I can go, covering every step I can take before I get too close. Third, I slowly speed up until I get close enough to tap the bumper of her car. She swerves and drifts left to right as if a semi-truck hit her. Dang, she should really pay attention to her surroundings.

An airiness fills my chest and I chuckle to myself.

Her right blinker comes on and she tries to move over into the right lane before I quickly tap the back of the car again. She swerves. On her tail, careful that she cannot see my car in her rearview or side mirrors, I switch on and off the high beams. On. Off. On. Off. Revving the engine, I take one more shot and jab the gas with my foot and sweep the left side of her bumper. Her car swerves and she plunges right into the ditch on the side of the road. And that's the fourth and final step. *Prey captured.*

Ooops.

I adjust my rearview and peep behind me.

Dang. Her lights are busted. The entire front of the car is crushed. She just might not come back from that. *Oh well.*

As Genesis lays his head in my lap while we watch "Us" by Jordan Peele, my phone lights up next to me.

Kendrick's name pops up.

What's he calling for?

Not wanting Genesis to see me get a call from another man, I tap him off me and go to the bathroom. Might as well freshen up a little bit while I'm in there so I can be right for my man. This movie night is about to be over once I come out.

Sitting on the edge of the toilet, I answer the phone.

"Hey, Kendrick. What's up?" I whisper.

"Azra…Your grandmother just had a heart attack."

I grab my chest and grip my phone. "What? No. No, she didn't, Kendrick. Stop playing."

"Azra, you need to get to the hospital. Now. We're at PG."

With trembling hands and a cold core, I shake my head. "No, Kendrick. Stop. How do you know?"

"She called me, and I called the ambulance. She was trying to call you, but you weren't answering your phone."

"She didn't call me. I would've known…" I say, pulling my phone from my ear to check my call log.

Four missed calls from Mom-mom.

"Azra…" Kendrick says. I don't have the strength to bring my phone back up to my ear. I listen from a distance. "Just come to the hospital. They're saying she might not make it through the night."

I drop from the toilet seat to the floor. My body goes limp. My phone drops out of my hand and lands on the fuzzy shower mat. I toy with the cross-necklace Mom-mom gave me. Hold it. Squeeze it.

This can't be real.

"Azra? Azra?" Kendrick mutters on the phone.

I can't move. Can't talk. Can't breathe. I'm numb.

No…no. Not Mom-mom. Not this way.

The door bursts open.

"Azra, I got to go," Genesis says, putting his arms through a fresh t-shirt. He stops a moment and gets a good look at me. "You alright? What's wrong? Did you hear, too?"

Holding my chest, I gulp in dry air. My mouth is a desert.

I stare at him. I don't know what to say. What to think. This has to be wrong. I glance down at my phone, Kendrick's still on the line. But I don't care.

Worry fills Genesis's eyes, "I got to go, baby. Andrea's in the hospital. Some asshole ran her off the road. You gonna be okay?"

He saunters closer and glares down at the phone. He picks it up, looks at it, and ends the call.

"What are you talking to him for?" he asks.

I shake. My hands. My feet. My body trembles.

Genesis comes closer and kneels. "What's wrong? Did he tell you something? What's going on?"

I gasp. Inhaling is all I can do. My chest burns. My stomach quakes.

He rubs my shoulder and holds me into his chest. "Breathe, babygirl. Just breathe. What's happening?"

My eyes burn. Ache with a fountain of tears forming behind to push through. "Mom-mom," I rasp out, "S-she's gone."

TWENTY-SEVEN

LOLA

Churches give me the creeps. The only times I've been in one was for a wedding of a friend of my mother's when I was six, and a funeral for the same friend who later died from pneumonia when I was eight. I honestly never could tell the difference between the two. Weddings signify the figurative death of an individual, and funerals celebrate the literal death of an individual. Now that I think about it…funerals might not be *that* bad.

Unfortunately, this time, Ms. Annette is upstairs in the casket, and me and William are here in the basement, a.k.a., family room, trying to be a shoulder for Azra to cry on.

I knew she'd be hurt, but I never thought I'd see Azra like this. Before I got ahold of her this morning, her hair was everywhere. Skin breaking out in red bumps that freckled her face. And she smelled like all hell turned upside down and rotted. Though I feel her pain and know she can barely lift a hand to wipe the tears from her eyes, I couldn't let my girl go out like that. After I made her shower, I combed her hair back into a bun, brushed her edges down, and spritzed some hair perfume on it so it didn't smell too bad. I grabbed her sandy-colored foundation and smeared it across her face, covering every red blemish. A sharp eyebrow, a bit of blush, and setting powder was enough for a funeral. I didn't even bother with mascara or eyeliner since she'd probably cry it off anyway. Since Ms. Annette's wish was for everyone to wear white to her funeral, I picked out a white, cape-sleeved, *below* the knee-length dress for Azra to wear. Finally, some chic sunglasses that—even though she couldn't care less about looking fierce— definitely made her look like the diva she's turned into. She was cute. Presentable for church. Yet, none of that matters to her, and I understand.

Losing the only piece of flesh and blood you know, is hard. I remember that feeling when my mother died. Only difference is that Azra loved Ms. Annette, and Ms. Annette *really* loved Azra. Not spending time with her in her last days has got to be eating her up inside.

Right now, she sits in the corner as we wait for everyone to file into the sanctuary. The vacant stare in her eyes focuses on nothing. She's like a shell.

"I'll be right back," I say aloud, yet William, who's scrolling on his phone, is the only one that responds.

I stand outside for a moment to escape the muggy stench of the old basement but receive little relief. The heat of August decided to seep into September and any chance of a cool breeze is just a fantasy.

I fan myself with my clutch and watch people file into the church. Although Azra said her Mom-mom didn't have many friends, there are a lot of people showing up to pay their respects. Must be members of the church.

Amongst all the somber faces and dresses with flats that almost gives me an aneurysm, here struts Kendrick in a fitted white suit, white dress shirt, and a black-tie. Wow.

"Hey, Ken. How're you doing?" I ask as he comes in for a hug.

"I'm fine, still a little surreal that she's gone," he says drawing me up into his muscular chest.

"Oh no. You know what? I completely forgot you and Ms. Annette were close. I'm so sorry. I should've asked if you wanted to take some time off from work."

"Don't sweat it. I was close to her, but she's in a better place now. She was strong in her faith so she's better off than any one of us."

"Yeah," I say not knowing what else to say.

"How're you, though? And how's Azra doing?"

"I'm doing fine. But Azra? I'm honestly worried about her. She hasn't done much since she got the news. She's not eating. Barely speaking. I'm concerned," I inform Kendrick.

Azra also hasn't seen Genesis since her grandmother passed. I've been checking in on her three times a day through video chat or dropping by and I haven't seen a sign of him. Good. He needs to be home taking care of his wife, anyway.

"Yeah. I figured. I spoke to her a couple days ago, and she didn't sound well at all. I dropped by to make sure everything was fine, and she was in the same place I saw her the day after Ms. Annette passed."

"Something's wrong. I understand she's grieving, but we need to make sure we keep an eye on her. I'm trying to find the right time to ask if she'll be open to getting grief counseling."

He shakes his head. "She needs something. I hate seeing her like this. I wish it was something I could do."

"Me too."

The small chatter of a few more people entering the church causes an awkward pause. I catch Kendrick gawking at me. I try to act like I don't feel his eyes burning holes through me, so I keep my gaze from him until he calls my attention.

"But you look beautiful, as always," he says with a slight smirk.

My stomach flutters. "Thank you," I giggle, tucking my chin to my chest. "You look dapper yourself."

"Thank you. You know this suit thing ain't really me, but I had to do what I had to do today." He fiddles with the buttons on his jacket.

I giggle again for some weird reason and look behind as if someone called me, but nobody called me.

"Well," he continues, "I should get inside. See how she's doing."

"Yeah, of course. She's right in the basement. William's there too. I just needed some air. I'll be back in soon."

He grabs my arm and gently squeezes it before leaving me where I stand.

My core shivers and tightens at his touch. "Oooh, chile, you at church, Lola. Get it together," I whisper to myself.

Before I can feel completely terrible about why I was thinking this way about Kendrick, I see ol' boy Genesis walking into the church like he owns it. Tailored suit. Shades. The whole nine. He's got a lot of balls showing up here.

My stomach turns but I quickly step my way inside and tap Genesis on the shoulder. He pulls his shades off and looks at me in shock before I whisk him behind a staircase.

"What are you doing here?" I grumble.

He furrows his brow and says, "What do you mean? I'm here for Azra."

"Why are you not at home with your wife?" I cross my arms, "She was *just* in a car accident and you're here trying to be supportive of your mistress?"

"Are you calling your friend a mistress?" he cocks his brow.

"Yes. I'll say it to her face. And I'm calling *you* a homewrecker and dimwit for thinking this is a smart thing to do," I flail my hands, wanting to smack some sense into him but I decide against it. "Genesis, Andrea is crippled—"

"Oh, God. She's not cripple. She sprained her ankle, which is a miracle because the car was totaled. But *she* is fine. She's only acting like she isn't, so I come home and take care of her."

Is this man serious?

"What the hell is wrong with you?" I gnarl, "Someone just tried to kill her by running her off the road for whatever reason and you got the nerve to stand here and act like she's a burden? Yet, you're here trying to comfort your *girlfriend?* Do you have adolescent hormones, or did you never grow up?"

"I see why you and Andrea are good friends. Y'all act just alike," he chuckles.

"I'm glad you think this is funny, but you need to go," I say, shooing him away with the back of my hand.

"Listen, Azra wants me here, okay? She told me last night she wanted me to come."

"Azra is out of her mind and doesn't know up from down right now. You don't know who's here. All because this isn't your crowd of people doesn't mean there aren't some people who know you. William is here. And you know he won't hesitate to put hands on you for messing around on his aunt, and you know he'll tell her. She'll be devastated. And with all Azra's going through right now, she doesn't need extra drama messing her up. She'll be thrown over the edge."

Dropping his gaze, he thinks about what I said. He lifts his head and asks, "So, what am I supposed to do? Just leave her by herself?"

"What am I? Chopped liver? She's not alone. Me, William, and Kendrick are—"

"Kendrick? What's he doing here?" His brow furrows.

I chuckle. "Nothing wrong, unlike you."

His nose flares and his chest heaves. He glares down and shifts his feet. He's jealous.

"So, as I was saying," I continue, "we're all here for her. So, I don't care what you do. Take a selfie and send it to her. Leave a note. Hell, you can even come by and see her later. But do *not* let her or William see you."

"Humph. For you to not like me, you sure do care a lot."

"Hold on now, chile. I never said I cared about *you.* But those two women you're juggling like bowling pins…those are my girls. I could kill

Azra for putting me in the middle of this crap, but I can't control what grown folks do and I can't control what you do with them. But hear me and hear me good. I will not let you hurt either one of them *this* way. Not today. Azra is out of control and for some ungodly reason is crazy about your arrogant behind. But Andrea? She doesn't deserve this. And you will not let her find out about this unless it comes from the horse's mouth. You owe her at least *that* much respect."

He drops his head and stuffs his hands in his pocket. Taking a deep breath, he peers at me, "I understand. I'll sit in the back, so nobody sees me."

My heart settles. "Good. And don't be obvious about *that* either. Just…lay low."

Walking in the sanctuary, the slow organ plays the woes of each crying heart. You can't help but feel sad when there's at least one hundred weeping sounds coming from all around.

As we approach the altar, Azra observes her grandmother lying in a beautiful gold casket. Not to be funny, but when they said casket sharp, they must've been talking about Ms. Annette. I didn't spend a bunch of time around her but dressed in her cream-colored, ruffled tiered, silk-chiffon dress, you can't tell me this woman didn't have style.

Surprisingly, Azra touches her grandmother's face and without a whimper, proceeds to the front bench on the right side of the church. Kendrick sits on her left side with his arm around her in an attempt to comfort her. I sit on her right and hold her hand, squeezing it every time I feel it tremble. She keeps her head down and without even a sniffle, goes through the service almost too quiet.

After the prayer, scripture readings, solo, and acknowledgments, the door to the sanctuary opens. Not many people turn around, but I do.

Of the sea of white suits and dresses, with a few white t-shirts in the crowd, here comes a woman dressed in an extravagant black gown. A black veil covers her head and big, bourgeoisie glasses cover her face, leaving her unrecognizable. She must've not gotten the memo. Swiftly, she drifts to the left corner pew in the back of the church. Being the only one turned around, as she sits, she scans the crowd, almost catching me staring at her.

I swiftly turn my head and face forward, so I'm not recognized.

"You okay?" William whispers in my ear, pulling me into him by my shoulder.

"Yeah. I'm fine," I say with a fake smile. I'm already creeped out by being in this church, and seeing what looks like the grim reaper coming to collect, I'm beyond ready to get out of here.

"And now, we will have the final remarks from the friends and family, with the reading of the obituary and the eulogy to follow," the pastor says before taking his seat.

Not many people jump up to speak, but a scattered wave of gasps breaks out amongst a few people when the grim reaper from the back glides up to the front.

For some reason, my heart throbs and although Azra still doesn't look up, I feel her hand trembling like crazy.

I can't take my eyes off this woman in black.

Without skipping a beat, she pushes back the veil covering her face and pulls down the large sunglasses.

My heart stops.

"Is that Andrea?" William whispers in my ear.

Not able to summon up the words, I look at him in disbelief.

"Bonjour," Andrea says in her usual sweet tone, staring down at a piece of paper in her hand.

Azra shoots her head up and turns beet red, even through all the foundation she wears. She shakes so violently I fear she might have a seizure. Before I know it, she shoots up from the pew, rips off her glasses, and bellows, "What the hell is she doing here?"

"Azra, please sit down," Kendrick says trying to calm her down.

"No! What the hell is this *bitch* doing here?" she yells again.

Gasps erupt through the crowd. Their virgin ears must not be able to take the profanity Azra spews.

The pastor stands and walks behind Andrea, supporting her back. "Ms. McKinney, I understand you haven't been in church in a while, but this is a house of *worship*. This is no place for that kind of language, young lady."

Andrea stands behind the microphone with her mouth agape. Her eyes are glossy.

Why *is* she here?

Kendrick tries to sit her down. "Azra, please—"

She swats him away and stares at Andrea with the evilest stare. Seething. What's gotten into her?

"Az," I say standing up, grabbing her face so she'll look at me. "Please. Just let her say what she came up to say."

She's panting like she just ran a marathon, but somehow, she listens to me and takes her seat. I take her hand in mine and squeeze just as hard as she squeezes me.

"I, uh..." Andrea begins again. "I'm sorry for those whose presence I've upset. But I have a letter to read," she says, holding up the paper in her hand.

Genesis was right. She isn't as cripple as she claimed to be.

"Go ahead, sweetheart," the pastor says, taking his seat.

Unfolding the letter, Andrea clears her throat and wets her lips before reading. "Annette was a woman of great standards," she begins, "Standards and a moral code that nobody could touch. She was heavily involved in the church and did everything she could to prove not only to the church but to God, that she was perfect. But that moral code was sometimes even hard for *her* to follow. But still, she always seemed put together. Smiling. Never letting anything bother her because she knew God was good all the time, and so was she. But that grandiose idea of perfection ran a lot of people away from her. Even made her cut people out of her life. So, I'm writing this to tell a story many of you may or may not know." Andrea quickly glances over in our direction.

Azra is steaming, but I squeeze her hand to keep her somewhat calm.

"As some of you may know," Andrea continues, "Annette had fraternal twins when she was in her early twenties. She was devastated. Not because she was pregnant, but because that perfect image she always wanted to keep up for her family and friends, seemed to be tainted, especially because she wasn't married. But she kept the babies because she thought God would never forgive her for killing her unborn children. So, she had them. Named them Aaron and Abigail. And provided for them very well.

"One day, while not paying much attention to her children playing outside, Aaron was struck down by a drunk driver. Annette was devastated, but for some reason, always blamed Abigail for the accident. Years passed, and without getting the love and affection Abigail craved from Annette, she found it somewhere else. With a man ten years her senior. She had no idea how protection worked, and the man didn't care, so consequently, Abigail got pregnant. This pissed Annette off because she'd done everything to make sure Abigail was *perfect*. She stopped taking Abigail to church. God forbid anyone found out she was pregnant. Annette told everyone in the congregation that her daughter was out of control, disrespectful, and needed prayer because the devil had gotten ahold of her.

"A few months passed and Abigail had the baby two weeks before her fifteenth birthday. Though she was a baby herself, Abigail instantly fell in love with her child. Sadly, she wasn't able to properly name the baby because a couple of days after popping it out, Annette told her to hit the road faster than Jack. She did her job of keeping Abigail safe during the pregnancy and now she was done. She wasn't gonna take care of another child, so she got rid of the old one and wanted to start fresh. Apparently, she told people Abigail ditched the baby and ran away. Annette was deemed a saint because she took the baby and raised it as her own.

"As for Abigail, she caught a couple of buses to her father's house. A beautiful two-story home in the upper-class suburbs. She was terrified to tell her father she'd had a baby and got kicked out the house, but she knew she had no other place to go. So, when she saw her father at the doorstep, she omitted the baby part and begged to stay with him. Of course, he said yes. And although his wife didn't necessarily like the idea of having the offspring of a salacious affair living with them, she proved to be the honorable woman in the situation and raised Abigail no different than her other two kids. Although I knew Annette differently than many of you may have known her, I can't write this to solely knock her off the thrown you all have put her on. She took care of and raised a woman, who I'm sure is beautiful, inside, and out. And for that, I'll always say thank you. And although we haven't seen each other in twenty-five years, no matter what happened between us. I will always love you, mom. With love, Abigail Andrea Rogers."

What? Did I just hear what I think I heard?

Azra's hands feel like cold jelly in mine and if I didn't see her slow and faint breathing moving her chest up and down, I would've thought *she* was the deceased.

Tears stream from Andrea's face as she steps away from the altar. She looks over to Azra, and although Azra is zoned out into oblivion, Andrea croaks out a heartbreaking, "I'm so sorry. I didn't know."

Slightly limping down the aisle, Andrea opens the doors to leave the church.

"I'll be right back," William whispers in my ear and jogs out of the sanctuary in an attempt to catch her. Not that she can get too far too fast with that little sprained ankle of hers.

I glance over at Azra who looks like she's about to pass out.

"Are you okay?" I ask, not expecting a response. But instead of not answering, she begins to laugh. Hysterically.

Kendrick and I look at each other with raised eyebrows. Loss for words, we silently agree on one thing: it's time to go.

He takes her left arm and I take her right, making sure to pick up my handbag before leaving the pew. Azra's laughing slowly switches to shrieks and squeals of disbelief, making my ears ring.

We take the longest walk down the middle aisle of the church. Everyone is dead quiet. No movement. Not even a murmur from the children who sit as mute as a mouse. Although it's quiet, I'm sure that's just code for the mothers of the church planning which way to gag this Sunday.

TWENTY-EIGHT

AZRA

"Az, you sure you're okay? Because I'll stay if you want me to. Evvie's got her dress and she loved it. She doesn't need any adjustments. Everything is good. I can get my stuff from the office and come back to do some work here. It's gonna be a slow day anyway so I can stay with you." Lola says, placing a peanut butter and banana sandwich in my hands as I sit up in my bed. Apparently, it's the only thing she knows how to make. But at least she's trying.

I'm living in a nightmare. There's no escape. No sign of hope. All I want to do is to wake up. Run to Mom-mom and find her frying her greasy bacon. Inhale her lemony scent. Hold her. Cling to her frail body and make all the sickness and death disappear. I want her to tell me, "It was nothing but a dream, sugar," and kiss me on my forehead. I want her to hold me in her arms and tell me everything will be okay. I just want her. But I can't. This isn't a nightmare. This is life. There's nothing I can do to change it.

I haven't cried in about two days. Might be because I've used all my tears up, or maybe I'm just growing numb. But I'll admit, today I kind of feel good. As good as I can feel.

"I'll be fine, Lo. I need some time alone anyway," I say, picking up the sandwich and nibbling the crust off.

Lola sits on the edge of the bed. "Yeah...you have had a crazy couple of weeks. But don't you think I should just—"

"Lola, I'll be fine. Besides, I need to bathe and just rest a little. It's no need for you to miss work for me."

She narrows her eyes and chews on the corner of her lip. "Okay, I guess. You sure you'll be okay? You remember those breathing exercises I taught you whenever you feel yourself getting overwhelmed—"

"For the last time, I'm. Fine. I remember the exercises and I'll do them if I need to. Promise," I grab her hand and give the best smile I can muster up. I haven't genuinely smiled in weeks. Feels so foreign.

"Okay, okay," she giggles, standing from the bed and smoothening out the wrinkles on the comforter with her hands. "Well, Kendrick will be over after work to bring you something to eat. William and I have a session tonight, so I'll be over some time tomorrow, okay?"

I nod and try to stomach another bite of this sticky sandwich.

Grabbing her purse from the other side of my bed, she asks, "I know it might be kind of early to ask, but have you thought about when you'll be going back to work or school or anything?"

"I'm not sure. Honestly after all of this. I'm considering doing something different. I'm not sure what I want to do."

"Isn't Ace holding your position?"

"They are but...I don't know if I want to go back there. I just don't know yet."

Flinging her bag across her shoulder, she swats the air with her hand, "Well, don't even think about it too much right now. You just worry about feeling better sis. And like I said, Kendrick will be over around eight or so with dinner. So, answer the door for him. You know he doesn't have a key, so don't be a Stubborn Stacey, okay?"

I chuckle. "Alright."

"Kay. See you sis. Love you."

"Love you, too," I mutter, putting the small plate on the nightstand.

Waiting until the door shuts, I jump to retrieve my phone from the charger and swipe it open. Going straight to my messages, I text Genesis. He wants to come by and talk, but between Lola's video chatting and texting, watching my every move like a hawk, and probably making sure I didn't have time to see him, we haven't had the chance. But today is the day.

I type:

She just left. You can come now.

He responds:

OMW

After showering, brushing my teeth, and zhuzhing myself up as best as I can, I lethargically lie on the loveseat. Man, not eating enough will definitely have you feeling weak.

Three metallic knocks at the door, and I perk up.

"Come in," I sing.

Emotionally, I've felt nothing. But now, I feel butterflies. Faint. But butterflies, nonetheless.

The day of Mom-mom's homegoing, I was hurt I hadn't heard from Genesis. He hadn't reached out, called, stopped by. Nothing. He ghosted me again. I couldn't understand why. I still don't get it. But the anger dissolved and blended with numbness. But now, that numb feeling dissipates as I see him walking in.

He saunters over with his head down. I want to jump up and hold him. Kiss him. But the lack of energy prevents me from doing anything.

"Hey," he says, rubbing me on the shoulder and sitting on the arm of the love seat.

No hug? No kiss?

"Hey," I mutter back, sinking into the seat. Drawing my knee up, I turn to look up at him. He doesn't pay me any mind.

"How're you doing?" he asks, looking at his fingers.

"I'm fine. You?"

He shrugs. His sedated manner scares me. Although I may not be much different, I have a reason. What's his excuse?

We sit in silence for a moment before I break the ice. "So, what did you want to talk about?"

"Honestly. I don't even know where to start, babygirl."

Whew. He's still calling me *babygirl*. That means we're good.

I perk up a little more and touch his leg. "Does this have to do with....you know?" I ask, referring to *her*: That attention-seeking, delusional, lying whore he just so happens to be legally bound to.

He moves his leg away from my hand ever so slightly. Adjusting himself on the armrest, he crosses his arms. "I don't know how to say this, so I'm just gonna come out and say it." He heavily sighs and closes his eyes.

My heart pounds as every second takes eons to pass. He opens his mouth then closes it. Finally, he utters out, "We can't see each other anymore."

What? A tightness forms in my chest and my thoughts freeze. He didn't just say that. Did he?

"Did you hear what I said?" he asks, still not making eye contact. "We can't see each other anymore," he repeats himself.

Is he being funny? Because I know he isn't seriously breaking up with me right now? After all I've been through and he chooses *now?*

Lost for words, heat rushes from my feet to my head. I shake my head back and forth, trying to rattle myself back to reality only to realize, this *is* reality.

"Why?" I ask.

"Babygirl—"

"Don't—" I yell, throwing my hand up to stop him. Taking a deep breath and trying the breathing exercises Lola taught me, I continue in a whisper. "Do not call me babygirl right now," I say, lowering my hand and glaring at him. "Is this because she's not giving you a divorce?"

He gazes at me with a bunched brow. His head tilts to the side as if I have five snake heads sticking out of my neck.

"No, Azra. It's because you're Andrea's daughter."

"No," I shake my head, "she's not my mother, and that woman is a liar among so many other things. There's no way I'm her daughter. My mother ran away because she didn't want me. She *decided* to leave me. She wasn't forced. Okay? So, what? You're calling my mom-mom a liar now?"

My blood is boiling. How dare he believe anything that comes out of that me-me-me Jezebel's mouth?

He squinches his eyes at me and then drops his head. "Azra," he exhales, "Andrea is your mother—"

"She is not my mother!"

He sighs. "Azra…I love you. I can't deny that. But I can't, in good conscience, leave Andrea. Especially with everything we just found out. I had no idea you were her daughter—"

"She's not my mother, dammit!"

"Yes, she is. I heard it just like you and everyone else did."

"How? You weren't even at my mom-mom's funeral, Genesis. Even after I asked you to be there."

"I *was* there, Azra. I was in the back on the balcony. I saw and heard everything."

"Then why didn't you tell me you were there? Why didn't you comfort me when I was sitting up there having a nervous breakdown? You just sat there and watched? You didn't even have the decency to call me later to let me know you cared. You abandoned me, Genesis."

His eyes soften. "I didn't—" he inhales, pinching the bridge of his nose. "I didn't want to leave you alone, Azra. This has been just as hard for me as it is for you. You don't think I felt bad not being able to comfort you since that day? All I've been thinking about is you. But I couldn't sit up there with you and you know that. William was there and you know how that would've ended. And I didn't say anything because after everything that happened...I didn't know how to come to you."

"Like a *grown man*. Oh, but let me guess, you had to be there for your lying wife, huh? Had to bow down to her and her rules? Just forget about little ol' Azra. She'll be fine."

He takes a deep breath and stands from the armrest. Taking a few steps away, he turns back around. "Azra, this is the problem. You've completely lost touch with reality. Whether you like it or not, Andrea is my *wife*. I'm married to *her*. Not you."

My heart aches at those words.

"I already feel terrible for what I've done to both of you," he says, sitting on the barstool by the kitchen. "But I can't keep this going. I love her. We have our problems but that's still the woman I chose to share my life with. We talked things out and it's so much I didn't know was going on with her. I can't divorce her, Azra. Not because she won't give me one, but because I don't *want* to. And I especially can't keep on seeing her *daughter*."

Jumping off the couch and storming over to him, I yell, "That bitch is not my mother! And if breaking up with me was your plan all along, you could've just done it like a normal person and shot me a text. You just had to come and say this to my face?"

"Watch who you're calling a *bitch*," he says, pointing his finger in my face.

"Bitch-bitch-bitch-bitch-*bitch*! What'chu gonna do?" I twist my lips.

Red. That's all I see. My body shakes with a raging heat of anger and pain that I never felt before.

"Listen," he dips his head down and sighs. Moving me back by my arms, he continues, "I'm sorry about your grandmother. I'm sorry about how you found out about you and Andrea. And I'm *really* sorry about even letting this affair happen and get this far. But we're stopping this right now. And although you might not like it, this way is better than doing it over the phone or through text." He backs up and moves towards the door. "Azra, I really do love you and I need you to know that. That isn't gonna just go away. But I couldn't end this over a text, one: because I'm a man. And two: because you deserve so much better than that. You're a good woman. It's a good man out there for you. But I'm not the one."

Stepping backward, I stumble into the coffee table. Catching myself, my legs shake and lose strength. The room spins. I force myself to focus my vision and breathe.

Shaking my head, I plead, "Don't do this."

"I never meant to hurt you with my selfish actions," he says, moving his way to the door.

"Genesis..."

"And I pray you can forgive me. I wish you all the best and I pray God heals you from this."

"Genesis, stop," I grab my aching chest. Pushing away the tears that compress to be released. They forcedly find their escape, "Stop talking like this. You can't leave me."

"I have to."

"No, you don't."

"I do. This wasn't right from the start, Azra, and you know that."

Leaping off the sofa, I scream, "What happened to you making me your wife? Huh? You promised me!"

"I wasn't thinking clearly. And neither were you."

"No. I was and *am* thinking very clear." Shuffling over to him, I grab him by his black short-sleeved t-shirt. "You are *mine*! You can't—you will *not* do me like this."

Looking up and trying his hardest to avoid eye contact, he says, "I paid on the rental for another month. That should give you enough time to get things together with finding a new car."

Is he for real? All of this and all he talks about is a rental? Speechless, I squint my wet eyes at him.

Emotionless. Stoic. Just like he was when we first met. Is he some sort of robot or something? Where the hell is the emotion?

"I'm gonna leave now," he states, trying to peel my hands off his shirt, but I squeeze tighter. Digging my fingernails into the fabric.

"No. You're staying right here and we're gonna talk this out."

"Azra, let me go!" he shouts, still trying to pry my hands from his shirt.

Kicking and screaming, I push him against the door but only push myself back to the ground.

With wide eyes, he watches me fall.

He thinks he can just break up with me like that, and everything will be fine? *Oh, hell nah.* He's gonna sit and talk this out with me if it's the last thing he does.

He paces over to me to help me up, but I scramble onto my feet and run to my bedroom. Diving under my bed, I search. Moving shoe boxes out the way, I search. Less than a few seconds, I find it. I pull out that long-lost friend of Lola's. Just sitting there under my bed. Waiting for this moment. Without thinking, I run back into the living room and press Poppy right into Genesis's forehead.

"Whoa," he holds both hands up and backs away, "Where'd you get that from?"

"You're not leaving me, Genesis," my voice shakes uncontrollably. Adrenaline rushes through my body. My tears stop. Loud pounding in my ears drown out every other noise around me, including him.

"Azra, just give me the gun."

"You're not leaving me," I say, holding the gun tighter so it stops shaking.

Slowly, he raises his hand over the barrel of the gun. "Alright, babygirl. I'm not leaving. I'm staying right here. Just…calm down, okay?"

Lowering the gun from his face, I see right through what he's trying to do. I nudge the gun up, knocking his hand off.

"I love you, Genesis. I love you so much. I gave you all I could give, and this is what you do? You treat me like some kind of whore you met off the street?"

Tears resurface.

What am I doing? It's like I'm in a fog and have no control over my actions. I can't do this. But for some reason, I keep the gun aimed at his face because there's no way he's gonna get away with pissing me off like this.

"I'm not doing anything. I'm not leaving," he says. His voice is light and reassuring. He gulps down a mouth full of saliva and whispers, "Just give me the gun and we can talk this out, okay?"

His eyes are sincere, and my heart softens. Lowering the gun on my own, Genesis skillfully disarms the gun. The clip falls from the gun and bullets pop out as it hits the floor. Without a second thought, I lunge at him. Clawing and hitting him in his chest, he turns me around and holds my arms down.

"Get off!" I rage.

"Azra, just stop!" he yells, picking me up off the ground and holding me in the air from behind.

I kick and throw my head back but all to no avail.

"You need to relax, Azra."

I thrash my body back and forth to get from his hold, but his arms are firmly wrapped around me. I've never despised his touch until now. And before I know it, I scream out, "I hate you! Let me go!"

I donkey kick my way out of his arms.

Falling from his grasp, he bends over. I hit the release button. He grabs himself and grunts in pain.

Scrounging around the ground I pick up the gun. I have no idea how to reload it, so I grab some bullets and chuck them at him.

"What the hell is wrong with you, Azra? You're acting like you're possessed," he bellows, trying to dodge the bullets with his forearms.

"You drove me to this. This is your fault! You fed me all those lies. You told me I was your future, Genesis. Remember that? Talking about *'I love you. I'm leaving Andrea for you. We're getting married'*. Knowing damn well you were just using me for your sick fantasy of being with a young girl! You caused this, you big ol', sick, perverted bastard!" I scream, pushing him into the door.

He snaps. With a growl, he ricochets and plummets into me. Picking me up, he runs me to the couch and slams me down.

Twinkles of light shine in my eyes. The door opens, and I jump up. He edges his way out my apartment.

"Genesis, you better not walk out that door!" I yell, jumping to my feet. Lightheaded, the room goes dark for a moment and I fall back on the couch.

Posted at the door, he looks back, and everything drags by. He glares at me with disgust in his eyes. My heart splits in two.

Shaking his head, he sighs before fixing his mouth to say, "Goodbye."

I sit on the couch paralyzed. "Gen—Genesis! Get back in here! Genesis!" I scream.

The door shuts. He's gone.

The rage subsides. Tears take over the burning wrath that I felt not even a minute ago. The longer I sit the sicker I feel. What just happened? What is my life right now? My heart is pounding through my chest. Heat recedes from my head to my feet and a nauseating grumble rocks my core. Gagging, I cover my mouth and jet to the bathroom.

Raising my head out of the toilet, I struggle onto my feet and steady myself on the sink. Washing my mouth out, the room dims and spins around me. I shuffle to my bed, grab my sleeping pills from the drawer of my nightstand, and secure them to my chest. Hot tears roll down my face, but I don't care to wipe them.

I have no Mom-mom. No Genesis. The woman who claims to be my mother was a victim of a car accident *I* caused. I could've killed her. I wish

I did. Then none of this would even be happening. I don't even have God. God? Where are you?

I cry out, "Mom-mom, why is this happening? What has happened to me? Mom-mom, I need you. I need you so bad. I can't take this by myself. Why did you leave me? I know I've been bad. I know I've been distant. Even God doesn't want me after all I've done. But I at least thought I'd have you, Mom-mom. Please, Mom-mom. Come back! Come back, please. I need you. I can't live with myself. All I want to do is sleep. Sleep, and never wake up. I'm so tired, Mom-mom. I'm tired."

TWENTY-NINE

LOLA

"Lola, I'd like for us to get into your childhood a little more," Dr. Henderson says.

Although I'm glad my counselor is a Black woman and I'm comfortable speaking to her, I still can't bring myself to go deeper into my life with her. She's here to help. That's her job. But talking about my past is never easy.

It's been seven weeks and I've held off on speaking about my childhood. But here we go again. Trying to get all in my business. I know this is the point of counseling but still.

"What about it?" I huff and cross my arms. I glance over to William sitting to my left. He grabs my knee and tenderly rubs it, bringing a calming sensation to my heart. He smiles to loosen me up and I flash a smile back. I'm so happy he's here. But opening up in front of him is harder than I expected.

"Well, would you say you had a good childhood? Was there a certain activity you and your mother or father did that brings a smile to your face now?" Dr. Henderson asks with her notebook on her lap and her pen in hand.

Sucking my cheeks in and taking a deep whiff of the pumpkin spice scent that fills the room, I anxiously tap my foot on the ground.

"Lola, it's safe here," she says, clearly seeing me tense up, "this is all a part of the process. Last week you told me you wanted to destress and learn different coping mechanisms to handle your anxiety. To do so, I need to know how we got here, today. Usually, childhood is where most anxieties start. So, I'll need to know a little more about your childhood so I can help."

I hear her. But I shake my head and hug myself tighter. William stretches his arm out around me and holds me. I already shared the main part of my childhood with Kendrick weeks ago. I'm definitely not looking forward to telling a complete stranger *and* William about it. How will he see me afterward? Will he be disgusted with me?

I bite my lip and shake my head once again.

"That's fine," Dr. Henderson says, turning her head to William, "Sometimes it helps when others share their experiences out loud. I know this session is about Lola, but would you like to share a bit of your childhood, William?"

"Sure," he says straightening himself up.

"Awesome. So, do you have any special memories about your childhood? An activity you used to do? Any family members stick out to you in a positive way?"

"Actually, my childhood was kind of lonely. It wasn't bad or anything, it's just my parents didn't spend much time with me. They were busy people and worked a lot of crazy hours."

"What kinds of jobs did they have?"

"Well, I come from a long line of doctors. My dad is an anesthesiologist, and my mom is an obstetrician. So, you can imagine how disappointed they were when I became a chef," he chuckles.

"Do you feel like you let them down? Or have they expressed that to you?" Dr. Henderson asks.

William pauses. Bunching his brow and tilting his head, he glares down. "They didn't like the fact that I was a chef. But now since I'm becoming recognized and making good money, they seem to be okay with it. They accept what I do, but never really supported me while I was getting it. That's why I'm so close to my aunt. She supported me in what *I* wanted to do. My dad is about eight years older than her, and they didn't really have a close relationship with each other until I was about a year old. That's when my aunt started babysitting me and she became like a big sister to me. She taught me how to cook and bake. She was always there for me, so I have a lot of respect for her. I'm glad she introduced me to culinary arts because I can't see myself doing anything else."

"That's good," Dr. Henderson smiles warmly at William, "So, do you feel at peace with your relationship with your parents, now?"

"Yeah, definitely. We have a good relationship. I just feel closer to my aunt."

"And you're okay with that?"

"Yeah, I'd say so," William says.

"Very good." Dr. Henderson grins then turns her gaze to me. "So, Lola, do you feel more comfortable sharing a little now?"

I shift in my seat. Keeping my head down, I mutter, "I guess."

"You got it, Bean." William rubs my shoulder with his arm still around me. He's never let me go, but the fear of him knowing what happened to me as a child unsettles me.

"Whenever you're ready. Just remember, this is a safe place," Dr. Henderson says.

Closing my eyes, I center myself. I flash back to seven-year-old Lola standing in front of my mother.

She was in the mirror. Getting dressed. Slathering on her red lipstick all over her wideset lips. Her tight black dress fit snuggly around her petite, yet voluptuous, frame. She pinned her hair up on the top of her head. Loose, jet-black tendrils fell down her face. She was beautiful. Though she never came home that way. Her hair would be everywhere. Makeup smudged. Mascara running down her cheeks. But to me, she was still pretty.

"Momma, where you going?" I asked, sitting on the floor watching her dance as *I Get Around* by Tupac played from the stereo.

"Out. And no, you ain't goin' wit' me." She sprayed her perfume between her legs.

"But you promised me we could see 'Hocus Pocus' tonight."

She snapped, "Oh my god Lola, *damn!* I told you I'll take you when I got the time. Stop askin' me 'bout it. You 'bout to not see it at all."

"But mom—"

"Shut up! I don't wanna here it no' mo'. Now, go be a good girl and play in your room. Uncle Randy gonna be here in a little while to watch you."

My heart dropped. "But I don't want to stay with him—"

"What I say?" She tightens her upper lip, "Get your butt in that room now and shut up."

"But Mom—"

"Go!" she yelled, pointing out the room.

I stood from the floor and shuffled to my room. Called my mom everything under the sun, in my head.

"Cramping my style," she continued, talking to herself. "Shouldn't have got pregnant so damn young. Now I gotta deal with this stuff the rest of my life."

I choke through how my mother would often speak to me. Not wanting to look over at William, I keep my eyes cast down.

"Take your time," Dr. Henderson says. I glance up at her and though she tries to hide it, she seems mortified.

Taking a deep breath, I continue, "That night is when everything went downhill. Randy. He…She allowed him to do things to me…" my voice shakes, and a pain in my throat constricts me from speaking.

I close my aching eyes. William's hand rests on my leg and squeezes. I place my hand over his and regain the strength to push on. I swallow before continuing, "I never told her because I guess deep down, I felt like she knew. And if she didn't, I was afraid to tell her because *he* always told me it'll hurt her to know her baby was a…was a…" My throat cramps again and I sigh.

Although William's grasp on my leg is strong, I grow weaker. Tears leak from my eyes, "He called me all kinds of things. Made me do things to him that…" I stop. The heaviness on my chest feels real enough to cave it in. I can't talk about this anymore. I cover my face and swallow. William pulls me back into him and hugs me tightly.

"Very good, Lola," Dr. Henderson says, handing William a box of tissues to give to me. "But if you can, please stay right there. I know it's painful, but this process is about healing where it hurts. Don't fight what you're feeling and do this for me. Try to identify three or four words to explain how that made you feel as a child?"

Sniffling, I tap back into the hyperventilation and racing heartbeat that pumped through my chest as I awaited Randy's visit late at night and sometimes in the afternoon. The dizziness that resulted into temporary paralysis whenever I was violated. The mixture of heat flashes rushing through my body, and fury of wanting to give him what he deserved once he left my room. Four words are all I need to sum up how I felt as a child.

"Unsafe. Afraid. Sad. Angry," I grit my teeth.

"Mmm. And you do feel any of those feelings in your everyday life, today?"

"Not that I can recall," I lie, knowing every time I think about my past I want to re-kill Randy until I can erase everything he did to me.

"Are you sure?" she asks.

I shrug and nod while dabbing away a final stray tear.

"Why do you think that may be?"

"Well, about four months ago, my mother died," I confess. William's head turns to me and I meet his bulging eyes. "I didn't tell anyone," I assure him, "not even Azra. I thought I could handle it alone. I thought losing her would give me the clarity I needed to move on from all the guilt and anger and sadness I felt while she was alive. I felt like I could let go of my past because she was no longer here. And because I never talked to anyone about her, I assumed nobody cared. So, I kept it to myself, but now I realize it only made my anxieties worse."

"Why didn't you tell me? You know I care about everything dealing with you," William interjects.

"I know you do. But you didn't know anything about my past, and honestly, I didn't want you to, because that's not who I am today."

"But it is, Lola," Dr. Henderson jumps in. "You're here today *because* of your past, am I right?"

I nod and glare down.

"Listen, I'm not saying you *are* your past. I'm just saying your past can affect you so much that you allow it to define who you are. I'm not saying this is what you're doing. But you mentioned in our last session that you know for a fact your past has affected and is affecting your life and relationships today. Many times, early-onset anxiety doesn't go away on its own and is usually triggered and worsened by different anxiety provoking events that happen throughout one's life. So, now that we know when your anxiety has started, we can find different strategies and coping mechanisms for handling potentially triggering situations and to help reduce your anxiety levels."

Feeling a bit tense at the truth Dr. Henderson is speaking, I roll my shoulders and say "Okay." Clutching my hands together, I glance up at her quickly skimming her notes.

"So, you said you felt your sadness, anger, and guilt went away after your mother passed. What about the feeling of being afraid and unsafe? I'm assuming those feelings carried on?"

"Well, kind of. Not when *she* died, but when my ex died. I felt unsafe because I knew that when he got out of prison, he'd come looking for me. But after a few weeks of him being released and he didn't come, I got a little comfortable. But now that he's gone, I feel like I'm free from that."

"That's great. So, you don't feel afraid and unsafe anymore?"

I search the air for answers. "Not for my *life*," I respond.

"Mmm," she hums, "Can I suggest something?"

"Sure."

"Last week you mentioned you haven't said you loved William."

I shake my head and scrunch my face up, "Yeah, and?"

"Well, by the looks of it, you two are inseparable. And although you haven't said the words—I can only go by what I see—you two have a connection."

"Well, yeah. He's my guy. He's good to me. And he's the only person in my life other than Azra, that I feel I've been vulnerable with," I admit.

Peeking over to my left, William is smiling from ear to ear. I giggle and turn back to Dr. Henderson grinning back at us. "But what does that have to do with anything?"

"So," she says as all of our smiles fade, "based on your past with your mother and your ex, whom we talked a bit about over the last few weeks, do you feel William will be just like them and disappoint or hurt you physically or emotionally?"

Searching the air again, I shrug. "I don't know. I feel like my judgment of character is all jacked up," I chuckle but really don't find anything funny.

"Now, Lola. I want you to hear me out on this, okay?" Dr. Henderson places her notes on the coffee table and uncrosses her legs.

I sit on the edge of the seat and bite my lip. Why do I feel like she's about to give me some test results on a life-threatening disease?

"Though you claim to have let go of the feelings of insecurity and sadness deriving from your past, that it's possible you've simply grouped them under the umbrella of fear?"

"What do you mean? Isn't fear and being afraid the same thing?" I narrow my eyes.

"Well, yes and no. Being afraid is the feeling that comes from fear, which makes fear the emotion. A feeling is an acute response, whereas an emotion is a chronic adaption. So, in other words, you can live in fear, but not be *afraid* twenty-four-seven. Fear encompasses our feelings of being unsafe, sad, and even doubtful of others. So, I ask you, do you think that your life and relationship with William is affected because you carry the fear of your past, into your present? Do you feel you've pushed away or withheld your feelings from others because you're trying to ward off the possibility of being disappointed and hurt again?"

If *mind blown* was a person, it'll be my face right now.

With the simplicity of how she just read my complex life in a matter of seconds, I feel embarrassed that I couldn't figure it out myself.

A smile emerges on my face and I shake my head. Rolling my eyes from her to William and then from him to the ceiling, I scoff. "Whatever, Doc. You don't know me."

William laughs and rubs my back.

Dr. Henderson tilts her head to the side and giggles. "Listen, Lola," she begins, "I can't tell you what to do. But as I tell many of my patients: you can't change the past, but you can learn from past experiences to fuel the change that you want to see in your future. It may not be easy, but you must learn how to move on with the knowledge and experiences that you have. Don't count them as a loss or stain on you, but as a gain to what you can add to make sure your present and future will be richer due to those circumstances. Your past is what made you who you are today. Just from our sessions, I know that you haven't been dealt a great hand in life, but you can't let your past define your present. You've been resilient thus far, there's no doubt with the tools and coping mechanisms we'll go through in our remaining sessions and your homework, that you'll be successful in improving the quality of your life and relationships moving ahead."

Smiling and holding back tears that I'm honestly sick of shedding, I whisper out, "Thank you."

⁎⁎⁎

"That food was bussin'," William says as we come into my apartment after dinner.

"It was. But that small lobster tail and three pieces of shrimp just didn't do it for me. An extra-large pizza and some cheese fries are on my radar for tonight," I chuckle, going into my room to get a few more outfits to take back to William's place a.k.a, my temporary home.

William laughs as he follows me into my room, "We can order some when we get back. But you deserve all the fancy things in life, woman. Watch, one day you'll be so accustomed to it you won't even be able to stand the *smell* of fast food."

"Highly doubt it," I giggle throwing a lace bra and pant set into my duffle bag. "I'm gonna call Azra to see how she's doing."

"Cool. Don't take too long, though. You know the first episode of the competition is airing tonight at nine-thirty."

"How could I forget? You've only been reminding me every half second," I laugh while picking up my phone.

"You laugh, but you gonna see how your man was knocking them out. Left and right." William punches the air like he's boxing.

I smile but get distracted by the relentless ringing on the other end of the phone.

Pressing the end button, I look at the screen for a moment.

"No answer?" William asks, sitting on the edge of the bed and checking his phone, something he's been doing all day long besides when we were at counseling.

He's been on his phone a lot lately, but I'm not quick enough to catch what he's doing or who he's talking to. Not that I should have anything to worry about. I don't think. But being the type to let things slide a few times, I just ignore it…this time.

"Nope. She's probably sleep," I say, tossing my phone on the bed.

"Wasn't Kendrick supposed to drop by there?"

"Oh, yeah, I forgot about that. Well, knowing him, they're probably in Bible study right now," I chuckle, throwing a pair of fluffy, comfy socks into the bag.

"Maybe. But Kendrick is cool people. We've been talking a lot since that incident at the boutique."

"That's good," I smirk.

I owe Kendrick for putting his butt on the line for me. I never had anyone do that for me. But what makes all this disturbing is the fact that I actually find myself thinking about him. A lot. I think I have that syndrome that people get when they fall in love with their rescuer. But the thing is: I'm not in love with him, and Kendrick didn't *physically* rescue me from anything. But *acting* like he did is making me *feel* like he did.

Shoot. What is that syndrome called?

"You good?"

"Huh?" I snap back to reality.

William's dimpled grin greets me. He laughs. "You're just standing there dazed out. You alright?"

"Yeah. I didn't even realize it," I chuckle but make a mental note to ask Dr. Henderson about the name of that syndrome. I continue, "I was just thinking how weird it is that Azra's your cousin."

"I know, right? That's crazy," he says looking at his phone.

"Yeah. That reminds me though. I haven't heard from Andrea like that. I spoke to her a couple days ago, but she was short."

"Same here. I tried to drop by to see how she was doing but she's been working a lot. You know she's expanding CocoDrop, so it seems like she's throwing herself into her work."

"That's not good."

"Well that's Andrea. That's how she's always been. You'd never know something was wrong unless she tells you. But this time, we know exactly what's wrong and she still acting like it's nothing. It's crazy because my dad always said something about her having a baby nobody knew about, but I thought he was just talking."

I shake my head and walk over to my dresser, "Well, now you know he wasn't lying."

"Yeah. Unfortunately."

"I feel bad for them, though. Andrea deserves so much better than the crap that she's been going through."

"Yeah, finding out your child has been right under your nose all this time has got to be something else."

"Not only that, but the fact that her relationship with—" I gasp.

Almost let the cat out the bag. Good thing my back is turned because this *oop* face would've given me away. Ugh. I want to tell William about Genesis and Azra's affair, especially knowing that Azra is sleeping with her mother's husband. Yikes. I don't think it can get any worse than that.

Damn Azra for putting me in this position.

"Her relationship with who?" William asks.

Dropping down to retrieve a few tank tops from the bottom drawer, I think quick. "Um, her mother." Whew. "Andrea's baby was taken away from her and then Ms. Annette turned around and bad mouthed her to everyone. That's messed up. And poor Azra. She thought her mother didn't even want her. On top of that, she finds out who her mother is at her grandmother's *funeral*. It's all a hot mess. But oddly enough, she acts like none of it is resonating with her."

"It's probably hard for her to process it all."

"Yeah. I guess so."

Standing back up with four or five black and white tank tops in my arms, I kick the drawer closed and walk to the bed. William gazes at me but doesn't say anything.

I flash a smile and shyly look away as I stuff my shirts in the bag.

He continues to stare.

"What?" I giggle.

"Nothing. Just wondering…how're you feeling?"

"What do you mean?" I furrow my brow.

"Well, I know you don't like talking about your sessions once we are done, but…are you okay?"

"Oh, goodness, William. I'm fine. Please don't make it weird," I chuckle, feeling exposed.

He stands and comes behind me. He wraps his arms around my waist and rests his chin on my shoulder. "I'm not making it weird, woman. I just want you to know that I'm here. I'm already *at* the sessions with you. You can talk to me when we are out as well. I'm always here for you."

Scoffing out a laugh, I place my hand on the side of William's head and kiss his cheek as he remains rested on my shoulder. "Thank you," I whisper. "Now. Let's go. If we don't leave now, we'll miss the *one* episode you're in."

"Hol' up now. It was *nine* episodes, and I only lost the last one because of you."

"Of course, it's all my fault," I laugh, zipping up my bag and pressing it against William's chest.

My phone vibrates on my bed. Quickly picking it up, my heart skips a beat.

Kendrick

Not waiting another second, I swipe to answer. "Hello?"

"Hey, Lola. I know it's kind of late to be calling, but have you heard from Azra?"

"This morning. I called her not too long ago, but she didn't answer. Why? What's up?" I stand, not knowing what else to do, but I dare not look at William. Instead, I try to slow my breathing that sped up when I answered the phone.

"I left her place about twenty minutes ago, but I forgot my key card on her kitchen counter. I tried calling and texting, but she isn't answering."

"Well, she's probably fell asleep. William and I are on our way out of my place right now. We can drop by and I'll let you in to get it."

"That'll be great, Lola. Thank you," he says with deep appreciation.

I smile and glance at William on his phone standing in the doorway of my bedroom, not paying me or the dumb grin on my face any mind. What is he doing on his phone anyway?

"It's no biggie. We'll be over in a few minutes."

Hanging up the phone and walking towards William, he quickly closes out whatever he was doing on his phone.

"You got some business to handle? You've been on your phone a lot lately," I ask.

"A little bit. Nothing important," he says.

Humph. Could've fooled me.

Rolling my eyes, I brush it off. "Okay, well, Kendrick needs to get something out of Azra's place, so we have to drop by there before going home."

William's eyes light up and his brows heighten. "Home?"

"Listen," I say, holding my hand up, "don't get excited now. That was an accident. *Your* home," I clarify.

He smirks and nods, "Mm-hmm. If you say so."

THIRTY

LOLA

"Azra? Open up," I yell, banging on the door. The door latch catches as I try to peep inside Azra's darkened apartment. As William sits out in the car waiting for me to come back from letting Kendrick in Azra's place, I check my phone for the time.

8:56 p.m.

Four minutes from the time I unlocked the door, only to find the chain lock was locked as well. Three minutes and thirty seconds too long for Azra not to answer.

Kendrick stands behind me and worry grows on his face. "If she doesn't come to the door in five seconds, I'm busting it down."

"Wait, Ken. She'll come, she's probably just in a deep sleep. You know she hasn't slept well since Ms. Annette died. She's exhausted," I say, trying to calm him down, but also trying to stop myself from obsessing about what could be going on, on the other side of this door.

I press my ear as deep into the crack of the door to see if I can hear anything, like breathing or snoring. Instead, beyond the gripping silence, trickles of what sounds like water drips in the distance.

"Do you hear that?" I ask Kendrick.

He puts his ear in the position mine was and his face tightens.

Our eyes meet and a sour taste forms in my mouth. An ache in the back of my throat makes it difficult to breathe. My stomach roils. Though my mind goes to the worst-case scenario, I stop myself.

Azra wouldn't dare. She was doing better this morning. And Kendrick was just here less than an hour ago. She was fine then, and she's fine now. I stop thinking the morbid thoughts and break the uneasy glare between me and Kendrick.

Banging on the door, I shout, "Azra! Open the door right now!"

Chills run through my body and my knuckles turn numb and white from the knocking.

Kendrick roams back and forth before curiosity kills his patience. "Back up, Lola," he says, picking me up and moving me out of his way. Taking two large steps back, He rolls his shoulders, turns to his right side, and rams the door, breaking the chain lock.

One attempt and we're in.

With a quick glance around the hall, it baffles me that none of the neighbors have come out of their homes. But as soon as I see the door bust open, my feet move faster than I can comprehend. Knowing the layout of Azra's apartment, I maneuver my way in the dark. The blinds are drawn and there's no light other than the dim glow from underneath her bathroom door. It guides me.

With tunnel vision, I race Kendrick to the bathroom.

Azra's not dumb, I think to myself as we come to a screeching halt at the door. Kendrick and I look at each other before I extend my hand to brace the knob. A shudder shakes me from the inside. I close my eyes. Turning the knob, I push the door open.

Drip, drop. Drip, drop.

Each droplet of water dribbles from the faucet of the porcelain bathtub. I swallow heavily as the door swings open. My sluggish heartbeat pounds. Everything moves in slow motion. Finally, a dangling hand lying on the side of the tub causes my chest to twinge.

"No, no, no, no," I scuttle toward her.

Spotty vision and tingling legs, I drop to my knees. "Azra? Oh my God! Azra. No, no, no, no, no, no! Azra, wake up!"

Adrenaline shoots through me and I stand to pull her naked, partially limp body out of the hot, overflowing water. A couple empty prescription bottles topple over onto the floor. I flop her body on the fuzzy shower mat and rest her head on my legs.

"What did you do!" I wail.

Her eyes flutter but don't open. Dried tears stain the sides of her face. Her lips are purple, and her skin is so pale. *Oh, God. Please don't take Azra away.*

I open her mouth and begin to stick my finger down her throat.

"No, Lola!" Kendrick yells, moving my hand from her mouth. His other hand holds the phone up to his ear. "Don't do anything. Put her on her side and just keep her comfortable."

"Are you crazy? Kendrick, she's *dying!* " I scream. "She needs to throw up or she's gonna die!"

"Lola, please just—Yes…yes, I need an ambulance. My friend appears to be overdosing." Kendrick's voice remains calm, but he paces back and forth as he speaks to dispatch. He grabs a few towels from the towel rack near the door. Cradling the phone between his shoulder and his ear, he gives dispatch the address and he covers Azra with the large towels.

Losing my mind, I turn Azra on her side but keep her head lying on my thighs. Why would she try to do this to herself? Blurred and spinning vision, I close my eyes. My heart palpitates. Rocking back and forth, I whisper,

"It's gonna be okay. Please God make it okay. You can't take Azra away from me. Please don't do this. Please, please, please." Hot tears stream down my cold face.

Kendrick walks around the bathroom with the phone still to his ear. He quickly stumbles over to pick up one of the medicine bottles. "Um, I'm not sure...uh...Z-O-L-P-I-D...Uh, yes, that's it. What is it?" he asks. "Sleeping pills?"

As Kendrick repeats what dispatch told him, my stomach drops even more.

When Azra told me she's been taking sleeping pills, I didn't think she meant prescription sleeping pills. Oh god, this better not have anything to do with that bastard Genesis. Ooh, I'm gonna kill him. Heat flushes through my body just thinking about him.

I rock back and forth, rubbing Azra's wet hair. Breathing through my nose and blowing out my mouth I wipe my tear-soaked face.

"Hang in there, girl. You can't leave me like this, okay? Please just...stay with me, sis."

"They're on their way," Kendrick says as he slips his phone in his back pocket.

Dropping into a squat, he glares at me. His body loses its power. His strong shoulders droop over. All the wind looks like it's been knocked out of him. Crossing his arms with his elbows on his knees, his eyes swell up and turn red. Though he tries to hold it in, he bows his head and finally breaks down.

THIRTY-ONE
AZRA

One word: Pain.

Physical. Emotional. Spiritual. Mental.

My stomach is heavy. An agonizing, dull, and pressing pain radiates from my stomach to the point I feel it in my kidneys. The beeping machine blasts my eardrums. Head pounding like my brain is waiting to explode through my eyeballs.

Fluttering my eyes open, the debilitating strain of the fluorescent light shining above me hurts.

This can't be.

My heart beats faster, deeper. Like a bass drum. *Why God? Why am I still here?*

The shutters are open, yet the most blinding light is the one shining above me.

A light, floral fragrance fills the air. I turn to my left. The aroma strengthens. It comes from a nurse dressed in yellow scrubs. Knotless braids pulled back into a bun. The corners of her lips slightly upturned. She takes an empty saline bag from the hook until she notices my movement.

Her eyes widen, "Wow, you're up! I'll be right back," she smiles, placing the saline bag on a silver tray and rushes out of the room.

Seconds later, she comes back in with a tall, thin woman dressed in a long white coat.

"Ms. McKinney. We're so glad you're up," she comes near and rests her hands on the right handrail of the bed. "I'm the doctor watching over you today. It's nice to meet you."

Opening my mouth to speak, I wince. Every inhale is like a punch to the gut, so I breathe lightly and close my eyes.

"It's fine," the doctor says, placing a hand over mine before she snatches a clipboard hanging on the wall. "You don't have to say anything. You may not be in the mood for talking but let me know your pain level." Holding up the clipboard with a chart of different colored smiley faces and numbers underneath them, I point to the last face that's beet red, crying, and looks as if it's about to lose its hold on life.

"That's normal," she says, circling a few things on her own chart and doing other doctorly things I have no interest in trying to understand. "Discomfort is expected but that's just us trying to make sure all of the medicine is out of your system. Unfortunately, we won't be able to administer any pain medication at this point. But we'll try to make you as comfortable as we can."

Not feeling like opening my mouth, let alone making any sound, I croak out, "How'd I get here?"

Holding her clipboard in front of her, she takes a deep breath and says, "Your friends brought you in last night. They found you in a bathtub after taking a lethal dose of sleeping pills." She pauses. Looking at the nurse who stands on my left side of the bed, she asks, "Do you have any recollection of that?"

Hesitantly, I shake my head.

I waited to do what I did. I didn't want anyone to find me. At least not while my spirit was still in my body. So, I cleaned up the bullets and tucked away Lola's gun beneath my bed. I waited for Kendrick to come over. He brought some Chinese food. Broccoli and garlic sauce. I didn't eat. I couldn't. My stomach was in knots. Queasy, I refused, though he tried convincing me how good the food was. After he left, I got in the tub. Took the last bit of sleeping pills I had. And dozed off.

Trying to sit up, a pain shoots through my stomach. Clenching my hand over my lower abdomen, I groan and lay back.

"Easy," the nurse says, helping me get into a more comfortable position.

"Friends?" I ask.

"Will Rogers!" the nurse responds with a huge smile on her face. "I'm sorry doctor, but I'm a huge foodie and I watch all the cooking shows, and *everybody* knows about Chef Will. He's the foodie's heartthrob," she gushes.

The doctor gives her a squinty sneer.

"Anyway," the nurse calmly continues, "he came with a woman named Lola? And they were with some tall, muscular guy. I can't remember his name, but he was definitely a cutie," she whispers and giggles, clearly trying to amuse me but I frown at the description of the very person I did *not* want to see me in this state: Kendrick.

Oh, Lord. He probably thinks I'm weak. If he's in any relation to the people at Moriah, then he's turning his nose up at me with judgment coming from every angle. And Lola. I can hear her now, *"If you ever try to take your life again, then you better succeed, or I'll kill you for even trying."*

I'm sure they're all scared. Pissed, too. Probably think I'm selfish. I just want the pain to stop.

I huff and close my eyes. This is so embarrassing.

"They're actually still here," the nurse continues, placing the new IV bag on the hook. "They never left. You want to see them?"

"No," I answer holding up my hand but not having the strength to raise my IV-bound arm off the bed.

"That's fine," the doctor interjects, seeming a bit annoyed by the nurse. "You don't have to see them at all if you don't want to. It's your choice. But you'll still have to be seen by our mental health professional today. She'll be in shortly to go over a few things with you to see how you're feeling and to make sure you're in a safer headspace before you're discharged." The doctor speaks as if this is an everyday occurrence. For her, it probably is. She gathers herself. Smiles. Tries to make me feel like she cares. Says her goodbyes and whisks herself out of the room as fast as she came.

"I'm sorry," the nurse says, moving out of the glare of the sun. Staring at me with her hazel yet, sorrowful eyes. I finally see her. Not one blemish nor ounce of makeup covers her bronze, satin-like skin. She flaps her curly eyelashes.

"About what?" I rasp out. Throat is on fire.

Sitting on the end of the bed, she turns around, "Well, first of all, my name is Meko."

That's fitting. Looks carefree. Happy. Peaceful.

"Nice to meet—"

"Ah-ah," she gently taps my leg, "You don't have to speak. I know it's uncomfortable after getting that tube stuck down your throat. And the discomfort in your abdomen. Don't talk. It's fine."

I muster a weak smile and let her continue.

"I'm sorry you're in this situation."

I drop my gaze.

"Judging by the cross around your neck, I take it you're a believer?"

God is probably looking down on me with such disappointment right now. After all I've done. All the bad decisions I've made. He doesn't want me. If he did, I wouldn't be here.

Hesitantly, I nod as tears well in my eyes.

"I figured. I just wanted to make sure before I go any deeper," Meko says. Taking a deep breath, she goes on, "Listen, I see this stuff every day. Most people aren't as blessed as you. And I'm not just saying that because you're a believer or because I'm trying to stop you from potentially trying again. I'm saying that because I was where you are, ten years ago. I couldn't stand it when someone would tell me I had *everything to live for*, because I didn't feel that. I was clinically depressed, and nothing made me feel better. No medicine. No CBT. Nothing. So, I was tired of feeling the way I felt. And at eighteen, I decided I was done. I took my father's razor blade and..." she pauses and looks at her wrists. Faded keloids scars both her arms.

Furrowing my brow, I pout.

"Don't feel sorry for me. The Lord allowed me to keep these scars. It's a reminder of what he brought me through. And how deep his love is." A glint in her eyes sparkles as she talks about God.

I want that.

"Anyway," she continues, "my father found me and rushed me to the hospital. When I woke up, I was still depressed. Still wanted to die. And I told myself the second I got home; I would try again. But when I was in the hospital, a nurse gave me a Bible. Completely against policy and so many laws, I'm pretty sure," she chuckles and tilts her head to the side. "But although I didn't grow up in a religious household, I opened that Bible that night...and it changed my life. From there on, I decided the only way I ought to live was by living for the One who gave me a second chance."

Her eyes remain steady on mine. Uncomfortable, I close mine to escape from the awkwardness, but also to stop the tears from falling. It's too late.

"Now," she says, placing her hand on my leg that's covered by piles of blankets, "I'm no therapist. But I know what you're going through. It may be under different circumstances but we both ended up here. In the hospital. Able to pull through and get another chance at life *only* by the grace and mercy of God. And although you may not feel it right now; with the pain and the thoughts that are going through your head, you're a miracle, Azra. God is giving you a second chance because he has a purpose for your life only *you* can fulfill."

Tears stream down my face, but I don't care to wipe them. Her energy reminds me of Mom-mom. God, what I wouldn't do to see her again. To hold her and smell her. To hear her nag my ear off about how I need to be in church and on prayer call. To run just one more errand for her. What I wouldn't do to make life so simple like it used to be.

Meko stands to grab a tissue from the tissue box on the right side of the bed and hands it to me. "I don't mean to make you cry," she lays a delicate hand on my shoulder, "but it's something you need to hear. I know when I woke up, all I wanted was for someone to encourage me. Someone who went through what I went through to tell me the road may not be easy, but with God, anything is possible. And no matter what we do or the bad decisions we make; nothing can separate us from the love of God. I'd be a liar to say I've been perfect. I've been everything but. But I've also learned God doesn't want perfection. He wants us to try. Yes, we'll have slip-ups. We'll blatantly choose to do wrong. But he's always there. Even when we don't feel Him. Even when we don't *want* Him to be. He's *always* there."

Dabbing my eyes and nose, a painful smile spreads over my dry lips. I whisper, "Thank you."

"You are so welcome." She smiles and walks over to the other side of the bed to get the used IV bag and other equipment. Walking towards the door, she turns back around, "I should be here for another couple of hours. So, if you need anything, just push the call button on the remote and I'll be in to assist you. The mental health professional should be in shortly, so afterward—if you want to—you'll be able to see your friends. I'm sure they're still waiting."

Nodding my head as the tears still leak from my eyes, I take a deep breath, and do what I haven't genuinely done in a long time. Pray.

The visit with the mental health professional was alright. She asked questions like: Do you look forward to the future? Are you on any prescription or illicit drug of any sort? Have you recently experienced a life-altering change in your life?

I could've lied. Could've told them I see a bright future for myself. That the only drug for me is life and love. That nothing has changed, and I took a jab at taking my own life just for the heck of it. I could've lied.

And I did.

I was only honest about Mom-mom's passing since she died in this hospital. Left out the life-changing news I received about who my mother is. Left out the heartbreak that ultimately landed me here. It's not their business.

They gave me six hours until I'm discharged. Six hours. That's a total of eleven hours after being admitted for attempted suicide. Since the attempt wasn't grisly enough, they said I should be fine having some friends look over me while I recover.

Six hours.

As if any suicidal ideation would have dwindled by then.

I fear even if I did tell them the truth—how I still don't understand why things are the way they are; how confused I am about *who* I am; how sleeping pills are the only way I'm able to sleep most nights; how I still don't want to be here but I'm too afraid to try again—they'd still discharge me early.

It's because I'm Black. They can say it isn't, but I know the truth. This healthcare system never loved us and why would I be any different?

I would feel better if I could say my prayer lifted my spirits, but all I did was cry. Too ashamed to ask for forgiveness. Too ashamed to even talk to God. Why would God forgive me for what I've done? I'm a horrible person.

"Hey," Meko pops her head in before opening the door completely. "It's a shift change, and I'm headed out. Just wanted to drop in one more time."

"That's sweet, Meko. Thank you," I smile.

Reaching into her purse, she pulls out a church program and hands it to me.

"What's this?"

"I know it might seem kind of weird, and let me know if I'm crossing any lines, but, you wanna go to church with me one day?" she grins. Perfectly straight teeth spread temple to temple.

I press my lips together. What is this girl's angle? Does she like me? Like...*like* me? Or does she just want to get close to William? Lola will drag her. She don't want none.

She's nice, but...Okay. Maybe I'm overthinking it. It's just church.

I sit up and smile, "Sure."

"Great! Oh, my goodness. I'm so glad you're down for that. I was afraid you'd think I'm weird or something. But anyway, here's my number." She pulls out a pink gel pen and takes the program from me. She writes her number on the top. "Now, you can text me whenever. I'm good at texting back, but don't call. I can't stand it when people call without asking first." She giggles, handing me the program.

"Well, I'll hit you up soon," I say, giving a closed-mouth smile.

"Cool. So, before I go, do you want me to send any of your friends in? They're all still out there. Even Will Rogers," she sings, wiggling her eyebrows up and down.

I laugh, but the discomfort in my stomach stops me in my tracks. "As a matter of fact. Can you send him in?"

"Really—I mean—of course."

I giggle through my throat, "Listen. You ought to know, he's taken. And his girlfriend—Lola? She has a bedazzled pistol. Or Glock. Or...I don't know. Some sort of gun. So..."

"Oh, Jesus," she raises her brow and chuckles, "well you don't have to worry about me, then."

I try to keep from laughing.

"Well, I'll send him in. And you take care, Azra. I'll speak to you soon?"

"Yeah. I'll text you as soon as I'm out of here."

"Cool. See you later."

Closing my eyes, minutes seem like seconds before William knocks on the door. He comes in with a smile.

"How you doing?" he asks, putting his hand on my shoulder and giving it a tender squeeze.

"I've had better days. Tired. Pain is an understatement. I won't even get to the emotions I'm feeling," I keep smiling. Holding back tears.

"I hope you feel better, Azra. You scared us all," he squeezes again.

We sit in silence for a moment.

"I'm sorry. I...I didn't mean to...I just...I don't know what to say," I stutter.

"You don't have to say anything."

"I know, but...I don't know. I just wanted to see you. I feel bad for putting y'all through this. It's my fault."

"Hey," he sits on the edge of my bed and lays his hands on my leg. "It's okay. For real. Don't stress yourself out over it. We're not the ones to worry about. We're just happy you're okay. Seriously."

I hold the back of his hand and sniffle. "Thank you. That's why I wanted to see you. You're calm," I chuckle, "And you're family," I say, finally accepting reality.

"I am." He smiles.

Dipping my head, I ask, "Does *she* know I'm here?"

"Nope. Only me, Lola, and Kendrick. But don't worry about that. I think the main thing to worry about is Lola."

My mouth parts. "Why? Is she okay?"

"She's fine. Pissed. But fine."

"Why?"

"Because you wanted to see me first."

We chuckle.

I cover my mouth, "Oh, my goodness. I can imagine she's probably having a fit. But family first, right?" I smile.

We chat a little before silence falls between us.

I sigh. "I don't know what to do, William."

"Well as far as I'm concerned, you're a Rogers." Flipping his hand on top of mine, he holds it tight, "And we take care of each other. Whatever you need. Money. A place to stay. Food. Even if it's just to talk. We got you. And if the rest don't, I do. Andrea is like a mother to me and as far as I'm concerned, you're my sister now."

My stomach flutters and I weep.

Fixing my mouth to say thank you, William smiles and shakes his head. "Nah. You better not. You're family." He squeezes my hand once more before letting go and standing up.

I chuckle and wipe my tears away.

"So, should I get Lola or Kendrick? You want to see them both?"

"Lola. Can you tell Kendrick I don't want him to see me like this?"

He chuckles, "I got'chu."

He bends over to hug me and says goodbye.

Seconds pass. And nobody. Absolutely nobody.

"Why would you do some stupid crap like this? What is wrong with you, Az? You better be glad you're not dead otherwise I'd kill you myself." Lola bursts into the room, tackling the door down like a linebacker.

"With that warm welcome, I should've called you in hours ago."

"Azra. Why?" The closer she gets, the redder her eyes and nose appear. "I'm glad you're okay but why did you do this?" her voice breaks.

Jutting my chin, I blink uncontrollably. Dropping my head, I hide my face.

"Hey," she whispers, sitting close to me on the bed and grabbing my hand. "Don't worry about it. We'll talk about it later, okay? But Azra, please promise me you'll never do this again. Please? I can't...I can't lose you." She sniffles.

Gazing from under my brow, I mouth, "I promise."

"Good," she snatches her hand back and pulls her leg up on the bed. "'Cus I'll beat out the little bit of holy water and oil you got left in you."

THIRTY-TWO
LOLA

The steam from the curling iron goes right up my nose as I do a quick spiral curl on my natural hair. Regret sinks in already. I should just wear a wig, especially with how humid it is today. Why is October this hot? Makes no sense. But William likes my natural hair, so…whatever.

We're going on a date tonight. He hasn't told me where but by now I've learned to accept and enjoy the surprises as they come. But one thing I'm not willing to accept is the fact he has yet to call me today.

Texts are fine, but this is William we're talking about. He needs to hear my voice. Not to mention his responses are delayed. That man has been on his phone like he's a teen who just got unlimited minutes. Why he's taking forever to text me back is beyond me.

Usually, I wouldn't be bothered by his phone use, but what makes my antennas perk, is the fact he's being so *sneaky* about it. On one hand, he's giving me hella cheater vibes. But on the other, he's still the same, if not *more* loving than he was before the phone became an issue. But let's be real. What faithful man do you know keeps his phone faced down, dims the backlight whenever he uses it and rushes off the phone before you come into a room?

I'll wait.

Exactly. The same 'faithful' men in these streets talking about *Black men don't cheat.* Give me a break.

But this ain't nobody's fault but mine. I'm in too deep.

My phone shivers on the bathroom sink. Barely paying attention to who's calling, I swipe to answer.

"Oh, *now* you got time to call me? What you been doing all day that you can't call to say hi? Were you with somebody?"

"Uh, Lola? It's me."

My heart jumps as Kendrick's honeyed voice catches me off guard.

I cover my mouth. "Oh, my god. Ken, I'm *so* sorry. I thought you were William," I blush.

"No worries," he chuckles, "I was just calling to ask if you needed anything from Target. I'm picking up a few things before shooting over there and wanted to know if you needed anything, like toilet paper? Paper towels? I know between me and Azra being over there lately, you might be running low."

I smile, "No, Ken. Thank you, but it's honestly not a big deal. I'm just glad you're able to spend time with Azra. That means a lot to me. Y'all aren't a burden of any sort. If y'all were, I wouldn't have her staying here with me."

"You sure?"

"Don't you think you've done enough? Yes, I'm sure," I giggle, tucking my phone between my shoulder and ear. I pick up the curling iron and finish curling the remaining pieces of my hair.

He laughs, "Well if you need anything, just let me know. I got you."

"You've got me so much that I won't ever ask you for a single favor as long as I live. I'm still trying to figure out how to pay you back for…" I lower my voice, "you know." Putting down the curling iron, I grab my phone and switch it to my other ear.

"I told you, Lola. Don't."

"Alright well *you* don't bring any paper towels and we'll call it even. I'm already indebted to you. I don't need another twenty-five dollars added onto that."

"Twenty-five? Baby, store brand is only $9.39 for six rolls. You can't beat it."

"Sounds like you've been talking to William a little too much," I laugh.

"I actually have. I just got off the phone with him not too long ago."

Oh no he didn't.

He has time to talk to Kendrick but not me? Hell nah. I take my phone from my ear and go straight to my messages.

"He called you?" I ask. Thumbs ready to fire.

"Yeah. He told me y'all were going out tonight."

That's it. I text:

> *Oh so you can't call nobody?*
> *How you gonna call Kendrick but not me?*

I press send. Now I feel stupid. I could've just called him…but no. He's supposed to call *me*. He's the man. What in the world is he doing? He better not be trying to play me.

"Yeah…supposedly," I mutter to Kendrick. "I haven't really heard from him today, so we'll see if he even shows," I stare at my phone. Bubbles appear but quickly disappear.

"I'm sure he will," Kendrick assures me.

I roll my eyes and draw the phone back up to my ear.

"We'll see," I chortle, "Because if not, it'll be three's company up in here tonight."

"Hmmm. That don't sound too bad. Being around two beautiful women at the same time? Let me tell him to cancel," he jokes.

I laugh and my cheeks warm.

"I thought you were supposed to be a Christian, good sir."

"I'm a man first," he chuckles.

"You're a mess," I smile, shaking my head. Glimpsing at myself in the mirror, I ruffle my hair before flicking the bathroom light off and heading to my closet.

"I'm messing with you. But I'll be there in about a half-hour."

"Cool. I'll let Azra know you're on your way."

Hanging up the phone, I scrape the plastic hangers across the metal rod. I come across a red wine, off-the-shoulder, wrap midi dress. A string of diamonds cuffing at the wrist. A split that stops just below my thong line. I decide to wear it.

William doesn't even deserve to *see* me, let alone see me looking *this* good. I just don't know what's going on with him. I check my phone to see if he responded. Nada.

Throwing my phone on the bed, I proceed to find Azra.

"Yo, Az—" Walking past my sewing room turned guest room, I catch the doorframe and draw myself back. Azra lies across the air mattress, texting. She's smiling.

"Ahem."

Shooting her gaze from her phone, she grabs her chest and sighs in relief. "Goodness, Lo. I didn't see you there."

"Now you know how I felt when you would barge in without announcing yourself," I laugh, leaning against the doorway. "Who're you talking to?"

"None of your business, Mom. Dang." she chuckles and rolls her eyes back to her phone before locking it and flinging it beside her on the bed.

"I'm just asking. You're smiling and everything. Just hoping it isn't—"

"It isn't. Trust me. It's Meko. You know, the nurse I met in the hospital. We've been texting since I left. She's cool people."

"Whew. That's good. I was thinking it was another dude," I maunder over and flop on the edge of the firm, and quite uncomfortable blowup mattress.

"What do you take me for? I know how to let grass grow."

"I wouldn't know. Since I've known you, you've had a jungle before you met...you know who."

"Yeah. Let's not go there." She pushes up to sit Indian-style. Leaning to her side, she grabs her composition book and pen from the sewing desk on the left side of the bed. She opens it and begins to write.

Drawing my knee up, I turn to her, "Listen. It's been a few weeks now, and for the seriousness of all you've been going through, I kept quiet. But I have to ask. And because you're staying here, you need to answer me. I can't go on any longer not knowing."

Dropping the pen in the notebook and sagging her body, she gives me a blank stare.

"Don't look at me like that."

"What do you want to know?" she shrugs.

I blurt out, "What were you thinking trying to kill yourself?"

"Wow. Just plow right through that wall, huh?"

"I don't have time to tip toe around the bush, okay? I can clearly see over it, but I want you to tell me what's there, so I don't have to keep wondering."

She rolls her eyes. "Not your best analogy, but why not just ask if I tried to take my life over...him?"

"Did you?"

She glares at her notebook before closing the pen inside and setting it on the bed. She crosses her arms. "If you can see over the bush, then why ask? You know the answer."

"Why can't you just tell me?"

"Becau—" she sighs. "Because it wasn't just behind *him*, Lo. I felt lonely. You got to remember I just *lost* my mom-mom. I know that isn't enough reason to do what I did, but strictly saying it was because of him sounds so freaking stupid. I felt lost. Still do, to be honest." She glares at me with tears brimming her eyes. "It was stupid. I wish I never did it but…it happened. It's nothing I can do about it now. It's embarrassing. It's shameful. It's…downright disappointing."

I pause for a moment. I'm not good at this comforting thing, so I'll continue the way I know how. "So…just for clarity's sake: *He* broke up with *you*?"

"Yes, Lola. Why are you even asking me this?"

"Because sometimes the best way to heal a wound is to rip the bandage off and douse it with peroxide. It's gonna hurt, but it'll help the wound to not become infected and possibly get worse."

She sucks her teeth and sniffles, "Something your therapist taught you?"

"*Counselor*. And yup. Now you're getting free counseling. You're welcome."

She chuckles and moves from Indian style to sitting on her legs.

"Peroxide alert," I warn.

She bows her head to let me continue.

"He broke up with you because…Andrea's… your mom? Right?"

She gives me a *duh bih* look.

"Don't look at me like that. You put me in this position of not being able to talk to anyone about it. So, the least you can do is tell me what happened and how it went down."

She loosens her jaw and takes a long exhale. Nodding her head, she tells me *everything*. And I mean everything. Kind of wish I never asked. I can't believe *she* ran Andrea off the road. This child about to go to jail. And poor Poppy. For Azra's sake, good thing she didn't know how to use a gun. But Genesis definitely needs a whooping for the crap he did. He's lucky *I* wasn't the one with Poppy.

I try my hardest to keep my emotions from spilling out onto my face, but I'm failing like a college dropout. I wish I never even asked.

"I-I don't know what to say," I stutter. "Sounds like something out of a movie."

"I don't think you can make this up," she says, hanging her head in her palms. "Ugh! I just can't believe I lost my mind like that. It felt like something inside of me snapped. Like I was being controlled by something."

"You were."

She glances up from her palms.

"The D," I giggle. She laughs, too. "I'm serious, girl. The D can be two things: The D, and the Devil. They'll have you out here psychotic. Looks like both drove you crazy."

Shaking her head, she mutters, "Unfortunately."

We sit in silence for a moment, but I need to get dressed for this date that may or may not happen. Either way, I need to get ready.

Standing, I look at Azra.

"What?" she asks, "You look like you want to say, *I told you so.*"

"No. You look like *you* want to say, *you were right.* But I'm not looking to be right in this situation. I just want to know if you came back to your senses. You know that man was nothing but trouble, right? And come in my room, I need to get dressed," I walk out.

Following behind, she says, "Well, okay. You *were* right, and I can admit that. But I still don't feel like he's the dangerous one. Honestly, it was me—"

"Don't you dare go blaming yourself. It was only *fifty* percent your fault." But in reality, it was like seventy-five. Maybe eighty. I mean, she was the one running people off the road and sticking guns in people's faces. Sounds pretty dangerous to me. Yeah, it was definitely Azra's fault. But *she's* not the one that's married. But she *did* pursue him. But *he* had an obligation to stay faithful to his wife. Alright, sixty-three percent.

This is exactly why most marriages are trash.

"No, Lo. I messed with a married man. I knew he was married but for some reason, I didn't care. I was just so tired of doing good and getting nothing from it. I wanted to know what it felt like doing what *I* wanted to do for once. Guess it drove me a little crazy."

"A little? Girl, I thought you were shape-shifting for a moment," I chuckle.

I slip out my silk robe and let it cascade onto the floor. I pick up my dress from my bed and slip my arms into the sleeves. I proceed to dust my face with my favorite powder foundation.

"Ugh. I'm sorry," she chortles, pressing her hands against her cheeks as she sits on the edge of my bed.

"No need to apologize. It is what it is. I'm just glad you're alive. But one thing I *do* think you should do, is to see my counselor. It'll be good for you."

She wrinkles her nose. "Nah. I'll pass."

"Az, no disrespect, but you got a lot of crap to work out. I mean, between your Mom-mom, Genesis, and Andrea being your mom, I think that all qualifies you to get professional help." I coat my lips with a light layer of lip balm before applying my matte, dark-red berry lipstick.

"That's for you. Not me. I'm good. All I need to do is go to church and continue getting my relationship back on track with God. I'm alright."

"Well promise me one thing?" I glare at her through the reflection of my body-length mirror. "You'll give Andrea a chance?"

She huffs and puffs, rolls her eyes, and crosses her arms.

I turn around and double down. "Azra, you have to. I know you don't like it, but she is your mother. She knew as much as you did, which was nothing. But she wants to be there for you. She asks about you every time I talk to her."

She shakes her head. "It isn't that easy."

"But it could be. If you just try," I say, walking over to her on the bed. I pick up my phone. William texted back:

Last time I checked, the phone works both ways.
BTW I'm outside talking to Kendrick rn

I scrunch my brow and text:

So that's your boyfriend now?

"Alright. I'll promise to *think* about it. But only if you go to church with me this Sunday with Meko." Azra says.

Peering up from my phone, I say, "Done."

"Done?" she furrows her brow.

My phone vibrates with another text from William:

Woman just come out when you're ready

I snicker and throw my phone back on the bed. Going into my closet, I grab a pair of nude-colored, strappy lace-up heels and yell out, "Yup! What'chu think I'm some sort of heathen? I'll go to church. Besides, Kendrick's rubbing off on William, and unfortunately, he's rubbing off on me, so we can all go. Invite Ken while you're at it. Let's make a date out of it."

"Oh...*kay*?"

"Mm-hmm. Didn't see that one coming, did you?" I giggle, making it back to my bed and tying up my heels. "But for real, I'm here for you, Az. I got your back no matter what. Whatever I can do to help you get back to normal, even if that's going to church every Sunday, I'll do it."

She gives a pouty grin and hangs her head low. "Thank you for being so understanding, Lo. You really don't have to be, especially with how crazy I've been—"

"Chile please," I shoo her away. Standing up, I strut to the mirror to see just how good I know I look. "I told you to leave it alone. We've been pass—Oop!" I get sidetracked as I catch a glimpse of my backside in the mirror.

Azra darts her head up. "What?"

"You see that?" I run my hands down my hips.

"See what?"

"My butt! Girl, you don't see how juicy it looks?"

She titters, "First of all, what butt?"

Snatching my gaze from my gorgeous reflection, I pivot on my heel. "You're a whole hater."

We both laugh.

I pick up my robe from the floor and drape it on my bed.

"Where're you going anyway?" she asks.

"I don't know. Romeo's taking me out tonight but per usual, didn't tell me where. He hasn't called me today either so…" I roll my eyes.

I pick up my phone and throw it in the nearest handbag from my closet. Thankfully, it matches my shoes.

She smiles, "I knew y'all were gonna stay together."

"Chile, the jury is still out on that one."

"Who else you gonna be with?"

"Me, myself, and—"

"Yeah right. You can stop acting like you don't want William, 'cus you're terrible at it. You know he's your future husband."

I suck my teeth, "We'll see," I say spritzing myself with my flowery perfume.

"Mm-hmm, you're in love with him."

"Girl, please."

"Awww. Lola's in love, Lola's in love." she sings.

I playfully draw a fist back and bop toward her. "Don't make me punch you. I never said I loved him."

She giggles, "You don't have to. It's all in your face."

A knocking at the door draws our attention.

I grin, "Well, it's about to be all in *your* face because that's Ken," I prance out of the bedroom.

Azra jumps off the bed and yanks me back. "Kendrick?" she angrily whispers. Hand brushing her hair and wiping off her clothes, she panics. "Why is he here?"

"Don't act like he hasn't been over every day since you've been staying here. He's watching you."

"Watching me? I'm not a child, Lo. I'm fine. And yeah, he's been over but that's when I *know* he's coming! You can't let him see me like this. Besides, I don't need to be babysat. I can handle myself. What about when I go back to work? You gonna still keep an eye on me then?"

"Where? You know you're not going back to Ace. I'm surprised after pulling Poppy out on him, he didn't fire you."

She glares down. "He did. Well, Trish did. I'm supposed to file for unemployment soon, actually."

I sigh. "Listen, don't even worry about that right now. You're just lucky Ms. Annette left you a good amount of money, so you don't have to worry about working right away. But this doesn't have anything to do with your feelings. When I can't be around you, Kendrick will. That's how it's been and that's how it will be at least for another month. End of story. The doctors and the mental health professionals said someone needs to be around at all times until we feel you're better. Why do you care what you look like anyway? I thought you didn't like him."

"I don't like him like *that*. But I still don't want him seeing me like *this*."

"Well go get yourself together then," I say pushing her down the hall and into her room.

She stops and turns to me with narrowed eyes. "Is this a setup or something?"

"Nope. Just trying to keep you alive, sis," I touch her cheeks with mine while kissing the air. "Love you. And I may or may not be back home tonight."

"Wha—He's staying the night?" her eyes bug out.

"Well, that's up to you two," I wink and back my way out of the bedroom. "You know what they say: *The best way to get over one man is to do Bible study with another.* Bye." Shutting the door behind me, I chuckle and make my way to let Kendrick in.

Opening the door, Kendrick's jaw drops. Awestruck. His eyes meet mine.

"Hey, Ken."

Walking in, he slowly smirks and curls his lips in his mouth while running his free hand over his beard.

"Does William know how blessed he is? Because he'll be a fool to mess around on you."

I drop my head and feel my heart quiver. "I clean up alright, I guess."

I don't know if William is aware of how blessed he is to have me. But this phone situation has me a step away from second-guessing myself.

I look at the Target bag in Kendrick's other hand. He bought that pack of paper towels.

I laugh, "Just couldn't help yourself, huh?"

"You can never have too many paper towels."

I shake my head and roll my eyes, adjusting the slit on my dress. "William's downstairs?"

"Yup. Waiting on you." Kendrick says, placing the large bag on the kitchen counter.

"Cool," I lift my keys from the key holder near the door, "Well, you two have fun with those paper towels. Azra will be out in a minute. She wasn't exactly decent," I giggle, dropping my keys in my handbag.

"No worries. I'll see you later. Have a good time. And remind him how blessed he is." Kendrick smiles. His biceps, triceps, and whatever-other-ceps flex as he unloads the Target bag. I've never seen someone place a bag of chips on a table so sexily.

Ugh! Goodness, who put the heat on?

My heart flutters. Without another word, I give a toothless smile and get out of Kendrick's sight and presence as fast as I can.

Coming out of my apartment building, I see none other than Mr. Does-the-most-and-I-love-it.

He leans against the back car door of his brand new, black Escalade. Checking out his fitted black slacks and his collarless button-up shirt; both hugging him in the right places of his perfectly lean physique, I forget what I was mad about.

I smile.

He holds out a small but stunning bouquet. One stands out: A white chrysanthemum smack dab in the middle of the arrangement.

"My, my, my," William says, sounding like Billy Dee Williams in one of those movies he played in with Diana Ross.

"Well, don't you look dapper," I smile.

I take the flowers and wrap my arms around his neck. A certain calmness comes over me when he grabs me and holds me close. Our hearts beat in harmony. All muscles relax. I breathe so easily with him.

Pulling away, I hold the bouquet with both hands and take a deep whiff. A fresh, lemony aroma tickles my nose.

William walks around to open the passenger door. "I'm speechless," he says from behind me. "Damn!"

I glance back before stepping up into the vehicle.

Eyes set down, he steps back and rubs his hands together with an ugly yet pleased expression on his face.

"See! I knew I wasn't trippin'," I laugh, rubbing my plump-ish derriere. "That's all that good food you've been giving me. Putting in work."

Lost for words, he smacks my butt as I step up into the car.

Giggling, I sit in the large seat and take one more smell of the flowers as he shuts the door.

THIRTY-THREE

LOLA

This man is crazy. He lost his mind.

"Are you high?" I ask William, pulling back as he hauls me forward. "You're delusional if you think I'm getting on that thing," I raise my voice as we get closer.

I tense, stopping both of us in our tracks.

My ears ring as the loud fire filling the humungous balloon blows. Yup. He booked a hot air balloon ride after we had a beautiful, fine dinner at The Capital Grille. Although I'm pleased with the fact he hasn't bothered to check his phone today, I still can't help but torture myself over who he's been talking to. To be honest, I'm afraid to ask.

What if he's seeing someone else? Maybe he's planning to let me down easy because he realizes he doesn't want to be with an older woman.

My stomach clenches at the thought of losing him. So, for now, I'll push that thought out of my head.

Anyway, I never rode a plane. Never entertained the idea of crossing bungee jumping or skydiving off my bucket list. Never desired for my feet to be off solid ground. I'm terrified of heights, but how would William know that? *I* didn't even know until now.

"Bean, do you trust me?"

"Trust ain't got nothing to do with this. Can you stop that thing from blowing up when we're a jillion miles up in the sky?"

Laughing, he pulls me into him and wraps me in his arms. "It's the experience, woman. It's beautiful. And I promise I will never put you in any danger. I've taken plenty of rides before, and nothing's happened to me." He kisses my forehead.

I whine.

Dawdling forward, he practically pushes me into the balloon basket. No one else is here. Just a few men who got the balloon together.

"So, we're the only ones who signed up to die today?" I humor the operating men. My body trembles from the inside out but I keep my balance and strength by hugging William's arm.

"We're not gonna die, Lola," he chuckles, caressing my chin with his other hand. "Just close those pretty eyes as we lift off. I'll tell you when to open them."

Kissing me on my lips, a glimmer of love shines in his lowered eyes.

I press my lips together to suppress a smile and purr, "Okay."

Laying my head on his shoulder and closing my eyes, gravity lifts from beneath us.

"You feel that?" he whispers in my ear.

"Mm-hmm," I hum, trying to hold my dinner down. A slight chill comes over me and I squeeze my eyes closed.

He chuckles.

We stand in silence. The loudness of the fire is still relevant but subsides the higher we drift. Pulling his arm from my grasp, he instead wraps his arms around me from behind. He kisses up and down the side of my neck.

I smile and tilt my head to give him easier access to peck his lips on my flesh.

Keeping my eyes closed, I murmur, "It feels like I'm floating."

"Mm-hmm," he says, laying one last smooch on my ear. "That's how I feel every time I'm with you."

My heart melts as his breath brushes my ear.

"Shut up," I giggle. He chuckles too.

My heart steadies. I no longer fear the oysters and filet mignon making an encore performance on all the civilians we hover above, so I'm good.

"Alright," William whispers, "open your eyes."

My breath stalls at the beautiful sight. Land for miles. The soon-to-set sun gleaming on the tall trees and buildings. The water glitters with soft movement as the rays of the sun hits it, giving an iridescent illumination to everything around.

"Oh, my God," I utter. My skin tingles at the sight.

"I told you," he grins, moving from behind me.

I slowly tiptoe closer to the railing of the basket. I don't look down, but I focus on the beauty of the sparkling water.

"Champagne?" William says, standing behind me. He holds two glasses of cold wine. I look around to see where he pulled them from. A small wine bucket sits in the corner of the basket.

I take the glass and smile. "Where'd that come from?"

"That's my secret," he jokes. Must've had someone slip it in when I closed my eyes.

I take a sip of the wine. Sparkling. Sweet, yet a bit tart. Green apple notes. My nerves rest even more.

I giggle. "You know me so well."

"Yeah. It took a while to get here, but I'm glad I did," he sips. " I actually wanted to tell you something."

My stomach trembles. "What is it?"

"I've been holding off on telling you because I wanted it to be the right time."

"Right time for what?"

He takes a deep breath and looks down at his drink. "I got offered a job."

"That's good. What kind this time? A competition? Or are you judging again?"

He shrugs. "Neither," he glares at me from under his brow. "They want to give me my own cooking show."

"Oh, my god!" I shriek, "Really? Romeo that's great." My stomach relaxes.

I hug him but he limply wraps his arms around me. Pulling away, I search his face for any inkling of happiness, but he looks sad.

"Why are you so upset about it? That's like the pinnacle of what you've been working for, isn't it?" I ask.

"It is. But it's gonna require a lot of my time to be spent in Cali. I wanted to tell you, but I didn't know how you'd respond."

"What are you talking about? Of course, I'm happy for you. I know with your kind of work you're going to be busy. That's just life. We have our own thing. We can work it out. But you don't seem happy about it."

He shifts his feet and leans on the edge of the balloon. "Well…we won't be able to see each other like that. For at least weeks at a time."

The logical part of me wants to ask him why that's such a big deal. We have FaceTime. I can take time off work and visit. It's an easy fix. But the emotional side takes over, and I utter, "Are you breaking up with me?"

"What?"

"Are you breaking up with me, William? Is this because of counseling? Do you see me differently now or…what? Is this why you brought me on this extravagant date? Like a farewell type of thing?"

He knits his brow, "What? No, woman. I don't see you any differently than I saw you before. If anything, I see you *better* now. I feel like I know *you*. Not what you try to put out for everyone else."

"Then why are you making such a big deal about the time we'll spend apart?"

"Because honestly, I don't want to leave. I don't want anything to happen to you while I'm gone. But now since I won't be around as often, we'll need to get Clyde back, or some kind of security. I'm still not comfortable leaving you without having someone to watch your back. But why'd you think I was trying to leave you?"

"Because," I sigh, watching the bubbles of my champagne pop one at a time, "I feel like things are different between us."

"They are," he says, "but in a good way. You know I used to be nervous around you?"

"Yeah right," I tuck my chin and brush my hair from my face.

"It's true."

Avoiding eye contact, I settle my nerves with a sip of wine. I feel foolish. Letting my emotions get the best of me. Assuming. My cheeks flush with heat and I nervously smile. "Aww, did your stomach get bubbly? Heart fluttered at the sight of me?"

He chuckles, "You're joking, but yeah. Ever since I approached you that night, I was afraid you were gonna reject me. I just knew you were gonna tell me you had somebody already or wasn't interested."

"*You* were afraid of rejection?" I furrow my brow.

"Yeah. Most men are. Which is probably why men don't chase after the woman anymore and the roles are reversed. But I believe in the old-fashioned way of doing things. Taking risks and going for what you want. Sometimes when you take risks—like this one, two thousand feet up in the sky—you realize the beauty that lies on the other side of that fear. That's how it was when I first saw you. Something told me I'd be rejected by you a lot. But I knew I had to take that chance because I knew I'd eventually get you." He leans his elbow on the wicker railing of the basket and peers at me.

His stare and confession embarrass me. My stomach quakes as I pull my gaze away from him and take a hefty gulp of the champagne.

"So, you think you *got* me now or something? Like I'm just wrapped around your finger?" I ask, downing the rest of my wine. Although what he's saying sounds good, I can't seem to shake who he's been talking to lately that's so important.

"Are you?" he bites his lip.

Squinting my eyes at him, I hand him the empty flute and cross my arms. "Can I ask you something?"

"Sure."

My heart beats fast. I sweat profusely. But I have to ask. "Who've you been talking to? I mean, aside from today, you've been occupied on your phone. You rush off when I come around. You hide it from me, which is weird because you know I don't snoop. If it had anything to do with you getting offered your own TV show, then I understand you didn't want me to find out, but it seems like it's more than that. I just...I *need* to know what's going on. Because if we want to talk about risks, it's a possibility I might be taking the ultimate risk with...fall...falling in...love...with you. And I don't want to even take that step without knowing for sure what is going on with you. I don't care if you'll be on the road more. I just want to know you're really down for me and not trying to play me." My heart pounds and a knot forms in my throat. I can't believe I just told him that.

Pushing up from his elbow, he takes the flutes by the stems in his right hand and looks out at the sun. He's unfazed.

"You noticed that, huh?" he asks.

I rub away the goosebumps on my arms.

He drops his head. Bending to set the empty flutes down, he stands back up and sighs.

Pressure builds up behind my eyes. "William, listen. If there's someone else, don't string me along. Please. I'm getting too old and, quite frankly, too soft for these kinds of games. I can't do it. So just be real with me."

"Be real?" he raises his brow.

I nod and squeeze my arms, bracing for impact.

Adjusting his body to face me, he takes a deep breath. "Alright. Lola, I—" He double-takes at something over my shoulder and narrows his eyes.

"You what?" That nauseous feeling is coming over me. "William—"

"You don't see that?" he interrupts, pointing behind me.

I snap my head around for a split second, see nothing, and snap back. "Are you seriously trying to deflect right now? William, if you don't want me then just—"

"Woman, if you don't look!" He lets out an exasperated chuckle and turns me around to look out of the adjacent side of the balloon.

My stomach drops. An effusion of warmth swells my heart. Miles away, a broad flower bed of white and red flowers in the middle of an empty grassy field spells out the words, 'Will you marry me?'

I cover my mouth with my hands. Tears prickle my eyes, stinging to burst through. And they do. Hard.

Astounded, I spin around to find William on bended knee. Ogling at me, he reaches into his pocket. Pulling out a small turquoise box, he smiles at me.

"I love you, Lola," he begins, "I will *never* do anything to hurt you. All that texting and phone calls I was making, went to this moment right here. So, that risk you're thinking about taking with loving me, won't be in vain. And I'll take that risk to be rejected by you a hundred times as long as I know the one hundred and first time, you'll say *yes*. I don't want, nor have I ever wanted anybody more than I want you, Bean."

My heart is beating so fast. I'm becoming light-headed.

"So, I'll ask you again..." he opens the box, revealing a dazzling and blinding, three-stone engagement ring. Pear-shaped diamonds enclose a large round cut diamond in the center. He breathes deeply, "Will you marry—"

"Yes!" I scream without a nanosecond of thought, surprising myself. Never have I ever thought I'd gladly accept a proposal from any man, but William has worn me down. Warm tears run down my face and my hands shake uncontrollably.

He flinches his head back and frowns. "Wait…For real?"

"Yes," I giggle, wiping tears from my eyes with my right hand. I hold my left hand out and he takes it in his.

Lazily holding my hand, he grins and looks at me. "I don't know. That was just *too* easy. You ain't gonna pull back before I slip this ring on, are you?"

We laugh.

"William if you don't—" I waggishly snatch for the ring, but he jerks the box away. "Put it on," I giggle.

Taking the ring out of the box, he rubs my hand in his before gliding the ring on my finger. It's perfect.

My breathing is staggered but I'm squealing like a mouse.

Kissing my hand, he grips it in his like it's his lifeline. He leans his forehead on it.

Squatting, with tears running down my face, I pull my hand away. Placing both hands on each side of his face, I lift his head to look at me. Tears form in his eyes, but he holds them in.

Looking into each other's souls, my heart pounds. "I love you, William," I profess, willingly and permissively. And it feels so good.

He drops his head from my hands and chuckles. Lifting it, he says, "Say that one mo'gin," he jokes.

Laughing together, I wrap my arms around his neck, and we stand up. Holding me tight, we kiss. Long. Deeply. Intensely. Devotedly. Lovingly.

"Wait," I pull my lips from his. "I still haven't met your parents yet. Do they know about this?"

He smiles and grabs my face. Resting his forehead on mine and gazing into my eyes he says, "Nope. Looks like we got some arrangements to make."

THIRTY-FOUR

AZRA

"And so the Lord says, 'These people say they are mine. They honor me with their lips, but their hearts are far from me. And their worship of me is nothing but man-made rules learned by rote'."

Of course. Fake Christians. The title of the sermon today. Of all days, we go during the time the pastor is in the middle of a series about fake Christians.

I feel my whole life and belief system was categorized under 'fake Christian status' and it stings. But I still wonder, *am* I a fake Christian?

When I think about it…probably.

I've not only lived in sin with Genesis, but I *enjoyed* it. Even now, I kind of wish I could go back. Relive every moment that took my breath away. Made my heart race. My body tingle. My soul melt. To relish in the sin I knew was no good for me or the relationship I claimed to have with God. I crave those feelings. And for some ungodly reason, I still want Genesis. Those feelings are strong. Though I've never done drugs, I can imagine it's similar. Survived my whole life without that high, but that first hit hooked me for life. I barely know how to live without it.

Genesis had me inebriated. Infatuated. Entranced. The devil led me into a lustful rapture just to abandon me. Drug me deeper and deeper. Had me at my lowest. Yet, I still *crave* it.

That scares me.

What is wrong with me?

"You good?" Kendrick asks with a smile growing on his face.

He, Lola, William, and I decided to go out for brunch after church. Meko had to make it to her three o'clock shift at the hospital, so decided to split after service.

She hit it off nicely with everyone. Especially Kendrick. But I don't think he was feeling her. Lola likes her but feels her naturally *nice girl persona*, as she calls it, is everything but natural. I think she's just jealous because I have a new friend.

A nudging on my knee rips me from my thoughts. I peep at Kendrick in the corner of my eye as he sits next to me in the booth.

The sun shines through the large windows of the restaurant, hitting Kendrick's face in all the right places. His usually dark brown eyes turn a shade lighter when it's sunny. The skin that isn't covered by his thick black beard is silky. Makes me want to drink an entire fountain of water to achieve his level of skintimacy.

"Huh?" I ask, coming to my senses.

An attractive, young waitress interrupts, placing our drinks down on the table.

Lola and William sit across from us. They're so into each other they don't even notice the waitress. I'd be on cloud nine too if I got proposed to in a hot air balloon. Or a restaurant. Or a room. Or a space. Any space will do. I'd do anything for a slither of the happiness Lola has.

"Thank you," Kendrick smiles at the waitress and drags our drinks closer to us.

She blushes and walks away. What's up with everyone crushing on Kendrick today?

He looks back at me, "I asked if you're cool. You've seemed out of it since we left church."

"Yeah...just thinking," I say, hitting my straw on the table to break it from the paper covering.

My eyes tighten as I watch Lola grin. A dazed glint of love sparkles as brightly as that iceberg on her finger. She reaches for her glass...with her left hand. She rips away the paper from her straw...with her left hand. She crumbles the paper up and sticks her straw in her drink...with her left hand. She swirls the straw around and around and around...with her left hand. Lola's a righty. She tries to act like being engaged isn't much of a big deal to her, but she's hype. As she should be. I guess.

Kendrick leans in and speaks close to my ear, "What about?"

Taking a long sip of my strawberry lemonade, I glare at him and sigh. "Well, I feel like they were talking about me at church."

"Who?"

"The pastor."

He furrows his brow. "Why would you think that?"

"You didn't feel attacked today?"

He chuckles. "No. But it did make me think about what I can do in my relationship with God, but I didn't feel attacked. Why do you feel that way? You've been in church your whole life. You have a relationship with God. Your Mom-mom taught you right—"

"No, she didn't," I say under my breath.

"What do you mean?"

I take a sip of my drink and roll my eyes. Shaking my head, I place my drink down. "My Mom-mom lied to me. My *life* is a lie, Kendrick," I grit my teeth.

The stench of greasy, fried, dirty swine causes a dull wave of nausea to hit me. Mom-mom used to say not to speak ill of the dead or they'll haunt you. Maybe it's her telling me to stop talking about her.

My stomach clenches as I gag.

Kendrick furrows his brow. He glances over to Lola and William, in their own world. "Do you want to go talk about this somewhere else?" he asks.

Hesitantly, I grab my purse and take Kendrick by his large arm. I pull him out of the booth and we retreat to the back of the restaurant by the bathrooms.

"What's going on?" he asks.

I fold my arms and dig the ball of my foot into the floor.

"I just...I feel like...No. I *know* I've been living a lie. All this time. Mom-mom lied to me about everything. She lied about who my parents were. She lied about why my mother didn't want me. She made me live in fear of God my whole life. And not the *reverence* kind of fear, but that bone-chilling, *if-I-think-the-wrong-things-I'll-be-thrown-to-hell-immediately* kind of fear. Mom-mom didn't teach me how to have a relationship with God. She condemned me for asking questions. She stopped me from living a normal life because she had me believing normal was sinful. The only thing she taught me was to be perfect and to *talk* and *act* Christian without actually understanding what it means to *be* a Christian. I'm a fake Christian, Kendrick."

"You're not a fake Christian, Azra."

"Then why do I feel worse for *who* I hurt rather than what I actually *did*? I mean, if I'm a Christian, I should feel some remorse for what I did."

"Because you're human, Azra. And that's sin for you. It has a way of making us want to go back to it even when we know the consequences aren't desirable. But that doesn't make you a fake Christian."

I glare up at him. Heart heavy in my chest and nausea growing in my stomach, I ask, "How doesn't it?"

"Well, who have you hurt?"

"Everybody. Lola. I stopped talking to her for months because she was calling me on exactly what I was doing. Andrea, though I don't believe she knows anything solid about me and…you know who. My Mom-mom. I'll never be able to get that time I wasted not spending it with her. I've hurt myself by trying to take my life just because I felt I had nothing else to live for. I mean, even you. You stopped talking to me for three months behind what I did," I swallow a lump rising in my throat and quickly blink my lids over my aching eyes. *I'm not gonna cry.*

"What about God?" Kendrick asks.

I close my eyes and nod. "That's my biggest regret. I even find it hard to pray because I'm too ashamed."

"Have you asked for forgiveness?"

Staring at the ground, I slowly rattle my head side to side.

Silence. Clattering amongst the people in the restaurant seems to go quiet as well.

I wait for what seems like minutes for Kendrick to respond. I should just walk away. He's judging me. But the way my stomach is set up right now, maybe being close to the bathroom isn't a bad idea.

Kendrick sighs and then speaks. "*If we claim we have no sin, we are only fooling ourselves and not living in the truth. But if we confess our sins to Him, He is faithful and just to forgive us our sins and to cleanse us from all wickedness.*"

First John one, verses eight and nine. I know that verse like the back of my hand but never paid it much mind.

"Okay?"

"That's to say we all sin, Azra. And it also says you're not a fake Christian. We sin because we like the way it makes us feel. It's all about pleasing the flesh. But the Spirit is stronger than the flesh. And with God, we're able to fight sin. Now, I understand what was going on with you and Genesis. But the consequences could've been far worse than what they were. But now that y'all are done, confessing to God, and asking for forgiveness is the next step. And that's not to say you won't have those desires anymore, but that's where you got, not only me and Lola to keep you accountable, but you got the holy spirit. Listen beauty, you don't feel bad for what you did, because you liked it. It made you feel good. But feeling bad about hurting those around you, especially God, *is* remorse. And remorse leads to repentance, and repentance is a form of *reverence*. So, whether you know it or not, you're on the right track. You're not a fake Christian, but you've gotta pray."

"But after all I've done, Kendrick? I still have a hard time believing God will even forgive me. I mean, I can hardly forgive myself."

"What can't you forgive yourself for?"

"Everything," I flail my arms.

Kendrick takes a breath, runs his hand down his beard, and retorts, "Do you love your Mom-mom?"

I squint my eyes, "Of course, I do."

"Do you forgive her for lying to you?"

"Yeah. I mean, it's hard to understand why she did it, but I forgive her."

"Do you love yourself?"

"I...I don't know where you're going with this."

"Just answer."

"I-I guess so. Yeah, but...I just hate what I've done."

He nods and raises his brow, "Listen, Azra, we could go back and forth all day about this. But let me say this: You've got to start learning how to love God. Not how your Mom-mom taught you. But how God wants you to love Him. And the only way you can do that is by praying. Learn how to love Him and learn how He loves you. And then once you love yourself the way God does, then maybe you'll be able to forgive yourself. But you must love to know how to forgive. You might not forgive yourself. But God already has."

Wow.

I *haven't* loved myself. Not like I thought I did. I guess trying to take my life is an indicator that I need work in the self-love department. But I never thought of it that way.

To love is to forgive.

I inhale the truth. Exhale the years of deception I was fed. About God. About myself. About life. Meaning to thank him for the breakthrough I receive, nausea interferes. Strengthening and rising in my belly, it threatens to break the surface.

I grab my stomach and my mouth. Turning to my right, my eyes land on the bathroom door, and before Kendrick can ask if I'm okay, I'm in a stall with my head in a public toilet, releasing nothing but bile.

My stomach cramps and aches. Weak, I push myself from the ground and flush the toilet.

The bathroom door bursts open.

"Az, you okay?" Lola yells. Her heels clicking against the marble floors. She finds the stall I'm in without any problem. Thank God nobody else is in here.

I open the stall door. Lola's brow creases with worry.

"What's going on? Did you just throw up? In a public bathroom? Oh, God—"

"I'm fine, Lo. It was just the smell of the bacon. Turned my stomach," I push past her. She moves away like she doesn't want me touching her.

Turning the knob to the sink, I wash my hands with soap. The lavender smell of the soap soothes my stomach. Rinsing my hands with water, I bend over to rinse my mouth out. Lola slowly clicks up behind me.

Looking in the mirror, I catch her with her mouth wide open. Her hand covers the bottom half. Her eyes are in shock.

I furrow my brow and shut off the water. "What?"

"You're pregnant."

"No, I'm not," I pull a paper towel from the dispenser and wipe my mouth, then my hands.

"Yes, you are."

"Stop with the nonsense."

"When was your last period?"

"I just had—" I stop to think. *Was it...no because the beginning of September was...Shoot. I can't remember.*

"My period just ended yesterday. And I don't remember seeing you taking any ibuprofen last month, so unless our periods are no longer in sync anymore, you need to take this." She pulls out a long blue piece of plastic from her purse.

"Why do you have random pregnancy tests on you?"

"Chile for situations like these." She stretches out the test to me and bugs her eyes. "Go on!"

"Lola, I'm not pregnant. My body...it's been under a lot of stress lately. I'm probably just trying to get back to normal. Besides, if I was, I don't think any baby would've survived what I went through a few weeks ago."

"When's the last time you and Genesis had sex?"

"Gosh, Lola—"

"When?"

"Well...the day...the day my mom-mom died. Earlier that day."

She mumbles to herself, "So, August twenty-fourth," she counts on her fingers and says, "that means you're about...eight weeks."

"I'm *not* pregnant."

"Take the test, then."

"Fine," I snatch the test from her and rip it open. "This is so stupid. How in the world could I be pregnant after everything that's happened?"

She crosses her arms, "Stranger things have happened."

I go into a stall, hike my dress up, slip down my panties, and release the test from the wrapper. Popping the top off, I squat over it and relieve myself. I wonder how long I should pee on it. For safe measure I'll saturate it until I'm done.

Once I finish, I pop the top back on, wrap it in toilet paper, lay it on top of the toilet roll dispenser, and then take care of myself. I pull my panties up and flush the toilet. I look at the pregnancy test.

One flashing countdown bar.

"You done?" Lola yells.

"Yeah. Just waiting," I yell back.

"Well, wait out here. I want to see."

Picking the test up, I unlock the stall door and see Lola, jittery. Pacing back and forth as if we're waiting for *her* results.

I walk over to the sink and place the test down.

Two flashing countdown bars.

My heart flutters. Beats irregularly. Sweat beads form on my forehead. I wash my hands and pat them dry.

Lola bites her lip, still pacing.

I glance back down.

Three flashing countdown bars.

Lola stops pacing and rests her butt on the edge of the sink. The test sits in between us.

"Az, what if you *are* pregnant?"

"I'm not."

"But what if? What are you gonna do?"

"I...I don't know. That's...not even something I've thought about."

She furrows her brow. "Clinic?"

I shoot her a *you must be crazy* scowl.

"Just saying."

"Saying what? You know how I feel about abortions, Lola. I'll never get one. I don't care what the circumstances are."

"Is that because Ms. Annette raised you that way?"

I want to say yes, but that would make me just as bad as Mom-mom. She lied. She had kids by a married man and kept them. And for what? To treat one of her children like crap after losing the other? All because she thought God would punish her? Do I want to be that girl? Resentful of the decisions *I* made so I take my frustrations out on an innocent child who doesn't deserve it?

Without responding, I glance at the test.

Four flashing countdown bars.

"Az," Lola scoots close to me. Our eyes meet. "There's nothing wrong with getting an abortion. It's better than struggling and treating your child like dirt. Letting hellish things happen to them because you never loved them. If you are pregnant, it's still early. Maryland doesn't allow abortions after fourteen weeks, so you'll still have time to do it if you want to."

I remain silent.

She continues, "I know your Mom-mom raised you a certain way, but this is *your* life. You gotta make the best decision for *you* and your relationship with Andrea, if y'all create one."

On my peripheral, I see the blinking has stopped. My heart pauses with it. Frozen in time. Lola glares down her side to the test. I close my eyes.

Silence. Pure silence.

Lola's breath catches.

My eyes are closed, yet the room feels like it's winding like a whirlpool. I hang onto the edge of the sink and hold on for dear life.

My breathing becomes erratic. My heartbeat thumps in my ears. I'm going to vomit but not too sure I have any more bile to release.

The door bursts open and Lola and I jump.

"Oh! Hello," a woman smiles, rushing to one of the stalls.

I glare down at the test on the sink.

Pregnant.

A word I never thought I'd see before I was happily married. Living in a two-story, single-family home. A dog. Garden. Established in my career of songwriting, ghostwriting or any kind of creative writing. Trying for a child. Tracking my ovulation so my husband and I can know when we'll need to have extra time to get it on. Finding out while he's at work. Surprising him with the test and a cute little onesie from Target to announce we're having a baby.

All of that. Gone.

A bulge grows in my throat. I bite my lip hard. I fear I might draw blood.

A toilet flushes and the woman comes out. Washing her hands, she sees the test on the sink. Her face turns red. She forces a smile once more while she dries her hands and rushes out.

"Az?" Lola whispers.

I blink. Tears try to break through, but I won't let them. I'm cried out.

"Azra. It'll be okay, sis. It will."

I gaze at Lola. My breathing is faint. I grab my phone from my purse and unlock it.

"What are you doing?" Lola asks, watching my fingers find Genesis's contact.

She swipes it away. "Nope. No ma'am. Not on my watch."

"Lola, I have to tell him."

"And accomplish what? Huh? What do you think he's gonna do? Leave Andrea and marry you instead? That fantasy is over, Azra."

"He needs to know I'm having his baby."

"No, he doesn't. Him knowing you're pregnant isn't going to do nothing but make matters worse. It'll be a telltale sign y'all were having an affair. Your possible relationship with Andrea will be no more. You'll be dividing a family that already has enough issues as is. And say you do want to consider abortion—"

"I'm not getting an abortion."

"Adoption?"

I drop my head and squat to the floor. Covering my face, I rest my head between my knees.

"I'm sorry. I know this is all a shock. You shouldn't have to make this decision right now. But sis, I'm telling you, telling Genesis about this isn't the answer."

Rubbing my eyes, I feel them heat up, but tears don't flow. I look at Lola. "What if I decided to keep it. He could help me. At least with child support."

"Azra, you have me. You have Kendrick. And you have a full family of Rogers, including Andrea, who will be willing to help you take care of a child. You don't need no lowlife to do that."

I pout.

Lola's eyes soften and she squats beside me, placing a hand on my shoulder. "Anything he could do; we can do better." She smiles.

"I don't want my baby growing up without a father."

"Do you think William or Kendrick will let that happen? Especially Kendrick. Chile knowing him, he'd probably claim the baby as his. You know he's in love with you. You do no wrong in his eyes."

"Just like William is with you," I dryly chuckle.

Lola nods and smirks, "Yup. Just like him. We've got ourselves some good men around us. But they can't shine if we keep putting them in the shadows of toxicity like Angel and Genesis. They might be first-class F-boys but that doesn't mean we keep the good ones from stepping up and being who they are."

"I can't put this child on someone else. That's not right."

"It's not putting it on him if he offers. And you know doggone well Kendrick is going to offer."

I sigh and cover my face.

"Listen, Az. You have options. You still have time. Weigh your options. Pray about it. And I'm sure you'll choose the right thing to do. But whatever you do, *please* don't tell Genesis." She holds my phone out to me.

Eyeing my phone, I take it. "Okay."

She comes closer and wraps me up in a hug. "I love you, Az."

"I love you, too," I mutter, not wanting to let go.

We hold onto each other for a few moments before she backs away and stands up.

"We're going to get through this. Everything will be okay. I promise you." She assures me.

I nod and take a deep breath. "Okay."

"Now, let's get back out there before these guys think we both got sick," she chuckles.

I stand and put my phone in my purse. "Go ahead. I'm gonna get myself together. I'll be out soon."

Lola smiles. She primps in the mirror before making her way out of the bathroom.

I lean against the edge of the sink and take the pregnancy test in my hand.

My hands sweat just holding it. Tremble. I grab some paper towels and wrap them around the test, making sure it's secure. Sliding it into my purse, I cross my arms, drop my head, and close my eyes.

"Lord," I whisper, "I need you. I need you now more than ever. I need you to guide me. Show me the way to go. Father, these past few months have been crazy. I've done things I never thought I'd do. I've found myself in dark places I never want to go again. But through it all, I learned truth. My eyes have been opened. I've seen the light but I'm not sure how to approach it. Lord, please teach me how to handle this newfound light you have opened me up to. Teach me your love. Your wisdom. Teach me how to love you. How to love myself. How to love the ones who have lied to me, hurt me, done evil things to me. And forgive me for being that person who have lied, hurt, and done evil things to others.

"Forgive me for turning my back on you. For making others and myself gods. For putting you on the back burner to fulfill my own wicked desires. And though it's hard, please help me learn how to forgive myself. Help me heal from the wounds people have caused. Heal me from the wounds *I* have caused. Help me treat this child as the blessing it is, rather than a consequence of my sin. Help me love this child with the heart you love us with. To not project any of my resentment towards their father onto them, but to provide kindness, patience, love, and contentment. I don't know where to start because I don't know where to go. But I trust you'll get me back on track. I love you, God. I love you so much. And I'm ready to come back home. In Jesus name, amen."

Opening my eyes, a weight has lifted. My chest is lighter. My feet hover. I look in the mirror. Dab my nose, under eyes, and T-zone with a napkin. Grab my lip gloss out of my purse and lather it on my lips. With a pop of my lips, I breathe. In and out. In and out. My heart calms and beats at a normal pace. Stomach is settled. Peaceful. I throw my lip gloss in my purse and grab my phone. Go to my contacts, find Genesis's name, and press delete.

Who needs it?

Everything's going to be okay. As long as I got my life, my friends, my mental health intact, and God on my side, I'll be fine.

THIRTY-FIVE

ANDREA

My phone chimes. I pull my hand out of the water, dry it on a towel, and pick up my phone from the sliding bamboo bath tray that extends across me. A number rolls across the screen that I don't recognize. I put it up to my ear, "Allo oui?"

"Uh...Andrea?" A soft, almost baby-like voice answers.

Sliding the bath tray to the other end, I rise out of my freestanding, egg-shaped tub. The bubbles have all vanished, so there's no need for me to soak any longer.

"This is she," I answer.

"Hey, this is Azra."

My heart palpitates. I smile, stepping out of the tub, dripping wetness onto the white and gold cotton bathmat.

"Azra? What a beautiful surprise. How are you, darling?"

"I'm fine. Listen, I was calling to ask if you'd like to meet up this weekend. You know, to talk."

Jittery, I fumble my white cotton bathrobe and fling it around my body. My hands shake. I stutter, "Y-you want to meet this weekend? With me?"

"Yes," she giggles, "that's the next step, right? That's if…you want to."

I chuckle, "I will be delighted. Absolutely delighted. Where do you want to meet? Because if you don't have a place, I know this beautiful café we can go to. Their croissants are magnifique," I feel myself wanting to ramble, but I decide to keep it short and sweet. Don't want to scare her off.

"Sure, wherever you want."

"What day? Time? Saturday works for me. I have a few things lined up in the afternoon, but I can move the times around to meet you. Even cancel a few things—"

"Oh, no. That won't be necessary. Saturday will work, but if we can meet early, around eight a.m.? I've been getting up way earlier than I used to and that would be perfect."

There's an uncertainty in her tone but I ignore it. Who am I to be the tone police? I barely know her.

I switch the phone to my left ear and hold it with my shoulder. Sitting on the bathroom ottoman in the middle of the room, I pump my rose-scented lotion into my hands.

"That'll work. Is this your cell?" I ask.

"Yes, it is."

"Perfect. I'll send you the address of the café. It's called Exquis Pâtisserie. It's a quaint little cafe right on Wisconsin Avenue. You heard?"

"I don't eat many French pastries so, no. But sounds good."

Lathering my right leg, a warm, tingly feeling rolls through me. I shiver, then smile.

"Azra, you have no idea how happy you've made me by calling. I was too afraid to reach out to you myself because I didn't want to be pushy. I know all of this is hard for you as it is for me. But I'm *so* glad you called. I have so much to say but I don't know where to begin."

"Well, write them down. Because I have a *lot* to tell you, too."

"Really? Good things, I hope."

"Uh…Subjective."

"Oh, well, now you've got me all excited to know. Maybe you should write some things down, too."

"Oh, trust me. I won't forget."

"Marvelous."

I hear no smile in her voice. Maybe she's nervous. Doesn't talk much when she's in an uncomfortable situation. If she's anything like me, nerves, excitement, and pretty much anything will cause her mouth filled with cotton. Unable to salivate. Needing water. For her, it may be nervousness. For me, it's pure enthusiasm.

Silence lingers on the phone for a moment. I don't know what else to say. I stand from the ottoman, craving a bottle of Fiji right now. I can get water from the tap but I'm not a tap kind of girl.

"Well, Andrea," she breaks the ice, "I won't hold you for too long. Just wanted to see if you were available. I look forward to seeing you this weekend."

"Absolutely! À bientôt. I can't wait to see you either, Azra. You have a beautiful day, darling," I swallow.

My chapped throat screams: Water.

Hanging up the phone, I burst through the door, rush to my nightstand, and grab the mini-Fiji water bottle. Taking gulps with my eyes closed, I sense Genesis staring at me, wondering what the heck is going on.

I swallow the final gulp of water and sit on the edge of the bed.

"You okay?" he laughs, sitting in the bed.

He looks so fine. His beautiful dark skin, contrasting with the cream velvet duvet cover that shields all the lusciousness that lies underneath.

I shake my head and bite my lip as I take him in.

He chuckles, "Who was that?"

"You wouldn't believe me if I told you."

"Try me."

"Azra. Oh god, I still can't believe Annette named that girl Azra, but yeah. She said she wants to meet me this weekend. We're gonna go to Exquis Pâtisserie."

He stares at me.

My jumping heart rests but not for good reason. That's not the response I want. I want him to leap for joy. Scream at the top of his lungs. I want his energy to match mine. But it doesn't.

"Oh," he speaks before I can ask what's wrong. "That's the place you always asking me to get you croissants and tarte Tatin from? You love that place, don't you?" he drops his head.

"I do. Other than CocoDrop, it's my favorite bakery. But anyway, she wants to talk. She wants to meet me. Can you believe that? After all this time, I thought she was never going to want a relationship with me and here she goes. Calling me up to meet. That's unbelievable. I remember when I first saw that girl at Lola's opening. I couldn't keep my eyes off her. Part of me felt a little intimidated because of how friendly she was with you, but then I had to get out my own way. Little did I know, I was feeling something deeper. Isn't that crazy? It's like mother's intuition. I didn't know but something was weird. Like something was calling me to her. But now we know, and she really wants to meet me. This is the most bizarre, amazing thing that has ever happened to me. I'm just…I'm rambling. Am I rambling?"

"No baby, you're fine. I know this has been something you've wanted," he gives a feigned smile.

I draw my knee up and tilt my head. "What's wrong? You don't seem too happy."

"I am happy. I'm *really* happy for you, baby," he adjusts the pillow behind his back. "Just tired."

I lick my bottom lip and draw it in with my teeth. "Well, after last night and this morning I can't say you're alone. I ain't complaining, though," I blush.

My cheeks get warm when I recall how intimate Genesis and I have been lately. We've been spending more time together, kissing more, hugging more, doing more of that thing ladies like myself keep on the hush-hush. Let's just say, still waters run *very* deep.

He chuckles and drops his head. He looks shy. Like he used to be when we first met. When we were mad about each other. That feeling of guts twisting, sweaty palms, tingles reverberating through the body. That feeling is back. It's been a few years, but we got it back.

I climb completely onto the bed. Untie my robe and expose my bare, tight curves. I cuddle next to my husband and rest my head on his chest.

"Genie, I can actually say that for the first time in my life, I'm happy."

"Really? Ever?"

"It might sound bad but, yeah. I mean look at this. Look at where we are. We have thriving businesses. We're relaxing in our beautiful condo in Baltimore. The sun is shining. We just had two ethereal nights together. You and I are in an amazing place in our marriage. I feel like I can be open and honest with you. You know everything about me now. I don't feel like I'm hiding anything from you. And you know how hard that was for me. Holding on to everything about my past. I didn't want to tell you, but I'm so grateful you're the way you are. You listened to me. I was just afraid before."

"Afraid of what?"

"That you'd see me differently. Like I was damaged goods or…a whore. Annette always told me how nobody was going to want me. How, when someone found out I had a child, they'd be disgusted with me and never love me the way I would want to be loved."

"Well, that's not true. Even if you did tell me when we first met, my mind wouldn't have changed about how I felt about you."

I look up at him. "Really?"

"Yeah, I'm glad you told me. But I got to say, for years I knew something was missing."

"Like what?"

"I felt like you were only giving me pieces of yourself. I felt like an outsider."

My mind is wandering. Going back to places I never wanted to revisit, but if there is a time to do so, it's now.

I clear my throat and swallow. "Is that why you…cheated?" I ask.

He grunts, like I punched him in the gut.

"Didn't we talk about that in therapy? You know I don't like talking about that."

"And you think I do? I know it isn't pleasant to talk about but what's done is done. We got through it in therapy but that was right after things transpired. We should still talk about it so we can really get past it."

He huffs.

"So, is that why you got with Crystal?"

Crystal. That's a story for another day. But long story short: mentee, divorced at twenty, stays with me and Genesis for two months just until she got back on her single feet.

Bad, bad, *bad* idea.

My husband and that slore turned up missing on multiple occasions, but my slow behind didn't notice anything until she was moving out of our place and was caught in the back of a U-Haul with my wedded husband.

The cliche forbidden romance between mentee and spouse. I mean they could've been more original, at least discreet.

Anyway, she's Exodus's lady now. Having a baby boy. Leviticus. Levi for short. Ghetto, I know.

Genesis and I got counseling and it isn't until now that I can freely bring it up without imagining myself on trial for murder.

"It doesn't justify anything, but yes." He sighs. "That's *part* of the reason why."

"Well, what's the other part?"

"You really want to know? Right now?"

"What made you want to cheat, Genie? I wouldn't ask if I was gonna get mad," I lie. But I promise to keep my composure.

"Well, let's get this straight. I didn't *want* to cheat. It just happened. I didn't want to hurt you but...the lack of validation I got in our marriage was the main problem. The lack of respect. You sometimes treat me as if I know nothing about nothing. I want you to trust my decisions without putting down everything I say and fact-checking me like I'm some politician. I want you to let me be in control sometimes. I know what I did was wrong, but she made me feel in control. Competent. Trusted to make decisions. She gave me space when I didn't know I needed it and an ear to listen to me when I didn't know I wanted it. She made me feel like a man. Like I meant something to her. Like I was part of the reason why she breathed every day."

My heart race as I hear my husband speak about his ex-lover as if it were yesterday. He speaks nostalgically. As if he misses it.

Heart pounding in my chest, my sinuses opening, everything seems magnified. But I take a few deep breaths. *Calm down.*

I swallow back the familiar anger I felt five years ago. That anger is trying to overshadow the positive moment we are in now. I can't let that happen.

Calm down, Andrea.

"I'm sorry. I didn't...I didn't know you felt...emasculated," I whisper, never thinking I may have stripped him from his manhood. Made him feel like my servant. My PA. My flunkie. That's not what I want.

"I didn't really know either, baby," he says, circling his fingers on my shoulder. "But when you told me about your past. About your mother. About your child. How you let me hold you and comfort you. How you needed me. Not only physically, but emotionally. Spiritually. It made me feel good. It made me feel like a husband. And that's all I want to do. I want to make you feel good, Dre. I want to love you and give you all you need as a husband. But that's hard to do when you reject the things I really want to do with my life."

I lift my head from his chest and look into his eyes. "What is it that you want to do, baby?"

He glares down and shakes his head, "I don't know if you'll understand."

"S'il vous plait? Tell me?" I beg.

He huffs again, lifts his eyes to meet mine, and says in a low, controlled tone, "I want to sell Ace. The bakeries, Lola's boutique, and the restaurants we can keep. But the club got to go."

I sit up, closing my robe shut, "Why? That's our first business together. It's rated three on the top ten nightclubs in the country. Why would you want to give that up?"

"There's nothing but sin at the club. It's…it's like a breeding ground for everything sinful. You know I'm trying to get my life on track. My spirit can't take it anymore. I can't be the owner of that place. And as my wife, I don't want you to be a part of it either."

My lips tighten. I tilt my head to the side and close my eyes. I've heard this story time and time again. I'm tired. We're not selling the club. But I have an offer he will never be able to refuse.

I force a smile, "We can discuss that. We'll give it some thought. Talk about it some more. But only if you can give me one thing," I counter.

He rolls his eyes, "What?"

"Hear me out," I chuckle.

He crosses his arms over his bare chest as he catches my contagious grin, "I'm listening."

"Well, we're not getting any younger…"

"Uh-huh."

I crawl over top of him. His lower body still buried beneath the sheets. "And we're going to need our energy to handle what I'm about to propose."

"Yes?"

"I was thinking, how would you feel if we gave it a shot?"

"Gave what a shot?" he furrows his brow, unlocking his folded arms to bear the softness of my booty through my robe.

"A baby," I sing in a hushed tone.

He narrows his eyes on mine. A slight smirk plays on his lips.

"Listen, I know this seems to all be coming out of the blue, but I've been thinking a lot lately and...ever since I saw Azra at Annette's funeral. I've been considering the idea of starting over. Not letting my past control me, or my marriage. Or *your* happiness. I know how badly you want kids. And since I'm learning to become more submissive to you—"

"I'd rather the word *accommodating*."

"To-may-to, to-mah-to," I giggle, "But since I'm becoming more *accommodating* to your needs, I don't think starting a family of our own will be half bad if *you* still want to. You do still feel the same way, right?"

He sucks in his bottom lip. Taking a gripping hand off my rump, he runs his hand down his face and heaves a sigh. "Yeah...I do. Just...thinking."

"About?"

He stares at me. Love in his glare. He smiles, then responds, "When to get started." He gently pinches my chin. Caresses it. Gives me butterflies all through my body like he did when we were in our twenties.

I giggle. Cupping his face with both of my hands, I kiss him. Slip him some tongue. He loves that. I rest my forehead on his, rub our noses together. Our eyes closed. I roll my hips back and forth. His thrilling anticipation provokes me.

I whisper, "Now wouldn't hurt."

He draws in a breath and exhales in a tender moan, "I love you, Dre."

Those words weaken me. His soft deep voice. So heartfelt. It dissolves all inhibitions. I'll sacrifice my figure. My freedom. My life. Those three words come from a man that will make me glad to bear all his children. His first and his last. Every single one. Willingly. I will never, ever, let him go. I've worked too hard to let this man go. He is mine. And I am his. Nothing in the world can break us apart.

I rub my nose against his. Peck him on the lips, softly. I open my eyes, meeting his. We stare at each other. Earnestly. Without a question of my heart, I proudly whisper, "I love you more, Genie."

ABOUT THE AUTHOR

B.D. Hendrix was raised in the small town of Wilmington, Delaware. She began writing in grade school and enjoys creating complex, loving, and relatable characters everyone loves. She strives to encourage, enlighten, and intrigue readers with exciting but realistic and thought-provoking stories that highlight mental health, faith, and simple common sense. She now lives in Virginia and is currently working on her next novel.

Learn more at:
Briahendrix.com
Instagram: bd_hendrix
Facebook: AuthorBDHendrix
Twitter: bdhendrix

Note to My Readers

Hey everyone! If you made it to the end of this book, I want to tell you just how much I appreciate every single one of you.

This is my first novel/book-baby, and I was so nervous but also very excited upon releasing this book to the world. To everyone who has supported me throughout this journey of beginning my writing career, I want to thank you. The excitement and love that you all have shown has been the inspiration and motivation for me to keep going, even when times were hard pushing through (and they were sometimes).

I cannot tell you enough how much I appreciate you. I really hope you all loved Heaven Can Wait and the crazy characters. Can we talk about them though? My goodness! They have occupied my mind and heart for the past year of writing this novel and I cannot love them any more than what I do, but dang! Talking about a rollercoaster ride. They are family (in my head) and I really hope at least one of them resonated with you as you read this story.

I didn't want this book to end, and if any of you are like me, I'm sure you didn't want it to end either. But don't worry, I am working on book two to this series! And let me tell you…book two is going to blow your wig off. I'm still trying to wrap my head around it.

I hope you all are excited to continue navigating the lives of these beloved characters of mine. Stay tuned and don't forget to follow me on all social media platforms to stay up to date and to communicate with me!

Also, let me know your thoughts! Feedback, reviews, everything! I'm open to it all. Lay it on me! Until then, I'll see you all in book two!

Love and Blessings to each and every one of you,

B.D. Hendrix

www.ingramcontent.com/pod-product-compliance
Lightning Source LLC
Chambersburg PA
CBHW032133190626
46814CB00005BA/1678